Mags pic

Maybe needing someo... y they had kidnapped Bear . . . and maybe the reason they had kept him in the Archive was because they had no place else to put him, and they needed things to clear out after the blizzard before they could escape. It would have been very hard to move a prisoner and their raving lunatic quietly until the snow cleared off. Maybe they had been hoping no one would bother coming to the Archive. Maybe they had figured on drugging Bear and smuggling him out with their baggage. Maybe—

A sudden shout of unknown words made him glance to the side with alarm. And there, not more than the length of a horse and wagon away from him, was another of the bodyguards. One of the ones who he had humiliated, and who was not likely to have forgotten his face.

The man shouted again, and pointed at him, as the one he had been following shoved the Valdermaran aside and reached for a knife.

Oh hell!

:RUN Mags!:

Novels by MERCEDES LACKEY
available from DAW Books:

THE NOVELS OF VALDEMAR:

THE HERALDS OF VALDEMAR
ARROWS OF THE QUEEN
ARROW'S FLIGHT
ARROW'S FALL

THE LAST HERALD-MAGE
MAGIC'S PAWN
MAGIC'S PROMISE
MAGIC'S PRICE

THE MAGE WINDS
WINDS OF FATE
WINDS OF CHANGE
WINDS OF FURY

THE MAGE STORMS
STORM WARNING
STORM RISING
STORM BREAKING

VOWS AND HONOR
THE OATHBOUND
OATHBREAKERS
OATHBLOOD

THE COLLEGIUM CHRONICLES
FOUNDATION
INTRIGUES
CHANGES

BY THE SWORD
BRIGHTLY BURNING
TAKE A THIEF
EXILE'S HONOR
EXILE'S VALOR

VALDEMAR ANTHOLOGIES:
SWORD OF ICE
SUN IN GLORY
CROSSROADS
MOVING TARGETS
CHANGING THE WORLD
FINDING THE WAY

Written with LARRY DIXON:

THE MAGE WARS
THE BLACK GRYPHON
THE WHITE GRYPHON
THE SILVER GRYPHON

DARIAN'S TALE
OWLFLIGHT
OWLSIGHT
OWLKNIGHT

OTHER NOVELS:
GWENHWYFAR
THE BLACK SWAN

THE DRAGON JOUSTERS
JOUST
ALTA
SANCTUARY
AERIE

THE ELEMENTAL MASTERS
THE SERPENT'S SHADOW
THE GATES OF SLEEP
PHOENIX AND ASHES
THE WIZARD OF LONDON
RESERVED FOR THE CAT
UNNATURAL ISSUE

INTRIGUES

THE COLLEGIUM CHRONICLES
VOLUME TWO

MERCEDES LACKEY

DAW BOOKS, INC.
DONALD A. WOLLHEIM, FOUNDER
375 Hudson Street, New York, NY 10014

ELIZABETH R. WOLLHEIM
SHEILA E. GILBERT
PUBLISHERS

http://www.dawbooks.com

Cover art by Jody A. Lee

DAW Book Collectors No. 1524.

DAW Books are distributed by Penguin Group (USA).

First Printing, October 2011

1 2 3 4 5 6 7 8 9

DAW TRADEMARK REGISTERED
U.S. PAT. AND TM. OFF. AND FOREIGN COUNTRIES
—MARCA REGISTRADA
HECHO EN U.S.A.

PRINTED IN THE U.S.A.

With thanks to Rudyard Kipling for inspiring the Kirball match.

MAGS slapped the palm of his hand against the blue-painted wood of the stable door, and it banged open, whacking into the frame as Mags hurried through it. The noise echoed through the stable, startling the Companions that were huddled together in the aisle nearest the door into backing up a pace or two. Brick walls didn't do much to deaden sound. The chill wind that followed him through chased down his neck as the last icy grasp of winter clawed at him. Behind him, a few stubborn patches of granular snow lingered at the bases of trees and under bushes, but most of the ground was bare, which was a welcome relief after a winter season that seemed as if it would never end. The huge blizzard that had virtually closed down Haven, Palace and all, had been followed by snowfall after snowfall until Mags began to wonder if spring was ever coming.

Then, finally, the snow stopped, and began to melt. And now the weather was changing, but winter was definitely not going quietly. Occasionally a frigid wind showed that it wasn't quite done yet.

Mags pushed the door closed, leaning into it as the wind whistled around the edges, before the spring latch dropped into place with a snick. He took a long deep breath of the comforting smell of the Companions' stable; clean straw, clean "horse," a hint of damp wool, another hint of woodsmoke. If "home" had a scent, this was it.

All of the pristine white "horses" in the building looked in his direction for a moment before going back to whatever it was they had been doing. For a moment, Mags was the focus of a sea of blue eyes.

The largest stallion in the building, who had presumably been chatting with two other Companions in the middle of the aisle between the stalls, gave him a long look down his aristocratic nose that Mags read as disapproving.

Bad manners to interrupt. *Just Not Done. Besides, You Let The Cold Wind In. Also Not Done. Hmph.* It wasn't in Mindspeech, but it might just as well have been. The stallion's ears were slightly laid back and he swished his tail in irritation.

"Sorry, Rolan," Mags said quickly, ducking his head as the King's Own Companion continued to give him the Stern Look of the Elder. He strolled under the watchful gaze down to the end stall near the door to his own small room and came face to face with his own Companion, Dallen. Horses—or Companions—couldn't grin, but he sensed more than a little amusement from his bondmate.

:Don't worry about Rolan; he likes to think that he stands in one place and the universe revolves around him,: Dallen said. Dallen's blue eyes shone with amusement, and while one ear twitched in Mags' direction, the other pointed back toward Rolan.

A snort from the other side of the stable told Mags that Dallen hadn't bothered to keep that little comment "quiet." Rather than Mindspeaking directly to Mags, Dallen had communicated it openly so that every Companion in the stable could hear it. Mags grinned. There were times when Dallen's cheekiness didn't just border on impudence, it jumped right into the middle of impudence and splashed it all around.

:Rolan's just being prickly. People have been banging through that door all day; and of course they let the freezing cold draft in every single time it starts to get a little warmer.: Dallen reached over his shoulder and tugged his blue-and-white blanket a little higher on his shoulders with his teeth. *:This is why I am sporting my natty little rug, here. Of course some people don't want to wear their blankets because they can't show off their muscles, so when a draft roars in, they are the first to complain.:*

There were whickers from all over the stable at that one. And another, louder snort. Mags smothered a giggle with both hands.

:THANK YOU FOR YOUR AMUSING OBSERVATIONS, DALLEN,: came a very loud, ringing mindvoice, one that was probably heard all the way down to the edge of Haven. *:I'LL BE SURE TO RECOMMEND YOU FOR COURT JESTER.:*

Now there were whickers from virtually every stall.

Including from Dallan, who had no problem poking fun at himself. Dallen tossed his head and somehow managed for just a moment to cross his ankles and his eyes, inducing more giggles from Mags.

:Until this weather breaks, when I don't need to be out with you I'm staying right here in my stall hugging the hay—it shields me a little from the blast of cold air each time someone comes in,: Dallen continued complacently, as King's Own Companion Rolan went back to whatever important thing he had been discussing. *:But I am well known as a lazy lout.:*

"Not lazy," Mags replied, getting a brush to get whatever invisible bits of dirt and hay might be caught up in his Companion's shining mane and tail. "Just practical. If I didn' have to go back and forth t' classes, I'd hole up in m' room an' not move till it got true-warm." He sighed a little. "Been so long since I seen a warm sun, I'm beginnin' t' disbelieve in it! Don' wonder that Rolan's tetchy."

Dallen nodded vigorously. *:Oh I heartily agree with you. All those days of dark cloud and endless snow made people depressed and edgy, and now I think maybe some of us are losing our patience as well. It's hard to be cooped up in here, knowing that spring is taking its time in getting here properly.:* The stallion stretched, arcing his neck so that Mags could get at all the itchy spots with the brush as he did so. *:I'm not the only one wanting a nice walk out on a lazy hot day with the sun blazing down. Too bad that won't happen for at least a couple of moons yet. And when I think about how it feels to have a good roll in long grass, and a gallop on a warm summer night—bah, I start to feel out of sorts too. Especially when I think about* *those gallops on summer nights, because I do look so splendid by moonlight!:*

Mags had to smile at that, and his mood lifted. He leaned into Dallen's neck and continued to brush, letting the motion soothe them both. It had been another slightly edgy day for him, and maybe Dallen was right about people being out of sorts because they were cooped up. He couldn't understand why—well, he couldn't until he thought about it from the point of view of the other Trainees. Most of them thought being "forced" to stay warm and indoors was a trial, and not a hitherto unimaginable luxury . . . actually he was probably the only one who felt that every day was spent in luxury.

Eh, not quite. There's a couple *from sheep-country. An' a couple farmers. An' that gal whose da is a blacksmith . . .*

Still, he was the only Trainee who came from what—to the others—was unimaginable poverty. The vast majority of the Trainees came from the highborn families, or at the very least, the prosperous. Even the poorest shepherd was appalled when he heard about the conditions Mags and the other younglings with him had endured.

People were always complaining about something—the food, the work, the beds, the uniforms didn't fit, their rooms were too hot or too cold, or so-and-so was too hard a teacher. Sometimes he wondered if they just made things up to complain about.

Whereas . . . he was grateful to wake up in any kind of bed at all. Doubly grateful that it was a warm bed in a warm room, a clean warm bed on top of all of that.

For most of his life, his bed had been filthy straw in a hole under the barn floor, and a blanket with more holes than cloth, a bed he shared with a dozen other slave-children. It had never been warm, even in the heat of summer. It had never been clean.

He had never been clean, not even when they were all given the rare good meal and apparent good treatment on the occasion of a show visit to satisfy those who were supposed to ensure their well-being. Baths? Never heard of them. The only time dirt got washed off was by accident, as he worked the sluices, washing the gravel from the mine for tiny bits of gemstone.

Having a warm, soft bed—that was obvious, of course anyone would like that. But following his rescue and subsequent "civilizing," he had quickly discovered he liked being clean. And after that first bath it had just gotten better, although initially the experience had terrified him.

To put on clean clothing that wasn't rags, eat good food that filled you up—it was, by the standards he had grown up with, the stuff of which dreams were made. No, not even dreams. When he'd been a slave, he hadn't even known that such things were possible, so how could he have dreamed about them?

Dallen was the reason all this had happened to him. Dallen had Chosen him, Dallen had come for him, and when the Companion couldn't get him away from the man that had kept him and the others in terrible slavery, Dallen had fetched help in the form of another Herald—Jakyr.

Of course, at the time, Mags had been as terrified of

the Herald as he was of his master, though in a way that had been good, because his fear had kept him too paralyzed to move or run until Dallen got him sorted out.

Then, oh how his life had changed!

Becoming a Trainee had changed his life so dramatically that he sometimes thought he had become an entirely different person.

Take the food. No more thin cabbage soup and bread that was mostly chaff, or even sawdust. No more digging into garbage pits and the pig-slop for food that was too spoiled for the people living in the "big house." As a mine-slavey, his highest ambition had been to hit a richer vein of "sparklies" to earn himself one more tiny piece of bread than anyone else had.

And the living conditions. No more sleeping in a pit on rotting straw in a heap of other dirty children. Or trying to keep warm with only a thin blanket and the body heat of the rest. Or wrapping his feet in straw and rags because he hadn't ever put a pair of shoes on his feet. No more chilblains. The Trainees here, at least so far, didn't even know what a chilblain was!

And no more spending virtually every waking hour on his belly in a mine shaft, chipping out gemstones by hand, penalized by having some of his food withheld when the "take" wasn't good enough—as if he had any control over what the rock yielded to him!

That was the biggest change of all, at least, on the inside of him. Now he was using his head for thinking and learning all the time. His world had gone from the confines of the mine and yard to—well—a whole world. His days were spent doing things that were difficult but rewarding, and there was no punishment meted out if he wasn't good at them. Instead of punishment, he got help.

Unbelievable.

No, the others had no idea how good they had things here.

And to be honest, he didn't want them to know, the way he knew. No one should have to live like that.

But the differences between his life and theirs still made the adjustment hard for him in ways he suspected no one really understood. He didn't even understand it, except that he was always in a state of vague discomfort except when he was alone with Dallen. He felt like a kitten being raised by chickens. It was obvious that no one here reacted the way he did to things, and everyone here knew from their own experience how people were supposed to treat each other.

He hadn't been raised like a human being, he'd been raised like—no, worse than—an animal. He knew how to read and write, because it was the law, and the owners of the mine he'd worked at grudgingly made sure the children learned that much, but he didn't really know how to conduct himself among people who had what he now knew were "normal" lives.

He stumbled and fell in so many situations that required an understanding of how people were supposed to be. That got him in trouble—or at least, garnered him odd looks—so many times in a day that he didn't bother to keep track. He was never quite sure of exactly what it was he had done or said when he violated some code or guideline for behavior that others just took for granted.

At least, not until after the fact when Dallen would explain it to him.

And no matter what he did, how much he learned about behaving like other people did, simply because he was so grateful for the smallest of things—and so completely unused to them—he often had the feeling he was never going to fit in.

He'd been a Trainee for months now, and he still felt as if he was running in a race in which he would never catch up. That no matter how hard he tried, everyone else was always going to be smarter, faster, stronger than he ever would be. It went without saying that everyone, from the lowest servant to the highest in the land, was used to simply having more things than he did. The most that one of the mine children could claim was a ragged scrap of a blanket, and then only if someone bigger didn't take it. The idea that he actually owned things was sometimes preposterous to him. Under it all was a fear he could never quite shake, that someone would find him out and it would all be taken away from him. That fear had faded over the months, but it was still there, an undercurrent to everything.

:You know, all I can do is to keep telling you is that you do belong here, I Chose correctly, and no one is ever going to send you away,: Dallen said, breathing warm hay-scented breath into his hair affectionately. *:Eventually I'll wear all that away, like water wearing away a rock.:*

Mags sighed, and patted Dallen's neck. Even Dallen didn't quite understand it. He couldn't help it. This was the way he had lived forever and ever, and . . . maybe the rock was just too hard to wear away.

And then there was . . . well, his position here. Most of the people around him, his fellow Trainees in particular, were used to a lot of deference from those of lesser rank, and of course, most folk outside the Collegium were of lesser rank. They were self-assured, they expected that people would speak to them respectfully. He was in the habit of expecting as many blows as words, and no one, ever, had spoken to him with respect until he had put on Grays.

The Trainees were used to treating each other with a casualness that came hard to him, while he had to battle to keep from giving them the same deference the servants gave them. That, of course, was viewed as "sucking up."

And last of all, he truly admired the Heralds, and many of the older Trainees. He really wanted them to know that. They had earned his admiration. Hellfires, the Heralds had saved him and all the younglings at that mine! Life was short there at the best of times . . . at the worst, well "accidents" had happened to the youngsters who got the least little bit rebellious. There were always more unwanted orphans to replace them.

Manners, deference, knowing how to act around other people, all these things were absolutely alien to your thinking when you had grown up fighting over kitchen scraps, and sucking up was a way to keep from getting beaten. There had been plenty of times at the mine when he would happily have done almost any degrading thing in order to get just a little more food, or a blanket that was a tiny bit larger. Anything. So how could he relate to people who thought he was trying to curry favor when he was only thinking how much he appreciated being here?

But there was one thing he could always count on. Somehow Dallen always managed to make him feel better, no matter what happened, no matter what faux pas he managed to commit.

And the moments when he was sure he would never, ever go into Whites were getting fewer. Most of the time he thought he was actually getting close to acting like everyone else, even if he didn't actually feel like everyone else.

:Just keep on acting. Pretend long enough that you belong, and eventually even you will believe it.: Dallan nudged him with his nose. *:You might also think about that spot right under my chin . . . :*

He grinned a little, and gently ran the bristles of the brush along his Companion's chin. Having Dallen as a comforting and persistent presence in the back of his mind kept him steady. It was only when the invisible pressure got too much that he needed to physically come to Dallen for relief.

Just now, the trigger that had sent him here had been a brush of a resentful thought that he was somehow trying to become the teacher's pet, when in fact all he was doing was trying to stay even with everyone else in class. He couldn't help it. He was grateful to the teacher for taking the extra time to explain. Why was saying so wrong?

"You allus make me feel good," he murmured to Dallen's shoulder. "I dunno why you don' get tired of me."

:I'll forgive you if you actually hand over that apple

pie that you promised,: said Dallen, nosing at Mags' pocket urgently. *:You know pocket pies are far and away best when still warm, and you said you'd bring an extra from lunch.:*

Happy to have something to take him away from thoughts that were always uncomfortable, Mags reached into his pocket and pulled out the two small rectangular pastries—a special treat for the colder day from the kitchen staff. They were a handy way to take the dessert out of the dining hall and eat it later, they kept your hands warm, and the students always appreciated them. It took a little more effort to make the individual pies, but then again, the dining hall tended to clear that much faster if the food was taken out. That meant the dishes could be worked on faster, tables wiped, floor mopped, and the whole job done that much sooner. Everyone benefited.

The door banged open again, showing that Mags wasn't the only Gray-wearer that had thought to take the chance of a few stolen moments with his or her Companion. Possibly with an extra pie to share as well. Companions did have a sweet tooth. He didn't bother to see who it was; if they wanted to talk to him they'd already know he was here. And if they wanted privacy he wasn't going to invade it.

Mags watched the pie vanish as Dallen practically inhaled it.

"I got no idea why you like 'em so much," he said, "considerin' that you couldn't possibly taste it. I'd be surprised if it e'en touched yer tongue."

Mags took a bite out of his own pie. It was delicious;

it tasted as if the apples had been picked today, which was remarkable, considering it was probably made from dried apples from last year. The head cook did pride himself on making food for well over a hundred people still taste as though it was made for a small family meal. He almost always succeeded. Luncheon today, for instance . . . Mags licked his lips, thinking about it. Thick bean soup with bacon in it, winter greens cooked with ham hocks, lots of bread so fresh from the oven it burned your hands a little as you cut open the rolls and spread them with butter. "Good plain food and plenty of it is what these younglings need," was what he'd overheard the man saying. "And if the highborn are too good for it, they can go and eat elsewhere." Well, if this was "good, plain food," he really didn't want to eat with the highborn. His head would probably explode.

And, of course, after this luncheon there had been the pocket pies waiting to be taken away at the door instead of regular pies on the table. There were always pies. The cook reckoned pie was a good way to share out fruit now that it was winter, and make it last. Another undreamed-of luxury. At the mine, the only time he ever tasted anything sweet was chewing the ends of clover-blossoms, stealing honey from a wild-bee nest, or grubbing something sweet and burned out of the pig-food.

:I taste my pie just fine, thank you. So, do you feel that you are getting on in classes now?: asked Dallen, his enormous tongue licking teeth and lips and curling up around his nose in an effort to retrieve every crumb and speck of sugar, honey, and spices. *:Sometimes it's hard to*

separate your general air of anxiety from things you and I genuinely need to address.:

:Not doing too badly,: responded the boy in kind, thinking, as he took another bite from the pastry, how he was glad to be able to use Mindspeech. It allowed him to "talk" and eat at the same time. *:I think I'm gettin' better at the history. An' I like figurin', but today they started givin' us this stuff they call geometry, an' it just makes my head spin. Lena's not as much help there as she is with history. I can't imagine why we need anythin' past sums and all. I ain't going to be an artificer!:* The thought of the morning maths class made him sweat a little. Angles and unknowns and calculations, and nothing as straightforward as adding or subtracting.

:No, you aren't, but you still need to have a grasp of such things when you go out to the villages. It's not just artificers that need geometry. It's part of a Herald's duty to reset boundary markers after a flood or some other disaster, and to check them when there is a dispute over land.: Dallen nodded thoughtfully, and Mags got one of those mental glimpses of a Herald—as usual, someone he didn't know—laboring over calculations, then going out to reset boundary stones while two farmers watched him, waiting for the slightest hint of favoritism. *:All too often, especially well away from Haven, a Herald is the closest thing to an expert that some villager may have to depend upon for help. That's why, for example, you take quite a lot of wound-tending and basic healing classes. Nobody expects you to be a Healer—but there might be times when someone is hurt, and you're all they've got.:*

Try as he might, he couldn't picture himself in that

position of authority. It still made his brow knit, and sometimes his head hurt, to think that some day someone would be depending on, listening to, him. Impossible. Who would ever believe in him?

:I believe in you. And anyway, it's not whether people believe in you, personally. When you turn up on Circuit, they won't know you, and they don't have to. They believe in the uniform and what the uniform represents. They don't care who is inside that uniform as long as he makes good decisions, because the uniform is what they trust.:

Mags chewed thoughtfully, and swallowed. There was one thing he could imagine himself doing. He could easily see himself standing between danger and people who couldn't defend themselves. After all, he'd already done that, hadn't he? He'd put himself in danger to save Bear. And before that . . . he'd given all the information that the Heralds needed to shut down the mine and save the rest of the slaveys.

He shuddered involuntarily when he thought of the revenge his old master might take, if ever he discovered who had betrayed him, and said, with forced levity, "I reckon I might, one day, need th' healin' stuff for m'self. I heerd wha' th' real Heralds call th' Whites. 'Oh Shoot Me Now.' "

Oh, yes. Being a Herald was dangerous. Sometimes he was glad of that . . . it was rather like an "I have good news and bad news" scenario. "The good news is that you are going to be respected and all your needs and wants will be taken care of forever. The bad news is that your new name is 'Target.' " Sometimes he was relieved because he just could not bring himself to believe in this life unless there was a steep cost attached.

And sometimes he was terrified. So despite his casual words, there was a little chill down his neck when he thought about using the Healing skills he was getting on himself. It had gotten dreadfully close to that when he'd helped save Bear.

Dallen gave Mags a piercing look. *:I won't pretend it's not possible, but it will be a good long time before you ever need to worry about being in that position. You have years of learning ahead of you. And who knows? You might end up being stationed in Haven or some other city and never go out on circuit at all. All right?:*

Dallen's mind-voice had an undertone of anxiety. Mags smiled, and rubbed his cheek against his Companion's neck. "I'm not gonna worrit 'bout it. Just—s'ppose 'tis a good reason t' keep payin' more attention in harder classes, belike. 'Specially if they involve bandages!" He laughed a little. "I got a long ways t' go afore I'm catched up wi' ev'one else, anyway. By time I get Whites, I'll prolly be white-haired t' match!"

He worked on Dallen until the Companion's thick winter coat was as soft and clean as the down from a new pillow, and his mane and tail as shiny as silk. He carefully saved away all the long mane and tail hairs for later braiding, now that he knew just how much people valued the little trinkets Dallen had taught him to make with Companion and horse-hair. He even had a little net-bag hung up on a nail in the stall to collect the hair in. He'd wind what he collected into a little circle and carefully stick it into the bag, as he did now.

With Dallen clean and under his blanket again, Mags looked out of the stall. "'Tween you and me, when I come in like that, Rolan looked as though I'd spoilt his best chat-up lines. Was he on 'bout business—or pleasure?"

Behind him, Dallen made a noise that closely resembled a snicker. *:It wouldn't surprise me in the least if you did interrupt him flirting, you know. Not that he would ever come off his dignity to admit it. I'm pretty sure that most of the mares have a crush on him.:*

Mags turned and cocked his head. "Reckon he's poachin' in yer woods, Dallen?" He grinned.

Again the stallion snickered. *:I'll have you know that, pure resplendent perfection that I am, I'm in no danger of losing a light'o'love even to Rolan. It's not as if I'm languishing away in this this box waiting for you to visit.:* He managed to curvette and prance in place like a showy parade horse.

Mags had to laugh.

:Though I must admit that it does help that you are so attentive with the grooming. It puts the polish on what is already exquisite.: Dallen curved his neck and struck a pose.

"An' modest too!" Mags chuckled.

:But of course. It is part of what makes me so lovable.: Dallen batted his enormous blue eyes at Mags.

He had to chuckle even more. "I swear, yer worse'n one'a them court fellers. Next thing, ye'll be wantin' me t' find ye a silk'n'velvet blanket 'cause wool just don't show off yer coat good 'nough."

:Hmm. You think?: Dallen paused just long enough

for Mags to begin to wonder if his Companion was serious, then whickered his laughter. *:I shall recommend one to Rolan. He'll need it to compete with me.:*

"Rolan's gonna pull yer tail off one 'a these days." Mags shook his head. "I dunno why he ain't yet."

:Because no matter how miffed he pretends to be with me, he likes my tweaking his vanity. And I like to let him get all huffy with me. It's how we muddle along.:

That was a word that was unfamiliar. He shook his head. "Muddle along? Whassat mean?"

:Muddling along is an art form, dear boy. It's the great secret to life. You can't plan for everything, so you take the good and the bad and cope as they happen and even though life gets muddled you somehow manage to get by.:

Mags thought about that. It was true that he mostly lived in the moment, without thinking about good or bad times, at least not on purpose. But that was because when he thought about such things, then although the times were good, there was always, somewhere under everything, a feeling of certainty that they couldn't go on being good. All his experience had taught him that. So was that, just thinking about today and not worrying too much about tomorrow, what Dallen meant by "muddling along?"

:Not exactly,: the Companion corrected. *:You get hope in the bad times that there are better ahead, and there are. You temper the good times with plans for the future because you know there will be bad ones. And, sadly, there will always be bad times; it's in the nature of things.:*

Well he could certainly agree with that.

Dallen nudged him. *:The rule is that most things don't*

matter as much as you might think. So long as you keep that firmly in mind, then neither foe nor loving but misguided friend can hurt you—at least not so badly that you can't recover.:

Mags regarded him dubiously.

:We're none of us quite so sure of our place in the world that we can't be rocked off our feet by bad times. It's the getting back up again that counts. Not that you fall, but getting back up again counts for more in the long run.:

Mags snorted. "You ought to set up shop in the Mindhealer's area and charge a penny a customer with all that."

Dallen raised his head and looked regal. *:You can mock. But answer me one important question, if you will.:*

Mags nodded.

Dallen lowered his head and looked his young trainee hard in the eye. *:Are you actually going to eat that other half of your pie?:* he queried, pointedly. *:Because if you're not . . . :*

Mags sighed, then laughed, and gave it to him.

WHEN Mags left the stables, he hadn't so much as a hint of a crumb anywhere about his person. Dallen had even made big eyes at him until he turned all his pockets out, proving there wasn't even a fragment of crust left. As he pulled the door closed against the wind, he caught a glimpse of someone approaching out of the corner of his eye. He turned, and saw an older man, a full Herald, in pristine whites, walking toward the stable door. He was holding a half-eaten pocket pie in one hand. Mags grinned at him.

"I see yer had the same idea I had," he announced. "Don't let my Companion—Dallen—see ye have that, or ye might lose it. And fingers too."

The Herald blinked in surprise, and then let out a rich mellow laugh. "Ah, you're Dallen's Chosen? That would make you Mags, yes?" His cultured accent showed that he was highborn, but he seemed quite relaxed and utterly friendly. Most of the time when Mags saw a full

Herald, unless it was a teacher, it was usually someone in a tearing hurry.

Mags nodded and smiled back, noticing that the man had curiously colored eyes, a very light gray. Silver, he would have said, if he'd been asked to put a name to it. They looked very odd and striking with his dark hair. Mags wondered if he could be newly assigned as a teacher—or perhaps just in from Circuit. There were new Heralds coming and going all the time.

"We've been hearing very good things about you, Trainee Mags." The Herald nodded as if to emphasize that he agreed with the assessment. "I'm glad I had the chance to run into you. You came to the Collegium with no expectations, and no memory of how we used to teach trainees. Are your classes going well under the new system? Is there anything about them that you think is giving you and your fellow Trainees trouble?"

Mags gave a surprised chuckle of his own; given how many Heralds were still against the "new system," he was pleased to find one that seemingly wasn't. More than that, he was pleased to find one that was actually interested in improving the system rather than just criticizing it. "Well, I'm not as good at figurin' past sums as I oughtta be, I think. But I'm catchin up with folks 'n doing pretty good wi' history, I reckon. If I was t' say, though, I reckon some on us, like me, yah, but some others too, needs extree help, an' not all on us is brass 'nuff t' go find it. Them highborns, they kin go to ma or pa an' say, 'get me a tutor, eh?' But we cain't. We cain't pay fer 'em, an mostly we kinda shy off askin' teachers." He pondered a moment longer. "So . . . mebbe jest find summun's willin' t' give the help an' hev' 'em say 'bout it in class? No hevin' t' ask fer help, nor tryin' t' find summun willin' t' give it, 'cause some on us is shy 'bout askin', or shamed t' admit it. Jest hev summun a-waitin' ina room after classes. An them as needs the help jest shews up, an' teacher's there t' get 'em over the rough spots."

The older Herald nodded, looking oddly pleased. Mags had a nagging feeling of familiarity; he was sure he'd seen this man before somewhere. Unfortunately, he realized he was at that awkward point in the conversation where stopping to ask a name seemed a little odd. He groaned inwardly. Proper manners were very hard. Would it be wrong to ask now?

His hesitation cost him his chance. The older Herald smiled. "Well said, and a fine idea. I'll have a word with the right people. I am even more pleased now to have run into you."

Mags flushed a little. "Eh, I jest say things. Don' mean I'm right. Jest say things 'cause I'm too dumb t' know I shouldn'."

The Herald laughed. "And there is a very wise saying that only the young are unsophisticated enough to see past the mask to the truth and brave enough to speak it aloud. I'm sure we'll be seeing each other soon." With that, he opened the door and went into the stable, leaving Mags staring after him, still trying to pin down why he was so familiar.

Then he shook his head and pelted for the Collegium at a dead run, vaulting the fence around Companions' Field rather than taking the time to open the gate, and scrambling up the path with his book-rucksack banging on his shoulders. Fortunately, his next class was at the nearer end of the building; he wasn't the last person to dash in through the door, though he was the last to fling himself behind his desk. Still, Mags managed to arrive without being late, getting into place mere moments before the teacher entered the classroom.

The class itself took all of his concentration, and managed to drive all thought of the odd encounter right out of his mind. It was one of "those" maths classes, the ones where he was supposed to figure out angles and the like. It made his head hurt, he was concentrating so hard, and feeling altogether like the stupidest person in the class. Sums were so easy, but this . . . there were so many things he had to keep track of.

Thank goodness the next class was history. He was always ahead on history. It was—well, not logical, exactly, because history was people, and people weren't always logical. But it was like stories, there was a beginning, a middle, and an end.

But as he was going into the door for his last class, he was approached by a page boy and handed a piece of paper. It was a note from Herald Caelen, the head of the Collegium, asking him if he'd come by after classes were over for the day.

His first thought, immediately, was *what did I do wrong?* His second was to think back to that encounter at the stable with the Herald. What if the Herald had been offended at his forwardness? What if he'd insulted the Herald by not addressing him by name? What if the Herald was one of those who didn't approve of the new system? What if he did, but was offended by Mags' implied criticism? His head spun, and he felt that all-too-familiar old reaction. Back in his old life, the only reason someone in authority would want to see him would be because he was in trouble or that someone was looking for a scapegoat to punish.

He reminded himself that he wasn't in his old life. He'd never had that sort of thing happen to him here.

But it was hard to break his old ways of thought. He could all too easily imagine a hundred things he would have done or said wrong. As he worried them all through, the class dragged along.

He tried to reason with himself. Maybe Caelen wanted to see him for a good reason rather than a bad one. Probably Caelen wanted to see him for a good reason. Maybe that Herald had told Caelen he had a good idea, and Caelen wanted to ask him about it. Finally he managed to convince himself that this was the most probable—a sign that at least, if he had not overcome his instinctive reactions, he could finally reason his way past them.

Regardless, everything about the impending meeting kept him distracted during a lesson that was not one of his best subjects. This was the language class, and language, with all of its rules about grammar and spelling—made no sense to him. Nothing about it was logical, and just when he thought he'd gotten a rule straight in his head, it all went out with some exception or other. And as for his spelling, well, it was . . . creative.

This generally made for a long lesson at the best of times, and being preoccupied made it longer.

At last the teacher dismissed them, though unfortunately with a writing assignment. Just what he needed, with his head all of a muddle. Mags wondered if Lena would help him put it together, and then wondered if he was going to be too busy trying to make up for what he'd done wrong to ask her.

Once again, his mood dropped, and he had convinced himself that he was in trouble. He pulled his books together into his shoulder bag, suddenly wishing the lesson had been even longer. What could Caelen want?

As he walked along the corridor, feeling as if he was under a dark cloud, and wondering if he should pretend he never gotten the note, he felt a familiar presence in the back of his head. *:It's probably not bad, you know,:* his Companion assured him, *:I would have warned you if I'd seen you doing anything that was that bad. But you aren't going to find out unless you go.:* There was an amused chuckle. *:No matter what, you'll muddle through. Besides, how do you know Caelen isn't going to thank you for coming up with a good idea?:*

That was enough to lift his mood, at least a little. And give him enough courage to head for Caelen's office and knock tentatively on the door.

"Come in," called Caelen through the door.

Mags pushed it open. The block-like Herald was, as usual, rather buried in things on his desk. There were sheafs of papers stacked precariously around him, and it was impossible to tell which were things he was done with and which he had yet to work on. Mags blinked owlishly at the piles. How did Caelen ever get through all the work that was piled on him? Every time he thought that he was piled high with work, he would get a glimpse of what Caelen faced, and know that the work of a Trainee was nothing.

Caelen looked up and gave Mags a warm smile, and then followed his gaze, and made a wry face. "Budgeting," he sighed. He waved vaguely at the piles. "I have to account for every penny spent in Herald's Collegium, and my procrastination has come back to bite me. Again." He stabbed a finger at the paper in front of Mags. "It doesn't help that I have no idea sometimes what I'm signing for. Here it says we ordered a bale of dried marrow root." He rolled his eyes. "I have no idea what marrow root is, or, since this order is missing half of its information, where it came from. And yet, I have to sign to say it's justified. And if someone comes to ask me what in heaven's name I was thinking when I signed for it, I will be sitting here looking like a fool."

Mags peered at the paper. "Bear would prob'ly know," he suggested, trying to be helpful.

Caelen laughed. "Well, since he's the one that put in the request for it, I sincerely hope so. I gather it is something that he feels would do you lot good in the winter." He put aside the piece of paper, and looked Mags over. "You're growing," he noted, nodding approvingly. "It's good to see you filling out, considering the size you were when you arrived. I won't say you were the smallest Trainee we have ever had, but you were certainly the thinnest, and certainly the shortest for your age."

Mags looked down at himself. "Can' really help it," he said, shrugging. "Sorta happens all by itself."

The Herald rubbed his greying temples. "I suppose it

does," he replied with a nod. "Well, that brings me to the reason I brought you up here. I was reminded today that you are in a room that is usually used for the grooms that care for the Companions, and I thought, now our building work was getting closer to completion that you might like one of the newly built rooms that are free. It would get you out of the stables and in with the other trainees."

Mags was shocked, and his jaw dropped. "Move away from Dallen?" he asked, aghast.

Caelen gave a chuckle. "I can see, if you put it like that, that it would be a wrench. But it would stop you from standing out as . . ." he gave a wry smile, "the Trainee that we stuck off in the stable."

"How's that bad?" Mags asked, adding as an afterthought, "Sir? Not like it bothers me."

"You'll recall that bit of an altercation over you being there in the first place," Caellen said with a grimace. "You know already that there are many of the adults who would be certain any boy out in a room alone far from adult supervision is certainly up to no good, Trainee or not."

Well of all the things he'd heard here, that took the prize for making no sense. "But I got 'dult supervision!" Mags protested. "Companions! Bunches on 'em! If I was t' get t' jiggery-pokery, ye know they'd be callin' in t' their Chosen!" He could just imagine it, too. Say, purloining a couple of bottles of wine to try out what being drunk was like. He'd not get two cups into the first bottle before half the Collegium, including all the teachers, would be at his door. And he didn't even want to think about what would happen if he was up to anything worse than that. And what Dallen would say to him—he'd rather be whipped.

Caelen shrugged. "You have a very good point about the supervision. Well, if that is how you really feel, I won't make you move. I thought a boy your age would be a little worried about how the others might think of him. It might be thought a little odd to be down there all alone. People are very likely to wonder why you are there, if there is something, that makes you antisocial, or if—oh, say for example, your Mindspeech is less than controlled, and we are keeping you apart from the others to prevent problems from it. Or as if you are some sort of pariah, and we want to keep you away from the others to keep you from contaminating them."

Mags shook his head. "If'n I can stay, I want to," he stated firmly. "It ain't like I'm in the way. It's the warm end o' the stables, 'n I think the Companions like me being there. If somethin' was t' happen, I'd be right there, 'fore even someun's Chosen could or one'a the grooms, 'cause the Chosen 'd haveta run down from Collegium an' Dallen'd wake me afore a groom knew there was aught wrong. I dun mind bein' alone; I'd druther, actually. It's quiet. Easy t' study. Easy t' sleep, ain't no one larkin' about an' makin' noise. I never had no privacy afore, an' . . . an' I like bein' where no one kin bother me. An' I definit'ly like being next t' Dallen."

"Well. I suppose if you feel that strongly about it." Caelen sighed. "I suppose it can't hurt to have someone in the stable as we come toward foaling season anyway. The Companions usually keep everyone aware of when foaling is likely, but once in a while it's a surprise." He cocked his head and looked Mags over. "I reckon you'll be able to keep a level head in an emergency—and of course, the Companions will help. Even though Dallen is a jokester, he's solid in a crisis, I understand."

Mags grinned with relief—and a little at hearing Dallen described as a "jokester." Evidently his "tweaking of Rolan's tail" had gotten around. "Aye, sir. That I reckon 'e is."

Caelan blinked. "You know—you are a little young for this, but something just occurred to me. I've something I'd like you to consider adding to your lessons. It's a good thought, actually, and something that will . . . get you working with some of the other Trainees a good bit more."

:He means he thinks you need to be socialized,: Dallen said wryly. *:He thinks you ought to be running about with a herd. That's all right, he means well. And perhaps whatever it is he just thought of will be fun. You have been sorely missing out on fun.:*

Caelan carried on, oblivious to Dallen's comments; well, after all, he couldn't hear them. Companions rarely Mindspoke to anyone but their Chosen. It was unusual that Rolan had let Mags hear his sarcastic remarks to Dallen. "You and Dallen have an exceptionally close bond—I'm told your Mindspeech is remarkably strong. According to your records you and Dallen are also two of the leaders in the riding lessons. Those two things would make you a pair of ideal candidates for what I have in mind." The older Herald grinned like a young boy. "Think you'd be up to being part of a Kirball team?"

Mags frowned. "Kirball?" He'd heard the term bandied about, mostly during meals, but hadn't really gotten any notion of what it meant besides that it was some sort of game. A brand new game, one that several of the Heralds themselves were devising for the Trainees—but Mags had no idea what was involved. Well, other than the fact that, judging by the exuberant hand-gestures and pantomime, it was probably going to be very exciting for those who were in it.

"It's a new game that the Heralds are trying on the students this year. They are rebuilding the obstacle course out in the field and running it over that. It's part goal scoring, part capture-the-flag, and part team building." Caelen was oblivious to the fact that none of this meant anything to Mags; fortunately, Dallen quickly provided his Chosen with images of what Caelen meant. "We think it will be a good learning exercise for the Trainees. I believe it originally got its name since Herald Kiri came up with it. She's always one for inventing crazy ways to test the trainees, but this one has definitely become popular. The name seems to have stuck. It doesn't hurt that one could say it was meant to honor King Kiril as well."

Something nagged at the back of Mag's mind, but he couldn't quite put his finger on it, and the thought ran away as Dallen rang in loud and clear.

:Oh, I would like that! Just think, you'll get to compete on the fastest Companion in the city!: came an eager comment, showing Mags that Dallen was still listening in. *:We'll be fantastic at this!:*

The Herald continued, leaning forward and becoming animated as he did so, "Here's the basic idea. Now, we've done a lot of games on Companion-back in the past, but what is new about this is that the students form teams from all three Collegia. Some will be on Companions, of course, but some will be on horses, and then some afoot. It's a twelve-person team, and the way we have planned to run it is that competition can be two teams against each other, a three-way, three goal arrangement or even four teams all in. Though for now, while we work play and rules out, it will just be two teams against each other."

:It'll be chaos on the field, and if I understand Kiri's Companion correctly, that's sort of the idea. It's supposed to show how well you deal with a fight, and get you used to something like a battle without actually being in one. It's wargames by any other name,: noted Dallen. *:That said, it should also be a lot of fun.:*

Mags frowned. "Wargames?" he repeated aloud.

Caelen winced visibly. "Well, that's part of it. I can't pretend it isn't, but it's a combination of riding skill, teamwork, communication and how well you use your Gifts in a pinch. There will be people on each team that don't have Gifts, don't have Mindspeech, don't have Companions—which is just like a battlefield. This will test and train your abilities to put together an effective small force of all sorts of folk, setting things up so that each uses his strengths. That said, I think it's going to be fun, and it's going to be something for all the students to get involved in."

Mags' thoughtful frown deepened. "Gifts are allowed?" he asked, pondering how that would work.

Caelen nodded vigorously. “Within reason. I think we might have issues with someone using Firestarting to burn someone, since we don’t want actual combat as such, but I should think most Gifts will be useful. I suspect the people with the Fetching Gift are particularly going to be in demand for this. And those that don’t plan on a counter to it are going to find flag and ball scored against them without the other team even moving.”

Mags furrowed his brow. “Huh. I think I see. That’s gonna to take some thinkin’ about.” Actually, it looked as if the amount of planning was going to equal the amount of playing. Well as long as it wasn’t him having to do the planning. . . .

“Yes, it certainly is. Anyway, the riding instructors are going to be pushing people onto the teams as I permit. We don’t want people getting onto teams that aren’t fit for a bit of roughhousing, after all.” Caelen raised an eyebrow at him.

“ ’M pretty tough, sir,” Mags said, since he could sense Dallen’s excitement in the back of his mind, and didn’t want his poor Companion to explode. “Reckon this’d make me a mite tougher, too, an’ that ain’t bad.”

Caelen nodded. “Once this gets well underway, I suspect that your weapon instruction might be more focused on defending yourself from the back of a Companion as opposed to merely on foot this year. And if what I hear about the way you ride is correct, you’re going to be a popular pick for one of the two Heraldic positions on a team. Ordinarily I’d eliminate a first-year Trainee just on the basis of lack of skill and experience, but you have more than enough skill to make up for any other lack."

That startled him. The idea of being popular and wanted for something was quite unexpected. He had never really thought of himself as excelling in anything other than riding, which was, face it, a rather solitary occupation; oh he was good enough with weapons, the hand to hand ones, but he wasn't brilliant. And the riding, well, that was mostly Dallen's doing, and he had figured everyone knew that. He didn't quite know what to say in response.

Caelen looked pleased at his reaction. "Didn't think you were any good, eh? Still worrying about not measuring up." He gave a soft chuckle and tousled Mags' hair. "Don't worry about it. And don't stand there gawping like a fish gasping for air. Go now, off with you. And if you change your mind about rooming up here in the main building, you let me know. All right?'

Mags closed his mouth, still blinking and tried to exit the room gracefully. He leaned against the wall outside, feeling a little breathless.

Dallen was amused. *:Of course you're a good rider. You're on me! Who wouldn't be brilliant on the fastest, sleekest, most handsome Companion in all of Valdemar?:*

That broke his shocked mood, of course, and made him laugh. Still laughing, he headed on toward the dining hall.

He clattered down the stairs to the main hall, and joined the thin stream heading in the direction of food. Savory scents were already filling the hallway, making everyone hurry. On the way, amidst a gaggle of other students, he spotted the dark, curly hair and rust-colored uniform of his best friend, Lena, herself a Bardic Trainee. He called her name and she waved, and weaved her way through the crowd toward him.

"Mags!" she greeted him. "I'm sorry I've been so busy—"

"You better've been eatin'," he chided her. "I ain't seen ye fer two days!"

She ducked her head, guiltily. "I'm sorry. I got caught up in a special project; it's a four-person performing group. And yes, we were eating; our teacher had food brought in so we could eat while we worked. Did that history paper go over well?"

He grinned at her, relieved, as she tucked her hand into his arm and they breasted the crowd together. "Aye. It did, and thankee kindly, miss teacher. King Tyrdel and the war of the harvests, and how after 'e died, his daughter Elspeth made peace and expanded the borders wi' treaties and a marriage." He patted her hand. "I reckon a Bard coulda tole the tale better though."

She smiled back. "Well, it sort of is our job to be historians, Mags. Bardic talent goes hand in hand with a love of stories; and it doesn't matter if we make them up ourselves, nor if they are modern or from deep in history. At least so my tutors keep telling me."

He cocked his head to the side. "Huh. I cain't 'magine why anyone'd haveta keep tellin' you anythin'. You never seem t' ever stop workin'."

"Oh they tell me plenty," she replied, making a face. "Like I need to quit trying to write pieces with arpeggio if I'm no good at doing it myself. But I like arpeggio."

He squeezed her hand as they got within sight of the door of the dining hall. "So, wha's the answer?"

She sighed. "Practice I spose. As usual. Practice seems to be the answer to everything."

The crowd in the entrance thinned as students filed into the dining hall and took seats for the meal. Lena started to pull Mags along.

"What's the hurry?" he asked.

"It's roast beef tonight, and beans with bacon. There'll be nothing left if we don't get in there," she said. "Honestly, some people are just like locusts!"

She was exaggerating of course, and Mags had no fear of that. It hadn't happened yet, and he didn't think it was likely to in a hurry.

On the other hand, she was right about some people being like locusts. It was entirely possible that the choicer portions would have been snapped up if they didn't get to a seat quickly. He increased his pace to match hers.

A figure in a full Bard's outfit stepped in front of them, from one of the staircases that led to the upper stories. A tall and very handsome man, with dark hair that was greying at the temples, held out his hand imperiously, forcing them to a halt. "Ah, Trainees. Excellent. I need one of you to take this note to the King's Own Herald. I shall be performing for an entertainment for the King this evening, and he needs to discuss with me which pieces would be best for the audience." He held out a folded piece of paper.

Mags expected Lena to take it, since she was the Bardic Trainee, and this was definitely one of her expected duties. He glanced at her, and was surprised to find her white-faced and unmoving. He reached forward and took the paper from the man, and nodded. "I know Herald Nikolas, sir. I'll take it." The Bard nodded, and turned on his heel without a further word. Mags turned to Lena.

"That was rude." he muttered. " 'E coulda said please at least."

Lena was staring open-mouthed at the retreating figure. Mags looked from her to the man, curiously. "D'you know him or summat?" he said, "Doesn't look like he knows you too."

Lena blinked slowly and shook her head. "He ought to have recognized me," she said, in a strained tone of voice. "He's my father."

Mags stared at the note in his hand and looked at the retreating bard, nonplussed, and then back at Lena.

"But . . ." was all he managed, looking at the shaking girl. He just couldn't think of anything to say.

She made it easier for him—in the sense that she abandoned any pretense of conversation when she turned and hurried back down the hallway the way they had come without saying another word to him. He went after her, but when she broke into a sprint, that made it quite clear that she didn't want him around. Or, knowing Lena, anyone around.

She dashed around a corner and was gone before he reached it. He slowed to a halt, and caught his breath, looking down the corridor, but she must have run out the door. Probably heading back to Bardic and her room.

If she was determined to be alone, he was going to have to give her that, even though he really doubted that she should be alone right now. He gave a frustrated growl and stared back the way he had come.

Her father? But the man hadn't recognized her! Surely Lena's father couldn't have failed to recognize his own daughter. . . .

He glanced back at the vacated corridor ruefully. Lena certainly seemed to believe he could be capable of that. Her shock had been real . . . but there hadn't been any surprise. Just bitter unhappiness.

He thumped the wall, frustrated. Here he was, stuck between two duties, torn between going after his friend and taking the note in his hand to Herald Nikolas.

Or, a rebellious part of him said, *hang the note and go have dinner, and take the note when you're done . . . Bards be damned*. He sighed at that thought. But this was supposed to be about something for the king. And if he didn't deliver it in a timely manner, that just would show that he was too stupid to be trusted with more important matters. Definitely more trouble than he needed to have hounding him.

With a second sigh to match the first, he turned away from Lena's direction and considered where Herald Nikolas could be found. He eyed the entrance to the dining hall, listened to his stomach growl at the wonderful smells coming from it, and then almost kicked himself for missing the obvious.

:Dallen? Could yer fin' out from Rolan where Nikolas is?: and then a moment later, for politeness' sake, he added, *:Please?:*

A wry chuckle came back. *:And bother his high and mightiness? Since he seems to be just fine with talking to you as well, why don't you just ask him yourself, hmm?:*

Mags was rapidly feeling irritated enough by this entire mess to do just that, but he mentally counted to three and tried again. *:Dallen, I can' do games reet now. I got a note from a Bard t' take, an' Lena says yon Bard's her pa, an' he didn't recognize 'er an' she's mortal upset an' ran off. An' it's beef night. So you know that's upset.:*

:Ah. In that case . . . : There was a pause. *:He's coming to you. Stay where you are.:*

Well that was easy enough; Mags relaxed a little. Perhaps Nikolas would be able to explain what was going on. At any rate, it meant he wasn't going to have to run all over half the Palace and Collegia to try and find the man.

The King's Own Herald appeared at the end of the hallway shortly, recognizable by his silver-trimmed Whites, and Mags trotted down the long polished expanse to meet him, holding out the note. There was a look of faint annoyance on Nikolas' face, and once again, Mags felt himself shrinking back in guilt. *Ah bother. I went an' interrupted him in something', an' now—*

"Wretched Bards," Nikolas muttered, taking the note. "Think that they stand in one place and the sun rises and sets just to illuminate them properly. Thank you, Mags, you should never have been bothered with this." He read it quickly, after flashing Mags a hint of an apologetic smile. And as he read, his brow furrowed again with exasperation. "Just as I thought. There is nothing here that I needed to be bothered about. He could just as well—and more appropriately—have gone to the Steward with this nonsense."

Nikolas looked as if he very much wanted to crumple up the note and throw it away. He wasn't angry, at least not that Mags could see, but he was clearly very much annoyed.

"I dun understand, sir," Mags said, humbly.

Nikolas shook his head, and grimaced. "It's a kind of status game Marchand plays every time he turns up at Court. He just wants an excuse to make the King's Own jump through his ornamental hoops. Conceited popinjay that he is—he wouldn't get away with this kind of behavior if he were less Gifted, I can tell you that."

Mags was still puzzled. "Does havin' a lotta Gifts make that much on a difference in how folks're treated?" he asked.

"It shouldn't, but it does." Nikolas rolled up the note with exaggerated care and slid it back and forth between his fingers. "Then there is the 'artistic temperament' that Bards are supposed to have that Marchand milks like a prize heifer and which has thus far spared him from censure. Lita has been much too indulgent with him. And I am strongly considering seeing to it that steps are taken to give him a reprimand."

" 'E ain't Gifted 'nough to tell when his own youngling's standin' in front of him," Mags replied, feeling much relieved that Nikolas wasn't annoyed at him. " 'E looked at Lena like she was a stranger. Didn't e'en notice how upset she was."

"Of course he didn't notice. He'd have to remove some of his attention from himself for a moment,"

Nikolas replied crossly. "Never mind. I'll get this dealt with, and I will make sure it is the *last* time Marchand does anything like this again, one way or another. Mags, you properly did exactly what you were told to do. Now I want you to get some dinner, then go to the kitchen on my authority and have someone make up a dinner basket for Lena. You take it to her room; if she won't let you in, and she might not, find the proctor for her floor and tell her what happened and leave it with her. Meanwhile, I'll send a servant with a message for Lita, and she'll deal with Bard Tobias Marchand and Lena too."

Mags sighed with relief. Good. He wasn't in trouble, and Lena was going to get sorted out. And he was going to get some dinner after all, and maybe a chance to get into that new book he'd found, if Lena was still too upset to come out of her room. She probably would be. Over the course of the past several moons, there was one thing he had noticed. Though girls at the mine had mostly been indistinguishable from the boys so far as how they behaved was concerned, girls here had a whole different set of behaviors from boys. One of them was to go lock themselves in their rooms for candlemarks or even days when sufficiently upset. When they did that, only other girls could get near them.

Nikolas wasn't done, though. "Also, when you're done with Lena, I want you to come up to my rooms. I have a little task for you."

Well, so much for the book. Oh well. Whatever it was, it wouldn't be trivial. Strange as it seemed, Mags was the King's Own's private information source, and even sometimes a sort of spy. Books could wait. "Yessir," he said, and waited to see if there was anything else Nikolas wanted him for.

"Well, don't dawdle or you won't get anything but the crusty ends of the beef!" Nikolas said, tapping him on the top of the head with the rolled-up message. "Get!"

The kitchen was buzzing with gossip when he went to get the dinner basket. From the sound of things, the arrival of Bard Marchand was going to be a nine days wonder. Everyone was agog at his presence back in Haven, and all that anyone could talk about was how brilliant and how handsome he was. Mags sat on a stool out of the way and waited for one of the undercooks to put that meal basket together and listened.

Notice no one's talkin' *'bout how nice he is,* Mags thought sourly. To his right, serving maids helped collect the leftovers and sort them into what was going back into the larder, and what was going out to charity. Nothing was wasted in the King's kitchens.

"Do ye think we'll get a chance t' hear him, like?" one of the serving maids sighed, her eyes all dreamy-sparkly as she deftly combined the remains of three pies into one pan.

One of the undercooks rapped her on the top of the head with a spoon. "He's not for the likes of you, gu-url," she growled. "So you can pull that little thought right out of your head. The most you be like to hear is a snatch of song while you be servin' the wine, an' if you go all moony and spill the wine, it'll be the pots an' pans for you for the rest of the year."

"Well put, Una," the head cook rumbled, from where he was supervising the making of porridge for breakfast on the morrow, and he cast a dark look around the kitchen. "That goes for all of you. If I hear of one incident that happened because you were gawking at the Bard, the gawker will find herself demoted to scullery maid if she's lucky!"

That didn't stop the gossip, but at least it went to whispers behind hands, as the head cook shoved the finished dinner basket at Mags.

So across the lawns and gardens he went—the gardens still slumbering under their layers of carefully raked leaves and compost. Like Herald's Collegium, Bardic had separate sections for the girls' and boys' rooms. But the moment he turned up at the door to the girls' rooms at Bardic Collegium and asked to see Lena he was told to "wait right there."

He sat down on a bench in the little entryway, thinking that it was a very good thing that there was an extra hot plate in the bottom of the basket keeping everything warm. He had been here before, now and again; people were allowed to have other people in their rooms. He knew that the Dean of the Collegium had her office quite nearby, and shrewdly reckoned it was to keep any mischief from happening in the girls' section. Bards were not known for keeping regular hours and the head of Bardic was no exception to this rule. If you didn't know for sure whether or not the Dean was in her office you would probably think twice about getting up to something.

And that was when he heard it . . . Master Bard Lita Darvalis, Dean of Bardic Collegium, and head of the Bardic Circle . . . sounding off in full voice. And she was not singing. Oh no.

"I am appalled! Appalled, Tobias! If you were a Trainee, you'd be in the kitchen peeling roots at this very moment, with an assignment to analyze all three hundred verses of 'Maddy Graves' to follow! How *dare* you order Trainees about as if they were your personal pages? Not even Bardic, but a *Herald* Trainee, over whom you have precisely no authority!"

There was a moment of silence, which Mags, his ears burning, assumed wasn't silence at all, but the Bard attempting to answer.

"Well if you are going to act the fool in the middle of a crowded hallway at dinnertime, you had better anticipate that the gossip is going to be all over all three Collegia before the pie is served!" Mags let out his breath. Oh good. He wasn't going to be the one Bard Marchand was going to blame for being hauled before Bard Lita. "And above all else, how dare you try and turn the King's Own into your personal flunky? I have children in this Collegium that were raised in barns and fostered by sheep that have better manners than you displayed—in public no less! And you a Master Bard!"

There was another moment of silence. Whatever it was that Marchand said, it only made Lita angrier. "You are a disgrace, Tobias! Dear gods above and below, did every single bit of what you learned in Courtly Graces fly out of your head the moment you left the Collegium? No one, no one, sends the King's Own a note about a performance unless it's about a suspected assassin in the audience! If I could do it, I swear I would break you down to Journeyman at this very moment! What in the name of the Seven Hells were you *thinking?*" Lita didn't give him a chance to reply this time. "Never mind. I would rather assume that you weren't actually thinking at all. It's far preferable to knowing that this was some twisted little trick of yours to prove your inherent superiority to mere Heralds."

Mags was very, very glad that he was sitting politely in the entryway and right where he was supposed to be, because he really did not want anyone to think he had placed himself deliberately where he could overhear this. Mind, Nikolas would probably be interested to know exactly what had been said . . .

Then again, the entire Collegium was probably hearing this. Lita was making no effort at all to keep her voice down. Now that he thought about it, she might well be projecting it on purpose.

"You are damned lucky that the King specifically requested your presence tonight, or by all that is unholy, I would send in a trained dog to take your place and tell Kiril that I had found a better performer! And you are damned lucky that Nikolas is not the sort to react in kind to such a piece of petty behavior, or this little incident would be all over the Palace by tonight, and what do you think that would that do to your fine reputation, hmm? How many of your noble patrons would welcome you if they thought they'd be treated to a display of such insolence in their own homes?"

If the Bard replied to this, as before, it was inaudible. And Mags was saved further discomfort by the proctor of Lena's floor arriving to come take the basket from him. It was a girl he knew vaguely, a hearty blond who seemed concerned enough. "Lena's upset, but I'll see that she eats," the girl told him, in a not unkindly tone.

"Thankee," he replied, and quickly made his escape before he could overhear anything else. It had been uncomfortable enough to overhear a grown man being dressed down like a misbehaving youngling, and he just didn't want to hear any more at this point.

It could have been a trick of acoustics, something that made what was said in Lita's office clearly audible in that entryway and nowhere else. It could have been . . . but he doubted it. Lita was a Master Bard, and he would be very much surprised if she wasn't aware of the acoustic properties of every inch of Bardic Collegium. No, she wanted people to hear what she was saying, and he was just—accidentally—the only non-Bard to do so.

:Of course she wants them to overhear,: said Dallen, as he made his escape down a path swiftly darkening in the twilight. *:Marchand's behavior really was appallingly rude with even the best possible interpretation. With the worst interpretation—well, you heard Nikolas. Bards are supposed to be examples of deportment and they are supposed to be extremely good at protocol. Lita wants everyone in Bardic Collegium to know that not even being extraordinarily Gifted nor extremely famous and popular is going to save you if you act badly, because your bad*

behavior will reflect on the Bardic Circle as a whole. By the way, I was passing all that on to Rolan directly. I thought that would be more discreet.:

Ah, another relief; Mags hadn't been looking forward to a question-and-answer session that was likely to be as embarrassing for Nikolas as it would be for him. He shook his head as he ducked into the closest door, a chill breeze chasing him inside. *:Well then, is he stupid, or what? I mean, he had to know this was gonna get 'round and he was gonna get told on.:*

:Well, it's not stupidity,: Dallen replied ruefully as Mags paused long enough to take off his cloak and drape it over his arm. *:If I were going to guess—and it has to be a guess, because I don't know his thoughts—he's been out of Haven for quite a long time, and he's been very much made the pet of by several houses of the high-born. They are flattered that he comes to their homes, they fawn over him, and quite frankly, he has gotten used to being treated as if* he *was practically royalty, so much so that now he thinks he is the equivalent of the King's Own. You know, I think I have even heard of him being called the 'King of Bards.' So perhaps in his own mind, he is a sort of King.:*

:Ye kin paint a crow white, but that ain't gonna make it a dove,: Mags replied shrewdly, nodding at one of the other Trainees as they passed each other in the hall.

:I must remember that one. Well, there is a bit more to it than that. Besides his Gifts and talents, it is true that he has Projective Empathy, and he has used it in several crisis situations, making him something of a hero at the time.:

:Huh,: Mags said. *:Still—:*

:Indeed. Still. He did stop riots three times. And he did manage to save an innocent man from a mob. And he did hold an entire troupe of brigands spellbound until help could come, twice. But. The thing about Projective Empathy is that it is a very good tool to ensure that the wielder is safe.: Dallen's mind-voice was more than a bit sarcastic. *:If things start to go badly, you can just narrow your focus down to convincing your opponents that you are their new best friend.:*

:So it ain't like throwin' yerself inta harm's way, then.:

Mags could feel Dallen's snort. *:The average Guardsman sees more danger in a single incident than Marchand did in all six of his encounters together. Oh, I am not going to say he wasn't brave, but it is easier to be brave when you know you have a gigantic shield to hide behind if you have to.:*

Mags plodded down the hallway and pushed open the door at the end that led into the Palace proper. *:So people think he's a big damn hero, an' he's an amazin' Bard with a lotta Gifts. An' he reckons now he's back at the Palace, 'twere time ev'body realizes he's the Second Comin' of Stefan, an' acts like 'tis a privilege t' breathe th' same air as him?:*

:In a nutshell. And again, I must be fair, part of this is a desire to see Bardic Collegium regarded with the same respect and value as Herald's and Healer's,: Dallen said reluctantly. *:You've heard Lita on that subject.:*

It was Mags' turn to snort. *:But most on it is there ain't 'nough space for him an' his ego t' be in th' same room at th' same time.:*

There was an astonished pause, then a flood of mental laughter. *:Oh my. Oh my. I'm relaying that to the others. Mags, every once in a while you do have a way with words!:*

:Tell that t'me language teacher,: he replied ruefully, then he was at the door of Herald Nikolas' small suite, and there was no time for chat.

MAGS was a little nonplussed. Although he had known he was going to escape a sort of interrogation about what he had heard, he had fully expected Nikolas to say *something* about the Bard, if only to assure his protégé that Marchand was not going to come looking for Mags in reprisal. And he had been morally certain that Nikolas was going to ask for Mags' own thoughts on the matter, and correct them if Mags had come to the wrong conclusion. But aside from asking how Lena was, Nikolas appeared to have dismissed Bard Marchand from his mind entirely. It was odd. It seemed as if the *Bard* was obsessed with proving he was every bit the King's Own's equal, but the *Herald* was utterly indifferent to the supposed rivalry.

Back at the mine, rivalries like this generally ended badly, when they weren't dealt with firmly by a superior authority.

Take the Pieters siblings, just as an example. The boys all seemed to have been born quarreling with each other and jockeying for position. They were always at each others' throats, trying to gain ascendancy in their father's eyes, and it was only the knowledge that their father would have the hide of anyone who interfered in what made the mine profitable that kept them confined to informing on each other or trying to make sure that the blame for anything that went wrong fell squarely on shoulders other than their own.

Well, things were different here, and he was always reminding himself of that. Maybe—probably—the Bard would confine himself to petty annoyances that Nikolas could just shrug off.

"I will say this much, that man does not deserve to have a child," Nikolas said darkly. "It is heinous enough that he clearly spends so little time with his family that he cannot even recognize his own daughter on sight—but the fact that she is one of the more promising Trainees *and he isn't even aware of it* is just—" Nikolas shook his head. "I have no words."

Mags nodded. Nikolas actually had a daughter of his own, a bit older than Lena. Amily was one of Mags' few friends, and Mags knew how much the two cherished each other.

"I dunno," he replied. "I ain't exactly real good at knowin' what families supposed to be like."

Nikolas coughed apologetically. "Well . . . the reason I asked you here tonight is because I would like you to take some of your training outside the Collegia and do a bit of outright spying for me. You remember what I said about people ignoring a young lad like yourself."

Mags nodded. "Yessir." This was sounding very interesting indeed. He hadn't had any sort of overt assignment from Nikolas since the disappearance of the foreign envoys. Granted, he and Bear had spent some time recovering from nearly being killed, but they really hadn't needed more than a fortnight for that. The lessons had resumed in Nikolas' quarters after that respite, but they hadn't taken place quite as often, and truth to tell, Mags had been a little disappointed.

These had been lessons in how to be unobtrusive, and in how to observe. Interestingly enough, the lessons in "how to be unobtrusive" were not always about being quiet. Nikolas had shown him how to gauge the mood of people around him, what the King's Own had called "reading the room." He'd learned to tell when being somewhat boisterous would be more useful than being quiet, and how to counterfeit looking careless and utterly oblivious to what was going on around him.

Or rather, he had just begun those sorts of lessons. He knew very well that he was a long, long way from mastering them.

On the other hand, these were things he *could* practice on his own, and really should. He couldn't expect the King's Own Herald, who was, after all, the very literal right-hand man of the King himself, to spend hours tutoring him through simple practice. That would be as rude as—as what Bard Marchand had done.

But there were a lot of times when he wondered if Nikolas had decided he wasn't worth wasting any more effort on.

"I've been watching you, and you're coming along well. Well enough I think that for something simple like this, you can handle it on your own." Nikolas smiled a little as Mags sat straight up, eagerly. "I'm counting on your youth, your appearance, and the fact that our quarry is the sort of man who regards servants as furniture."

Mags grinned a little. "There's a mort' o them, sir."

"True enough. Well, here is the situation. Councilor Chamjey is up to something, and I should like to find out what it is. He has gotten a virtual flood of messages lately, far more than is normal for him at this time of year. He has missed several Council meetings, and been late or left early for others." Nikolas coughed. "Chamjey is not exactly subtle, or he wouldn't have made such a series of fundamental mistakes."

Mags tilted his head to one side. "That don't seem all that suspicious-like t'me, beggin' yer pardon, sir. I mean, could be anythin' from plannin' a party t' surprise 'is lady, t' jest making a really good deal he don' want anyone t' know 'bout. I mean, he's a merchanter, right?"

Nikolas nodded. "That's correct. And all of that would be in keeping with a merchant working some sort of shrewd bargain. The problem is two-fold. The first is that Chamjey is probably the one person least suited to being a Councilor on the Council; most of the others will at least make an attempt at altruism, and at thinking for the greater good of Valdemar. Chamjey has never let the greater good get in the way of his own personal interests in all of the time I have known him. The second part of the problem is that Chamjey has a habit of boasting about deals he has in the making to some of his colleagues, usually in the form of oblique hints. There has been nothing this time, although Soren says he has been incredibly smug of late. So both Soren and I are concerned. We want to know what he's up to. It might be nothing. But if there is anything going on that is counter to the interest of the kingdom as a whole, not only do we want to know what it is, we can use that to dismiss Chamjey, or demand his resignation, and have someone more honest put in his place."

Mags nodded. "Am I gonna need t' get leave t' skip some classes?" He both hoped for and dreaded the idea. Hoped for, because he would certainly not be at all averse to missing a complex maths class or two. And definitely not averse to missing a language class.

Dreaded because if he did miss the classes, he would only have to make them up. Ugh.

"Perhaps. I don't know yet, but I'll take care of the arrangements for you. In the meantime—" Nikolas handed him a slip of paper. "This is his address, if you care to scout it out. Perhaps it will give you some ideas for following him without being observed."

Mags took it, and smiled. The address was not far from Councilor Soren's home, and the Councilor—and more especially, the Councilor's niece Lydia and her friends—were acquaintances of his. No one would think twice about seeing him ride past, and he was overdue for a visit.

Now he just had to somehow squeeze time in for that visit. From somewhere. And make sure Lena was all right. And help find some way to make her feel better if she wasn't.

And then there was that Kirball thing that Caelen wanted him to look into.

He sighed. Things were just never simple. "Yessir, I'll hev a look, soon's I kin."

"Chamjey?" Lydia said, with curiosity. "Why don't you ask Uncle about him instead of me?"

"Cause yer uncle'd tell me what he was. I wanna know what he does." Mags grinned at her. It was pure luck finding her alone like this, and he'd snatched it up. "Yer servants all talk to ye, so I wanta know what they tol' ye. They prolly wouldn' tell me, cause I ain't family."

He was "paying" for his information by serving as a yarn-holder while Lydia wound skeins of extremely fine, soft yarn into tight little balls for the lace shawl she was planning on knitting. Lydia and Soren had an unusual relationship with their servants—unusual by the standards of the wealthy, that is. They knew all of them by name, about their lives, and treated them as people rather than furniture. If there was anything more to Chamjey's mysterious comings and goings than Nikolas already knew, the servants would certainly have told Lydia.

"What he does, well, hmm," she said thoughtfully. "Ana was telling me the other day that some of the servants think he is having an affair or keeping a mistress, but she doesn't think so."

"Huh." That would be a bit of a laugh on Nikolas if a clandestine affair was the cause of Chamjey's behavior. "Why not?"

Lydia smirked. They were sitting in her solar, with lovely sunlight pouring through real glass windows down onto both of them, and with a crackling fire on her hearth it was almost as warm as summer. Lydia had pulled back her tumble of red curls with a green ribbon, and was wearing a deceptively plain green wool dress to match. But Mags knew, thanks to Lydia's own expert ongoing tutelage in such matters, that appearances were indeed deceptive. The wool was the finest of chirra underfur, the gown was expertly tailored, of a design that would not fall much out of fashion, ever, and green was a very, very hard color to dye. Only red was harder. Lydia's "plain" gown probably cost more than some of the velvet and satin outfits that the highborn paraded around in at Court. This was the sort of thing that was passed down through generations as an heirloom, for it was easy enough to put it in fashion with a new collar, belt, trim, undergown, or overgown.

Lydia had even explained to him why it was that red, green, and white had been chosen respectively for the Bards, Healers, and Heralds. All three colors were expensive and difficult to dye—or, in the case of Heralds' Whites, to bleach and keep pristine white. All three were, as a consequence, immediately recognizable at a distance. And all three would be very, very hard to counterfeit properly, in no small part because they *were* expensive. People who were trying to pull scams generally spent as little as possible to do so. It wouldn't be impossible for someone to try, but it would be unlikely.

Even Lydia's gown was not the brilliant green of Healers' robes, but a much more muted, darker color.

She set the ball of wool—dyed to match in the same batch as her dress, she had told him—down in the basket at her side, put another skein on his outstretched hands, and began winding again. "Well, the first thing is, according to my maid, Chamjey isn't going out at an hour when his wife wouldn't miss him. When he goes, he's dressed very quietly, not his usual style." She made a face, which told Mags that the "usual style" was probably flamboyant and ostentatious. "A man going to see a new mistress would dress up to impress her. He doesn't bring any presents, either, which a man with a new mistress does. But the big thing is that Chamjey's wife is sporting some very expensive new presents herself, and she is looking uncommonly satisfied about them. Now, that might mean that Chamjey has a new mistress, and his wife is getting expensive gifts in an attempt to mollify her. But that only works if the wife is perfectly happy with her husband going off with another woman. That's not true of Mira Chamjey; she is very jealous, and if she knew about a mistress, she would scalp him and skin the woman. So he *is* bribing her, but it's not to let him have his fun."

Mags nodded, now very glad that he had come to Lydia before he had scouted the ground himself.

"So—" he prompted.

"I think it's a business deal, and I think it's one that's

underhanded, and I think he's trying to work it through a third party." Lydia nodded decisively, the ball of wool growing in her fingers as if by magic. "The fact that he is trying to do it through a third party makes me fairly certain he thinks he would be in trouble if he got caught at it."

"See now, tha's where yer losin' me," Mags admitted. "I dun see how a sharp deal could get a man in trouble wi' Crown."

"It depends on what kind of a sharp deal it is," Lydia replied. "Suppose—just suppose—someone had had an absolutely accurate idea of when that blizzard that caused us so much trouble this winter was going to strike, how long it would last, and how badly food and wood supplies would be hurt until everyone dug out. First of all, it would be his duty to report that, so that all of Haven could have gotten prepared. But let's just suppose that he didn't. Let's suppose that instead, he got several warehouses and filled them up with staple foods and firewood and didn't sell them until just before the blizzard was going to hit. And then he opened them up and began selling things at twice their normal value, and once the blizzard hit, then sold them at three times their normal value. That would be a sharp deal, but it would also get him in a lot of trouble."

Mags nodded. That made sense.

"There are other things, too, that's just one example. So have you got any ideas?" she asked.

"Think mebbe. Reckon I'd better be right careful 'bout how I follow 'im. It'll be hard t' do it the usual way. This street ain't crowded, so I'd stand out no matter what I looked like." He scratched his head. "Round here, ev' servant has house uniform, an' ye cain't jest wander about 'less ye got the right uniform, or ye look like ye belong here."

Lydia tilted her head to the side. "If that's all that's stopping you—" then she paused. "No, that wouldn't work, would it? If Chamjey is doing something underhanded, seeing someone in Uncle's livery following him—"

Mags chuckled. "Which's why I ain't asked ye," he replied.

"I'll leave it to the expert then," she said with a grin. He made a face at her.

"Ain't no expert. More like 'prentice. 'Prentice bein' set his first task t' do on his own." He laughed self-deprecatingly. "So I reckon this ain't anythin' like—really important. More like t' see if'n I kin find out anythin' on m'own."

Lydia blinked solemnly at him. "I think you're probably underestimating yourself, but—" She shrugged. "Well, maybe not, maybe you're right. So how is poor Lena?"

He refrained from rolling his eyes. "I dun know why she's so upset. Weren't like she ever saw her pa, or he saw her."

Lydia wound up the last of the wool deftly. "I'd say ask Amily. She has a father that's just as famous, so maybe she can explain it."

With his hands now freed he could scratch his head. "Reckon I will," he said. "And thankee, Lydia."

She grinned at him. "You made a very good winding

spool, and a much more entertaining one than my usual. Good luck with this job, and I hope you impress Herald Nikolas."

He laughed, and took himself off to the stables where Dallen was waiting. *:So what d'ye think?:* he asked, as he saddled his Companion. *:I'm thinkin' that followin' this feller ain't gonna be too easy. Leastwise, not up here.:*

:I tend to agree. We need to do something other than the usual. Move the blanket a little higher on my withers, please.:

Mags got the distinct impression that Dallen was waiting for him to come up with . . . something. Something creative. Something that wasn't . . . usual.

He sensed Soren's head groom approaching from behind and reached back without thinking about it for Dallen's bitless bridle. "Thenkee, Roben," he said, and that was when it struck him.

He always knew where someone was, if he knew that person. Was that some aspect of his Mindspeaking Gift?

:Yes it is,: Dallen said promptly. *:You don't have to know what someone is saying to recognize his voice. He could be in another room and all you need to hear is the cadence to know it's him. It's the same with Mindspeech. You don't have to know what they are thinking to know it's them. So . . . :*

If he knew someone . . . he would know what they "sounded" like . . . so . . .

He swung himself up into Dallen's saddle. *:So, it'd be all right if I followed Chamjey by that? So long as I didn't actually listen in on what he's a-thinkin'?:*

Dallen tossed his head in the way that told Mags he was pleased. *:Exactly so. So?:*

:So I reckon I'd better find a reason t' lurk around 'im and get t' know 'im.:

They headed up the road to the Palace and Collegia.

:How convenient that you'll get your chance today,: Dallen told him, with a hint of amusement. *:There is a Council meeting going on right now, and it is going to go long, according to Rolan, Chamjey is showing no signs of wanting to slip away. And I expect if you were to put on a page's uniform and go serve wine for a candlemark or so, no one would object.:*

Mags groaned. As if he didn't already have enough to do. Oh well. Best get it over with.

Evidently there had been a great deal of silent communication among Nikolas, Rolan, and Dallen, because when he arrived back at the Collegium, there was a page waiting with an impudent grin and a spare set of pages' livery in approximately his size.

He then spent the most boring pair of candlemarks in his life, standing with the other two pages while the circle of old men droned on and on about—well, it involved a lot of maths. Trade things, it seemed. Fortunately he was not there to understand what was going on, he was there to get himself familiar with the feel of Chamjey's mind.

Chamjey himself would have been utterly ordinary if it hadn't been for the flamboyance of his dress. And that was the oddest thing. Because judging by that "feel," Chamjey was using that very flamboyance as a kind of . . . mask? No, a distraction. He was using it to make the other Councilors underestimate him. Not that he was brilliant by any means, but he was shrewd. He knew exactly what he was doing.

The outside was a plainish man, average in height, weight, and facial features, with thinning hair and a bit of a belly, who appeared to be desperately trying to make himself look more important, attractive, and wealthy with his rather too elaborate clothing.

The inside was a shrewd calculator, who never did anything without studying it from as many angles as possible. If Chamjey had been an animal, he would have been a crow. Not highly intelligent, but clever. Very clever.

And very much on the lookout for himself and no one else.

When the set of pages that Mags was with was relieved of duty by another trio, he wandered off to his room to try and make up for missing two candlemarks worth of study time, wondering if he had somehow stumbled onto something not even the King's Own was aware of.

Strange.

:What's strange?: Dallen asked.

Mags leaned idly against the side of a building and waited while his quarry, all unaware, approached him. This was a relatively busy corner, where young men with nothing better to do—or who hoped to pick up an odd, easy job or two—loitered in the shadow of an inn. He was wearing the same set of mismatched cast-offs from various Guardsmen that he had arrived at the Collegium wearing—although, now that he had a bit more weight and height, they fit him a great deal better.

:Clothes. Funny how they make ye feel. Yon fancy stuff I have, tha' I wore t' Midwinter . . . feel like there's allus someone watchin' me, an' I gotta be extra careful and quiet like so's I don't make mistakes. Like if I open m'mouth I'll get found out an' kicked out, even when it was just Master Soren what invited me in the first place.:

:I can see that,: Dallen replied.

:Reg'lar Trainee uniform, I feel like I gotta just try hard all the time, not waste a drip of a candlemark, better measure up, no slackin', no slouchin'. Like . . . like I gotta live up t' the Grays, belike. This . . . : He chuckled to himself. *:This, y'know, I dun feel like there's all that pressure.:*

:An amusing observation. Is that why your posture is so poor?:

Dallen was—somewhere. Somewhere that Chamjey wouldn't see him from the street at any rate, and somewhere that a Companion alone would not excite much interest. Nowhere near Mags. Probably waiting in an inn-yard somewhere nearby, one where Heralds or Trainees might leave a Companion while they went on an errand. Companions were not exactly unobtrusive after all—horse-sized, horse-shaped, brilliantly white with silver hooves and blue eyes—you couldn't mistake them for anything else, and their white coats literally would not "take" dyes. So having a Companion visible on this street, when he was already nervous, would immediately put Chamjey on alert.

But one more lounging youth leaning against a wall and watching several other wastrels at a game of dice wouldn't alert him to anything. Except, perhaps, an irritated observation about wastrel youth and wasting time.

:Nay. Just blendin' in.: Mags had picked this spot very deliberately. It was the first place where Chamjey would be able to choose a direction once he came down off the street that led to his manor. So Mags was going to wait here, see what direction it was that Chanjey chose, then ride forward on Dallen, getting ahead of him, to the next spot where the same choice was likely to happen. Chamjey would never see anyone following him because no one would *be* following him. It was all about staying within range of that faint "feel" of the man. As long as he did that, he would know exactly where Chamjey went.

And in this case, as he leaned over the game intently, Chamjey reached the intersection and went west without even a glance at Mags and the gamers.

After he was gone, Mags sauntered off, looking as if he was going nowhere in particular. But he met Dallen in the alley behind the building; making sure no one had seen either of them, he hopped up into the saddle, and off they went.

It was a very good thing that Companions were a common sight here in Haven, and an even better thing that he had brought the cloak that went with his Grays to conceal the very non-uniform clothing he was wearing. No one gave him more than a cursory glance. The most that happened was that traffic parted a little to let them pass, with perhaps a smile or a wave.

It became apparent that Chamjey was headed in the direction of the Trade Road—and probably was going to one of several extremely large and busy inns on the outskirts of the city, all situated on either side of the Trade Road, and all devoted to merchant-travelers. These inns catered to everyone from the simple peddler with a donkey to merchants specializing in gems and other small and extremely valuable items. If you were going to have a clandestine meeting with someone, you had a choice, after all—you could slip away in the dead of night, try and find a secluded spot, and hope no one had followed you, or you could "hide" in the sort of place you had every right to frequent and do it at the busiest time of day. Chamjey had picked the latter, which was very shrewd of him.

:Now that we know where he's going?: Dallen said suggestively.

Mags knew exactly what Dallen was going to suggest. *:Aye. Might's well cut straight there, then you disappear whilst I lurk and figger out how I kin get close 'nough to listen.:*

Dallen moved into a canter; at this point the best thing that they could do would be to get far ahead of Chamjey and minimize his chances of spotting them.

When they arrived at the spot, it was the busiest time of the day. It wasn't going to be hard to hide amid all the noise and bustle of the inn-yards. The inns swarmed with people; travelers arriving, travelers leaving, local merchants turning up for a meeting or merely a meal. And as for the animals, there were horses, donkeys, even a chirra or two—small carts and enormous "show wagons" where the side could be let down to form a stage—there were so many draft animals and vehicles that moving them in and out was a science. The practitioners of that science were grooms and servants and in at least two of the inn-yards, a blacksmith.

Mags had no idea how anyone kept anything straight, but amid the chaos no one was going to notice one slightly undersized, slightly shabby young man. Especially one that walked as if he had somewhere to go and a purpose. You didn't want to loiter in a place like this, that made you look suspicious, and you might be thought a potential thief.

Mags even had taken the precaution of bringing a "messenger" bag with him, a flat satchel that went over one shoulder and was used by paid runners in the city to convey documents and small objects. That, all by itself, would insure his invisibility.

With Dallen safely tucked away in one of the out-of-the-way stalls reserved for Companions—for, yes, Heralds came here too—Mags walked the inn-yards, looking like a young man with an errand, bag prominently on his hip. The air was thick with the scent of horse and hay, sweat, dust, and the occasional whiff of something good from the kitchens. There were boys with shovels and buckets scampering about just to get droppings from the animals before they got stepped on—the last thing you wanted was for your inn patrons to come into your common room with manure from something they'd trodden on in your yard. And the noise—you had to shout to be heard over it. Hooves clattering, wheels rolling, music and laughter from the inns themselves, and people in the yard talking or yelling at one another.

He sensed Chamjey coming closer and closer, and finally positioned himself at the crucial moment right where he could get a good view of the road. As a result, Mags caught sight of the man himself going into one of the inns that catered to the prosperous, but not wealthy.

But that might be a ruse. Chamjey had proven himself quite clever at such things already. So Mags moved around through the crowd at that inn, making sure that Chamjey was, indeed, in there to stay. Then he retired to the back of the stable and the relatively quiet alley to think. How to get close to the man?

:Server?: Dallen suggested.

:Too risky. He mightn't order nothin', an' he'll spook if somethin' he didn't expect turns up.:

:Well you don't need to get in the same room he's in, you only need to get near enough to overhear.:

:Server's still too risky. Some'un might catch me lurkin'. An' I ain't had a chance t' talk t' the keeper an' get permission. Reckon I'd be taken fer a thief.:

:And you need to be doing something that will keep you in one place for a good long while as you listen.: Dallen pondered this. *:I wonder . . . can you just nip in and look at the fireplace in the common room?:*

Mags was baffled by the request, but Dallen obviously had a reason for it, so he did as he was asked.

The common room was full, but not so crowded he couldn't get next to the fire. He glanced into it. It looked like a fireplace. But Dallen, looking through his eyes, obviously saw something else, something he had been hoping for.

:Aha! The ashes haven't been collected. Good. Come on out. We're going to pay a quick visit to a soapmaker.:

Now Mags was even more baffled, but from the "feel" of Chamjey, the person he was waiting for had not yet arrived, so there was no reason to balk at Dallen's orders.

:Why a soapmaker?: he asked, getting himself up into the saddle again.

:Because soapmakers need ashes, and inns produce a lot of ash they don't need. Most households save their ashes—they make their own soap, they use the ash on their back gardens, or they use it to polish metal, like silver and brass, with. Inns don't. So soapmakers go around to collect it. Here we are.: Dallen stopped at the front of a little shop that had a workshop in the back. *:Go in and ask which soapmaker has the concession for the ashes at The Splendid Table. Be friendly and casual.:*

Mags walked into the shop, which was a little like walking into a wall of scent. There was a counter just inside the door; behind the counter were shelves full of soap cut neatly into wrapped bars, or stacked in great multicolored chunks.

The pretty young blond girl about his age behind the counter, dressed in a light blue gown with an embroidered apron, stared wide-eyed at him. She knew what a Companion was, of course; every child old enough to walk in Haven knew what a Companion was. But it wasn't often that you saw someone not in Whites or Grays riding one.

"Evenin' missus," Mags said, "Wunner if ye kin tell me who has concession fer the ashes from Splendid Table?"

"Oh!" The girl got two very pink spots in her cheeks, and her voice went up in a squeak. "That would be us—is something wrong?" Without waiting for an answer, she darted through a curtain into the back of the shop, and returned with a woman that was an older version of herself in tow.

"I'm Mella Amise, Herald," the woman said, wiping her hand carefully on her apron before offering it to him. "You wanted to know about the ash concession?"

"Trainee, missus," said Mags, clasping her hand briefly, but firmly. "And aye—"

:Ask her if she's due to collect.:

"Are ye due to collect?" he repeated.

"Overdue by a day or two," the woman said with a sigh. "I've been right busy sending our boy out with deliveries."

:Ask her if you can.:

But before Mags could repeat what Dallen had told him to say, the woman cocked her head at him with a shrewd look in her eye. "Reckon you want an excuse to be in there?" she offered.

He hesitated. She looked out the door, straight at Dallen.

"This isn't some prank is it?" she asked Dallen directly.

Dallen shook his head vigorously, and gave her a long and penetrating look.

"Something he's doing—he needs to be in the inn—"

She stopped. "Something . . . a Herald knows about this?"

Dallen nodded just as hard.

She seemed satisfied. "I won't ask Herald business, and I'm more than willing to help." She eyed Mags a moment. "Aye, those clothes will do; I expect that's why you're in them and not proper Grays. Tellie, go get the ash-collector kit."

The girl went behind the curtain again, and returned with a dusty, heavy canvas apron, a covered bucket, a dustpan, and a small hand-broom. The woman helped Mags don the apron. "Now, it's easy enough. Tellie will have the barrow out front for you. Just sweep the ashes into the pan, dump them into the bucket, when it's full, take it downstairs to where you've left the barrow and dump the bucket in the barrow. No one will look twice at you. When you've got what you came for, just come straight back; the boy can do the rest of the job tomorrow."

Mags nodded, feeling a little astonished that this was going so smoothly.

:She's a law-abiding citizen of Haven, you silly boy. My presence and my confirmation tells her you have the authority to ask what you want from her for help.: Dallen's mind-voice was amused. *:My presence and the fact that I told her a Herald knows about this also assures her that what you want won't be anything wrong, because I would kick you into the next city if you did abuse your authority.:*

"All right then, off you go. You look like you're no stranger to hard work, so you should be able to pass as one of my boys." She made little shooing motions with her hands. "Your Companion can stay here if you like."

"That'd be good, missus, thankee," Mags managed to say. Dallen whickered. He carried the implements outside and there, as promised, a hand-barrow was waiting, but not one like he had ever seen before. This one, just like the bucket, had a cover. In fact, it looked less like a barrow and more like a crude chest with barrow handles and a wheel in front. He put his burden down inside, picked up the handles, and returned to the inn.

He was intercepted by one of the grooms, who sent him around to a side door where he could leave the barrow. He made certain of Chamjey's location and headed inside. He hoped that the meeting hadn't gone on too long. He hoped he could find a place where he could hear it!

Luck was still with him. He found a vacant room that shared the same chimney with the one Chamjey was in almost immediately; it was one of a long line of what looked to be private parlors. Getting down on his hands and knees, he removed the screen, the fire-dogs, the andirons, and the rest, and slowly began sweeping, listening as hard as he could.

The chimney proved to be an excellent carrier of sound, and Mags spared a moment to be grateful to Dallen for thinking of this.

". . . and it gets better for us. That last late blizzard did for about half the lambs; it caught the shepherds right in the middle of lambing season," someone was saying. "We haven't even gotten into the rains, and those always take a toll as well. Right now all the herders are thinking about is to wonder how they're going to survive without lamb to sell for meat until shearing time comes. And then, what with that wet-lung plague this past fall, they've all lost about ten percent of the adult flocks and the fleeces are going to be a bit dodgy this year, since a sick sheep makes a weak fleece. So they've been jumping at the chance to sell their wool as a future-speculation, while it's still on the sheep's back, and to sell lambs still trotting about and bleating." There was glee in the man's voice. "Buying up the fleece and lambs before they're harvested, so to speak, is brilliant, Chamjey. The herders think we are risking our money, paying for lambs that might die and fleece that is going to be poor. They don't know how widespread the problem is, and that we've rounded up the whole market and put it in our pocket. We'll be the ones setting the prices, no matter what."

"And you made sure nothing can be traced back to us?" Chamjey asked anxiously.

"Not a chance," the man assured him. "I've used so many intermediaries sometimes it makes my head spin. By the end of the fortnight, we'll have completely wrapped up this year's mutton, lamb, and wool market, and we'll be able to demand whatever we want."

"Brilliant," said Chamjey with deep satisfaction. "I'll see about imported wool. I think I can get a high tariff put on it, in the name of protecting our shepherds from cheap outside wool. There's just not that much imported right now that I think anyone will even blink."

As he swept up every single mote of ash, Mags was just—astonished. Somehow Chamjey—or perhaps, this unknown person—had discovered the misfortune that had befallen, not just a few flocks, but evidently the flocks across—what? Most of Valdemar? And now he was somehow going to make a lot of profit off it?

:I think we've heard enough,: Dallen said. *:I've already relayed all this to Rolan. Let's return this stuff to the soapmaker and get back up the hill.:*

Chamjey and the other person were deep in a conversation about wool, which Mags didn't think was going to interest Nikolas. *:Right. Sooner I get out, less chance I get caught.:*

He put the fire things back where they belonged—because not doing so would look very suspicious, and because he didn't want to make any extra work for the inn servants—and took his bucket of ashes outside. Once there he got his barrow and headed back.

The soapmaker greeted him with a nod, as if she had expected he would not take long. She took back her apron, and thrust it at a rather grimy boy who took it cheerfully enough. When the boy was gone, taking the barrow back to the inn, presumably, she turned to Mags.

"I hope you got what you were looking for, Trainee," she said. "And I'm glad we could help you."

"So'm I, missus," he replied with a little bow of thanks. "Ye saved me a mort' o'trouble."

"Well good." Then she grinned. "And you might think of sending here if you need soap."

He dusted himself off with the help of the girl, who brushed him down with a broom with a bit too much enthusiasm, and went to get Dallen out of their yard. Dallen was looking altogether pleased with himself, and Mags felt he had every reason to be.

"So what's Nikolas say?" he asked, as they made their way up the hill.

:Well, the long and the short of it is—you know that example Lydia gave you? It was uncannily spot-on. While we were aware that the blizzards were causing some hardship, and we knew there was a plague of something that was affecting the flocks in the south, we didn't know just how bad both were. Somehow, Chamjey found out, and rather than alerting the Crown via the Council, he decided that he was going to secure all the available wool and meat for this year to himself, so that he can command whatever price he wants.: Dallen, strangely, was not angry. He was not even annoyed.

Perhaps because Chamjey had been found out . . .

"Would that matter all that much?" Mags wondered aloud.

:For the meat and leather probably not. One could use goat, cow—even wild animals for meat and leather. But the wool is a life-and-death matter for the spinners, dyers, and weavers. Soren is going to be purple over this.:

"Well, we proved we kin do what Nikolas asks us to, eh?" he replied, still not sure why this mattered all that much, but believing that it was that important to Nikolas and Master Soren.

:More than that, Rolan and Nikolas really didn't think Chamjey was up to anything more than a minor peccadillo—oh, it would be worthy of getting him to resign from the Council in embarrassment, but nothing more. Instead we caught him in a major scandal.: Now Dallen sounded pleased again. *:This is good, this is very good. The only thing that would have been better would have*

been if you had recognized who it was that was meeting with him.:

"Oh—hellfires. Should we go back?" Mags swung around in the saddle to look back down the road.

:No need. This is important enough that they are about to be intercepted. We'll find out soon enough who it is.:

MAGS made it back to the Collegium in time to make his last two classes—or rather, one class and one exercise. Sadly, the class was the languages one. Happily, the exercise was riding. He didn't even have to think about riding anymore, and even though the wind was strong and bitter enough to cut right through his clothing, he and Dallen just romped over the entire course, staying warm enough through pure exertion.

Riding just felt right, in a heart-deep way. He knew what Dallen was going to do before the Companion actually did it. Dallen knew what he wanted the moment he decided on a direction. The two of them were physically melded so close together that they might just have been a single entity.

It was glorious. Even though they made a few mistakes—missing two jumps by knocking down the bars, and having to go around a scramble, losing time—it was still glorious. If this had been all they had to do, life would have been perfect.

Of course, it wasn't. But at least for that slice of time, it was as close to perfect as Mags could get, or had ever gotten.

He washed up at the Collegium, where there was all the hot water he could want, and tubs for soaking in when he had the time. The washing facilities at the stable were about the same as at the mine, the only difference being that the water came from a pump rather than the stream or the sluice. Once clean and feeling more civilized, he then went in to supper. Bear was there, but not Lena, who was still not talking to her friends.

:It's only been three days,: Dallen reminded him.

"Three days is a long time to sulk," he said out loud, and Bear looked at him oddly.

"Lena?" he said finally.

Mags flushed. "Aye. Sorry. Talkin' t' Dallen."

Bear shoved a bit of meat pie into his mouth and chewed thoughtfully. "She wants to impress her da," he said, after swallowing. "I mean, really impress him. Make him sit up and take notice. Been working at that all year. Hardly ever does anything but work on being a Bard. And then he shows up and doesn't even know who she is, which, when she's thinking he's at least seeing the reports on her and maybe seeing she's living up to him—"

Mags blinked, finally understanding what Lita meant. Trust Bear to put it into simple language even a dunderhead like him could understand.

"Oh . . ." he replied.

"So, likely she thinks she hasn't done enough. Or hasn't done the right things. Or, you know, she's done all the right stuff, but she's just not good enough to impress him." Bear gulped his tea, a glum look on his face.

"That ain't fair," Mags said slowly.

"It isn't fair and it isn't true, but that's what she thinks." Bear put his mug down. "I guess I know something about not being able to impress your folks," he added bitterly.

Belatedly, Mags remembered that Bear came from a family of Healers, of which he was the only member that did NOT have a Healing Gift. He licked his lips awkwardly.

"Well, she's here, not at home, and maybe the Bards can sort her out," Bear concluded. "Probably. I mean, after half Bardic Collegium listened to her pa getting the skin pulled off him, maybe she'll figure out that not everybody is as impressed with him as he is with himself."

Mags decided that a little duplicity was in order. "Bard Marchand? Getting' the skin pulled off him? What?"

Bear cheered up a little and proceeded to describe in detail the dressing-down that Lena's father had gotten. It was a lot more accurate than Mags had expected—but then, Bards were supposed to be able to memorize things that happened on the spot, so they could repeat them back accurately in song or story form later, so maybe that wasn't altogether shocking. That was cheering, too. It meant that, really, Marchand had no one to blame but himself for the tale getting around. Mind you, with someone like him, he'd probably look for any scapegoat rather than accept responsibility for his own stupid behavior.

Well at least this meant that Bard Marchand would not be looking for a single Heraldic Trainee to blame for word of this getting out. More like Trainees in his very own Collegium.

"I hope that cheers 'er up," Mags said, when Bear was done.

Bear just shrugged. "You never know what people are going to think when something like this happens to kin. Sometimes there's this, 'serves you right, I'm glad you got what was coming to you' feeling, sometimes there's this 'glad it was you and not me' and sometimes there's this 'how dare they say that about my pa' thing. Just no telling. Doesn't change that he didn't know her, either."

"No." Mags sighed. "Wish she wasn't so . . . easy t' hurt."

"That's Bards, I reckon, at least at the beginning." Bear shoved away from the table. "But they need to get a thick skin before they get into Scarlets, or they're gonna spend all their time maundering about feeling hurt by people what don't like their work or Bards that are better'n they are, or how their family don't understand 'em, and not getting the job done."

Mags couldn't have put it better himself. He nodded. "Well I hope she stops feelin' so poorly. I miss 'er."

"Me too," Bear said shortly. "See you later."

Mags sat there wondering what had made Bear so out of sorts. Maybe the same not-quite-spring crankiness that seemed to be affecting so many of the others. He stared at the remains of his pie and wondered if he ought to try and get to Lena and talk her around to a good humor.

In the end, though, the thought of the mound of study waiting for him back in his room decided him. He couldn't make anything better for Lena than he already had; sending her somewhat misspelled notes affirming that he (and Dallen) would like to take her out for a ride or a walk or just have a game of draughts or something. Not saying anything about needing her help with classes, because that would seem as if he only valued her for that help. What else was there to do?

Bah.

But when he got back to his quarters, there was a piece of folded paper waiting on the top of his books that he had not left there. He hoped it was from Lena—

But it was from Herald Nikolas.

Please come to my quarters after dinner. I need you to report what you overheard Chamjey saying for the King's ears.

Nikolas wanted him to report to the King.

To the King.

He was flooded with panic.

No, no, no—how kin I—I cain't—th' King—I nivver—

Suddenly, in the middle of the muddle, he felt Dallen in his head, coming in and firmly just squashing all that panic down for a moment, as if the Companion had actually sat on it, physically.

:He's just another Herald.:

"But he's the King!" Mags said aloud, his voice breaking at the end.

:Only in the Throne Room. That is why Nikolas asked you to come to his rooms. There, Kiril will just be another Herald.:

"But I dunno how to talk t' him!"

:You just talk to him. With respect, but that's all. Now hurry up, he's probably already there, and you don't want to keep the King waiting.:

That sent another spurt of panic over him, but it was panic that got him moving. Hastily, he made sure he was clean and hadn't accidentally dropped any food or sauce on himself at dinner, snatched up his cloak, and ran all the way back up to the Collegium. He arrived at Nikolas' door all out of breath, and before he could tap on it, Nikolas himself opened it.

"Ah good, Mags. You got my note." Nikolas put one hand in the center of his back and firmly propelled him into the room.

The Herald had three rooms, so far as Mags was aware. One was Amily's bedroom, although his daughter was apt to sleep overnight at the home of one friend or another, including Master Soren's niece. One was his own bedroom, and one was a "public" sort of room, with comfortable seating and a desk as well as a fireplace.

This was where Mags occasionally met with him, although usually the King's Own came down to Mags' rooms at the stable. Today there was a stranger sitting in the chair nearest the hearth, feet propped up to the fire. Sprawled, actually, rather than sitting, and looking just a little untidy.

"This is Mags, Kiril," said Nikolas, continuing to propel Mags into the room, since Mags' own legs seemed to have lost the ability to take steps forward on their own.

The man turned, and Mags blinked and did his best not to gawk. He knew this man. This was the Herald he had encountered three days ago at the stable. No wonder he had looked familiar! That profile was on at least half of the coins that Mags had handled since he arrived here.

The King grinned at Mags. "You were right. Dallen did try to take my fingers."

:Did not.:

"Um," said Mags, intelligently.

Nikolas got him seated across from the King by the simple expedient of positioning him in front of a chair and pushing down on his shoulders. He plopped down gracelessly then leapt to his feet and started to kneel.

Nikolas grabbed the back of his collar and hauled him back into the chair.

The King was laughing so hard he was bent over.

"Mags, Mags, please," he choked out around laughter. "No kneeling, no bowing, just the two of us having a conversation."

Mags gulped and sat gingerly on the edge of the chair. "Yessir, yer Majesty Highness sir," he gabbled.

"Calm down," said the King, making soothing motions with his hands. "Now, I want you to put your mind back to this afternoon when you first found where Chamjey was going. What did you do?"

"Tried t' figger out how t' get where I could hear 'im, yer Greatness," Mags said. "Dallen, he said t' get inside an' lookit th'fireplace. Twas fulla ash. Dallen, he tookit us t' the nearest soapmaker t' find out who got th' ash from thet Inn. Happen it was that soapmaker. Dallen said, ask if they'd collected. She said no. Dallen said, askit if I could. She—" He stopped and thought for a moment. "She askit me an' Dallen if this was prankin', we said no, t' wasn't. She askit Dallen if there was a Herald knew what we was about, an' Dallen, he nodded aye. So's she give me th' apron an' all an' tol' me how t' collect an' I went back t' Inn."

Nikolas and the King exchanged a significant glance. "They're starting to ask Companions questions," the King said.

"That's no bad thing," Nikolas replied. "Intelligent questions, not just 'hey boy, want an apple?' "

"Then what?" the King asked.

Mags closed his eyes, the better to remember, and slowly recited everything that he had heard, with Dallen prompting him. When he was done, he opened his eyes to see the King nodding thoughtfully.

"We've got a quandary," Nikolas said to the King, and Mags suddenly felt as if he was not even there, the two of them were concentrating so hard on each other.

The King nodded. "Two, actually. What Chamjey is doing is not technically illegal. Just immoral, but we don't regulate morals—or at least, not that sort of morality . . ."

"It . . . ain't ethical, your Majestic," Mags put in timidly. "Don't we got laws 'bout ethics?"

Two pairs of eyes suddenly made him the target of the same intense stare, and Mags felt utterly unnerved.

"We do," the King said, finally. "And members of the Council swear an oath when they accept a seat on it that they will behave with the interests of the Kingdom as a whole superseding their own. At the very least, Chamjey has violated that oath."

Nikolas drummed his fingers on the wooden arm of his chair as the fire crackled in the fireplace. "Chamjey is shrewd. And we don't have any actual proof of all of this. We have one Trainee who listened in on a conversation, but could not actually see the speakers."

"Ah! But we can get corroborating evidence!" the King replied after a moment. "We can canvass the herders, find out who invested in their wool and meat-sheep, and follow those leads up the line. It will take time—"

"Soon's ye get t' the fust guilty man, he'll get all nervous-like," said Mags, thinking of how that sort of thing had gone back at the mine. "Th' other feller, he said they went through lotsa people t' do this, but an' ye get the fust feller t' talk, it'll go up chain pretty quick, I bet."

They both nodded, and the King sighed. "I wanted to get this settled quickly, but I suppose I shall have to resign myself to getting it settled thoroughly." He stood up. "Mags, I'm getting some tutors arranged for you Trainees. There are a number of intelligent young people in Haven that are being interviewed, fine scholars, but poor, who would certainly benefit from this idea. In fact, the only reason we haven't got some tutors yet is because we are making sure that they are good at teaching."

Mags felt his eyes widening. "Twas a good idear then?" he said.

"Very much so. And I am looking forward to seeing you and Dallen trying for a Kirball team. I'd like to see if Dallen can run with the same eagerness that he eats pocket pies." The King's face split with a grin.

:Hey!:

Mags smothered a laugh.

"Now, I've taken up enough of your time . . ." the King hesitated.

Mags supplied what he thought the King was looking for. "Eh? I wuz never here, never talked t' yer Royalness 'bout nothin', an' I don' know nothin' 'bout sheepses and wool. Herald Nikolas, he jest wanted t' ast me 'bout what Bard Marchand said, 'xactly, when he sent me on that there errand he shouldn't of."

The King nodded. "Exactly so. Good night, Mags. It was good to meet you formally, so to speak."

Mags got to his feet, managing to control his knees, which still felt a bit weak, bowed, and let himself out. As he left, he sensed that the King and the King's Own had only begun an evening of intense conversation and decision-making.

He was very, very glad that he was never going to be in Nikolas's shoes.

:And between you and me, I am just as glad not to be Rolan. Now come on back and let's talk about this Kirball business. I've made some inquiries.:

Bear and Lena seemed to have forgotten the project that had taken them all into the Guard Archives this past winter—but Mags had not. Although his opportunities to go back and search had gotten a lot rarer, he still presented himself at the door of the Archives from time to time for a candlemark or two of research.

And the next day gave him one of those rare opportunities, as he finished an exam unexpectedly early and was dismissed with a smile. He headed for the Guard Archives at a trot, feeling as if he was getting very close to what he was looking for. The last time he had been through the reports, there had been mention of an unusually large bandit group, one that the Guard felt probably had a substantial encampment. "It would not be difficult here," the Guard Captain had written. "There are many caves and abandoned mines, and it would be possible to hide as many as fifty or sixty fighting men and their hangers-on in some of them. The raids we are seeing are growing bolder and more pernicious, and suggest that these miscreants have organized under a clever leader."

That sounded like what he was looking for, and Mags had already had enough disappointments that by now he was well over the dread of finding out who his parents had been. He just wanted some answers, any kind of answers.

Besides, if anything had shown him lately that just because your parents were something, it didn't follow that you were the same, it would have been encountering Bard Marchand. There could not possibly be a person less arrogant and self-assured than poor Lena, and there could not be a person more arrogant and self-centered than her father. So if his parents *had* been bandits—well—

So what.

Maybe he would at least find out *why* they had become bandits. Lena had spun all sorts of fanciful tales for him. His mother had fallen in love with one of them who was noble at heart, and had followed him to the encampment. His mother had been a captive who had lost her heart to one of the bandits. His mother had been an unwilling captive. His *mother* had been the bandit, and his father a poor shepherd she had seduced. He thought it was a lot simpler than that. Likely that his parents had been—something—shepherds, farmers, even traders—and had a bad run of luck. Turned to robbing and fell in with the bigger group. It was a common enough story, and he was living proof that you'd do almost anything when you were starving.

He nodded at the archivist at the front desk, who knew him so well by now that the man just waved him inside, and he went up the three stairs into the Archives themselves.

It was a huge barn of a building, not just a room, with floor-to-ceiling shelves packed very closely together. There were ladders at intervals along the shelves, for there was no other way to reach the upper shelves. On the shelves were identical wooden boxes. Shelf upon shelf, row upon row, up and down the entire room. There was nowhere to sit and study, since the Archives were rarely visited by more than one person. Instead, there was a single table with several chairs around it at the door end of the room. The place was heated the same way that Bear's indoor herbarium was heated, from beneath the floor. The room was a little stuffy, very warm, and very dry, and the air was scented with the smell of old paper, but not of dust. Now he knew this was because one of the duties of the Archivists was to keep everything dust free. The lighting was good too thanks to the narrow windows up near the roof all the way around, windows with real glass in them.

He went to the shelf where the boxes of records he had last gotten into were stored, and took down the one with his ribbon marker on it.

He was three reports further along when he began to feel a sense of excitement and anticipation. This was definitely looking like the right year. There was no doubt in the Guard Captain's mind—or in his reports—that he had a substantial and well-organized brigand group on his hands. They knew what they were doing; they weren't raiding randomly. They hit wealthy traders but ignored caravans of items that were bulky and hard to find a market for, they overran entire farms and looted the places, but only at intervals that suggested that these were re-supply raids.

He asked for help; his little Guardpost didn't have the manpower to take down a group that big.

He got the help he requested, in the form of an entire Guard troop, mounted and foot.

And then, there it was. In the middle of the reports, a fatter packet. Lists, lots of them. The roster of the Guard company that had come to augment his troops. The list of the townsfolk that had volunteered. Loot captured. Casualties. The list of the dead on both sides.

And the all-important after-action report. Mags hands shook a little as he opened the folder and read the first page.

From the beginning, we made our real plans in secret. The Fourteenth did not make a camp; they entered the town singly and in pairs, and were quartered among the townsfolk. Their scouts scoured the hills for a full moon, looking for the signs of the passage of men. They were clever, as I knew they were—the scouts found nothing, which told me that the hiding place was probably deep in the caves. Finally I sent out the sacrificial caravan, one with the rich prize of weapons and wine, and one I knew that the brigands could not resist. Of course, these were flawed; the swords weakened to break at the quillons, axes with handles drilled, bows that would snap at the first draw, arrows with heads that would shatter on armor. I was not minded that we give them that which they could turn against us. Furthermore, the wine was triple strength, but sweetened with honey, so that the taste would not betray the strength.

As I expected, the brigands appeared, and the scouts followed them back to their lair. Now we had them, and after a few candlemarks had passed, the Fourteenth assembled, all men at the ready and with the volunteer townsfolk making a rear-guard of pikemen, we marched on the caves.

The scouts found and silenced their outer guards, but given how cunning they had been, I did not expect to catch all of them surprised and drunk, and as I anticipated, an alarm was raised before we got to the entrance.

There was fierce fighting; first, at the fortified entrance, and then as we made our way through the rats-warren of tunnels, until all the brigands were dead or fled. The chief made his last stand at what we took to be the central cavern. There we found what was left of his loot, the stores he was putting up against the winter, what looked to be a surprisingly orderly camp. There was a handful of camp-

followers, some of whom fought the Guard with the same fierceness as the bandits, some of whom cowered in fear and could scarcely be gotten sense of. One of them, however, was a captive from an earlier caravan, and she led us to a hidden chamber that held other captives being held for ransom.

There were but three of these living, and two dead. The woman gave us to know that when the fighting began, one of the brigands was dispatched to the chamber to slay the captives, but the captives rallied and fell upon him. In the scuffle, two were slain before the brigand himself fell beneath a rain of blows and kicks.

The two dead were a woman and a man in foreign garb. The woman told us that no one could understand their speech, and they communicated mostly by signs. Their clothing was rich; presumably because of this, the brigands hoped to puzzle out whence they came and demand a ransom. With them was their child, a small boy of perhaps two or three years of age.

There was nothing else of value that could be pointed to as theirs except their clothing. Lacking any other clue, I placed the child with the townsfolk to be dealt with as an orphan without resources. We buried the captives within the chamber that had been their prison.

I then apportioned the loot as follows . . .

Mags stopped reading, the pages falling from his hands. So, there it was. His parents hadn't been bandits themselves; they'd been captives!

There was nothing whatsoever wrong with his blood. . . .

The dread he had been feeling fell away, leaving

behind a succession of emotions. A flash of rage that the Guard Captain should have so callously disposed of a helpless child. A strange grief for his parents who had come so close to being rescued. Frustration, that he still knew so little.

He quickly looked through the rest of the report, but there were no more details about his parents, not even a crude sketch of their "foreign" clothing. There was nothing to say what land they were from, nothing that had been found in the loot, nothing any of the captured brigands or the captives that had been imprisoned with them had said. Nothing at all.

He banged his fist down on the table and swore silently. So little—so little! Their clothing was "rich"—but what did that actually mean? How "rich" was "rich"—and was it "rich" by their own standards or by the standards of a provincial Guard Captain? If someone lived where sables were abundant and easy to trap, a sable coat could be the possession of almost anyone, but here in Valdemar, it would be an item only the wealthiest of highborn could afford.

So in a sense he was back at the beginning again. He knew only now that he was "foreign," and not a bandit brat.

:I don't see that it matters,: Dallen observed. *:You are still the same person you were before you learned all this.:*

Logically it shouldn't matter to him. But it did. He wanted to know.

Well, he had come to a dead end at this point. Anyone who might have known anything about him was either dead or had long ago forgotten about the nameless child. He wasn't about to try and find the cave and unearth what might have been left of the bodies just to see if there was a shred of a clue in their garments. Even assuming there was anything left but bones, which was not likely.

He put the report back in the box, and the box back on the shelf. On his way out, he turned over to the Archivist all of the little ribbons that he'd been given to mark where he was doing research.

"Hmm," the man said, one eyebrow raised. "Find what you needed then?"

"Nossir," Mags replied with resignation. "But I found all I'm goin' to."

Both eyebrows rose. "That has all the sound of a tragic ballad in the making. I'm sorry your excavations into the archives were not as fruitful as you would have liked."

Mags managed a wan smile. "Well, at least I know I ain't some bandit brat. Trouble is, that's 'bout all I know."

"Perhaps you can elaborate on that," the Archivist prompted, looking interested.

Mags shrugged. "M'parents musta been caught by bandits. They was dressed good, guess they was bein' held fer ransom. But nobody understood 'em, and they was dressed foreign, and they was killed when the Guard came after the bandits. An' that's what I know."

"Actually, I can tell you a little more than that," the Archivist responded. "They cannot have been Rethewellan, Hardornen, nor Karsite. Guard Captains have a smattering of all three languages, and the fashions of those places are either distinct, or very like

Valdmaran. I would also suspect they were not Hawkbrothers, nor Shin'a'in, since the Clans are not inclined to leave their own in captivity, and they have ways of knowing where their kinfolk are. Vanyel more or less closed the passage to the North. So that leaves you with beyond Rethwellan as the likeliest."

Mags blinked. "That's—far."

"And it begs the question of why your parents, who must have been traveling alone, came this far. What could possibly have driven them to come to a country where they didn't even know the language and evidently had neither friends nor contacts? Because you may rest assured, if foreigners who did have friends or contacts went missing in Valdemar, the Heralds, the Guard, and ultimately the Crown would know about it and be looking for them."

Mags felt that dread creeping back over him. The only reason he could think of was that they were running from something. "So mebbe I still am some kinda bad blood . . ." he said slowly.

But the Archivist only snorted. "Actually, I can think of a much better reason for running into a strange land, if one was young and foolish, as I presume both of them were."

"What' d that be, sir?" He held his breath, hoping for a sort of reprieve.

The old man shook his head. "One of the oldest stories there is, of course. They were in love, and their parents disapproved. And their parents were wealthy or powerful enough that only by fleeing far past the borders of their own land could they escape the long reach of parental authority."

Mags blinked. "You think?" he ventured.

The old man shrugged. "I have known many young lovers, and most were fools," he replied with more than a touch of cynicism. "Make of that what you will. I am sorry that you did not find all that you were looking for, Trainee, and I thank you for your courteous treatment of the Archival records."

Well, that was a dismissal if ever he had heard one. Mags nodded, and trudged out the door and back to the Collegium buildings and his room at the stables.

Both Bear and Lena were out—at classes for the latter, probably, and off tending someone for the former—so he left them brief notes outlining what he had found.

:Look on the bright side,: said Dallen. *:Now you won't have to spend time going through those boxes anymore.:*

"I suppose," he said aloud.

:Well now that you know, maybe this will unearth some sort of memory for you. Maybe a word or two in your parents' language, or a memory of what they looked like.:

"That don't seem likely. I'd'a thought I'd'a remembered somethin' like that afore this."

:Maybe not. Memory is a funny thing. You know . . . smell tends to trigger it.:

"But if I cain't remember what m'parents smelled like, I cain't exactly trigger one, can I?" he objected.

:Not what they smelled like. The caves.:

Huh. Now that Dallen mentioned it . . . he did seem to get nightmares more back at the mine when the sleeping hole got mucked out and the smell was more of damp, cold earth than it was of rotting straw and filthy children.

"I'll see if I kin 'member one of m'old nightmares," he said, finally. "Don' think I wanta bring 'em on me again. Useta wake up screamin', an' I reckon none of the Companion's'd thank me fer screamin' m'lungs out in middle of the night."

:Hmm. You are probably right. So what are you going to do?:

"Right now?" Actually—he kind of wanted to take his mind off all of this, and let it rest for a moment. And he had a good idea what would do that. "Right now—I think I'm'a gonna find out about this Kirball."

:HERALD Setham,: Dallen said, instantly, and with tremendous excitement in his mind-voice. *:You want Herald Setham. Wait a moment . . . :*

Mags waited patiently, shivering a little in the cold wind. Was the wind never going to stop blowing? There wasn't even a hint of spring on it yet.

Dallen was probably speaking to Setham's Companion. That always took time. Of course, it would have been possible for Dallen to allow him to "hear" Dallen's side of the conversation, but that would have ended up being confusing. It was also possible for him to listen to both sides, but that would have meant taking down shields, and getting permission. Companions were notoriously reluctant to let anyone but their own Chosen listen to them.

:Archer says Setham will meet you at the new Kirball field,: Dallen told him, finally. *:It's where they've been putting in all those new obstacles.:*

"Aye, I know it," Mags confirmed. He changed

direction to head for the field, which actually had been part of Companion's Field before it had been partitioned off. "Why ain't they using the old course?"

:Not big enough.:

By now it was late afternoon, the sun was making long shadows with the Collegium buildings, and his stomach growled. He hoped that either the explanation wouldn't take long, or that Herald Setham would be just as hungry as he was and willing to continue any discussion over food. It wouldn't be long now until the dinner bell.

"Why ain't the old course big enough?"

:Because they will have to fit two dozen or more people on it at the same time. They've finalized the rules, so we're in luck, whatever Setham tells us is exactly how things are going to go now.:

He saw the Herald—and his Companion—waiting for them beside the new rail fence that marked the boundary of this "ball ground." He had expected Setham to be young; it had seemed to him that anyone who was getting into something like this was going to have to be young. He thought that his expectations were confirmed when, from a distance, the Herald seemed to be shorter than even he was. He was surprised to see, as he got nearer, that while Setham was, indeed, a lot shorter than Mags, he was also well past middle age. He wasn't a dwarf, but he was certainly not much taller than twelve or fourteen hands. The top of his head barely came up to Dallen's shoulders!

Setham was wiry, and he kept his brown hair hair cut quite short, so that the gray at the temples was quite evident. He had a thin face, and intelligent brown eyes, and a mouth that looked as if it smiled often.

Mags smiled back at him, tentatively.

"I've been hoping you'd be one of the people to join us in Kirball, Mags," said Setham, without any preamble, sticking out his hand for Mags to shake. "I've been hearing a lot about how well you and Dallen work together. I think you'll be a cornerstone of my team."

"Your team, sir?" Mags said, surprised. "I thought I heerd this was all Trainees. An' mebbe Guard?"

"So it is, but teams need coaches, and that would be me." Setham grinned. "I was a jockey before I was a Herald, I rode steeplechases, and now that I am a Herald, I am one of the scouts and cross-country specialists. Archer and I are pretty well known for our ability to scramble over, under, or through just about anything."

The other Companion nodded and whinnied. On closer inspection yet, Setham was very short indeed, definitely no taller than twelve hands, and his Companion, Archer, was so compact and cobby he was almost pony-sized.

:We call him—Archer, that is—The Cat. He never seems to put a foot wrong,: Dallen confirmed. *:I may be faster across the straight, but even I can't move across bad terrain the way he can. And if you can believe it, Setham has never been thrown or pulled from Archer's saddle.:*

"So, the first thing I want you to do is cast your eye over the playing field," Setham continued. "Get a good impression of it. We chose the roughest part of Companion's Field for this."

Obediently, Mags did as he had been directed, and

the first thing he noticed was that this was even more challenging than the obstacle course. Instead of the usual rail jumps, this had—well—terrain, was the only way he could think to describe it. Gullies, a major ravine, little hills with abrupt drop-offs, stone fences as well as rail fences, culverts, bridges, even a stream he hadn't known existed, that led into the river. There were no big hills, but there were bits of very steep slope, enough to make even the most sure-footed Companion pause. No effort had been spared to create this thing—there were even lines where turf had been laid over what must have been raw earth after hills had been made and gullies created.

But unlike the obstacle course, there was no pattern, no obvious path you were supposed to take around this.

Something that the obstacle course did not have was two identical little stone buildings, with ramps up to the tops of them, one on either end of the field.

"What do you think of it?" asked Setham.

"Not sure what t' think sir," Mags confessed. He scratched his head. "Looks risky." Actually it didn't so much look risky as insane. He could scarcely imagine trying to ride over this thing at speed.

:I like it. It's a real challenge!:

"There is a lot of risk there, I won't deny it," Setham replied. "Only the best riders will be able to take this course full out. You and Dallen will take falls, I am sure. People are going to get hurt. But we have a big influx of Trainees right now. Historically that means that we are going to need those Trainees when they become Heralds, and that means Valdemar is going to be facing some trouble down the road. Better some bruises and breaks now than dead Heralds later."

Mags turned to see if he could read Setham's expression. This was the first time he had ever heard a Herald being quite that—blunt.

Setham looked deadly serious. "I'm not the first Herald in my family," Setham said. "I'm fourth generation in fact. My great grandfather was in the middle of the Karsite conflicts, and my grandfather knew Vanyel. Now . . . maybe the reason we're getting all you Trainees is because Valdemar is about to get a lot bigger. I won't deny that's possible—all sorts of little dukedoms and tiny kingdoms are looking at us and thinking they might want to throw in with us. We're all hoping this is why we have so many new Chosen coming in, so many new foals being born. But we aren't going to count on that. We're going to count on finding ourselves neck deep in war, and needing lots of Heralds, and if the other happens, we'll just be glad and feel lucky."

Mags scratched his head. "No way t' tell?" he ventured.

Setham shook his head. But then, he relaxed. "However, we also know whatever happens will be years away, and no rule says we can't make this training fun as well as risky," he continued. "So—that's why we are doing it this way."

"Yessir," Mags said. "I kin see that. But ye said, on'y the best. So what 'bout the rest? Ain't they gonna need the trainin' too?"

"Oh they'll get it," Setham replied. "They will certainly get it. The difference is that we want the best for the first teams, to get everyone excited and motivated. Then in the regular riding classes, we'll teach the Kirball technique and strategy instead of the old riding lessons, and I hope that will stimulate some more excitement."

Mags wrinkled his nose. "Not sure what yer aimin' fer, with all this excitement stuff. Sir."

Setham leaned against the fence. So did his Companion. It struck Mags that he had never seen a Herald and Companion who looked quite so alike before.

"Look, you seem like a serious young fellow," Setham said slowly. "I tell you that the Circle is looking at the current conditions and anticipating trouble in a few years, and you understand that. I can see it in the way you react to what I just told you—you squared up your shoulders, you looked a little resigned, but determined to meet the challenge. Am I right?"

Mags flushed a little with embarrassment, but nodded.

"But you've got to have seen how some of the Trainees just don't—seem to take things nearly as seriously as you do," Setham continued. "Knowing your background . . . your reaction is logical. Knowing theirs, well, so is theirs. They aren't what you would call 'grown up' yet. They're still thinking about things the way someone who has never had to face hardship thinks about them. Even that lot that helped you rescue your friend, Bear—within a fortnight or so, the fear of the rescue had faded, and it became just a fantastic adventure in their memories. Whereas you—"

Mags shivered. He still had the occasional bad dream

where he saw those mad eyes, and knew that he could, very easily, be dead in a few moments.

“Exactly.” Setham nodded. “You actually know, in your heart, that you could be killed or worse. They still think, in their hearts, that they are immortal. They’ll learn better, but they don’t know that now.”

“So . . . that’ d be why they don’t take some of the trainin’ serious-like.” This was somewhat unreal to Mags; he had seen death often enough that he could not remember a time when he hadn’t known, emphatically, that if he wasn’t smart and careful and clever all the time, the next corpse could be him.

Still . . . he had seen for himself how some of the others were. They talked, they acted, as if death simply didn’t exist for them.

It was just one more way in which he simply did not fit in. For a moment, it made him feel his isolation all the more.

Then again, Setham was not like that. Setham understood.

He fumbled his way in the direction Setham was trying to go, reasoning out loud. “So since they ain’t takin’ the trainin’ serious enough, an’ maybe not puttin’ ’nough effort inta it, ye reckon t’ give him—what’s it called? Motivation? Somethin’ that’ll make it worth it to ’em t’ fling thesselves inta it.”

Setham grinned. “Exactly. Nothing gets interest going like a game. Where going over and over the obstacle course gets boring, Kirball is going to be exciting. Some people will do very well at it. Those people are going to find their reputations going up, and they are going to become popular. Other people will want to have some of that popularity, and so they will strive more for it. It's just human nature. We like to have heroes."

Mags blinked at him. "I—you ain't thinkin'—"

"I don't know for certain, Mags, if you'll become wildly popular because of this. You tend to be solitary, and that will work against popularity." Setham looked at him shrewdly. "But you already have something of a good reputation, because of helping to rescue your friend. I think you should prepare for the fact that others will want to associate with you if you become a star player of Kirball."

Mags shook his head. "That don't seem right . . . I mean, be a hero for a game? Fer doin' summat important, mebbe, but not fer a game . . ."

Setham shrugged. "It is what it is. People become popular for lots of reasons. Even when they aren't very pleasant people to be around, like certain Master Bards I won't name! It won't only be the Trainees that will be following Kirball, it will be virtually everyone here at Court. So be prepared for that, and you and Dallen should discuss how you want to deal with notoriety." Setham smiled crookedly. "As I told you, I was a jockey, and I was a good one. Now there is something that makes no sense—being made much of because you happen to be able to stick on the back of a fast horse and bring the best out of him! Ridiculous. Nevertheless, being taken by surprise by success can be as hazardous as being taken by surprise by failure. Now. Back to the game. So you've seen the field. Now let me tell you the rules."

He pointed at the two stone towers. "Those are the goals. There will be three ways to score. The first is to lob a Kirball through the windows or the door of the opposing team's tower. That's one point. The second is to occupy the tower and hold it for a quarter candlemark. That's ten points, and it's going to be difficult to do that, and I very much doubt anyone is going to try it. Lobbing balls is going to be a lot faster and easier. The third is to steal the opponent's flag and get it back to your tower. That's fifty points, and pretty much game-ending, because you have to get the flag back to your home base."

Mags nodded.

"Each team will be of twelve players on the playing field," Setham continued. "Four Herald Trainees, four players afoot, and four mounted players, who can come from anything. The foot-players are supposed to guard the goal, but they are going to be allowed to move around the field, so who knows. The mounted players can do whatever the team captain wants them to do, as can the Herald Trainees. If someone gets hurt or tired, you can substitute a new player, but only if the one retiring from the field can get to the edge of the field and tag in the new player." Setham grinned. "We can't make this easy on you, after all."

"Nossir," said Mags, though privately he wished that for once, someone would. It would be very nice to encounter something easy for a change.

"What the mounted players and the Heralds do is entirely up to the team captain," Setham continued. "You can lob balls, you can go for the flag, or attempt to drive the opposing team off and occupy their goal. It's all up to you. You'll have to coordinate among yourselves somehow, which will be easier for the Herald Trainees and a lot harder for those without Mindspeech. Let's just pick one strategy as an example—an obvious ploy might be to pick someone with Fetching Gift and try to snatch the flag without getting near the goal."

"Aye, well, somethin' tells me anythin' obvious ain't gonna work too well," Mags said with a sigh. His stomach growled.

"Let's go back to the Collegium and we can discuss this over dinner," Setham offered. Just as he said that, the bell rang, calling them all to the meal.

"That was rare good timing, sir," Mags said with a chuckle. "Aye, that suits me. I was hopin' ye'd say as much."

Setham did not go to the common dining room. Instead, he led Mags around to a hatch that Mags had not even known existed. He rapped on it and the hatch slid up. It looked right into the kitchen.

"Two of whatever is going," Setham said casually, then with a glance at Mags, added "and extra pie."

The kitchen boy nodded and darted away. Mags watched him make up the same sort of food basket that he'd gotten for Lena, and a moment later came back with it and handed it to Setham.

"I would just as soon not be surrounded by three dozen Trainees all asking questions once they find out I am one of the Kirball coaches," Setham said, with a crooked grin. "There are going to be four of us to start, and we'll each pick our own teams. My preference is for outstanding riders; the others will probably have preferences of their own." He passed the basket over to Mags, who took it without a word.

"Now, I am going to be running trials just to make sure of the general skill level of my players, but I am fairly certain you are going to pass those handily, Mags," he said, as he led the way into the Heralds' Wing. "I don't, however, think you are going to be team captain. I am inclined to think it will either be an older Trainee or one of the Guards."

"I wasn' expectin' such, sir!" Mags exclaimed, shocked, as Setham opened the door to his quarters. Setham waved him inside what proved to be very spare rooms indeed, and just two of them. Plain wooden floors, bare walls, a simple desk with a lamp, two more chairs with leather seats, and a bookcase. The single window was covered with a shutter, and considering how it rattled, that was probably a good thing; this room must face the direction of the wind. Through a half open door Mags could just glimpse an equally plain bedroom. In fact, the place looked very much like his own room in the stable, and he felt immediately at home.

While they ate, Setham described more of how the game was likely to proceed. He already had two of his foot players—two young Guard recruits who were second-generation Guardsmen but not quite old enough to formally join the Guard itself. As was often the case with youngsters like this, they were acting as aides to the Captain of a Guard troop that did not include their parents or older siblings.

He also had one of his mounted players, the son of one of the Council members. He didn't say who it was, but from what Mags already knew, he recognized the person as Jeffers, the son of the head of the Printer's Guild. While not a member of Amily's immediate circle of friends, Mags knew the young man to have been among the visitors to Soren's house over Midwinter. He'd been quite affable there, and after identifying him, Mags had encountered him now and again up here at the Collegium where he was taking a few classes. Setham must know enough about him to trust him on the team, so that was good.

"I have my eye on a couple other Trainees, older than you, to round out the Heralds," Setham continued. "I'm thinking one of them will be the Captain. You don't have any objections to a girl Captain, do you?"

Mags shook his head. "Wouldn' dare," he replied. "They'd prolly smack me inna nose."

Setham laughed. "All right then. The four coaches are holding the trials for their teams over the next four days. I have tomorrow afternoon, someone else has tomorrow morning. Turn up at the Kirball field instead of your riding and weapons lessons; you'll have leave in advance. If I can't firm up the team tomorrow, I'll hold an open trial, but you won't need to turn up for that one unless you want to and you're free. Can't have you missing too many lessons, after all."

"Yessir," Mags nodded. "Nossir."

"Right then, off to your classwork with you. Kirball will be no excuse for doing poorly in class. And leave the dishes," he added, as Mags made to gather them up. "Someone will be along for them later."

Mags decided on impulse to go see if Bear was

about—and maybe Lena too. He wanted to tell them about Kirball and see what they thought of it. Had they heard the rumors, perhaps?

He left the Herald's Wing and headed toward Healer's, and saw to his pleasure that there were lights burning in the glass-walled conservatory that Bear called home. Now if Bear was just there and not out on some errand or other—

As he got closer, he saw that both his friends were there, deep in a conversation—and so was his friend he had met through Master Soren, Amily, the daughter of King's Own Nikolas! His spirits rose at that. He told all of Lydia's friends about Bear and Lena, of course, so Amily knew all about them. He hadn't any idea that Amily wanted to meet Bear and Lena, but to see her with them made him irrationally happy.

He'd wanted to introduce them some time ago, but just hadn't gotten the chance to. If she'd decided on her own to come introduce herself, that was marvelous!

He tapped lightly on the door to the outside, and saw all three heads turn quickly to the sound. He poked his head around to one of the windows and waved at them. Bear jumped up to let him in.

As always, Bear's pair of ground-glass lenses were perched on his nose, and he looked more like his usual self than he had of late. Instead of looking strained and cross, he looked like a sleepy, affable bear, with a round face, untidy short brown hair, small, but friendly eyes, a pug nose, and a generous mouth that was finally smiling again. He stood at the door, peering down at Mags, with a little bit of a stoop.

"Hope I ain't innerruptin' anythin'?" he said, suddenly wondering if, actually, he was. But to his relief, Bear shook his head.

"Come on in, got your friend Amily here," the Healer Trainee said, moving aside so Mags could come in the door. As usual, thanks to the heating under the floor, the conservatory was as warm as a summer day. The air smelled of clean, damp soil, with a hint of green and the faint, confused aroma of many, many herbs. Just now, rosemary was predominant

"Mags!" Amily said, waving him over to a stool at the table, "I missed you the other day at Lydia's. I'd been hearing rumors about how Bard Marchand got a right royal dressing-down, and I asked her about it. She told me all about your friend Lena and how rude Bard Marchand had been. I'd heard so much about Lena and Bear already that I thought it was just time for me to come around and introduce myself."

Amily was normally one of the most peaceful people to be around that Mags knew, but today she seemed even more so. She tended to wear soft browns, which with her brown hair and quiet face made her seem almost invisible at times, and yet she made her presence felt in the pool of serenity that was around her. Mags took a glance at Lena, and knew immediately that whatever had prompted Amily to come and talk to his friends, it had done Lena a world of good. Bear too, probably.

This visit wasn't just an impulsive gesture on Amily's part, either. Amily couldn't do anything impulsively; one of her legs was badly lame, and that made it difficult for her to move about. He knew now that it had been ruined in the same accident that had taken her mother's life, that she had been treated by the farmers that found her, and that by the time decent Healers had gotten to it, it had already set all wrong. She must have decided that Lena needed to be brought out of her unhappy sulks, and the best way to do it would be to make her feel that if she rejected the invitation to join Amily and Bear, she would be doing something unpardonably rude.

Mags wanted to hug her for her generosity. He settled for beaming at her. She seemed to understand his meaning, and smiled back at him.

"Well it's a good thing that she came down here," Bear said happily. "She and Lena are getting' on like anything, an' I've come up with some concoctions for that bad leg. Stuff to help her sleep better, stuff to make it ache less." He gave Amily a mock-stern glance. "You should have come see me before. You've never been seen by a good Healer that had something other than a Gift."

"You have a Gift, Bear," Amily chided. "It just doesn't happen to involve a personal power. Anyone with half an eye to see knows that your understanding of herbs and surgery is a Gift, and a profound one."

Bear flushed, and looked pleased.

"And Bear thinks that we ought to try re-breaking and setting it," Amily added. "They said they wanted to do that once before, but—" she shuddered "—I didn't even want to think about the pain. But Bear thinks he can keep me asleep while they break it, give me something to make sure I can sleep at night while it is mending, and he says there is a new Healer here that can do something about the pain when I am awake. If I can get Healing sessions so that the bones mend faster, it should all be done in a moon or less. I'm feeling quite optimistic now!"

"It isn't going to be perfect," Bear warned. "There's only so much we can do. While it's mending, you'll need help to do anything. Once it's mended, it'll still be some crooked. You'll still limp, maybe need a cane. It's going to be shorter than your good leg."

"But at least I'll be able to move easier," Amily countered. "And completely on my own." She didn't have to say anything more. Mags knew very well how much being able to get about without help would mean to her.

Lena patted Amily's hand in a consoling manner. Mags could tell that the two girls had made instant friends. This was excellent! Lena didn't make friends easily; when she was performing, she was wrapped up in the music and never noticed her audience, but when she was just being herself she was astonishingly shy.

He beamed at both of them. He couldn't have asked for anything better! Amily would have a friend up here and wouldn't have to try and get to Lydia's for company, and Lena would have a friend that was a girl and could presumably understand her—someone who was not in Bardic Collegium, and not a potential rival. They even looked a little alike, since both of them were small, thin, and dark haired. Lena was darker and smaller than Amily, but they could easily have been siblings.

Neither actually had sisters. Mags wondered if they would start to feel as if they had found a sister in each other. That would be good too, at least, as he understood these things. Families were supposed to make you happy.

Although Lena's father didn't seem very good at making her happy . . .

"When d'ye think this business'll happen, with yer leg?" he asked, to avoid such uncomfortable thoughts.

Amily shook her head. "We have only started talking about it. Bear needs to discuss it with the senior Healers, after all, he's only a Trainee still, and I need to talk to Father."

"If'n ye cain't get er done this summer, put it off till next," Mags advised. "People ain't as sick in summer, so th' Healers'll hev more time for ye. Things allus heal better in summer, an anyway, ye don' wanta be kempt up in bed over winter. What if there was another blizzard? What if we had one o them mortal cold streaks? An' there ain't as much good, healin' food in winter as in summer."

"Trust you to think of food, Mags!" Lena teased, but Bear nodded.

"No, he's right, you will need every advantage for this, and winter would be a bad time to take such an enormous risk. Even with Healers working on you and speeding the bone-mending. Mags is right that there are fewer people who are ill in summer as well, and fewer accidents. You'll be weaker, more likely to get some disease or other, and we shouldn't expose you to more than we have to." Bear sucked on his lower lip. "Best thing for it then, is to start discussions right away."

A moment of silence ensued, which Amily broke by saying, "Well, to change the subject entirely, I am going to kidnap Lena off to Lydia's the next afternoon that she is free. It would be marvelous to have a friend that can sing and play for us once in a while, and I want her to meet some of the others." She smiled. "I promise we won't ask much of you. None of us are likely to treat you as our private entertainer unless you want to be."

"Aye to that!" Mags said, and added, "An' take Bear too, an' ye kin pry 'im away from here."

"Pah, I haven't the time to spare," Bear objected, but he looked pleased that Mags suggested it and Amily nodded. "Well . . . maybe a little. But not often. Maybe I'm only a Trainee, but people here need me."

"Poor Mags, it used to be you that was coming down to Soren's house; you're going to feel quite neglected," Amily teased.

He grinned, for this was the perfect opening. "Nay, I'll be busy practicin'! Tis you that'll be missin' me, mebbe. Seems Dallen an' me got somethin' new t' do. Yon Herald Setham wants me fer his Kirball team!"

Bear gaped at him, Amily clapped her hands with delight, and Lena bounced up and down in her chair. "You're going to be on a Kirball team?" Lena exclaimed. "Really? Why, that's all anybody can talk about!"

"It's true," Amily agreed. "There is speculation all over the Court about it. Everyone wants to be able to watch, although I must say there are not too many people wanting to be players except for Heralds. Though if it is going to be as dangerous as I've heard, that is just as well."

Pleased, Mags told them all about it, from Herald Caelan suggesting he should look into playing, to the interview in Setham's room.

"I dunno," Bear said, looking worried. "It seems pretty dangerous to me. Real easy to get hurt. I looked over that field and I wouldn't want to ride over it, much less play a game on it."

"Well it's kinda supposed to be dangerous," Mags pointed out, and repeated what Setham had said about the huge influx of Trainees. "There kinda ain't a point to it, if it ain't dangerous. It's s'pposed t' wake the Grays up a bit. Make 'em figger out they ain't immortal."

"Still, dammit, I don't want to be dealing with your broken head or broken neck, Mags!" Bear said, looking a little desperate. "If this is supposed to just be training, it shouldn't be so dangerous that people come out of it seriously hurt. Bruises and maybe a break or two is one thing, but not a broken neck."

"I don' think Dallen'd let me break m'neck," Mags pointed out. "I'd be more worrit about them as is on foot or reg'lar horses."

"Point," said Amily, and smiled. "I think it's wonderful that the two of you were asked in the first place. Are there going to be trials? I had heard there were."

"Aye, an' I'm t' be in 'em fer form's sake," he told them and added shyly, "An I'd take it kindly if any of ye could get away t' watch. Unless it's too mortal bad weather!" he added, and sighed. "Knowin' my luck, twill be pourin' cold rain."

The morning of Mags' trial day threatened rain, but it never actually happened. By noon, the sullen clouds were reluctantly moving off without actually producing so much as a drop. Mags turned up at the Kirball field, though, prepared for the worst.

Prepared in more ways than one, as well. Although nothing had actually been said about armor, Mags had brought an open-faced helmet, a neck-brace, a stiff leather kidney-belt, shin-guards, arm-guards, and a chest protector. Having worn all of these in weapons' practice, he was reasonably sure that he could move and ride well enough in them to satisfy Setham.

The others had made no such preparations. Setham looked astonished at his rig-out, then pleased. "I hadn't even gotten into discussions with the other coaches about protection," he said, "But it looks as if you have anticipated a great deal of what we might need. Well done, Mags."

One of the older Trainees—the girl—raised a hand. "Permission to go raid the practice armory and bring things back here for the tryouts, sir?"

Setham looked pleased all over again. "Permission granted, Gennie. Take Halleck with you."

The two sped off. Setham surveyed the rest. "You footers and cavalry," he said after a moment. "You'll be at a disadvantage against Heralds. Even the ones that don't have strong Mindspeech will still have their Companions talking to each other and relaying. So, I want you to sort yourselves into groups of four, talk among yourselves, and work out a quick way to deal with that. When you've done that, I'll put you out there in your group to defend the goal, four at a time, and put two Herald Trainees against you. Now, divide up!"

There were about two dozen people trying out for both the foot and horse groups. One of them was Jeffers, who looked excited and a little sick. Maybe sick with excitement. He was on a cobby little bay that Dallen looked at with approval.

:That's good stock. And look how he sits, how easy his hands are. Let's just go over there and calm him down a bit, shall we?:

Mags was a trifle surprised. *:Why? He's pretty much gonna get on th' team, aye?:*

:Yes, but he doesn't know that. He could still make a bad showing out of nerves. Look at it this way, if this was before a battle, you'd be going about calming people down, right?:

:I would?: Mags blinked at that. He rather thought he was more likely to be the one needing calming.

:You would. It's part of what a Herald does. So go practice on Jeffers.:

Dallen ambled over to Jeffers' side, giving Mags no real choice in the matter. "Heyla," Mags said. "I seen ye at Master Soren's, aye? I'm Mags."

"What?" Jeffers started a little, then smiled weakly. "Oh, yes, probably. I mean, I don't know Lydia really well, but we shared some tutors back when we both took classes at Bardic, and we're more or less in the same circles." Belatedly he stuck out a hand, which was a little cold. Mags removed his gauntlet and shook it solemnly.

"This Kirball, seems people are takin' it important, aye?" he offered.

Now Jeffers' blue eyes lit up. "Well they should! I mean, it's not just a game, you know! This is going to be training in case, well, you know, combat training. I could never have gotten my father to agree to combat training with the Guard, but this! He thinks this is just a hearty, manly sort of game, and he thinks my playing it is a fine idea. I'm not about to tell him it's more than that!"

:Aha.: Dallen seemed pleased. *:Keep talking to him. Ask him why his father doesn't approve of combat training.:*

"So why's yer Pa not want ye fightin'?" Mags asked.

Jeffers sighed. "He's a pacifist. And that's fine for him. He really is quite good at negotiating settlements with people, and because of that, he thinks everything can be negotiated, and no civilized person should ever have to pick up a weapon. If he was forced to choose between grabbing a weapon and hurting an attacker or being hurt himself, and negotiation didn't work, he'd choose to be hurt rather than inflict harm." The young man knuckled the side of his head a little. "And I admire that, I really do. He absolutely has the courage of his convictions. But I can't live like that."

Mags nodded, although he couldn't understand someone not being willing to defend himself at all. "Well," he said, after a moment of thought. "When ye get on a team, reckon you an' me could meet up at salle afore or after practicin', an' I could give ye a bit uv trainin' like. Don' reckon Weaponsmaster'd mind. Ye jest tell yer Pa ye was practicin' extree wi' me and not what at. Won't be a lie then."

:Well done, Mags.:

Jeffers jaw dropped a little, and his eyes widened. "You'd—you'd do that? For me?"

"Dunno why not." Mags grinned a little. "Happen I kin get some on Lydia's friends t' come by too. So if I got stuff to do, we kin *start,* like, then they kin take over. So, ye know, won't be a lie."

Jeffers seized Mags' hand and shook it fervently. "Mags, thank you, thank you! You don't know what this means to me!"

"Eh, well." Mags flushed a little in embarrassment. "It's not like I cain't use extree practice m'self." He was saved from trying to think of anything else to say by the arrival of Gennie and Halleck, who had brought back enough miscellaneous armor to fit out all the riders.

Jeffers attached himself to a group of three horsemen, one of whom looked to be quite highborn indeed, if the quality of his tack and clothing was any indication. It wasn't flashy, in fact it was the opposite, but among many other things, being around Lydia had taught Mags how to assess what someone wore.

The fellow made no fuss at all about strapping on the worn and grungy armor, though, so he didn't seem to have any airs about him.

Then again . . . these people had all been invited directly by Herald Setham. So whoever they were and whatever their backgrounds, they had passed his muster.

It was Gennie and a third Trainee, Pip, whom Setham set off against the first group of foot-players. Mags very quickly saw why Setham was considering her for team Captain. She and Pip moved together in a way that Mags recognized had to be due to Mindspeech. Although the foot-players managed to keep them from lobbing the ball through the goal-windows for a while, eventually a clever feint on the part of Gennie caused them to concentrate on her long enough for her to flip the ball to Pip, and Pip to peg it through an unguarded window.

Then it was the turn of Jeffers and four of the riders against Gennie and Mags.

:Hullo Mags,: came the cheerful mind-voice as soon as he and Dallen replaced Pip on the field. *:Setham says you and Dallen are something special when it comes to riding.:*

:Uh—: he replied the same way, *:Dallen thinks he is. Tells me alla time.:*

She grinned, while her Companion snorted.

:I heard that!:

:You was meant to.:

:All right, I had something in mind for these fellows, so let's see if we can pull it off. They're already concentrating on me, which is good. Now, Pip and I play in-saddle ball games all the time for fun, so we're used to ball passing. I don't expect you to have that sort of coordination yet. You will, but not yet. So what I want to do is this, keep them concentrating on me, while you and Dallen run interference, and we'll see if I can get a ball in. If I can't, then on one of those interference passes, we'll brush by each other and I will pass you the ball, and while they still think I have it, you try lobbing it in.:

:We kin do that,: Mags agreed enthusiastically.

:Right then, here we go.:

What followed was barely-controlled chaos.

Mags and Dallen shouldered into the riders—carefully timing and gauging their bull-rushes so as to not actually put the poor horses in danger of a bad fall. They were only horses, after all. Meanwhile, Gennie made runs at the goal.

But the riders were good. And they had, somehow, in the short time they had been consulting with each other, worked out a strategy for communicating. Not as good as Mindspeech, but effective enough to keep Gennie away from the goal.

Dallen rushed Jeffers' horse and at the last minute, feinted left, went right, and shouldered him into a little rise. The hard smack of the impact of Dallen's shoulder into the horse's haunches shuddered through both of them, and the poor horse stumbled, but didn't fall. Gennie shot past just behind Dallen and made a run for the goal, but Jeffers shouted "Four!" and one of the others managed to intercept her. Dallen whirled on his hind hooves, put his head down, and went straight for the rider. *:Take off your blinkers,:* he said with glee, and hit him shoulder to shoulder. The taller horse skidded and slipped to the right.

"One, Two" yelled the rider, and the remaining two closed up to keep Gennie off the goal and force her to gallop off.

:That patch to the left under the hillock with the low stone wall on it is like a bog; try not to go there,: Gennie cautioned.

:It's slippery where I jest was, left of goal,: Mags replied, knowing both Companions would hear him, though it wasn't likely he would hear Gennie's Companion.

:Good place to shove them into,: she returned, as she

and Mags milled confusingly together, and the four riders lined up again.

There was a crowd at the fences now, and it made the four riders a little nervous, if not their horses. It made Mags a little nervous too, even though he knew that he was one of the first picks for the team. Out there—well, who knew who was out there? People who didn't like him and didn't feel he belonged, hoping to see him fail. Friends who maybe hoped too much. Bear, who didn't want to see him hurt.

:You in first,: Gennie said, and feinted with the ball. Mags made as if to take it and then Dallen dashed at the line. Two of the riders charged straight at him, without waiting to see if he actually had the ball, and Dallen compacted himself and braced for impact.

"Three, Four!" yelled the third rider, only now seeing that Gennie was the one with the ball, too late for the two heading for Dallen to change course. Mags closed his eyes and made himself as tight and small as he could. There was another smack, a bruising impact on his left leg, and Dallen's whole body shuddered, while the right-hand horse was forced right down on his own haunches and the left went staggering away, the breath knocked out of him.

Ninety-nine Trainees out of a hundred would have sat there for a moment, but not Dallen and Mags. Without a word being exchanged, the moment that Dallen felt Mags' weight shift, he was off again, rocketing straight for Gennie.

:The ball!: Mags said, as Dallen aimed for one of the two riders that had hemmed Gennie in.

Then they hit, and Dallen sent the off-rider stumbling into that bit of bog, and under the confusion, as they passed, Gennie shoved the ball into Mags' hands.

Then Dallen put his head down and ran for the fences, Gennie right at his heels, and all four of the riders streaming out behind them in a tail chase. *:I'll make for the goal on high right!:* Gennie called, looking back over her shoulder to be sure that she was still being followed and the riders thought she had the ball. She peeled away, taking three of the four with her. Only Jeffers was still on Mags.

Dallen reversed himself suddenly, pivoting on one hoof, and slammed into the chest of Jeffers' mount. The poor horse went staggering off, and sat down suddenly, dog-fashion, to avoid falling; Dallen ricocheted off the beast's chest and bolted for the goal.

"SCRUM!" yelled Jeffers, but too late. The others pulled off of Gennie, but were miles behind, and Jeffers' horse was too shaken for the moment to get up. With horses coming at him as fast as their well-bred legs could carry them, but a clear goal ahead, Mags and Dallen kept their heads down and their wits about them and drove for the open door and windows. As they passed, Mags pitched the ball in the doorway, as the biggest opening, and heard the cheers of the crowd just as the horses caught up with them and surrounded him.

"Goal!" shouted Setham. "Well done, Mags, Gennie, you are in! You too, Jeffers!"

A rush of elation filled him as the crowd cheered.

He and Dallen went out twice more, each time solo against foot groups. That was hardly fair; the best they could do was try and blockade the doors and windows with their bodies, and they couldn't be everywhere; the goal had been planned and built that way. Mags scored goals each time, but at least one of the groups of four made it hard enough on them that Dallen was lathered by the time they made their point.

When all four Herald Trainees were weary and their Companions lathered, Setham sent horse against horse, horse against foot, and foot against foot and sent the Trainees back to the stables. At this point, Mags didn't care. He knew he was on the team, and that was the important thing.

Physically, he was as bruised and battered as he had ever been since leaving Cole Pieters' mine, but he didn't care about that, either. He felt good, a good tired, and Dallen felt the same way.

They went back to the stable, walking slowly so Dallen had a chance to cool down. Actually, all four of them did, more or less together. Gennie glanced over at him after a while.

"Good job out there," she said.

He bobbed his head. "Thenkee," he said awkwardly.

"I mean it. You slotted right into teamwork without hesitation. There's a big difference between a good team and a team of good players—or good fighters." She raked her short brown hair out of her eyes with grimy fingers, and glanced over at Halleck, who flushed. "You've got to stop thinking of just what you can do, and think in terms of what *we* can do. That's why Jeffers' lot was good. Hadn't even been working together more than half a candlemark and were thinking about each others' strong and weak points."

Mags nodded, keeping quiet, but he was impressed with Gennie's observations. She was going to make a good Captain.

When they reached the stable, they were all starting to chill. Mags hustled Dallen inside, and rubbed him down within an inch of his life, getting both of them warm again. Once he was clean and dry, Mags threw his blanket over him, and buckled the chest and belly straps loosely.

:I must say, I am glad that they walled this place in with brick a few years ago,: Dallen said, blinking sleepily. *:Drafts are bad enough with people coming in and out of the doors all the time, and what with the windows only having shutters and no glass, but when our stable was wood, it was horrible.:*

"Next ye'll want wood floors," Mags said with a smile. "Or maybe on'y marble'll suit ye."

:You have wood, why shouldn't I?:

Mags laughed. "Same as th' reason why I'm goin' t' get me a hot bath an' you get a rubdown." He gave Dallan's ears a quick scratch, and went off to his quarters to get a clean uniform. He was going to claim a bathtub and not leave it until the water was cool and his skin looked like a withered apple's!

FOR days, all that anyone could talk about were the Kirball teams—who was on, who was *going* to get on, what the games were going to look like. This was especially true during the trials, and during them, Mags tried to keep himself as much out of the public eye as possible.

He was a little surprised to discover that Herald Nikolas was heartily in favor of his being on one of the Kirball teams. The King's Own made one of those stealthy visits to him the evening after the trial, right after Setham had confirmed that he had been selected.

Mags immediately started to apologize for getting involved in yet another time-consuming activity.

Nikolas laughed and silenced him with a gesture. "No, no, Mags, this is a very good thing. I'm quite pleased."

Mags blinked. "But—I thought th' ideer was fer me to mostly be not noticed . . ."

"Not . . . exactly." Nikolas steepled his fingers together. "The idea is for you to appear innocuous. Someone that can be safely ignored," he explained further, at Mags' bewildered look. "Now no one ever anticipates great intelligence out of a games player or a fine warrior. This is just how things go—people assume that anyone who is quite physical does not have as much going on in his mind. This is good for us. We can use this to our advantage."

"Then I should stop tryin' so hard in classes?" he asked, bewildered all over again now.

"No, no!" Nikolas laughed, his eyes crinkling up in the corners. "No one but your teachers will know how well or poorly you are doing in class, so just act as you have been. People will hear you talk and assume that you are not very bright; let them continue to think that way. In that way you become someone it is safe to ignore."

Well, this was all a little confusing, but Mags was willing to accept it.

Meanwhile, the teams were taking shape. He wasn't sure about the others, but their team got organized within a day. As Setham had suggested, Gennie was quickly made Team Captain; she set about ruthlessly finding out the weaknesses of her teammates, and structuring her strategy to minimize them.

It was a sound approach, and one Setham approved of. Their coach did not say what the other teams were doing, but Mags got the definite impression that at least one of the other teams was taking the opposite approach.

The hardest part was coordinating things with the

foot-players and riders. Or rather, it would have been hard except—for the second reason Mags was on the team.

His Mindspeech was powerful enough that he could be "heard" and understood by the unGifted. That meant Gennie could give him orders, and he could tell them instantly to the rest of the team. No one would have to think of codes for movements, or shout them across the playing field. As Captain, Gennie was going to stay where she could see everything, and prepare to dash in at need.

Or so the plan was. Mags had the notion that once games started, Gennie was going to be dashing in a lot.

It was too bad that without him reading the minds of his teammates, he couldn't tell Gennie what they were going to do. That was just out of the question; this was hardly any sort of emergency situation, this was a game and not a skirmish in a war, and it would be entirely unethical for him to violate the privacy of their thoughts this way—

Although if he could train them to—more or less—mentally shout what they were doing, that didn't count as "reading." So maybe he would suggest that, once things settled into place more.

Setham and the other coaches had decided that the teams needed names, and that the most innocuous would be the four cardinal directions, although they debated everything from colors to mythical creatures. Gennie had been very taken with the idea of calling their team Gennie's Gryphons; once the other three Captains had gotten wind of that idea there were almost fights breaking out over the best names. Dragons of any color, Firebirds, and so on were very popular. The coaches put their collective feet down over the ruckus, and that was the end of that.

"First of all, we are not having anyone's personal name being part of the team name, as if you were all some sort of mercenary company," Setham had told them all, quite sternly. "The team will, I hope, last long past when Gennie is in her Whites and out on circuit. Secondly, there is too much concentration on the name and its emblem and not on actually building the team itself. Your name is going to be one of the four directions, your team color will be the one usually associated with that direction, and there will be no totemic mascot. Now, let's not hear any more about this."

So Mags was on the South Team, and the color was red, and it was all settled. Even if from time to time he could hear Gennie muttering under her breath "they're still Gennie's Gryphons."

Somehow he was managing to stay relatively in the shadow of his other teammates. It did help that Gennie was outspoken, gregarious, and popular; she managed to eclipse anyone that did not have as powerful a personality as she did, and Mags was grateful for that. He basically portrayed himself as the quiet games-player, he carefully filtered all his ideas through Gennie, and if she thought that was odd, she said nothing about it. Maybe she thought he was shy, or had no self confidence. If so, that was fine, too.

The trials were over pretty quickly, and the teams set; with one or two exceptions—mostly when two of the coaches had tried to recruit the same person—people passed the trials and there were enough players and alternates that a second round wasn't needed. Once the trials were done with, some of the excitement drained away and life went relatively back to normal—except, of course, that Mags now had team practice every day along with everything else.

With four teams using the same practice ground some creative juggling of Trainee classes had to be done, because not everyone was free when his or her team was scheduled for practice. And there were some transfers, especially among the Grays. Mags found himself, to his profound relief, in a Language class that was composed mostly of the youngest of the Trainees from all three Collegia, and which, as a consequence, was not nearly so demanding as the one he had been taking. After some consultation, and a session in which he sweated over a stack of maths problems, it was deemed that he was proficient enough in geometry to get by, and excelled in everything else, so he was permitted to stop that class. He got switched to a different history class as well, one that was covering an entirely different time period than the one he'd been in, but that was all right; he knew he would catch up pretty quickly. And that freed his early afternoon.

His afternoons were going to be exhausting, though. All of his weaponry classes were held in late afternoon, which meant he would be going from Kirball practice to weapons work.

Well, if this was a wartime situation, it wasn't as if he would be able to take a break from the fighting.

Besides, as he told himself, so far nothing he had done had been as physically demanding as a day of mining on too little food.

There was one little problem, however. The first full day of team practice, he learned that the South team would have their session right after the noon meal, which was not such a good thing on a full stomach.

After thinking about it, he decided that what he would do would be to get himself a packet of things that would keep, eat very lightly, then have a second meal after the practice, dividing his lunch into two small meals.

So for the first day of practice, he sat down and warmed himself with a quite small bowl of soup, which he ate slowly, with a bit of bread. He was halfway through it, intently thinking over what Gennie might demand of them today, and what Setham might want them to do, when a tap on his back startled him.

Old habits died very hard, so when startled, he froze rather than yelping or jumping. While he sat there, Bear sat down on the bench next to him and eyed his lunch critically.

"I wouldn't say you needed to lose weight."

Mags grinned a little and shrugged. "Kirball fer m'team is right after noon."

"Ah!" Bear nodded back. "In that case, you're doing the right thing. You could get really sick if you ate like you usually do, then went out to practice. I don't think you'd impress anyone by losing your lunch suddenly."

Mags shrugged. "Happen ye learn a mite or two 'bout eatin' when ye ain't got a lot t' eat." He turned his attention fully on Bear, for something about his friend did not seem quite right. "Happen I ain't been payin' much heed t' friends lately . . . Bear, ye seem a bit fashet. Ye been frettin' bout somethin'?"

Bear looked uncomfortable and actually squirmed a little in his seat. "It's nothing," he said starting to stuff a huge bite of cooked greens into his mouth. Mags kept looking at him steadily.

Bear shoveled three more bites in, pretending to ignore the stare. But then he stopped, and put the fork down, and sighed. "You've got no idea how lucky you are to be an orphan."

Mags froze with the spoon halfway into his mouth. It felt like his mind was stuck in mud for a moment, because he could not imagine why Bear would have said anything like that. Finally he ate the soup, then put the spoon in the bowl. "Ye got any notion how crazy that sounds?" he asked.

Bear grimaced. "Very. But Lena's not the only one with parents that . . ."

Mags waited. When Bear didn't finish the sentence, he prodded. "What, I know they're all Healers, be they pretendin' ye don't exist cause ye got no Gift?" He snorted. "The more fools them."

Bear looked sick. "It's worse than that. We got into it over the holiday—or rather, they all sat and lectured me, one at a time, and then all together. They think I don't belong here, 'taking up a space that a real Healing Trainee could use.' They think if I were to leave here, someone from the provinces would get an open place. They won't understand that it doesn't work that way anymore, that anyone who can come here and be spared at home is free to come. They just refuse to believe that. They want me to pack up and come home and marry some . . ." he made a flailing gesture with his hands. " . . . some neighbor girl I supposedly used to play with that I don't even remember, so that I can maybe breed some children that will have the Gift."

Mags felt his jaw dropping. "Where—what—" He got control of himself again, but he felt a little as if Bear had suddenly announced he was going to become an Artificer.

"The Dean of Healers is stalling them. I mean, they can't exactly come up here and pull me out of the Collegium by the hair. They'd have to have my consent to come home. But . . ." Now Bear looked even sicker. "Here's the thing. I'm not sure they're wrong."

Mags felt his jaw unhinge. "Now *you* are th' one sayin' crazy stuff."

"No but look—most of what I do is with herbs. They generally won't let someone without a Gift do any cutting, because someone without a Gift can't See what they're doing and where they're going. So I probably won't be learning surgery. I can set bones, sure, but someone with a Gift can do it better. So that leaves just the herbs. And what good is that here?" Bear's face was bleak. "I can help a little, and I can take care of people who for one reason or another refuse to let a real Healer touch them, or the few people that Healing Mindmagic doesn't work on. That's all I can do, and I'm not sure I'm not wasting space. Maybe I'd be better going home and treating animals. Nobody would mind if I did surgery on them, and there just aren't many animal Healers."

"Didn' you even lissen t' Amily?" he asked, aghast. "She said ye had a Gift, an' don't ye think she's right?"

"Of course she would say that," Bear said bitterly. "She's the ungifted crippled daughter of the King's Own who has never been Chosen. She has to believe that people without Gifts are just as effective as those with them, or her own life would be unbearable."

Mags had never heard Bear talk like this before, and he was somewhat at a loss for what to say. He felt a little sick, and a little like crying. Bear was so clever, and so kind, that to see him in this state made him want to jump up and do something right now, and of course there was nothing that he could do.

"Well, I got a Gift, an' a Companion, an' I say ye got a Gift," he replied after a while, and laid his hand cautiously on Bear's shoulder. "What's more, I bet if'n ye ask the Senior Healers over there, they'd be tellin' ye the same."

Bear smiled wanly. "Thanks, Mags." He stirred his cooling greens, gazing broodingly down at them. "Oh, what was in that note you left me the other night? I haven't had a chance to talk to Lena, and I spilled a decoction all over it and it's illegible."

Glad to change the subject, Mags told him what he had uncovered in the Archives. "So all I know now is, I'm a furriner."

He hadn't made any effort to keep his voice down, although it wasn't as if he had any great secret to hide. But suddenly he noticed that he was getting odd glances from everyone within range of the sound of his voice.

And Bear's expression changed again, this time to wary. He hunched his shoulders and glanced furtively from side to side. "Aw hellfires, Mags, did you have to say that out loud?" he whispered.

"Uh . . ." Mags blinked. "There a prollem?"

Bear groaned. "Don't you ever listen to any gossip? It's all over the Collegia and the Court too."

Mags shook his head. "Ain't like I ever talk t' too many people," he pointed out. "An' I been pretty busy past few days. Why?"

Bear carefully removed his lenses and polished them with his sleeve. "Because this morning a lot of the Foreseers got visions. They saw the King covered in blood, a shadowy figure next to him, and the sense that someone had tried to kill the King and the feeling that the shadowy figure was foreign born. Which . . . you are. And the feeling is that only someone known to the King or otherwise vouched for could get that close to him. It's not as if he's ever unguarded, and he's a damn fine fighter on his own merits. So there's been a lot of speculation about who could be foreign-born and be able to get to him, and there's not a lot of people around that match those two things."

Mags blinked, and felt something very odd. Resentment. And some anger, but he didn't often feel resentment. "Well . . . that don't make no sense!" he said indignantly. "They got somethin' bad, the King in danger, an' someun' furriner an' they know 'xactly that, an' nothin' else! Ain't nobody got no brains 'round here?

Mebbe the furriner's there 'cause he came t' help! Maybe the furriner's there by accident! Mebbe nobody knows this feller is a furriner yet! Ain't 'nough in that vision t' make any kinda good guess 'bout what's gonna happen, 'cept that the King's prolly got an enemy, an' when ain't he got an enemy?"

Bear waved his hands at Mags deprecatingly. "Hey, I wasn't the one leaping to conclusions, all right? But you know how some people are."

Mags thought back to the Herald that had leapt to the conclusion that because he lived in the stable he was out there up to no good. Presumably with girls. Or liquor. Or both. Or worse things. "Aye," he growled. "Well. I'd sooner cut off me own hand an' bleed t' death than harm the King, an' there's an end to it! If'n ye cain't trust summun that's been Chosen, then ye might as well take 'way the Whites and turn all th' Heralds out. Right?"

He looked around defiantly at the people who were giving him sideways glances, and most of them looked away, flushing with guilt. A couple gave him nods of sympathy—but a couple of them gazed back at him with clenched jaws.

Great. Just fantastic.

:There have always been people like that here, Chosen. Idiots who can't even accept the judgment of a Companion, including some Heralds, who really should know better.: Dallen's mind-voice was soothing. *:We just have to deal with them as we always have...:*

Mags' only reply was a wordless growl of frustration. Bad enough that he already felt deep down that he didn't really belong here, but to have to deal with other people who felt the same? Unfair.

Then again, when was life fair? Ever?

"It'd be nice if some people'd think wi' their heads, 'stead uv some other parts," he muttered.

"If they did, the Healers would get a lot less work," Bear replied, with a tentative smile.

"Aye t'that." Mags sighed. "Well, reckon I gotta muddle 'long. An' I got practice. Hope we kin keep from brainin' each other."

Bear pulled a long face. "So do I."

Mags left his packet of food in his room. He reckoned he might just as well go down to the Kirball field armored up again; the worst that would happen would be that Setham would tell him to take it off.

So with Dallen saddled with his working saddle, he hoisted himself and his added burden up into place, and they trotted down to the playing field with Bear's unwelcome news shoved firmly into the back of his mind.

And certainly when he got there, it didn't appear that anyone else had heard the stories—or if they had, they certainly didn't seem to care.

Foremost in their minds seemed to be the number of bumps and knocks they had taken yesterday, for they were arrayed in as motley an assortment of makeshift "armoring" as Mags had ever imagined.

"Corwin, you look like you robbed your mother's kitchen," said one of the foot-players, laughing.

"Very near did," said the afore-mentioned Corwin, who was all but invisible behind all the stuff he had strapped to himself. "Half of this's stovepipe. T'other half's old bits of carpet. Thought of taking a pot for me head, but found a helm I could bang the dents out of."

"Great Kernos!" exclaimed Setham, as he approached with someone in tow. "You all have been . . . creative."

"That's being generous, sir," Gennie laughed.

"Well this is all rather interesting, because besides our first practice, I was going to get your help in designing what will be our specialized armor." Setham nodded at the solemn-faced young man that was with him. "My friend here will draw it up for me, I'll consult with the other coaches, who are doing the same, and we'll have the armor made up before the first match." He peered at Corwin's helm. "That miserable excuse for a helm—is that Karsite?"

"Aye sir, I think 'tis," Corwin replied. "Found it at a stall in the market."

"Well get one from the armory; those Karsite buckets are notorious. A baby could dent it, and a good hard blow will crack your skull right through it."

By this point, a cart had lumbered up, laden with what looked like the cast-offs and discards from the Guard armory. At least, it was all in dark blue and flaking silver.

"If you haven't ferreted out your own, or want to replace something, rummage through that," Setham said, waving a hand at it. "We can wait."

Corwin was first at the wagon, probably being very eager to replace his bits of stovepipe with something less makeshift.

When everyone was suited up, Setham went over the

rules for the game again. "Now, obviously, since you foot-players are less mobile, you'll be guarding the goal, both the flag and the 'castle,'" Setham said. "But don't think you will be confined to that by the rules. If there is a way for one of you to get a ball in the other castle or steal the flag, then your Captain will suggest it and you should try it. We decided to make the only rules of this game about safety. So no pulling a rider out of the saddle for now—although as you get better, that actually will be allowed. Riders, no running the foot-players down. That will never be allowed, because we can't trust the ordinary horses to do it safely."

They all nodded. Of course. *Nobody follows no rules in a battle*, Mags thought. *An' this's battle-trainin'.*

The rest of the practice session was confined to some very simple exercises with an end toward making them a team and getting them used to working with each other. Setham seemed satisfied. There was a lot of ball passing: Gray to Gray, Gray to Rider, Gray to Foot, Rider to Rider, Rider to Foot, Foot to Foot. There was a lot of goal blocking, first by just the Foot, then by the Riders, then by the Grays. Mags was kept busy "shouting" Gennie's directions into the heads of the UnGifted, though he quickly discovered that everyone reacted faster when he showed them a picture than when he used words. Useful, that. It was faster for Gennie to send a picture to him, and easier for him to send a picture out.

When they were dismissed, however, Mags was not done with the team. He approached young Jeffers, still on Dallen, before the latter could ride back into Haven.

"Reckon ye still wanta learn weaponry?" he asked diffidently. "I made some 'rrangements, if ye do."

Jeffers' eyes lit up, and his tired horse even raised his head, as if sensing his rider's excitement.

Mags held up a cautioning hand. "Got t' warn ye. Gonna be tedious fer a goodly while. But I got t' thinkin and I asked Weaponsmaster if he could be workin' out exercises ye kin pass off as Kirball stuff, that'll strengthen ye up i' the right way for weapons, an' 'e showed me some. This's all stuff ye kin set up t' do when ye're at home. So e'en though ye ain't actually practicin' with sword or whatnot, ye'll be practicin' fer 'em at home." He scratched his head. "Happen ye kin practice a-horse too, which ain't a bad thing. Yon cob of your'n is steady 'nough in Kirball so far, he'll be steady 'nough right off in this stuff."

Now Jeffers lit up even more; his eyes shone with happiness and he grinned for the first time since Mags had met him. "Mags, I can't even begin to thank you enough! No wonder Amily and Lydia think you are clever!"

Mags just shook his head. "Ain't clever. Jest used t' gettin' round rules and sneakin', ye ken? I mean, gettin' done whatcha need t' do, wi'out lyin' or getting' caught at it. That ain't clever, jest a way of thinkin' that ye got to learn when—"

He broke it off. Jeffers didn't need his story. Or Jeffers might already know it. In either case, telling him wouldn't serve any good or useful purpose.

"Anyway, I jest got figgerin' out how to get somethin' thet I want bad kinda ground inter me." He shrugged.

"An' I don' see no harm in you learnin' this, an' neither does Weaponsmaster. So, come on, an' we'll get ye started. Hellfires, prolly do ye good in Kirball too, top of ev'thing else."

"I can't stay too much longer," Jeffers warned. "My parents. And—they don't know anyone in the Foot or anyone in the Riders to ask, but—they might in the Heralds—"

Mags nodded. "Lemme check," he said.

:Dallen, kin ye make sure nobody rats on Jeffers? Covers fer him? Like, if there's an 'mergency an' someone comes up here fer 'im or sends fer 'im?:

Dallen engaged in that long silence that meant he was speaking to all of the Companions within reach, as the two of them headed up toward the salle.

:It's sorted,: Dallen replied finally. *:Some of the Heralds don't like it, but we reminded them that some of their parents weren't too happy about them being Chosen. We also reminded them that it isn't as if the young man is doing anything wrong—and that he is very respectful of his parents' choice, so they should be respectful of his. No one true way, after all. It seems to have worked.:*

"Dallen sez yer covered," Mags reported just as they got to the salle itself. He listened to what Dallen had to say and repeated it verbatim. "He sez if some'un comes up here lookin' fer ye, Heralds an' Grays'll say yer at salle getting' some tips on hittin' an aimin' from Weaponsmaster. Weaponsmaster'll say same. Ain't a lie, neither. An' afore anyone gets there, they'll be warnin', so ye kin get rid of weapon an' it'll look like ye was jest talkin'."

Jeffers dismounted, grinning ruefully. "And you say you aren't clever!"

"Hey, twasn't me," he protested. "That twas Weaponsmaster's ideer. Now, ye go 'long t' him, I'll rub down yer cob an' walk 'im cool. "

"Mags—" Jeffers was at a loss for words. "You are a star."

Mags knew he wouldn't be long. Not like his own practices—Jeffers' parents probably wouldn't quibble up to a candlemark for "extra practice" but they certainly would say something about more than that. He got Jeffers' horse and Dallen rubbed down and in good condition, and Dallen took the cob's reins in his teeth to lead him off to the horse stables.

Then Mags and the Weaponsmaster showed the young man the exercise they had worked out to simulate sword play. Normally this sort of thing was done by striking with a wooden blade—often weighted—at a padded pole called a "pells." Obviously that wasn't realistic for Jeffers to set up in a yard, since everyone knew what a pells looked like. So what the Weaponsmaster had decided on was for Jeffers to take swings with a weighted wooden club at a ball about the size of a melon, suspended at various heights to represent the various target areas on a human.

He could tell them it was Kirball. He wouldn't even be exactly lying, since one of the defensive moves they had all planned for was to smack the ball away from the goal with a much broader sort of club, more like a paddle, and the Kirball was about the same size. If he was ever challenged, he could say that working with a club instead of the paddle was to make his aim better, because it was harder.

When Jeffers had to leave, he took a club and a leather ball and its marked string with him, nearly falling over himself with gratitude.

But life continued to slide downhill into the mud. Aside from the Kirball practices, in which no one acted as if he was any different than he had been before all those ridiculous visions, that session with Jeffers was the last completely comfortable, happy moment Mags knew.

Gossip about the Foreseers' vision reached into every nook and cranny of the three Collegia, as did Mags' own revelation that he was foreign-born. He found himself the focus of far too many speculative glances, laden with suspicion. Granted, most of them did not come from Trainees or Heralds—but some did. And the most suspicious were from the Bards and especially the Bardic Trainees, who had far, far too much imagination for their own good.

He even started to hear wild tales about "Black Heralds" and "Black Companions," who could somehow pass as the real thing, but inside were evil incarnate. Was that even possible?

:No,: Dallen said emphatically. *:They're just making things up so they can frighten each other. What an incredibly stupid idea! It's too stupid even to make me laugh.:*

Still, the stories persisted, because the surest way to make some people believe almost anything was to deny it completely. "Can you prove that?" the doubters would demand. And of course, no one could prove that what had never happened before never could happen. After all, there had been Trainees who had been repudiated and everyone pointed to Tylendel as the primary example. So why not bad Companions as well? The Companions weren't infallible . . .

So went the so-called "reasoning."

Of course, no one actually said anything to him. They just whispered it behind their hands around him and their minds shouted it so loudly that it got past his shields.

Then there were the ones that turned up their noses in contempt at the wilder stories, but still thought, "what if it isn't him, but someone he knows?" Or "what if he somehow brings old trouble from his past into the grounds and the King gets caught in it?"

What could he say, to people like that, after all? He couldn't refute what hadn't happened yet. He couldn't even say anything, because they weren't saying anything to him.

It was aggravating. It was more than aggravating. It was sickening. He went around with his stomach in a knot most of the time now, feeling eyes on his back, as people watched him, hoping to catch him showing his "true colors."

He even got into a shouting match with some of the highborn youngsters and some of the Bardic Trainees. It all started over—of all stupid things—the fact that he was eating soup and a little bread instead of the regular hearty luncheon. Not that he had much appetite anymore.

"Is that what they eat where you come from, foreigner?" sneered one of the Bardic Trainees as he passed Mags' table. "Or are you too good to enjoy honest Valdemaran food?"

Mags gave him a stony stare. "Nah, I come from an honest Valdemaran mine, where we was worked worse'n donkeys," he said. "Mine soup was mostly water an' a couple cabbage leaves. Be good change for them as needs t' be able t' fit their uniforms, though, cause ye sure wouldn' get fat on't."

He knew he shouldn't have said that. All right, the fellow was packing on a good several pounds more than he should, and his tunic was straining at the seams. And yes, he did seem to have half a pie and a cream cake on his plate.

But it was a cruel thing to say, and he immediately regretted it.

Too late, though, because before he could apologize, the Trainee rounded on him furiously. "You need to learn some proper manners, foreigner!" he snarled. "Or better yet, just go back where you came from! We don't need your kind here!"

"What kind'd that be?" Mags shouted back. "Cause I reckon if'n yer talking 'bout kind, ye be talkin' 'bout ev'one in Grays or Whites!"

"And how do we know you didn't somehow bewitch that Companion into thinking he Chose you?" one of the others said viciously.

"Because, Jan, you incredible dunce, the other Companions would certainly have noticed." Lena ducked into the group and stood next to Mags, defiantly, her hands on her hips, her normally shy demeanor completely gone with her anger. "And because Mags can't even be as old as you. Since not even the most experienced Karsite priests who were four times Mags' age could manage to bewitch one Companion, much less the entire herd, I think you'd better give over that stupid idea. I wouldn't even accept that in a story-song." She gave him a withering glance. "No wonder you're failing composition. I'd fail you too, if that is all you can come up with."

"Maybe he's bewitched you too, Lena!" the fat fellow put in furiously, turning beet red with rage.

Bear shoved his way in to stand on the other side of Mags. Slowly he looked the overweight Trainee up and down, and then spent a long and pointed time staring at the laden plate still in his hands. "Ferd Lekson, I just got this to say to you. You insult a fellow out of nowhere, then get mad because he gives you back what you gave him, and even madder because he tells you to your face what your so-called friends won't, which is, if you don't quit stuffing your face five times a day, there won't be a Trainee uniform in all of Bardic that will fit you. Now, I got to say Mags was rude. But you were just as rude, and you started it, and you're making it worse for your side with all your dumb accusations." He put one hand on Mags' shoulder. "Mags is Chosen. That should be the end of it. But he also saved my life last winter, and a couple of other people's and you seem to have forgotten all of that."

Mags was astonished. He had never heard Bear talk like that before.

"Now, you and your friends just take your dinner somewhere else, because one more word out of you and I'm gonna have to decide you need to get treated for your own good and make sure you're on the special meals list."

Ferd went white at that. Mags knew what the special meals list was—it was for people who had troubles with some sorts of foods. There weren't more than a handful of people who were on it, and most of them were glad to be—it meant that the cook made absolutely certain that the foods that made them ill never got anywhere near the plates that were destined for them.

But if Bear put Ferd on it—Mags would bet nearly everything that Ferd would find himself restricted both in quantity and the kind of food he'd be allowed, and the only way he'd get anywhere near a piece of pie or cake would be if someone slipped it to him.

"You can't do that!" Ferd spluttered.

Bear got grim-faced, and his eyes behind his lenses grew cold as steel. "Try me. Maybe I'm only a Trainee, but when it comes to things like that, even the senior Healers listen to me, and I can have a list of twenty reasons why you need to be on it without even thinking hard."

Muttering to his friends, Ferd backed down and the lot of them slunk away. Bear sat down, Lena beside him, with a sigh.

"This's jest the beginnin' ye know," Mags said glumly, staring down into the soup he no longer had an appetite for. "They ain't done."

"I know," Lena said, looking after the lot of them

with a worried face. "And what's worse is, nobody else here said anything to defend you."

"You'd think some of the Grays would," Bear said loud enough for those nearby to hear him. "After all, it's Mags today—but who's to say it won't be one of them getting accused of ridiculous things tomorrow? Anything that can be used against him could be said about any other Chosen."

It was . . . very quiet. People kept their eyes on their meals, though no one seemed to be in the mood to eat.

"Reckon I'll go down t' practice early," Mags said abruptly, and shoved what was left of his meal away. "Thanks Bear. Thanks Lena. Least I know I got two friends."

Dallen said nothing as he stalked out of the dining hall, resolving not to eat another meal there until all of this was sorted.

But he had to wonder—why on earth was he here when so many people didn't want him?

Mostly cause I got nowhere to go.

That was the shame of it. There was no way he could just run away from here. Not so much for himself as for Dallen; the Companion ate a lot, and needed decent stabling, and all that cost money. What did he know, besides how to mine? Nothing. If Bear were in this position, he could just pack up and leave and set himself up as an animal Healer just about anywhere. Even Lena could go on the road as a wandering musician, even if she couldn't claim to be a Bard. Both of them had obvious talents and gifts or Gifts that would make them welcome anywhere they went.

He had—exactly nothing. Except mining, and where was he likely to get a place doing that? Even if Cole Pieters' mine was in better hands now, it was a sure bet that there were miners enough already. He didn't know any other sort of mining.

Beg on th' street, mebbe. Do odd jobs. He smiled mirthlessly as he trudged through the cold wind down to the Kirball field. *Get job as a ash-boy. Mebbe I should.* That nice merchant with the soap-shop had taken care of Dallen. Maybe she'd be willing to keep on doing so.

:I never thought you were a coward, Mags,: Dallen said sternly.

But Mags just rubbed his forehead; he reached the still-empty field and went and sat down with his back against the goal-castle. *:Mebbe ye don' know me as well as ye think ye do,:* he replied. *:Mebbe they're all right, an' ye're wrong.:*

:And maybe the sun will rise in the west tomorrow,: Dallen retorted. *:I can't prove it won't, but I think that is more likely than that I am wrong about you.:*

All Mags could do was sigh.

:WHERE are you going?: Dallen asked, as he went past Dallen's stall—wearing, not Grays, but the Palace page uniform he'd gotten through Nikolas. *:And why are you wearing that instead of your uniform?:* Dallen's head was up, and his ears pinned back.

Mags turned and looked his Companion in the eye. *:Goin' t' get breakfast. I ain't eatin' in hall till this gets sorted. An' I don' wanta get snubbed by kitchen staff neither. Figgered if I wear this, they won't look past th' livery. Gonna say I'm fetchin' food for Herald Jakyr, get the stuff an' bring it back t' me room.:*

Dallen went very still for a long moment. Mags shrugged, and moved on past. He was tired of a knotted stomach and ruined meals. At least this way he could eat in peace.

But before he got to the door, one of the other Companions intercepted him and shouldered him aside, then planted her ample hindquarters right in front of it and stood looking down her long nose at him. He recognized her as Pip's Litri. She didn't have to Mindspeak him; it was plain she was not going to let him pass.

:You get back in your room and put on proper Grays,: Dallen said firmly. *:What did Nikolas say about not making yourself conspicuous? This isn't going to solve anything. People are watching you now. If you stop showing up for meals, you'll only make people more suspicious of you.:*

He stared at both Companions. "I cain't eat wi' 'em starin' me down alla time!" he exclaimed in despair. "M'gut's all inna knot afore I even get in th' door!"

Litri snorted at him, as if to say she still wasn't moving. Dallen was not going to give in, either. *:Just do what I told you. We have a plan.:*

Shoulders hunched, Mags obeyed his Companion. He went back to his room, changed, and shuffled unhappily up the path to the Collegium. With heavy reluctance, he pulled open the door and went in, although he would much rather have been slouching his way to the worst Languages class ever than have to go eat under a sea of—

He stopped in the middle of the corridor, in mid-thought. There were half a dozen people waiting there for him. Bear, Lena, Gennie, Pip, Halleck, and the alternate Gray team member of the South, Meled. If it hadn't been friends, he'd have turned and bolted for the door, but since it was, he just stood there for a moment, baffled. Before he could say or do anything, they surrounded him, Gennie took one arm, Pip the other, and the lot of them bustled into the dining hall as a group.

As a group, they took up an entire table. Gennie and

Pip pushed him down on a seat between them, with Bear and Lena across from him. And as a group—Bear and Lena included—they started chattering about Kirball, immediately, doing absolutely nothing to keep their voices down.

". . . need a name for those clubs before we use them."

". . . neck brace, I think, but it ought to be flexible. Maybe a padded leather collar?"

". . . think we ought to all get together at lunch, every lunch, from now on, because we are going to need all the time we can get for planning."

". . . for goal tending . . ."

". . . someone with Fetching Gift could take the flag . . ."

". . . someone with Fetching Gift could lob the balls in and we'd never know it!"

Lena loaded a plate and passed it to him; he got so wrapped up in the Kirball discussion he only noticed when it was under his nose.

For once, even though he was still getting hostile thoughts from some of the others in the room, his stomach wasn't in a knot. He was in the middle of friends. No one was going to bother him or harass him, at least not right at this moment. The presence of the others pretty much guaranteed that.

Wonderful smells came up from the plate; hotcakes and bacon, hot porridge. His stomach growled and he dug in. The food went down easily and quickly and he was hungry for the first time since all this began.

Pip and Halleck got into a passionate discussion about the finer points of intercepting a ball—something that they hadn't even begun to work out in practice. Bear waded in manfully, pointing out that a ball going as fast as this one might when hit with a stick would likely break bones if it struck you. That triggered a discussion of more padding. Under cover of this, Gennie leaned over and caught Mags' eyes.

Her mind-voice rang out clearly in his head. *:If we'd known you were getting harassed, we'd have done this before,:* she said firmly. *:I'm sorry, Mags, as your Captain and as a Trainee senior to you, I should have been looking out for you. From now on, we get meals as a team. All twelve of us, plus your friends Lena and Bear if they can, at lunch at least. Those of us that live up here at breakfast and supper. You'll never come into the dining hall with less than six people around you. Nobody will want to lock horns with a group this big, we're Kirball players, which is starting to count for something, and seeing us four sticking by you just quelled any doubts the other Grays had.:*

He was so astonished that he could only blink at her. He could scarcely believe she was going to all this trouble.

She snorted quietly at the expression on his face. *:What? We're a team. And I'm almost as strong a Mindspeaker as you, with a lot more practice and training. You might be able to hold things back from me, but I would know you were, even if I didn't know what they were. You're good, Mags, but I have to tell you, you can't keep me out if I want in. And all these stories coming out of the Foreseers makes it ethical for me to rummage around in your head, because of the danger to the King, if I were so inclined.:*

:So did ye?: he asked solemnly.

She shook her head. *:No, because I trust and I know you. I'd ask first, if not you, then the Dean, and I wouldn't do it in secret. But others know that I am strong and trained, and they know I've had plenty of opportunity, and if they choose to assume I have had a walk around in your thoughts? Well that's good all the way around. Because they see me here and now and that is just one more shot in the heart of these stupid suspicions.:*

:Well . . . : he hesitated, because he really didn't want anyone in his head but Dallen . . . but if that was what it was going to take . . . *:You kin rummage aroun' in there all ye like.:*

She shook her head. *:Thanks, but no thanks. You've got nightmares in there I'd rather not see. Joy says Dallen told her so. But the mere fact that you offered either means you are the sneakiest and most underhanded and clever person in the Kingdom, or perfectly honest, and since you're Chosen, you can't be sneaky and underhanded, so you must be perfectly honest.:*

Her perfect trust in the Companions and their Choices shone through her thoughts, warming parts of him that had gone cold with rejection.

:I bin sneaky an' underhanded wi' Jeffers—: he said weakly.

:Oh, Jeffers. That doesn't count,: she said dismissively. *:In some parts of Valdemar, he'd be married and with his own family by now. He's capable of deciding for himself what he wants to do, it's honorable and honest, and all you are doing is helping him get it.:*

:All right then . . . I gotta thenkee . . . :

A flash of irritation. *:It's what we all should have been doing. But if the others won't man up and do it, your teammates will. So there.:*

He found himself smiling wanly, and went back to the conversation, which had moved on to finding ways of disrupting Gifts during the game.

While he talked, he let his Gift drift over all the projected thoughts out there. It was soon clear that Gennie's ploy had worked; no more hostile thoughts from anyone wearing Grays or Whites in this room—though he was getting plenty of curiosity and puzzlement.

Well, they cain't be any more puzzled nor me.

There were still hostile surface thoughts; the most worrying were the ones from the Guards, who, after all, were supposed to protect the King. He had to wonder if they would decide that it was easier to prevent him from being involved in this future calamity by, well, force if necessary. He didn't think they'd harm him but—they could find a nice dark prison cell to throw him in. Or they could drag him off and dump him on the other side of the Border.

It was the same problem, over and over. How was he to prove that he was not the one that was the cause of a future crime?

I s'pose I could ask fer Guard t' be there ev'time I meet w' th' King . . . or Nikolas or summun else that's good as a guard . . .

Yes, but look at how he had just run into the King by chance at the stables! How could he ever stop that sort of thing from happening? Well the Companions could coordinate, he supposed, but there was no accounting for accidents. Or a situation where they had to be in the same place at the same time.

It was just so frustrating . . .

And frightening, really, because even though he knew, he knew he would sooner die than harm so much as a hair of the King's head, what if it was the result of an accident, something terrible that just happened when he was in the vicinity? What if the King was attacked while Mags was there and he wasn't going to act quickly enough to save him? What if, what if—

There were just too many uncertainties, and in a way, he even felt some sympathy for those poor Foreseers, who were only seeing a corner of whatever it was that was going to happen. It must have been driving them mad.

I wisht I knew what in hellfire it was they saw, 'xactly. Might be able t' pick summat out. But right now, it was a lot more likely that Karsites would welcome Heralds and Companions with fruit baskets and flower wreaths than it was that any Foreseers would be willing to talk to him.

Ask your friends. Lydia, Amily, Marc and all. They'll know what's been Seen, ask them. Well, that was certainly an idea. He had been acting as their spy, why shouldn't they return the favor?

Well, he didn't exactly have the time to go down to Soren's house at the moment . . . but Marc was up here, at the Royal Kennels. And it wouldn't take too long to nip down there. He even had time before his first class.

They all finished their breakfasts, wrapped up the conversation, waited for Mags to finish his, and left as a group.

"Are you going to be all right until luncheon?" Gennie asked, as the others headed in several directions for classes.

He nodded. "Got a errand first, but it's t' see a friend. Nobody's bothered me 'tween classes or in classes."

Yet.

He pushed the thought down.

"All right then, we'll meet you here before lunch. Joy will set it up with Dallen." Gennie headed off, and Mags scooted out the door and aimed for the Royal Kennels.

Marc was feeding the gaze-hounds, and turned toward him with a worried frown when the dogs alerted on the stranger and he spotted that it was Mags in the building.

"Mags—"

"I know, I know," he replied hastily. "Thet is t' say, I know things'r bein' said 'bout me, but nobody'll tell me 'xactly what it is. Marc, I gotter know what them Foreseers saw. 'Xactly what they saw. Iff'n there's any detail, mebbe I kin figger out if I got any real connection wi' it."

Marc nodded, a lock of his red hair falling over his forehead. "All right, I can talk to Lydia and she can find out easily enough. Amily probably can too, and she's up here with her father. I'll talk to both, and have Amily get hold of you to tell you what she found. No point in passing things through too many hands, or having too many of us all asking the same questions. It all gets muddled."

"It does that," he said. His head hurt, trying to puzzle through all of this.

Marc sucked on his lower lip. "Amily can make out as

if she's asking on behalf of her father, and that will get her the stuff straight from the Foreseers."

Mags nodded, still wishing he could talk to them himself. There were supposed to be Foreseers among the Heralds, weren't there? It wasn't a common Gift, but surely there should be one . . .

"Bugger," he said aloud. All this, and he still had classes to deal with. And Kirball. He felt like a juggler with only one arm.

His unofficial bodyguard turned up at lunch, just as Gennie said they would, and universally declared that his habit of eating a very little before practice was a wise one. Gennie sent Pip off to the kitchens to explain what they needed, and shortly Pip came back with a heavy basket "for afters." There were pocket pies in there. Dallen was going to be thrilled.

The people in the dining hall who were not in Grays or Whites outnumbered those that were, and this time, despite the presence of the others around Mags, there was a lot of buzz of sullen conversation around them. And a lot of narrowed eyes and black looks.

Finally Halleck seemed to tire of it all. He stood up; Mags had no idea that he was going to do anything other than, well, leave, when his voice suddenly roared out like an angry boarhound.

"All of you. Shut up!"

Shocked silence descended. The attention of every person in the dining hall was riveted on the Trainee. And

Halleck was not a small young man; he was at least as tall, if not a little taller, than any other Trainee, and he had a truly impressive set of shoulders. Halleck looked around belligerently. "You people are like a bunch of nasty-minded old village gossips, you know that? Like a bunch of vipers. Hiss, hiss, hiss, and all that happens is you stir each other up over nothing. The Foreseers saw this. The Foreseers saw that. Well for one thing, the Foreseers have been too damn chatty about this, and they should bloody well know better. You don't go flinging dung around and act surprised when it hits innocent people. For another, my Gift is Foresight, and you know what I saw?"

He waited.

Silence.

"Nothing. That's right. Nothing. I haven't Seen a damn thing since then either, and it is not for lack of trying. I've done everything I can to get a glimpse; nothing. Now don't you think, me actually knowing Mags and all that, if he had anything at all for us to be worried about, I would have Seen something?"

More silence.

"Sometimes we See really detailed stuff. Mostly, we don't. The farther off it is, the more confused and unclear it gets, and the more we see things that are more like symbols of what's going to happen than the actual event. Now will you people stop acting like a crowd of hateful, vicious old gossips with too much time on their hands and too much venom on their tongues and start acting like responsible Trainees? People your Circles can be proud of instead of wincing every time your names are mentioned? Yes? No?" He waited for an answer.

Mags could still sense hostility and plenty of it.

"Bah, remind me never to rely on any of you for anything that actually requires thinking," Halleck spat, and sat down again.

"Well done," Gennie said warmly. He grinned at both of them.

Then he turned to Mags. "I'll tell you the truth, Mags. Foreseers—especially all the ones attached to Temples and the like, which is, so far as I know, all the ones who saw anything about the King and a foreigner—like to make out that they know more than they do." Halleck rubbed one eye, ruefully. "I guess it kind of comes with the whole priestly thing. Direct information from the gods and all that. Most of the ones that I know of are honest enough not to actually make stuff up, but then you get other people jumping to whatever conclusions they care to. I suppose it could all be construed as a kind of test of people's character."

Mags nodded.

Halleck shrugged apologetically. "Mostly what we get is glimpses. And those glimpses are exactly like glimpses you yourself would get if you were rushed past an event, fast, a little confused, and not all that clear. That is hard enough, but once a little time has passed—the visions become memories and memories get mixed up, blurred, changed by what other people tell us."

Mags nodded. Pip piped up. "That's why they tell us to get witnesses to give statements as detailed as possible right away. The problem with memory is that it's often mistaken."

"Eyewitnesses tend to see what they expect to see, too," Halleck reminded them. "Now, Foreseers do get special training so that we try and concentrate when we get a vision, and more or less turn off the thinking parts of our minds, but who knows what it was that gave those others the 'feeling' that the person with the King was a foreigner?"

"Enough of all this. We have practicing to do," said Gennie. "And I want to find out how many of the others can join us at meals. If we put enough teammates between Mags and the idiots, at least they'll be smart enough not to gossip in front of us and we can all eat in relative peace."

Mags sighed. "Relative" was the operable word here.

He thought about hiding in the Guard Archives to study, because he was all too aware when other Grays and Heralds came into the stable. Some of them didn't know, or had forgotten, that he lived out there—but most of them knew it, and it made them uneasy. But then he thought better of the idea. According to Tam and Liam, the two "not-quite-Guardsmen," there was plenty of speculation going on among their fellows about "what should be done about that Trainee Mags." He really didn't want to find himself cornered by Guardsmen who had decided that "what should be done about him" was to be locked up or sent out of Haven altogether, on the theory that if he wasn't *in* Haven then what had been Foreseen wouldn't happen.

Nice theory anyway. Because after all, the Foreseers couldn't tell where their vision had taken place, so he had heard. He could be sent out of Haven only to encounter the King by another accident.

It reminded him of a kind of morbid song Lena sang to him and Bear once, about a man who had his fortune told, and it was that he would meet Death in the village square the next day. So he flung himself on a horse and rode like the wind until at a few drips short of the appointed hour, and he dismounted in front of an inn in another city. Thinking he had escaped, he turned, and ran right into Death who said in surprise, "Oh thank you, you saved me a trip!" and took him.

But at any rate, it sounded like the Guard Archives, though quiet and warm, would not be a good place to hide out. Nor would the Collegium Library.

But the Heralds had Archives . . .

Not as big as the ones for the Guards, not even as big as the Bardic ones, but they had Archives, and almost no one ever went there.

:Actually,: Dallen said, after a moment, *:That's a good idea. You didn't look there for information about your parents, because you didn't know the exact dates or place where the bandits' camp was. Now you do, and there might be something in the Heralds' reports. More detail about your parents' clothing—perhaps even, if you look backward a bit, you'll find someone who ran into them on Circuit, maybe in a town, maybe on the*

road. Heralds are supposed to report on foreigners they encounter.:

In all of the unhappiness, Mags had quite forgotten why he had uncovered that information in the first place. He gave that some thought. *:Huh.:* He thought a bit more. *:Well . . . I got studyin'. Mebbe I kin look after I'm done wi' studyin'.:*

The Heralds' Archives were in the top floor of the Heralds' Wing, exactly where the library was in the Collegium Wing. Unlike the Guard Archives, or the Collegium Library, this enormous room was dark, and chilly. Like the Guard Archives, there were rows and rows of floor to ceiling shelves on either side of a passage through the middle of the room. Unlike the Guard Archives, it was rather untidy, with boxes left open on the floor, and books in piles. There were only a few lamps up here, and only half of them were lit, making perhaps four pools of light in the darkness, including one all the way at the end of the room.

This was why it was very obvious when someone moved a little at the end of the room. The shadow cast under the lamp there was quite long, and the movement did more than catch Mags' eye, it practically made him jump.

Bugger, someone's here already, he thought. But this was the most private place he was going to find, so he continued to move into the room. Whoever this was, maybe Mags could avoid him—

Which was, of course, right when his shin hit a chair he couldn't see, and knocked it over.

"Who's there?" cried out a startled voice.

One he knew.

"Amily?" he called back, incredulous.

"Mags? Oh good!" the relief and the welcome in that voice made him flush a little. "I'm so glad you're here, you couldn't have picked a better time. Please, come here, we found out what you wanted to know."

Being more careful this time, he hurried across an expanse of floor made treacherous by the piles of books, boxes of papers, and scattered chairs. Whatever else they were, the Heralds certainly were nothing like as tidy about their record-keeping as the Guard.

He found Amily curled up in what looked like her own private little nest, in a corner that was surprisingly warm and cozy. A good oil lamp was fastened up on what looked like—and proved to be, when he touched it—the back of a substantial brick chimney. It radiated warmth into this space exactly as the one in his room did. There was a heavily padded half-lounge here, a couple of padded chairs, two little tables within easy reach, and books and a teapot and cup on them.

Amily smiled up at him, her eyes twinkling. "I love my father dearly, but sometimes I just want to be somewhere that he's not," she said. "And no matter how polite he is about it, we live in three small rooms and there is never more than a single door between us. It's not hard for me to get up here, and no one minds my being here."

She patted the lounge, and he sat down gingerly beside her, flushing a little. "But enough about all that. I was actually just putting the last of the reports into order for you."

"Reports?" he said, feeling thick and stupid. She didn't know about his search for his parents, so how could—

"About what the Foreseers saw," she explained. "There's a protocol for such things, and a good thing too, considering how wild some of the rumors have gotten. All Foreseers are trained to either make notes on what they Saw immediately, when the vision or dream is over, or dictate to someone. And I have copies of many of them right here." She patted a folder on her lap. "I can sum them up for you if you want, though, since they are all nearly identical."

Mags nodded, not trusting his voice.

"Every vision was of the same thing, and every vision lasted about the same length of time—quite, quite short. They have the impression that this is the end of a fight. They first see the King, who is standing, but with a look of horror on his face, covered in blood, his hands also covered in blood. They then see what looks like a small, slight man, quite ragged, also covered in blood, with a knife in his hands. They get the impression that he is foreign-born. They get the impression that someone is dying and someone is badly wounded. And that is all."

Mags blinked. "That's it? Ev'think else is just what summon made up?"

She nodded. "Exactly. They don't see the other man's face. That's all. They don't know which of the two is dying, or wounded. They don't even know if there is someone else dying or wounded that they can't see, or even if there is an entire crowd there."

Mags didn't know quite how to feel. On this slender

thread was hanging all that hostility, all that anger—for what?

"I think I wanta hurt someone," he said finally. Amily nodded with sympathy. "I don't blame you. The damage is done and it's rather late to get things set straight."

He sighed and buried his face in his hands. After a while, he felt her slender arm around his shoulders, and she hugged him a little. "I'm sorry Mags, I wish there was something I could do. But at least—or, well, so I hear—Gennie is doing what can be done for now."

"Eh, she's a good sort," he mumbled. "Whole team is, akchully."

I cain't go back t' these people an' point out what's in the reports, cause that'll only make things worse. But I got to know— He steeled himself, because he knew this was only going to make more pain for himself. "Amily, kin you an' Lydia an' Marc an' all do me a favor?"

"Anything," she promised, still keeping her arm around his shoulders. And . . . it felt awfully good, that arm. Not like Lena, though Lena was a good friend, and could be quite comforting. No, this was something else. There was something about the warmth and pressure that made him feel odd, and a little light, and . . . well . . . tingly. He found himself wondering how long he could keep his head in his hands like this, as an excuse to keep her arm around him.

"Wouldja all tell me 'xactly what yer hearin' 'bout me?" he begged. "I mean, ev'thing. I'm mortal tired of seein' people whisperin' behind their hands. I wanta know the worst."

"Oh Mags . . ." she sounded as if she was going to cry.

"It's going to be nasty, I am sure of it, and I don't want to hurt you."

"I don' wanna be hurt, but truth's better'n not knowin'."

She sighed deeply. "All right. If that's what you want."

He echoed her sigh. "Ain't what I want, 'tis what I need."

"All right," she repeated, and finally took her arm away. Feeling vaguely disappointed, he sat straight up.

"Reckon I better go," he said reluctantly.

:Probably a good idea. You certainly are not going to get any studying done around Amily.:

:Hush, you.:

"I suppose you had better," she replied wistfully, then brightened a little. "Just remember, you can always come up here and share my nook with me."

"I thought ye said ye came here t' be alone," he replied, that odd, tingly feeling teasing at him again.

"I said I came up here to get away from Father," she corrected. "Alone—not necessarily." She smiled at him, and he felt all lightheaded. Then she reached out and gave him a little kiss on the cheek, and he forgot to breathe.

He didn't actually remember saying goodnight, though he was sure he had; she kissed him, and the next thing he knew, he was halfway to the stables.

:Well you're certainly not shaych,: Dallen said, amused.

:Uh, what?:

:Never mind. Come do your studying and go to bed before you float away.:

". . . and that's how you make an ankle-wrap that actually works," Bear said, finishing off the wrapping with a flourish.

Mags shook his head—and so did Lena. "I couldn't make head or tail of the diagram in the book," said Lena. "And yet it all seems so obvious when you do it."

Bear laughed, and shoved his lenses further up on his nose. "That's because the diagram is wrong," he said, and pointed to one picture in the middle. "See? That one there. Dunno what the engraver was thinking, but that's not part of the sequence."

"I knew'd we was right t' come talk t' ye," Mags said gratefully. "Uh . . ." he hesitated, then went on. "They still scratchin' at ye t' come home an' get shackled?"

Bear lost his good humor, and his lips thinned. "Aye. But I figured out how to stall them some more."

"How?" Lena demanded eagerly.

"So, they haven't got near enough Healers, right? Not anywhere?"

They both nodded.

Bear raised his head in triumph. "So where there are no Healers, if I've put together a standard medical pack that will treat just about anything, something every Herald can take on circuit—they can still get good treatment until help comes. It might not be as good as a good Healer, but it'll be as good as a weak one, and a damn sight better than nothing at all! I can put together a really big kit for—oh, say Temples and things, and all the instructions you'd need."

"Oh Bear, that's brilliant!" Lena enthused, looking happier. "How are you finding all the medicines you need?"

"That's where I become indispensible," Bear said smugly. "Maybe there are herb-Healers that know more than me out there somewhere, but they don't have my resources and most importantly, they aren't here. I know all the ways to treat things without a Gift, and I can write them down properly, not all wrong, like in that textbook you two brought me. I can make simpler, clearer diagrams. There are artists here that can draw them properly for me. The project has already been approved, and I'm formulating the medicines and figuring out how to pack them to give them the longest life." He hesitated, then added, a little awkwardly, "The Head of Healers says that when the standard pack is finished and it's been tested, if everyone is happy with it, they'll give me my Greens. They say this will be the equivalent of riding Circuit for me. Then my family can go—find someone else to marry that girl. I'll be a full Healer and I will be the one who says where I go and what I do. I figure I can stay here and teach people like me, find more medicines. Personally, I think we ought to be training more Healers that don't have Healing Gift. There are a lot out there, midwives and that sort of thing, but they don't think to come here for training. Or else, they can't manage to get the means to get here."

Then he drooped again. "I got to get it done, though. Could take a year, maybe more. That's the thing. I got to show plenty of progress, and some of this stuff is—hard. Coming up with medicines I know are going to be consistent, all the time. Writing out the directions. All that, and keep at my classes and—"

"And keep at my classes an' do whatever I'm sent off t' do by Nikolas, an' Kirball practice—" Mags interrupted.

"And try and figure out what will make Father proud, and memorize my ballad cycle and get ready for the solo and ensemble trials—" put in Lena with a sigh.

They looked at each other.

"Ain't we pitiful," said Mags. He shook his head. "Complainin' like that. Whine, whine, whine, like we was spoilt or somethin'."

"Well," Lena said, finally. "It just doesn't seem fair that we work so hard, and then we don't get rewarded for it."

"If'n I had all the sparklies I pulled outa that mine in m'life, I'd prolly have m'own weight in sparklies," Mags said sourly. "An' thet goes fer the other kiddies, too. Life ain't fair, an' that's that."

Bear's mind was heavily guarded, but Lena's surface thoughts were so strong he couldn't help but know what she was thinking. Her father now knew she was here, and he hadn't done anything at all about it. Not an apology, not a visit, not even a brief note. She could probably draw attention to herself by doing stupid things, showing off or challenging other students to music contests, but all that would do would be to disrupt other peoples' lives and concentration, and if her father actually took notice of it, she was pretty certain the reaction would be negative.

And that was not what she wanted.

She just wanted him to look at her once, and say, "Well done, Lena."

She'd never tell Mags that, though, and not just because she was shy, but because Mags would never have his father look at him and tell him he had done well.

Mags started to reach out to pat her hand—then he realized that Bear was awkwardly doing the same thing. He quickly pulled his own hand back, and let Bear complete the motion. "We'll make it through," Bear said, and rested his hand on hers.

"Aye, 'cause we gotta," Mags said, and stood up. "An thenkee, Bear, but I got to get."

They nodded. He let himself out, and looked back through the glass. They were still where he had left them, with Bear's hand still on Lena's.

THE Heraldic Archives proved to be the best place for Mags to go to get away from suspicious glances, for more reasons than one. As he had already known, almost no one came up there. The Archive room was above the Heralds' Wing, and no matter what their feelings were, Heralds had very disciplined minds and tended to not leak any surface thoughts. That made any place around the Heralds' Wing a very peaceful venue for someone like him. Proximity was everything when it came to what he picked up; the closer someone was, physically, the easier it was for him to "hear" them.

And third? Well, third was Amily.

It seemed that Amily did not spend her time up in the Archives merely to get some privacy. Amily was helping to put the Archives in order.

When Mags left Bear and Lena, he decided that he'd take advantage of Amily's little warm corner and get some more studying done. But when he opened the door on the Archives, instead of finding them deserted, he found all the lamps lit, and a very young fellow in Royal livery shelving several volumes under Amily's direction. "Over there," she was saying, as he carried what looked just like one of the boxes that the Guard reports were kept in. "Third shelf from the rear, south side, you'll see the one right before it up on the shelf where you put it two days ago." She made a little note.

"Hullo!" he called, startling both of them. Amily's eyes lit up.

"Mags!" she said, and waved him over. "Mags, this is under-Archivist Jonson; he's on loan to me from the Royal Library."

The young man was very young on closer inspection. He couldn't have been much older than fourteen; he was, however, extraordinarily tall. "More like a jumped-up page," the lad said. "I'm good for reaching the top shelves. But I want to be an Archivist, and I'll shelve stuff forever if that is what it takes."

Amily smiled. "Very good at it you are, Jonson." She spread her hands. "And this is what I do. Everyone needs a job, after all, and since I'm a Herald's daughter, I'm probably the best one to know how to organize things here."

"I kin see thet," Mags nodded. "An'—say, why don't I give ye a hand? I don' have heaps of time, but what I got, ye kin hev."

"Would you?" Amily asked, her face transformed by a smile.

" 'Course. Jest tell me whatcha want."

What she needed, it appeared, was for him to sort through piles of reports that had gotten muddled, either because they had been put back wrong or because someone had just tossed all the records in a box and shoved them up on the shelf. That had happened a lot. Amily wanted things to be as organized and tidy as they were in the Guard or Royal Archives.

So Mags would give the reports a cursory skim, and determine who had written them, and sort them by author. Then he'd go back and sort each author pile by date. Then he would actually identify the major events in each sorted pile, mark those on the outside of the box along with the author and the start and end date and major area of the circuit, and that was how they would be filed. First, by the geographic location of the circuit, then by date within that location, and last of all by the name of the Herald. Or Heralds, because often as not, it was the Herald and one or more of the Herald's Trainees. This was the old way, the way that was supposed to work so well.

Just skimming the reports, Mags found out that it didn't work all that well. It looked like the Heralds had to come to the rescue of their Trainees a great deal. Things that would have been minor problems here at the Collegium turned into much bigger problems when they were out there with—

Well, with no one to help.

Usually the situation wasn't really hazardous. Usually. Nine times out of ten it was something stupid, something they made a mistake about and mucked up whatever it was that they were supposed to be fixing. And nine times out of ten the Herald would sort things out.

But it took time, it delayed things, and to be honest, it made the Heralds look—

:It makes us look bad.:

:Aye, it do. Makes ye look . . . like ye cain't even keep yerselves sorted, so how kin ye sort out th' problems yer supposed to?:

Oh yes.

:You might want to keep that thought for the next time that someone tries to claim how much better the old system was.:

:Already thunk of that.: He pondered that a moment more, and turned his attention back to helping Amily.

Already she had made a lot of headway, and he found himself feeling ridiculously proud of her. The chaos wasn't going to get resolved quickly—and it was going to need some serious tending to, given that there was no one to keep a stern eye on things all the time the way that the Guard Archivists did.

But by the time he had to go off for class, he and Amily had made up another box, and young Jonson had shelved two rows of books again.

The Kirball practices were going well, at least for the South Team. They'd progressed to the stage of not only catching and throwing the ball, but hitting it with their paddles. Those who were supposed to try and catch it now had heavily padded gloves to spare their hands. Only one of the other teams had someone with Fetching Gift on it, and they had decided that the easiest way to deal with a "Fetcher," was to have Mags "shout" at him with Mindspeech, breaking his concentration.

For the rest, it was all coordination. They practiced patterns, riding and afoot, throwing the ball to each other, and then as one or another split off to gallop downfield, someone standing in the stirrups to give the thing an enormous *thwack.* And when the ball reached that far off player, he or she would catch it or bat it into the goal. They practiced sending the ball shooting across the ground, leaning down of their saddles to smack it with their paddles.

All this was conducted in relative silence, as Mags relayed their orders, the only other sounds being of the ball being hit and the drumming of hooves on sod.

Meanwhile it was also Lena's turn to face the first big challenge of her Collegium.

All Bardic students had to compete in a twice-yearly contest. There was no excuse that would get you out of it, other than being very ill indeed on the day of the competition.

And Lena was a nervous wreck.

She didn't have to say why, they all knew; she wasn't sure whether she was more overwrought about her father showing up, or him not showing up. She agonized about her competition piece—was it too short? Too long? Was it too simple? So complicated it looked as if she was trying to show off? Should she perform something original?

"Do you have anything of yours that is fit to sing for an audience?" Bear asked, as she sat on the floor of the conservatory, surrounded by a half a dozen music manuscripts.

"Yes! No! I don't know!" she wailed.

"Then sing something that ain't yers," Mags advised. "It ain't as if ye ain't gonna have more of these things t' perform at. So go easy fer the first one, eh?"

"But—!" she exclaimed, but never got past the word. Instead, she picked up and put down each of the songs in turn.

Finally Mags got weary of it. "Come out of there," he ordered, giving her his hand. "Leave them things on floor. We'll settle this for ye."

Bewildered, she took his hand and got up. He handed her off to Bear, who walked her over to a chair and made her sit down.

He looked around and finally picked up a bit of broken pot. Closing his eyes, he tossed it straight up to the ceiling. It landed on the floor with a clatter, then bounced about and ended up on one of the music manuscripts.

He picked the manuscript up and handed it to Lena. "There," he said firmly. "Tha's it. Tha's what ye'll do."

"But—"

"Seriously, Lena, they are all good pieces, and you do all of them well. Any of them will do, and it might as well be that one," Bear said, with just an edge of exasperation showing in his voice.

Lena sighed. "All right. You're right. It might as well."

"Hey," Mags offered. "Look at it this-a way. Nobody's gonna be lobbin' balls at yer head."

"I wish they would," she said, so mournfully that both he and Bear laughed, and then they had to fall all over themselves apologizing for her hurt feelings.

They were still apologizing when Amily arrived, hobbling along on her bad leg with her crutch to assist her. "Now what have you two done?" she asked, looking from their faces to Lena's, Mags held the door open for her. "Oh never mind. Listen, I just learned something you all need to know!"

Mags helped her to a chair, and they all gathered around her; given the mix of excitement and alarm in her voice, the importance of what she was going to say probably transcended any hurt feelings.

"You know that fuss that was raised late this afternoon?" she asked.

Bear and Lena nodded, Mags only shook his head. "Practice," he pointed out. "An' then I come straight here, after dinner."

"Well, it was trade envoys from Seejay arriving," Amily said breathlessly.

All of them frowned, since that was where the troublemakers of the winter had—

"And they were shocked to hear that there had been trade envoys from Seejay here this winter!" she continued. "Especially since those envoys didn't come with a Royal Charter!"

Mags sucked on his lower lip. "Well, we'd already reckoned they wasn't what they said they was," he pointed out. "So what was they?"

Amily shook her head. "The new envoys didn't know. Lady Adetha's daughter—you know, the one that's so good at drawing and painting—was even called to bring the sketches she'd made of them while they were here, and the envoys didn't recognize them. Not at all. And their clothing was nothing like what these new envoys are wearing. By tomorrow, this is going to be all over the place, Mags, and people are going to be asking questions all over again."

"Of course they are," Mags sighed. Because there was one big question that no one had been able to answer.

Why had that crazed assassin taken one look at him and exclaimed "You aren't supposed to be here?"

Sure enough, first thing in the morning, even before breakfast, a page from the Palace was tapping on his door.

He'd been expecting it, of course; Rolan had warned Dallen, who had gotten him up early. He'd put on his best set of ordinary Grays, and followed the page up to the Palace in a state of dread and resignation.

He was ushered into a small room crowded with people; there was a throne there, and the King was on it; he was surrounded by Guardsmen bristling with weapons and resentment, and besides the Guardsmen, Nikolas and the entire Council were there.

And so was a group of dignified looking men and one woman, all in long robe-like garments that at first glance were very unimpressive—

Until you realized, at second glance, that the subdued colors of their garments were woven in patterns so intricate that Mags had never seen anything like them in his life, and the threads that composed the fabric could not possibly have been thicker than a human hair.

One thing was certain. Their costumes looked nothing at all like those of the arrogant "merchant princes" who had so abused the Crown's hospitality.

They all studied him, as he stood there awkwardly. Everyone studied him. The Guards studied him in a way that suggested that some of them hoped he might try and bolt so that they could bring him down.

"Well, my lords?" the King said, when the uncomfortable silence had stretched on for far, far too long.

"Is beink chust ordinary boy, Highness," one of the envoys said with a shrug. "Is lookink nossink like anyone ve know uff."

"Not like some notorious assassin? Infamous thief?" Mags almost cast a sharp glance at the King, for even if his Councilors didn't detect the edge of sarcasm to his words, Mags certainly did.

"He is not beink look effen like native of our land, nor those around it," the Envoy said firmly. "He is beink little and dark, and ve are beink large and golden."

Well that was certainly true.

"He is not beink look like Shin'a'in, either," the woman observed. "They are beink dark, but tall. Werry tall."

The King spread his hands and turned to his Councilors. "There, you see?"

"This only proves that the real envoys from Seejay don't recognize this Trainee as looking like anyone they know, Majesty," said the Seneschal, with reluctance.

"And we still do not know where the false envoys came from."

"And I prefer to believe that poor Mags is the victim of that old saw, that everyone has a double somewhere," Nikolas put in.

The King laughed. "The most likely explanation that comes to my mind is that we don't actually know what the assassin thought he saw. The man was mad, and he might have been hallucinating. For all we know, he looked at Mags and saw his brother, his mother, or his worst enemy."

"And how likely is that?" the Seneschal asked, pulling on his beard a little.

"Very likely." The Head of the Healer's Circle had been mostly hidden by the others until he spoke. "Hallucinations of this sort are a common component of a deep level of insanity. There are even cases of people murdering beloved members of their families, convinced that the people trying to help them are mortal enemies, or demonic entities. I have known of sufficiently mad women who murdered their own infants, certain that the children had been taken away and demons left in the cradle."

"I'm satisfied," the King said. "You can go, Trainee Mags. Thank you for coming."

Mags bowed himself out hastily. So far as he was concerned, he couldn't get out of that room fast enough.

The team was waiting for him in the corridor, though not looking particularly anxious. Well that was the advantage of being Grays; your Companions kept you abreast of what was going on. Thank goodness. Pip punched him lightly on the arm, and Gennie threw him a smile, but nobody said anything until they all got inside and were seated.

"So?" asked Bear.

He told them what had happened. Or, more precisely, what had not happened.

Gennie raised her eyebrows. "Well, that's interesting, but it doesn't prove or disprove anything except that those men were lying, and we already knew that."

Mags nodded—then thought of something. "Mebbe one thing. They didn' seem ter recognize me, nor think I looked like summun else."

"True, true," said Pip. "Hmm. Well, put this in a logic tree." Pip, began tracing an invisible diagram on the table with his finger. "The real envoys didn't recognize Mags. The fakes didn't recognize Mags, but they did know him after being here a while. The assassin who was working with the fakes, did. Why?"

"Could be we've been looking at this all backward," Halleck said slowly. "Well, there's three possibilities. The first is what the Healer said. He was out of his head. That's the likeliest, and he could have thought Mags was anybody. I mean 'You're not supposed to be here—' that sound more like what someone says when he sees someone who really isn't supposed to be there, that it's impossible for the person he thinks he sees to be there."

"All right, and the other two?" Pip prompted as Mags listened intently.

"It could be the killer was from somewhere else, and actually recognized Mags as looking like someone he knew . . . but then you have to wonder why he was working for the fakes and how they found him. So the next likeliest is that the fakes told him about Mags, the killer went and had a look at him, did everything he could to keep Mags from finding Bear, and when he did anyway, had that reaction. That's even more likely if he was expecting the fakes to get rid of Mags. After all, Bear is Mags' best friend. If there was anyone likely to fight like a wildcat to save him, it would be Mags. So obviously, you wouldn't want Mags to find him."

Pip nodded. "And there's nothing mysterious or sinister about that."

"Why would the fakes wanta get rid 'a me?" Mags asked—then answered his own question. "Because I shamed 'em, they're bullies, and fellers like that likes t' get even."

"Exactly." Pip spread his hands. "Easy explanation, and you know what they say, the simplest answer is generally the right one." He grabbed a plate of bacon and began shoveling it onto the plates of the others. "So let's eat. I'm starving. We'll let the nags discuss it among themselves, then pass it off to their Chosen."

:Nag? I heard that!:

It was as if the gods were trying to muck up his life as badly as possible. The timing for this could not possibly have been worse. But he'd promised . . . and he wasn't going to go back on a promise. Especially not now.

As always, the team was waiting for him to escort him

into lunch. He approached them with his head hunched down. They weren't going to like this.

"Where's Lena? And Bear?" asked Gennie, craning her neck to see if they were somewhere in the corridor behind him.

Mags took a deep breath. "Lena got bumped on her Contest; she's comin' up right now an' Bear got called away. That Councilor Chamjey is s'pposed t' be answerin' charges, an' he took sick; reg'lar Healers can't make heads nor tails of it, an' they called Bear, so he's down in city. We both promised Lena we'd be watchin' her Contest. . . ."

He trailed off, just as Herald Setham approached their table.

"Mags, Dallen said you needed to speak with me?"

Mags blurted it all out a second time. "So—I know 'tis practice—" he said desperately. "But—"

"Hang all that, Lena's our friend too!" said Gennie, her eyes flashing. "Herald Setham, we'll make up the practice after supper, permission for the team to support Trainee Lena?"

Setham snorted. "You'd be damn poor friends if you hadn't asked for it. Of course."

Mags' heart leapt—Gennie slapped him on the back, and the group of them surged down the hall and out the door. If anyone had been taking notes, how they surged might have given them pause, for they moved as a unit, without anyone getting in anyone else's way . . . they really were a team, more and more as time went on.

They arrived at the Assembly Hall, where the Contest was taking place; Mags was the first one in, and he knew immediately that Lena was in trouble.

The Hall was absolutely silent, and Lena stood white-faced on the stage, clutching a lap-harp, with all eyes turned to her expectantly.

And it was clear she couldn't move. She was terrified, and she had forgotten the words of what she was supposed to sing.

And Mags saw why at a single glace.

Right in front, sitting at the Judge's table, was her father, Bard Tobias Marchand.

Looking unutterably bored, as if there was anywhere in the world he would rather be than there. Which was probably the case.

Oh bloody hell.

He didn't even think; he just acted. Gathered his mind, and "shouted" at her.

:Lena!:

She jumped a little, unfroze, and her eyes darted frantically around the room until he caught and held her gaze.

:Deep breath,: he said. *:Close yer eyes.:*

Convulsively, she did both.

:We're here. Th' whole team's here. We're b'hind ye. Now—le's make out like ye meant t' start this way. Deep breath.:

She gulped in another. He didn't say a thing about her Father. The last thing he wanted to do was make her freeze up again.

:Now, quiet. Real quiet. Make 'em strain t' hear ye. When rose the pole-star bright . . . :

She knew the song, of course, it was the Midwinter Song. Everyone knew the song. She'd probably have points deducted for choosing so common a song, but that was better than failing because she froze.

Her voice whispered out over the crowd, sweet, a little melancholy, soft. Sweet enough that, though it was scarcely more than a whisper, people leaned forward to hear her.

With each verse, as each of the birds in the song added its voice to the Midwinter Call, her voice strengthened. And finally, with her eyes still closed, she added the fingering of the harp to the song as she came to the final verse, her voice soaring in triumphant rejoicing over the notes that fell like drops of melting ice in the warmth of the newly risen sun.

From the rear, the team broke out in wild applause, joined a heartbeat afterward by the rest of the room.

Now she opened her eyes; caught Mags' gaze, and mouthed the words "Thank you!"

Then she flushed and ran off the stage before the judges could dismiss her.

"All right," Setham said, as the applause subsided. "That's over with, and there is still plenty of time for practice. Move out, Team South! Quick time to the field! Let's see those heels of yours."

"Yes sir!" they all said, and hustled out of the room before he decreed any penalty for the last one on the field.

It was a particularly spirited practice, and one in which Mags was moving too fast to even think about Lena or Bear. The rest of the team played with exceptional energy and exuberance, and it was clear that they all were taking credit for Lena's performance.

Damn right they should. He swelled with pride over it. She had seen them, and he knew it had made a difference to her. She'd been able to forget her father for a moment when she realized the entire team was there for her, not just him and Bear—even Herald Setham.

She wasn't going to get great marks for this, he was pretty sure about that. She wouldn't have fooled any of the judges about her stage-fright, and she hadn't managed to unfreeze enough to play the harp until the end. The song itself was simple and didn't show off much of anything except her lovely voice. No, she wasn't going to come in at the top of the Contest.

But she wouldn't be at the bottom, either.

When practice finished, they discovered that Herald Setham sent up the hill for food to replace the luncheon none of them had eaten. Swigging flasks of sweet, cold tea and munching on sausage rolls, they headed back up to the Collegium for their next classes or duties, all of them looking forward to seeing Lena at supper.

Mags was a little delayed by a note from Amily, asking him to meet her in the Heraldic Archives, and by the time he got to the dining hall, the team had surrounded Lena, though Bear was nowhere in sight.

". . . I can't believe you came out in the middle!" Pip was exclaiming indignantly. "You were so much better than that Bard that sang at my sister's wedding!"

"Well, it's a really common song," Lena said, shyly, and went on to explain everything that Mags had already figured—given how often she had told over the scoring method to him and Bear.

"I still don't think they scored you fairly," Pip grumbled, and spotted Mags. "Heyla! Let's get in there, those sausage rolls are wearing thin, and it's beef night!"

The room was full of Bardic Trainees, all of them ravenous. Mags had a feeling that Lena was not the only one who'd had an uncertain stomach before the Contest. Several of them still looked a bit green. Some looked triumphant or smug, some looked depressed.

Lena excused herself for a moment and went over to console several of the depressed ones, who had tucked themselves together around an out-of-the-way table. After a moment, Gennie joined her, and soon had them laughing.

When they both returned, and the group took the usual table, Mags gave the girls a look that invited explanation.

Gennie grinned broadly.

"You lot remember that incident with the presentation to the King?" she asked.

Pip rolled his eyes. "I thought you ordered us never to talk about that again?" he replied, mockingly.

"I ordered you never to talk about it again," she said, thumping him lightly on the top of the head. "And if you do, there will be a reckoning."

"Well, that's a double standard if ever I heard one," Pip grumbled.

Gennie turned to Mags. "It's pretty simple, I was supposed to present a cup of wine to the King when I was a First Year, at a thing where he was supposed to be giving out prizes for students with poor parents that had been sponsored up here by people like Councilor Soren. I got all tongue-tied, then my feet followed my tongue, I tripped and spilled it all over his Whites. Red wine, of course."

Pip smothered a laugh. She reached out without looking and thumped him again.

"Gor. That must' a bin—" Mags shook his head. He could just imagine it. "I'd'a gotten sick on 'is boots t' cap it off."

"I nearly did. And that is why the King never drinks anything but water and white wine in public, even though he loathes white wine," she said ruefully.

"And now, here you are, the Captain of the Team South Kirball players!" said Halleck.

"Well, yes." She shrugged. "You muddle through somehow—"

"Well, I wish someone would help me muddle through," said Bear, coming wearily up to the table. "I hope one of you saved me some beef. There's nothing left on the table but burnt ends."

Wordlessly, Mags pushed over the heaping plate he'd reserved for Bear. It was cold, but Bear didn't seem to care; he just slapped it between two bread-ends, smothered it in hot-root sauce, and tucked in.

"What happened?" Lena asked.

Bear groaned around a bite. "I am mortal sorry I missed your Contest, but I got called away midmorning and I've been at ex-Councilor Chamjey's house since. He was supposed to answer to the Council about those charges—"

"What charges?" asked Gennie, looking surprised.

"Ma—" began Bear, and cut off as Mags kicked him under the table.

Fortunately, Pip was more caught up on Court doings than Gennie was. "He was profiteering, or trying to, because of a bad season and a sheep disease," Pip replied, looking a little smug that he knew something Gennie didn't. "He basically cornered the market on mutton, lamb, and especially wool. The way he had it, if you'd wanted wool this year, you'd have been buying it from him or not at all, at his prices. He resigned, but when the Council looked into things and discovered just how much he was going to profit, and how much it was going to hurt some of the other Guilds, they decided to bring him up on charges."

"Huh." Gennie shook her head. "Now . . . that's something I don't understand. 'Cause no one would have faulted him for finding all this stuff out and making a reasonable profit. But no. He had to get greedy. What's the point?"

"So what happened?" Pip asked Bear, who washed down an enormous bite with sweetened tea before replying.

"Well, he got sick. They brought in a good Healer, who couldn't find anything, other than that he wasn't faking. He was bad sick too, so they finally brought me in. I dosed him good with all kinds of things, finally got him more or less cleaned out and resting, and I used a lot of those medicines I've been making up for that medicine chest I was talking about. But he looked like a beaten rug, and I still hadn't found anything, because he didn't have a fever or any other sign of a sickness. Well—"

Bear must have realized how raptly they were all listening to him, because he stopped talking and deliberately took another bite. And another. And another.

"Well?" asked Pip, Lena, and Halleck at the same time.

"Well . . . looked to me like he'd been poisoned, he had all the same symptoms of someone that's gotten something like wasp-bitten. By the time I saw him, he was starting to swell up. First thing I thought of was maybe something stung him, but there weren't any bites on him. I asked the servants, they swore he hadn't eaten nor drunk anything he didn't always have. Finally I went down to the kitchen, and I got hold of his tray. There wasn't anything poisonous on it, they'd tested everything on a mouse on the first Healer's orders, but thank goodness they had the wit not to wash stuff after that—the cook told me she wasn't going to wash anything without direct orders."

He paused again for another couple of bites. Mags got the feeling he was really enjoying this. And Mags didn't blame him in the least. By this point, the tables on either side of them were full of people leaning their way to eavesdrop.

"So?" said Pip, Gennie, and someone else at the next table.

"So, I asked the cook if there was anything she was supposed to keep away from Chamjey. 'Oh Kernos love you, duckie,' she said, 'Just the hint of chamomile makes him go all over green, and he's on the chamberpot for a day.' So I checked the teacup, and the teapot." He grinned. "Plain old mint in the teapot—but just a scraping of chamomile in the cup along with the mint. Might look like just leaves to anyone else, but not to me. Bugger tried to poison himself to get out of trouble. I went up, told the Healer in charge, who told the Guards, who searched the room and Chamjey and found bits of chamomile flowers in his pocket."

"Bear!" Gennie exclaimed. "That is excellent ferreting work! A Herald couldn't have done it better!"

Bear blushed and grinned. He blushed even harder when Lena beamed wordlessly at him.

"I'm mortal sorry I missed yer Contest, Lena," he concluded apologetically. "It took me a whole lot longer to do all that stuff than to tell about it."

"I'm glad you missed it!" she exclaimed, her eyes bright. "I'm glad because you just proved you can do things nobody else here can do. You're a hero!"

"Uh—" Bear said, blushing and tongue-tied. Mags just hid a smile.

:I CAIN'T b'lieve it's finally spring,: Mags sighed, as the sun baked his shoulders with gentle warmth. *:I thought it'd be winter ferever.:* Even though he was down in Haven, in the street, there were still hints of growing things in the breeze. And flower-sellers on the street! Everyone seemed just a little bit more cheerful too, and a bit less impatient.

:For a while there so did I,: Dallen replied. Mags got a mental glimpse of Dallen blissfully prone in a bed of young clover, basking in the sun. *:Enjoy this while you can. Spring is a treacherous creature. Tomorrow it could be pouring down rain that is near ice. Or we could be graced with a blizzard. Or, well, who knows. We might end up witn a three-day flood.:*

:Don't I jest know it,: he said ruefully. Such reversals of weather were all too familiar to the mine workers, and he never trusted the smiling face of a spring day until summer was within reach. He had spent far too many days working the sluices in rain that was just

barely above freezing, or worse, in one of those unexpected snowstorms. Those were times when the only advantage to wearing nothing but a few rags for clothing was that they dried on your body faster when you got out of the wet.

Ah, but today—today was the closest he had been to contented since the Foreseers began spreading their tales. Six days of the week there were classes, but not the seventh. There was no Kirball practice either—not that he would have objected to practicing, but Herald Setham wanted a day off as well. So that meant that, like most of the Trainees, the seventh day was one that was all his to spend as he liked. Lately, that had been holed up in his room, studying. However, today Herald Nikolas had a long round of discreet errands that needed to be run down in Haven—mostly messages to be hand-delivered, but a few items to be fetched from shops—and he had asked Mags to run them.

That had sounded just fine to Mags. A day like this one begged to be enjoyed, and the best way for him to enjoy something was to get as far away from people who recognized him as possible.

The errands took Mags out of the grounds of the Collegia and away from all those people who were still thinking daggers at him. There were a disheartening number who still were, despite everything that his Kirball teammates and even the King had said and done. Down here in the city, no one knew who he was—he would have been just another Trainee, if he had chosen to wear Grays.

Which he hadn't, actually; Nikolas wanted him to be

mostly-invisible, and that had meant not dressing in his Grays. He'd left Dallen behind and dressed in a set of clothing he'd gotten a couple weeks ago as a hand-me-down from Marc; very good quality clothing, though a bit worn, nothing to be ashamed of, nothing that marked him as out of the ordinary, all in various shades of brown. He blended in so perfectly with the folk in the street that he was practically impossible to pick out from the rest of the crowd. Exactly the way he and Nikolas wanted it.

Nikolas had not given him a time-frame for these errands, which meant that he was free to spend the entire day in the city if he chose. He was running some errands for Amily as well, which gave him even more of an excuse to stay down here among minds that were not wishing him elsewhere for the better part of the day. Later he could catch up with Bear and Lena, maybe . . .

Assuming Bear and Lena were not . . . "together." That was another reason for running the errands. He could take a hint. Even when they thought nobody knew how much they liked each other but they themselves, well, it was pretty obvious to everyone else. Today would be a perfect day for a picnic, and before they could hem and haw about whether or not to invite him, he had dis-invited himself, and nearly gave the game away by laughing at the guilty relief on both of their faces. That was another small bright spot; he was very, very glad that they were "getting on" so well.

He had spent the morning on the errands that required he pick up things; for Nikolas, this meant getting a number of small, mysterious, wrapped packages at various merchants around the city. "I'm here for Master White's parcel," he would say, having practiced the phrase over and over and carefully enunciating each word so as not to give himself away with his crude way of speaking and his dreadful accent. Instead, he sounded a bit slow, which was quite all right. There was nothing wrong with being "a bit slow" when it came to impersonating a servant.

A parcel would be produced, he would put it in his carry-bag, and go on to the next item to be picked up. He'd more or less mapped all of these things out in advance, interspersing Amily's requests with those of her father. That way, if against all odds someone actually was watching him, the pattern of errands would make no sense.

Amily's errands were much more straightforward, and not at all mysterious. He picked up more wool for her knitting; brought a bit of wool to match, and stood by while the shop-owner and her two assistants combed over all the skeins to find the closest. He got some scented candles at a chandler she specified, a quire of paper, a pot of a particular sort of black ink, and another of red, book-binding glue, and a cone of spiced nuts only found at one particular confectioner in the entire city. That last had amused him; now he would know what to get her if he wanted to buy her a little present!

And—she wanted soap.

She didn't specify where, or what, so the first thing he thought was the soapmaker who had been so helpful in the matter of listening in on Councilor Chamjey. It was a long walk and a good bit out of the way of the other errands—but that didn't matter, in the least. Not for Amily. He was not exactly an expert on soap, but he had liked the scents there, the shop had looked very good, and the soapmaker had asked he remember her up to the Collegia, which argued that she thought her goods were of high enough standard.

Besides, he wanted to see if he could be really inconspicuous without Dallen. Would the soapmaker recognize him? He was considerably less ragged than the last time she had seen him; then he had been dressed in a suitable fashion for an ash-boy, now he was dressed in a suitable fashion for a middle-class fellow running errands for a sister, or for the servant of someone really well off.

He considered what sort of soap he should get as he made his way through the increasingly crowded streets—for everyone else seemed to want to be out in the fine weather as well today. If he were a servant or a brother, he would surely have been sent with exact orders on what to buy—

He eeled his way between two carts that were blocking a lane and decided to go the easiest route. *:Dallen, what sort'a soap does Amily want?:* Rolan would probably know. Or maybe Dallen could tell, somehow, without asking Rolan.

:She always smells of lily,: the answer came back promptly. *:And Nikolas seems to favor juniper. Since she didn't say whether to get soap for her or her father, I would say get soap for both.:*

Trust his Companion's sharp nose! And it was true, she hadn't said whom she wanted the soap for; if he got it for both of them, that would make him look quite considerate. That was no bad thing, since, well . . . he rather wanted to "get on" with Amily himself.

He made his way in a leisurely fashion to the soapmaker, drifting with the crowd rather than trying to push through it, and absorbing the sights, sounds, and smells. You could easily tell where you were in Haven by your nose. It wasn't just places like the tanners and dyers, which had very strong smells indeed. You could tell where sausages and smoked meats were made or sold, where laundries were, where inns were, and what kind and class of inn it happened to be. You could tell a lot of things, if you paid attention.

His soapmaker was in the middle of a number of small shops that mostly dealt in household goods. It was on a side street, and since the doors and windows were open, the mingled scents of the soap drifted to the end of the block.

Spring meant cleaning, which meant scrubbing floors and a lot of laundry in the form of hangings and curtains, which meant that the soapmaker was very crowded indeed. She was mostly selling plain, brown, unscented laundry soap of the lowest quality, harsh stuff full of lye that made your hands dry out and the skin crack if you kept you hands in the water for too long. Mags remembered that very well. Spring at the mine had meant the little housemaids going about with sore and bleeding hands, since Master Cole was not minded to "waste" lotions and salves on the servants and slaveys. But this was the stuff that bleached the best, and so it was in great demand even in the best households.

The queue of shoppers stretched right out the door, which argued that this soapmaker was quite good indeed.

He stood in line with the rest of those waiting to be served, and when his turn came, asked carefully and quietly for a half a pound each of juniper and lily. The woman gave him an odd look, as if she almost recognized him, but the press of customers was far more urgent than her need to chase down that nagging memory. As it happened, lily and juniper were not so common that she was sold out of soap already cut and wrapped, and she fetched two cakes from the appropriate niches in the wall behind her. He paid her, she gave him the soap in neatly wrapped packages, and he made way for the next customer without any further flashes of recognition.

There were two more little packages to get for Nikolas, and then the fetching part of his errand-round was over. One he got at a blacksmith, the other at a maker of extremely delicate carving tools. Strange. Very strange. He couldn't imagine what it was that Nikolas would need at either of those places.

But if Nikolas had wanted him to know what he was getting, he would have been told.

:Are you still basking?: he asked Dallen.

The only answer he got was a sort of drowsy murmur, which pretty much told him that the answer was "yes."

With a laugh, he began the long trudge back up to the Palace on foot. *:Don' ferget I'm gonna need you to get i' the gates, right?:*

Dallen woke up enough to come for him just as he

got within eyesight of the Palace walls, which was a good thing, since Dallen's presence said "he belongs here" without having to produce any sort of verification. The Guards didn't even look at him twice. On the first pleasant free day since winter descended, Trainees were riding into and out of the grounds all day and not necessarily in their Grays, so he blended in just fine.

He left the satchel of packages in Nikolas' quarters, and thought about stopping for luncheon at the dining hall, rather than spend one of his rare coins down in the city . . .

Then thought better of the idea. He wouldn't have his team with him today; they had scattered to the four winds. Which meant there were good odds of unfriendly faces and minds in the hall—and seeing him without his group around him, they'd probably take advantage of the situation. No, getting something from a street-cart seemed like a better idea today . . .

:Are you going to need me?: Dallen asked, as he came out of the building that housed the Herald's Wing.

:Didja wanta come with me or lollygag 'round the Field some more?: he countered.

Dallen snorted. *:Lollygag? Me? I merely want to—:*

:Chase fillies, gotcha.: He chortled at the indignant look on Dallen's face. *:You jest stay here. I figger on takin' m'time 'bout this.:*

The errands that Nikolas had him running now—dropping off a series of sealed messages—could not possibly take more than two or three candlemarks. He had the entire afternoon to himself. Already he felt his shoulders loosening, his spine uncoiling from that hunched-over posture he'd been assuming without really thinking about it—

He knew that posture, for it had been the posture he had held for years. The posture that meant he was waiting for the blow to fall, the inevitable, inescapable blow. Back at the mine, that meant the cuff to the back of the head, the strike of a stick to the shoulders, for nothing more than catching someone's eye.

Here at the Collegium, the blows might not have been physical, but they certainly had been felt over the past moon.

Eh well, I kin enjoy t'day, an' try an' figger out what them Foreseers really are seein'. Or mebbe they'll see somethin' more, an I'll be outa it.

Since Nikolas had entrusted him, and not someone else, with the delivery of these messages, he assumed that the King's Own was probably concerned, at least a little, that a Royal Page might be followed. So just to err on the side of caution, he deliberately began to wander. He had done so merely by fact of interspersing Amily's errands with those of her father earlier, now he actually put some effort into it.

He began up among the mansions of the noble and wealthy. Some of them got messages, but he stopped at others to flirt with kitchen maids, admire a garden open for viewing, or discuss the points of a horse with a groom.

When he got down into the city, he got himself a sausage roll in one place, a pint of cider in another, a slice of cheese at a cheese-shop. He shopped a little, picking up dried apple slices dusted with spice for Dallen, a neat little ink blotter for Amily, and a strap of pretty woven stuff that Lena could use on her gittern from a street-peddler. He went in no particular direction, reversing himself often, until by the time he had delivered the last message, he had doubled back on himself so many times that he was surprised he hadn't met himself on the way.

At that point, he relaxed further, and simply sauntered along, stopping to look at whatever caught his eye. Once it was a clever little dog who had figured out how to steal from dried fish vendors by sneaking under the ample skirts of some of the shoppers and getting within tooth-range of the fish that way. Once it was a juggler who had set up on the corner and would literally juggle anything you threw at him. And when Mags threw him an apple, he not only juggled it, he ate it while he juggled, which earned him a great deal of laughter and applause.

Then, suddenly, something else caught his eye.

He stiffened involuntarily, not sure he had seen who he had thought—but a second glimpse through the crowd cemented the identification. He would know that profile anywhere.

It was one of the "bodyguards" who had been with the fake envoys. Here everyone assumed that when the lot of them had escaped the Palace, they had left Valdemar, but what if they hadn't? What if they hadn't even left Haven?

Now here he was quite by accident, encountering the man. And most importantly, the man hadn't spotted him.

Dallen sensed his alarm before he actually said anything. *:Mags?:* came the urgent call. *:What's wrong?:*

In answer, Mags let the Companion see through his eyes, and caught Dallen's recognition. *:Tell Rolan t' tell Nikolas,:* he said, urgently. *:I'm gonna foller 'im. I'll stay outer sight, but we cain't chance losin' 'em again.:*

A moment later, Dallen answered. *:Nikolas agrees. Be careful.:*

Heh. Like I'ma gonna rush up t' the man an' ask 'im ever so polite-like why 'e had Bear kidnapped. Aye, that there is a fantastic notion.

The difference between following this fellow and following Chamjey was that Mags knew the "feel" of Chamjey's mind. This man's mind—well, without actually reading his thoughts and getting inside, it was like the mind of pretty much anyone in the streets here that had a sword and knew how to use it. There was a lot of arrogance and restrained aggression. Mags hadn't had enough time yet to discern what made it unique, and with having to concentrate on keeping close, yet out of sight, he wasn't going to get the leisure to do so.

He had to fight his instincts in order to do as Nikolas had taught him. His instincts told him that as soon as the man turned toward him, he should duck out of sight. He didn't do that. The man was a trained fighter, and would alert on that sort of movement.

No, when the man turned to check his rear, he had to be doing something perfectly natural. Watching a busker. Reading an inn sign. Drifting off at a slight angle to the man's current direction, as if he intended to visit a shop or take a side street.

Then, when the man turned away again, Mags did something to change his own appearance a little. He bought a drab scarf at a stall, and when the man's attention was elsewhere, he switched how he was wearing it, putting it around his neck, tying up his hair, making a headband out of it, even a sling. All these things seemed to be working. The man only gave cursory glances behind him and his eyes never lingered on Mags.

They were heading to the part of the city where beast-drovers and small traders of the sort with a single cart went. It was crowded there, the more so because it was getting on to supper time, and people unfamiliar with Haven—or who were simply frugal—were going from inn to inn hunting for bargains for their evening meal. Every inn had a different "special"—sometimes it was because they had made too much of something that day, sometimes because they got a good deal on some foodstuff or other. The smart traveler sought these out to save a few pennies.

Mags felt as if every nerve was stretched as thin and tight as one of Lena's harpstrings, the closer they came to this inn-district. He felt sure that the man was staying here, somewhere—and maybe there were more of the foreigners than just the one. Mags tried to vary his posture as well as his appearance—even his gait, although in the crush that was less than successful. But when the scarf was on his head, he slouched, as if discouraged. When it was a sling, he limped. When it was around his neck, he swaggered.

The bawling of animals in enclosures, the cursing of the drovers, people being shoved out of the way and cursing back—you would have to shout at the top of your lungs to be heard in this din. It was all a nightmare of noise and heat and dust and smell. Dung and sweat stink mingled with food and beer odors, making him feel a little sick.

It was very hard to keep up with the man without shoving and making himself conspicuous. He had to take advantage of his small size, and duck through every available gap, and still keep track of the man.

The man definitely had a goal in mind, though—his movements were purposeful and a bit impatient. Mags was more and more certain by the moment that he was staying somewhere in this district.

This part of Haven was absolutely full of people who were strangers to the city and to each other. Innkeepers didn't bother to keep track of anyone, so long as the reckonings got paid and you weren't crowding more people into a room than you had paid for.

He realized that this was exactly what the foreigners needed; incurious landlords and a steady stream of strangers coming and going. Even in the dead of winter, this district had a fair amount of traffic; Haven was a big city, and there were a lot of mouths to feed, more than could be fed purely by the effort of the local farms.

Maybe—probably—they'd found a place to hide until things in Haven got back to normal after the blizzard. There were plenty of places in Haven that would have sheltered them, plenty of people as well, and not necessarily criminals, either. They could have posed as stranded travelers and stayed at a Temple Hostel, for instance. Or they might have thought far enough ahead and arranged for a bolt-hole down in the city when they had first arrived. They could even have done so through an intermediary, who probably wouldn't have cared what nationality they were as long as their gold was sound.

The inns here would have been better, though, for people not used to waiting on themselves, nor taking care of their own day-to-day needs, like finding food and cleaning their own clothing. *All they gotta do is move from inn t' inn regular, an' they're pretty much not gonna get noticed.* Inns would do virtually anything you wanted for a price. Presumably they had the price.

He hung back a little; it was actually easier to keep track of the man now because he was pushing his way through the crowd, creating a little area of disturbance—something else Nikolas had taught Mags to watch for. He followed that area until he actually saw the man mount the steps of an enormous drovers' inn—the Silver Bullock.

He gave the fellow some time to get away from the door, and sauntered inside himself.

He almost had his heart stop when he realized the man he had been following was still in the common room, but he steeled himself to show nothing, instead, peering around the room as if to try and find something, then fixing an "aha" look on his face when he spotted the bar. He went up to it, ordered a pint, and then ostensibly looked around for a place to sit.

There were several within earshot of the man he had been following; the best was a single stool against the wall. He wound his way toward it and sat himself down, fixing his gaze on a sturdy serving wench and sipping the potent beer. Clearly it was "Spring Beer," from the bottom of the barrel; it tasted strong enough to use for brass-polish. As such things went though, it was decent; the common-room here was clean and well-run, and the food smelled all right.

He kept his eyes on the rest of the patrons of the inn, and his face in a faintly pleasant expression. Meanwhile he strained his ears as hard as he could to overhear the conversation—it was in Valdemaran, and the man that the foreigner was talking to seemed to be local. The two of them were making no effort to hold their voices down, so obviously they didn't care if they were overheard.

". . . need more help than I can get from 'pothecaries with the crazy one," the native Valdemaran was saying. "The honest ones won't sell me what you're asking me to get, and the others—" he shrugged. "You take your chances. Maybe they'll sell you what you want. Maybe they'll sell you poison, or dried grass. Maybe they'll tell the Guard you've been asking for those herbs. There's just no telling."

The foreigner muttered something that sounded like a curse. "There must be something—"

"You can tie him up and gag him when you aren't feeding him. You can keep him dead drunk and hope that doesn't kill him. You can just let him rave—"

So it sounded as if the fellow that Bear was treating was still with them! They were probably trying to get hold of the same herbs that Bear had been using.

:Nikolas has alerted some of the Guard. We're on the way.:

:Are there any Heralds or Trainees nearer to me down

'ere?: He really didn't like the naked-feeling of being in this inn with no one else nearby.

:We're alerting them.:

Maybe needing someone to treat the lunatic was why they had kidnapped Bear . . . and maybe the reason they had kept him in the Archive was because they had no place else to put him, and they needed things to clear out after the blizzard before they could escape. It would have been very hard to move a prisoner and their raving lunatic quietly until the snow cleared off. Maybe they had been hoping no one would bother coming to the Archive. Maybe they had figured on drugging Bear and smuggling him out with their baggage. Maybe—

A sudden shout of unknown words made him glance to the side with alarm. And there, not more than the length of a horse and wagon away from him, was another of the bodyguards. One of the ones who he had humiliated, and who was not likely to have forgotten his face.

The man shouted again, and pointed at him, as the one he had been following shoved the Valdemaran aside and reached for a knife.

Oh, hell!

:RUN, Mags!:

He didn't have to be told twice. In fact, he didn't have to be told at all. He was already on his feet and heading for a door he expected led to the kitchen.

It did. With at least one of the two men practically on his heels, Mags ducked between two serving girls, rolled under a table on a floor littered with vegetable peelings, scrambled to his feet, and was out the door on the other side of the room before one of the two girls had finished her shriek of outrage and alarm.

The door led to a narrow hallway, with two more doors in it. He gambled and wrenched open the farthest.

He found himself standing on a set of steps above a brick-walled space used for storing things for the kitchen that weren't wanted yet and could stand weather. And for buckets of garbage. The place stank and was full of flies. There was a wooden gate opposite him, with a lock on it.

Hell. He made a running leap for the gate; his fingers just caught the top, and he hauled himself over it as the door behind him banged open again. He tumbled down into the alley on the other side, and looked wildly in either direction.

And realized he had no idea of where he was.

He picked a direction and ran.

He was in the middle of a rat-warren of walls and outbuildings and alleys going off in every direction, with huge walls and the sides of buildings on either side of him

The alleys were too narrow to allow anything better than the tiniest of donkey-carts to go by. And he could feel his pursuers right behind him. There was no time to think, no time to do anything other than react. He dodged down every promising escape route he could find, only to discover he was still in the maze. He felt Dallen trying frantically to get to him, but it was a long way down from the Collegium and the streets were packed.

He made another turn, his sides burning, and found himself in a cul-de-sac of windowless walls going up two stories on either side of him. At the back there was a bricked-up privy-aperture right above him. He turned, but it was too late. There was a man blocking the entrance. The same man that had recognized Mags and shouted. He was one of the bodyguards; very big, strong, and trained. And armed, which Mags wasn't.

Mags rushed the man anyway. Maybe if he took the bodyguard by surprise—

He dropped and rolled when he was almost on top of the man, hoping to knock his feet out from under them, but the foreigner must have been ready for that. The man dodged, and out of nowhere, there was a tremendous thwack to Mags' head, and he saw stars, then felt himself hauled to his feet by the collar and pinned to the wall by his shoulders.

The look in the man's eyes absolutely terrified him, because it was both furious and utterly impersonal.

"You, horse-boy," spat the bodyguard. "What are you doing here? How did you find us? Who sent you?"

"I don' know nothin'—" Mags began, and the man delivered a blow to his gut that doubled him over, and a second to his face that opened up a painful gash along his cheek. The pain that went through his body and skull drove all thought right out of his head.

"Who sent you?" the man repeated.

"I don'—" This time the blow to his gut was followed by a slam into the wall that rammed his head against it. He saw stars again, and his vision grayed out. He could hardly breathe.

“Tell me!” the bodyguard spat, and slammed his head into the wall again. He couldn’t even think well enough to defend himself.

“You will tell me!” A blow to the jaw loosened his teeth as well and his mouth filled with blood.

The trumpeting of an enraged stallion interrupted the interrogation, and the man whirled, dropping Mags, who slid down the wall, and slumped to the dirt of the alley, dazed.

Dallen’s bulk filled the end of the alley. The Companion shrieked with rage, dancing in place, but unable to wedge himself into the narrow space.

The man spat a curse and wrestled his sword out, banging it against the walls on either side of him. He plunged at Dallen in a fury. Dallen lashed out at him with forehooves, but had to give way. The man must have practiced fighting against a warhorse, if not a Companion, because he kept dodging the lethal hooves and getting in closer and closer with his blows, and it was clear he was aiming to slash open one of the big arteries or veins of the legs.

Mags fought off the dizziness, the dazzle in front of his eyes, and the nausea and pain of the beating, trying to get his breath again, trying to get up and fight back. After all, this wasn’t the first time someone had tried to beat him to death—and Dallen needed him! He fumbled for, and found, his knife. As he had been taught, he weighed it carefully in his hand for a precious moment. Squinting until the double images resolved into one, he flung the little blade at the man’s back.

The man howled and cursed in pain. The knife lodged

for a moment in his shoulderblade, then clattered to the ground.

In a fury, he looked from Mags to Dallen and back again, and evidently realized that where there was one Companion, there soon would be more.

He turned back to Dallen, but this time, the whirlwind strikes of his sword were meant to drive Dallen back, not to kill him. The moment that Dallen's bulk was clear of the cul-de-sac entrance, he darted away.

Mags dropped to his knees, then doubled over again, unable to decide what part of himself to hold, since so much hurt.

He wished he could pass out; unconsciousness would be very welcome right now. Unfortunately, his body refused to cooperate.

:Mags!: The frantic call rang through his skull and made more stars explode behind his eyes.

:Don'—think s'hard—: he gasped mentally. *:—hurts—:*

Slowly, he managed to get to his feet again. With one hand on the wall and the other on his gut, he stumbled to the entrance and fell against Dallen's neck. Dallen immediately knelt in the filth of the alley to let him drag himself over the Companion's back. He put both his arms around Dallen's neck, hanging on as best he could, balanced on the broad white surface like a sack of roots.

Dallen lurched to his feet without unbalancing Mags. *:Then others will chase him,:* came a whisper of thought. *:I am getting you back up to the Healers now.:*

And without another thought, Dallen sped grimly

back up to the Collegium, with Mags clinging dizzily to his neck.

:S'allright,: he managed, as they were about halfway there. *:Been beat this bad afore—wha's goin' on?:*

:The others are converging on the inn right now, with the Guard,: Dallen said. *:They'll try and catch the bastards.:*

:Shouldn' we—:

:No. We are doing nothing. You have done enough. You are in no shape to assist in any way at all.:

Dallen rushed through the gates, passing Guards that were nothing more than blue blurs to Mags, and into the Collegia grounds.

:I'm taking you to Healers' Collegium,: Dallen said, when they didn't stop at either the stable or at Heralds' Collegium.

Finally Dallen stopped. They were met at the door by a single Healer and by Gennie, and the flash of outrage in Dallen's mind that there was not a herd of Healers waiting for them was enough to set stars dancing in front of Mags' vision again.

:Sorry,: Dallen said, and damped down the connection between them so that less was getting through. But it was very clear that he was still enraged.

"Calm down," the Healer ordered, wincing, as Gennie helped Mags down off of Dallen's back. "He's one single Trainee who's been beaten up; he's neither bleeding to death inside, nor has any broken bones, I can tell you that much. Stop acting as if he was going to die at any moment, you big fool."

Dallen snorted and whinnied angrily, as Gennie held

Mags up so the Healer could peel back his eyelids and peer into his eyes.

"He has a mild concussion. His insides are badly bruised, but quite intact. I'm sure he hurts all over. Stop fussing," the Healer snapped.

"Tol' 'im—been beat this bad afore—" Mags managed.

"And you shut up. Companion, go to your stable. Trainee, you are going straight to a bed. Give him a hand, Trainee Gennie, and both of you follow me."

With Gennie keeping him from falling over, Mags followed the Healer into a part of the Collegium he had never been before—a big room with a great many beds in it, most of them empty. Gennie helped him down onto the nearest one, then when the Healer started to strip Mags' clothing off of him, flushed crimson and beat a hasty retreat.

The Healer peeled everything off him but his boots, singlet and hose, tossing the clothing aside. "That Companion of yours could stand to have better manners," he grumbled. "It's not as if you're the only sick or injured person here right now."

Mags thought about saying something, but his jaw hurt too much to move. In fact, everything hurt more and more the longer he sat here.

He winced as the Healer's hands moved over his body, probing the places where the blows had fallen. Then he sighed with relief as the hands rested on those spots, as warmth poured from the hands, and the relief from pain followed the warmth.

"Your assailant has done this before," the man said

laconically. "He was quite methodical about inflicting the most pain while doing the least damage."

" 's thet good?" Mags asked, as the room started to spin in circles around him. "Uh, I dunno'f'I'm gonna be sick—"

The man's hands rested on his head a moment, and some of the dizziness cleared away, and with it the nausea.

"Well, it isn't bad for you," the Healer said. "It means most of this is soft tissue damage, and I can tend it myself without help. One decent night and a day of rest and you'll be fit to go right out and Kirball to your heart's content. Yes, yes, I know you are on one of the Kirball teams, and I am very much aware that your captain wants you ready for the first game. And you will be. But not until you get that day and night. So—"

A hand to the middle of his chest shoved Mags down onto the bed. He wasn't expecting it, and fell right over.

"You need time for that concussion to clear up, and a number of medicines and some more Healing. You can talk to whosoever you want, but you stay there until tomorrow afternoon. Maybe even until the next morning, if I decide I have the time to continue treating you and you need it."

Mags blinked up at the man, owlishly. At least there was only one of him now, not two. "Dinner?" he said hopefully, for now that the nausea had begun to ebb, his stomach was growling.

The Healer lost that irritated look, and chuckled. "You're a resilient rascal. I think that can be managed."

He tucked blankets in around Mags, and left him with

a pitcher of water and a cup on a little table beside him. "Drink as much of that as you can—what I do tends to release a lot of nasty things that need to be purged out of you. The privy is right on the other side of this wall. Someone will come around with food for you in a bit. Someone else will be checking on you all night. Several someones, probably. Don't get up except to visit the privy; you'll find you are still dizzy if you do, and I don't want you undoing what I did by falling."

With that, the Healer left—

:I was listening. Are you sure you are going to be all right?: Dallen asked anxiously. *:If that Healer is neglecting you—if you are really hurt—:*

:I'm fine,: Mags reassured him, lying back and closing his eyes, because the room still had an unsettling tendency to move a little. *:'E's right, Dallen, I didn' get hurt that bad, thanks to you. Wha's goin' on down i' city? They ketch 'em?:*

Mags' unspoken prayer that the Heralds and Guards had caught the phony envoys was answered in the negative.

:No,: Dallen replied, sounding deflated. *:No, they ran. They left behind their insane fellow, but there's no sense to be gotten out of him.:*

Mags sighed, and cursed a little. So, they were back to where they had begun with nothing to show for it.

:Maybe Bear can get something out of him,: Dallen suggested, *:Or a really good Mindspeaker. And look on the bright side! They are foreign! Maybe this is what the Foreseers were on about!:*

:Mebbe. Hope so.: Mags sighed. *:Hate t' go through*

this jest t' end up wi' ev'one still angry at me fer something I ain't done yet.:

"Is it safe to come in?" asked Gennie from a little distance away.

"Reckon," Mags said shortly, because his jaw still hurt. *:Kin we talk like this?:*

:Surely. That Healer is the most terrifying man I have ever met in my life.: He heard Gennie come in and felt her sit down on the side of the bed. *:Are you really going to be all right? What happened?:*

:Was runnin' errands down in city. Saw one'a them phony envoy-bodyguards. Follered 'im, had Dallen tell Nikolas a'course, and Nikolas said t' keep follerin'.:

"Oho, so that's why people went boiling down to the city!" Gennie said. "I guess you got caught?"

:Aye. Ran fer it, got lost an' got trapped. Reckon I was driven now—if I'd'a been in their shoes, I'd'a learnt th' alleys 'round where they was like I could run 'em blind. Cornered me in a place Dallen couldn't fit.:

"You were lucky!"

:Don't I know it!: He sighed. *:Least I kin say I was follerin' orders proper.:*

His stomach growled and Gennie patted his hand. "I'll go get you some food. Something you can eat with a sore jaw."

:Thanks.:

She came back shortly with soup, mashed roots, and a custard. He managed to get his swollen and bruised eyes open enough to see to eat, and about the time he finished the Healer turned up again.

"Ah good, this isn't the thing to take on an empty

stomach, unless you want it even emptier." He handed Mags a mug. Mags knew very well it was medicine, it was probably going to taste nasty, and that he might as well get it down in a hurry.

It wasn't as nasty as he thought. In fact, the Healer had, very considerately, sweetened it with honey.

"Thenkee sor," he managed.

The Healer just grunted and sat down on the bed. "Hold still. I'm going to do something about those eyes and that jaw before I leave."

Once again, warmth spread out from the Healer's touch, and drove the pain away. Mags sighed with relief, and relaxed, and the next thing he knew, it was morning.

MORNING was absolutely lovely. His room in the stables didn't have glass panes, only parchment and shutters, and as cold as this winter had been he hadn't opened the shutters once. Every window in this big room had glass in it, and he was right under an eastward-facing one. He woke with warmth soothing his battered face, and just lay there enjoying it for a while.

Slowly he managed to get his eyes open. They weren't as swollen as he thought they would be, but he still couldn't get them open more than a slit. Still, it was nice. With sunlight pouring in the open window and now warming his bed as well as his face, Mags was feeling remarkably comfortable, considering that his chest and belly were so black and blue it looked like he'd had ink poured all over him. And he didn't want to think about what his face looked like.

He'd gotten off easy, and he knew it. Only the fact that the foreigner had wanted to know who had sent him and what Mags knew had kept the man from just taking out a sword or a knife and killing him on the spot. He could have gotten away with it too, before Dallen got there.

Strangely, that realization didn't make Mags feel frightened, just grateful.

There were birds outside the window, just ordinary creatures chirping cheerfully, but caught up in the lassitude of this morning, Mags found it very pleasant to listen to. Whatever had been in that medicine that the Healer had given him last night had left him still feeling pleasantly numbed and just sleepy enough to enjoy lying abed. Aside from the bruises, of course. He made a conscious effort not to move, because moving still hurt quite a lot. Not moving was nice. He even closed his eyes and dozed a little, and woke up a second time only when a voice roused him.

"Usually when I see someone with two black eyes, they tell me the other fellow looks even worse," said Bear, making him open those blackened eyes and squint at him.

The young Healer-Trainee was standing at the foot of his bed and peering at him somewhat anxiously through those thick lenses. He looked as if he had been awake for several candlemarks already.

"Nope. I barely nicked 'im," Mags admitted. He wiggled his jaw a little. It hurt, but not nearly as much as last night. "Least I kin talk this mornin'. Bastard 'bout broke m'jaw and tried t' knock out teeth."

Bear came close and peered at his face, moving his head from side to side. "Most of the swelling is gone from around your eyes, or I doubt you'd be able to open them," he observed, "Or at least, so I surmise. You'll look like a ferret for a while, but that's just looks, and I am pretty sure we can do something about the bruising so you don't look like Gennie beat you at the Kirball game."

Mags grunted. "'M not 'xactly anybody's sweetheart. Reckon that bruisin' won' keep the girls away anymore'n they already are."

"I wouldn't count on that." Bear grinned. "You're something of a minor hero. You spotted the bad fellow, you had the courage to follow him, and you moved in close to try and learn what you could. Plenty of people would have figured telling the other Heralds was doing your duty enough. Following him to the right inn was going above that. And going right inside isn't something I would have tried. Mind you, Dallen is a bigger hero."

"'E should be."

:Why, thank you!:

"Yer right there. 'E saved m'life. 'E came at that bugger e'en though the bastard was hackin' at 'im right smart." Mags put up a hand to touch his puffy face, and winced. "Me, all I did was get m'face in th' way of 'is fist."

The Healer from last night came in behind Bear, and theatrically clutched at his chest. "Dear gods. No boasting. I have a Herald Trainee in my care who isn't boasting about how bad his assailant looks."

Mags got a better look at him, now that there weren't two of him. Medium height, a sort of pleasantly-plain face, brown hair, brown eyes. Nothing very distinguishing about him, other than an expression of sour weariness that looked as if it was habitual.

:I'm sure his mother loves him,: said Dallen sarcastically.

:Hush, you.:

"I believe my heart will stop from the shock of such behavior, modesty, and good sense. I don't believe I have ever had a patient like you before," the Healer concluded. "Hello, Trainee Bear, you are just the person I was hoping to see. Have you any suggestions for me to help my patient look less like he landed face first in a vat of blackberries?"

Bear pursed his lips, and looked just a little surprised. "Aye, a few. Leeches won't hurt. Draw off some of that blood that's in the bruises."

The Healer nodded. "Leeches it is. If you want to run the treatment, you have my permission. I highly approve of things that don't require the Gift."

"Me too," Mags said fervently. "Like what 'f sommun was brought in so bad hurt 'e was tore up inside, an' ye'd wasted a mort' a Healin' on me?"

The Healer looked surprised and gratified. "Tell that to your Companion, would you?" the Healer replied. "If he doesn't stop ambushing me whenever I step outside the Collegium I am going to put in a strong recommendation that he be volunteered to haul firewood until you're on your feet and out of here."

:I heard that!:

:Ye been pretty rude.:

:He wasn't taking your condition seriously!:

:That's on account of it ain't serious.:

"Yessir," Mags said politely, though the only reason he didn't laugh was because he knew it would hurt too much.

"I'll do the leeching, sir," Bear said. "I've done it a lot."

"Then I'll put in an order for the leeches, thank you, Bear. Your breakfast is on the way, Trainee. Oh, something you should know. I think besides Mindspeech you either have, or are developing, a bit of Empathy. As strong as your Mindspeech is, it probably won't be much, but it might be useful to you to know you have it. If your shields aren't already handling it, come see one of us about it."

"Uhm . . . yessir," said Mags. What else was he to say, after all?

"And Bear, whatever you care to give him, I endorse." The Healer's faintly sour expression had faded, replaced by faint good humor.

"Yessir, Healer Juran, sir," Bear said, and the Healer bustled off, stopping to check someone in a bed at the far end of the room, before leaving through the door on that end, off on some other urgent task.

Mags gazed after him, thoughtfully. This was the first time he'd actually been treated by a Healer, but he'd watched a few, and to tell the truth, the man's straightforward sarcasm appealed to him. "I like 'im," Mags said. " 'E don't mess about. I don' like people what won't tell ye the truth. I don' mind him bein' a bit sharp; reckon Heralds don' make th' best patients."

"I like him too, but there's plenty that don't," Bear replied.

:Like me,: came the sulky comment. *:Haul wood indeed!:*

"He's good enough that I have the feeling he talks like that in order to keep troublesome patients away. You know, the ones that make out as if a bit of gout is going to kill them." Bear pulled back the covers to look at the bruises on Mags' belly.

"How bad are you hurting?" Bear continued. "Cause between you and me, I think you should sleep some more. Specially when I get the leeches, they really make some people feel sick to look at."

"I could sleep," Mags admitted. "I'druther eat first, though. An' I ain't worrit 'bout leeches. Had worse'n leeches where we all bedded down at th' mine, I reckon. All manner of bugs and creepies. Rats runnin' over ye in the middle of the night."

Bear shuddered. "Aye, that's worse. All right, I'll go make you a dose; you can have it after you eat."

One of the Healer's Collegium servants came in at that moment with a tray loaded down with soft foods—oatmeal, soft eggs, mashed apples and tea. Mags tucked into it while Bear went off somewhere and came back with one of those mugs that always seemed to hold medicine, and a pair of jars.

"Drink this, and if you really want to watch, I'll start now," Bear said.

Bear had not sweetened the stuff. Mags managed not to choke. "Sure, I wanta watch," he said, with some interest. "Mebbe I kin use this sorta thing if I gotta out in the field. So tell me why's ye do this?"

Bear fished a leech out of the jar and applied it carefully to a badly bruised and swollen part of Mags' belly. "The muscle gets all crushed, blood goes in but can't get out. That keeps things from healing as fast as they could. The leech pulls it out, watch."

Mags watched as the ugly little bit of black slime swelled up to a fat little pod of black slime. Sated, it detached itself. Bear caught it before it could fall into the blankets and dropped it in another jar. "It works really well where people have had fingers or toes crushed instead of broken—or well, lots of things, any time blood doesn't seem to be actually flowing."

"So—what's it do, now it's full?"

"We'll go put them where they can go make babies now they're fed," Bear said. "We try and breed our own, so we know they come from clean water and don't have anything nasty about them. Look at where he was."

Sure enough, the area was less swollen and not as blue. Bear applied a few more. Mags watched them, fascinated. "This is why some people call a Healer, especially one that doesn't have a Gift, a 'leech,' " Bear went on. "Animal Healers use leeches too."

"Huh." There was actually something rather . . . appealing about the idea. That this ugly little thing could help a person heal, without a Gift. "You gonna put those on m'face too?"

"Aye, if you don't mind."

He yawned. "I don' mind, but I'm feelin' like I oughta get flat."

"That'll help the leeches too," Bear said, catching one that was full and dropping it in the jar, giving it an oddly fond look.

"Huzzah, leeches, good fer ye," Mags said muzzily, waiting until Bear had taken the last one off his belly and chest, and scooting down in the bed. "Go make lotsa liddle leeches . . ."

Bear laughed, and he closed his eyes.

He didn't actually sleep, more like drowsed as Bear worked. He definitely felt Bear put the leeches on his skin; they were cool when they first were put on but quickly warmed up to his temperature, there was a kind of pinpricking sensation he wouldn't even have noticed against the general ache of his bruises if he hadn't been concentrating on seeing what it felt like. Then there was a numbing feeling and no more pinprick sensations. He thought about it, and decided that the leeches were probably doing the numbing themselves. After all, it was in their interest to make you not feel it when they were biting you and sucking your blood.

"All done," Bear said at last, rousing him out a lethargic, dreamy state. "You still awake? You look a lot better."

"Kinda," he mumbled. He opened his eyes with an effort. It felt as if he could open them more now. He blinked at Bear, who smiled at him. "So, ye know what happen, down i' Haven? Thet crazy feller?"

"They found him tied down to a bed in that inn when they broke into the rooms the men had been renting. The Guards brought him up here, and he's worse than before," Bear replied, shaking his head. "I don't know what his so-called friends were dosing him with, but it wasn't doing him any good, he's down to skin and bones and raving just as badly as ever. Besides that, he's suffering from not having whatever drug they were giving him, and the Mindspeakers don't want to come within a furlong of him. Maybe a really, really powerful Mindhealer could mend him, but we don't have one strong enough. So they gave him over to me."

"Well—thet's good, right?" He blinked again, trying to focus on Bear's lenses. "'Nother reason why yer family cain't drag ye home?"

"It is," Bear acknowledged, but looked unhappy, "The thing is I just wish I had more options for dealing with him. Right now all I can do is get him a little healthier and see if some of my remedies can help him out. I don't like not being able to do something for a patient. And, yes, I know, no one else can either, but . . . well, I really, really want to break him out of this. If Lena is right, and he's seeing *vrondi*, maybe I can find something, some medicine, in the old records that blocks magic. Or at least blocks Mindmagic. If he doesn't sense them watching him, maybe we can get through to him. All I was able to do before was to—well, dose him so that he didn't feel threatened by them watching him, if that makes any sense. I don't know, even if no one wanted me to try and help this fellow, I would do it."

Mags pondered this, drowsily, and closed his eyes. "I get it, Bear. Ye wouldn' be fightin' t' be a Healer if'n ye didn' feel thet way. Healer's a Healer, bone deep, Gift or no." He paused. "Am I a fool fer feelin' sorry fer 'im?"

"No. I do, too. He never did anything to either of us that I know of, and it was his so-called friends that kidnapped me, not him. Besides, I get the feeling he was forced to come here—and I am pretty damn sure he was forced to stay." The chair scraped against the floor as Bear got up to leave. "I need to take these little fellows back where they belong. I expect you'll be getting more visitors."

"Mebbe. An' if not, I kin sleep." He couldn't imagine who, besides Lena, would be all that anxious to see him. Pretty soon everyone would realize just what balderdash that "hero" business was. So long as everybody figured out that he wasn't the "foreigner" in those visions, he'd count himself a happy fellow.

Bear chuckled. "All right then, sleep. It'll be good for you."

He did just that, soothed by the stuff in Bear's tea, until a servant woke him for lunch, which was more soft food—pease porridge flavored with ham, but without any ham in it, mashed pears, mashed turnips. It was good. The cook had taken extra care with it all, he could tell. He winced a bit even so, as he ate; he supposed he was lucky none of his teeth had actually been knocked out of his jaw.

:Half the Collegium wants to visit you,: Dallen reported. Mags laughed.

:Reckon ye kin take that on yerself?: he asked. *:I think it oughta be you what gets all th' attention.:*

:Oh, I might . . . : Dallen temporized. *: Gennie and the team are on the way with a couple of your books, anyway. Healer Juran told them you won't be down long enough to need all of your studies brought in.:*

It hurt to smile, but he did anyway. The servant who had come to take his dishes smiled back at him. *:Then*

I'll tell 'em what kinda big damn hero ye are, an' let 'em spread it round.:

He chuckled at Dallen's astonished reaction.

:Juran is right. You really are ridiculously modest.:

:Or mebbe I jest don' like fussin' an' I know you eat it up. Jest think 'bout all those people tryin' t' bring ye pocket pies.: Just then he heard the sounds of a lot of boots in the corridor outside and turned his attention to the door.

It wasn't the entire team, but it was a fair crowd; it included Halleck, Pip, Gennie, and Jeffers as well as the young proto-Guards from the Foot, and he had to shush them more than once to keep them from disturbing the other people in the room. There were three other patients, though he couldn't see who, or even what, they were—only that they mostly hunched themselves up in their blankets and turned their backs on the "fuss."

"Dear gods, you look like a bad dyeing accident," Pip observed cheerfully. "Try not to heal too fast, we'll get lots of sympathy for our side at the first Kirball game."

Gennie pretended to smack him on the back of the head. They all settled around the bed. "Tell," demanded Gennie. "Or I'll leave Pip with you."

After he got done telling his part of the story—and being true to his word, minimizing his role and making sure Dallen got all the credit he deserved for trying to take on a skilled and armed fighter in a space where the Companion couldn't even move—he finally got to ask some questions of his own.

"Anyone sayin' wha 'appened down in Haven?" he asked.

Everyone looked to Barrett, who nodded. "No one's making any sort of secret about it," Barrett replied. "Your man managed to bolt before the Heralds and Guards got there, and vanished. There were at least five more besides the crazy one staying at the inn, according to the innkeeper. He had given them a couple of rooms over the stable that he was rarely able to rent out because of how noisy and smelly they could get when the inn was full—he'd done that because their crazy friend was given to fits of raving, and that kept him from disturbing anyone else. They'd only been there a fortnight or so."

"Huh. Wonder where else they'd been stayin' 'til then," Mags said thoughtfully. "They had t' be somewhere."

"Wherever it was, the crazy one hadn't been screaming his head off, or the other innkeepers would have remembered it." Barrett said. "Anyway, they stole horses out of the stable, left the crazy one behind, and disappeared. The inn was in an uproar when the Heralds got there, over the stolen horses."

"By now they're long gone," Pip said in disgust. "I wish I could get my hands on the one that beat up Mags." His eyes glittered dangerously and Mags was a bit taken aback. This was a side of Pip he had not seen before.

"Either they're really gone from Haven, or they stole the horses to make it look like they did," Gennie put in.

"Huh?" Mags blinked at her. "Ye think thet's likely?"

He couldn't imagine why they would stay, but the mere thought made his stomach feel odd. They'd had a grudge against him before he caught them out. Now? They'd probably want his hide tacked up on a wall.

Gennie shrugged. "It doesn't matter what I think, that's what older and wiser heads than mine are thinking. They say that given that we thought they were gone the first time, from what I heard, equal weight is being put on both possibilities."

"So . . . why'd they stay i' the first place?" Mags wondered.

There were puzzled glances and shrugs all around the group. "I suppose they didn't get something done that they needed to do," Gennie said at last. "And there's nothing they left behind telling us what that was—unless it was to kill the King."

"This sure matches up with that Foreseeing," Halleck said, speaking up for the first time. "Foreign blood—and an assassin. Let's hope you put an end to that, Mags."

"Eh," Mags shrugged. "Was more accident than anythin' else."

"Well what I want to know is, will you be ready for the Kirball match?" Gennie demanded. Mags chuckled. He had been waiting for her to say something.

"Healer says so. Says I'll be all green'n'purple, but I be good."

Gennie sighed with relief. "Well in that case, I'm happy!"

Supper came and went, and Lena followed it, with another dose from Bear and a request.

Well, not so much a request as an "I plan to do this and of course I'm sure you won't mind."

"No," said Mags.

". . . but . . ." Lena said, making big eyes at him.

"Nu-uh. No songs," Mags said firmly. "I ain't done nothin' t' make a song 'bout."

"But I need a subject for this week's assignment!" she protested. "It's perfect! I mean, I know you, and I know the story, and it's topical, which is important, because it proves it isn't something I've been working on all along on the side. Besides, it's mostly just about keeping your eyes open all the time and—"

She stopped, abruptly, and shut her mouth. But not before Mags realized what she had just said.

He stared at her accusingly. "Ye already wrote it, didn' ye?"

She dropped her gaze to the hands clasped in her lap. "Ye-es," she said reluctantly.

"Ye din' sing it fer anyone?"

"Um—"

He groaned. "Ye did. How'n hell did ye git a song wrote i' less'n a day?"

"I needed a song for an assignment and I couldn't think of a subject!" she replied pleadingly. "It was one of those 'make up a song in three days' assignments. Bards are supposed to be able to make things up on the spot, and this is supposed to train us in doing that. It was perfect! My class liked it!"

"Yer class." He groaned. An entire class of Bardic Trainees had heard the song and liked it. Which meant an entire class of Bardic Trainees had probably memorized it by now.

"It's very short," she said in a small voice.

"It'd haveta be." If his face hadn't been so tender he would have buried it in his hands. "An' since it's short, they all learnt it already. Cause thet's what Bards do."

"Um. Sort of," she whispered. "Sort of." Which meant she'd taught them. Even better.

"Wonnerful." Well there was no helping it. He had a song about him now. The best thing he could do would be to see if she could bury it with a better one. "Well, then, Lena Marchand, you owes me. An' I am gonna collect." He fastened her with a stern gaze, which was altogether ineffective since she was staring at her hands. "Yer gonna write 'nother song 'bout Dallen. An' yer gonna make it better'n the one 'bout me."

Now she looked up, with a slightly panicked look on her face. "I can't promise it will be better!" she protested.

He didn't relent. "Are ye a Bard, or no?" he countered. "Bards write t' demand all th' time. Ye jest said so. Well, I be yer first customer. Ye might's well start learnin' how t' please the customer now, an' be done wi' it."

She sighed heavily and dropped her gaze to her lap again. "All right," she replied unhappily. "I'll try."

He could hardly believe it. He'd only been tucked up in Healer's Collegium for a little more than a day and already this had happened.

Well, the best way to deal with it was to act as if it wasn't important—and neither was he. But this was certainly nothing like what Herald Nikolas wanted him to do.

His thoughts were interrupted by Lena, speaking in what was almost a whisper. "Don't you want to hear it?" she asked. "Even a little?"

He almost snapped out "No!" when he got a good look at her face.

Oh, how could he make her even more unhappy than she already was? That would just be the height of cruelty.

"All right," he said, trying not to show his reluctance. "It was damn nice on ye, Lena. 'S jest, I don' wanna fuss about me, an' I thought ye knew that. I didn' like the bad fuss, an' I don' like a good fuss about the same. Jest don' like any fuss, ye ken?"

She nodded.

He reached out and patted her hand. "Bet it's real good though. So le's hear it."

She lit up with a smile and reached down for the little gittern next to her chair. And Mags got to listen for the next half candlemark all about what a brave hero he was, when in fact, he was dead certain he was nothing of the sort.

"You're sure you can see all right?" Gennie asked anxiously. From inside the helmet, Mags nodded, the helm following the motions of his head and turning them into something ponderous. So did all the rest of them.

"All right, you lot. Remember. Play with your heads

as well as your hands and feet," she said to the team that had gathered around her. "Listen for Mags in your heads. But if you see something that opens up in front of you, think it as hard as you can."

They stood in a circle, with the horses and Companions on the outside, reins held loosely in their riders' hands. They could all hear the murmur of the crowd huddled up against the fence surrounding the field. A lot of people had turned up today; it was a gorgeous, sunny, warm day, perfect for just about anything. One enterprising fellow was peddling apples. Pip had taken a look at the crowd and remarked that before long they were going to need stands for the spectators. Mags had thought he was joking, but now he wasn't so sure.

They were all unmounted for the moment, the horses stirring uneasily at the ends of their bridles, sandwiched in between Companions to keep them out of mischief. The horses were mostly well-schooled and well-behaved, but they were horses, and one perceived nip or bump might start something, wasting energy that they would need for the game.

"Riders, we've got a disadvantage; the Riders on North are all well monied and they have a horse for every quarter. We don't."

They all nodded. Of them all, only Jeffers had three horses; the other riders had a pair apiece. That meant they'd be alternating, one to ride, one to rest. The second quarter each horse played was going to be hard on them—and even Jeffers was going to have to go with a barely-rested horse for the fourth quarter.

"So ride smart. Let your beasts rest as much as

possible, and see to it that theirs don't get a chance to. Just remember this, though, your horses are all tough and scrappy. Theirs are high-bred and all nerve and nose. Chances are we can make them or the riders lose their tempers, and if we do that, we win the game. Provided you can keep yours."

She turned to the Foot. "You lot have our secret, but remember to wait until we tell you to use it, because once we do, it won't be a secret anymore and everyone will use the trick. We have to plan this and plan it well. Right?"

One of the Guard boys saluted. No one found that funny. Gennie nodded. "Right then. Check the saddles, bits, and boots for your mounts. Check your paddle-straps. Check your armor. Let's play the game."

The South team lined up in the middle of the field. After a moment, the North did the same, opposite them. Mags noticed something immediately.

:The North Riders have whips in their hands,: he projected to all of them. *:They won't be able to manage reins, whip and paddle.:*

He saw Gennie nod slightly, and narrow her eyes.

:Tell them this again from me. Play together, play with your heads, and follow the ball. If North gets it, drive the ball to the Riders and let them fumble it. Keep it away from the Trainees.:

The "ball," a curiously soft thing about the size of a baby's head, lay on the ground between the two teams. It could be kicked by the Companions or by the Foot, it could be snatched up and carried, thrown, or hit with the paddles. Anything was fair. All eyes were on it.

"Ho!" shouted the referee, and the Trainees from both sides dove for the ball.

But Jeffers, on a pony barely big enough to be a mount for him, dove in under the nose of one of the North Trainees, leaning down out of his saddle, and scooped up the ball. The indignant Companion pulled up with a whinny. As he hauled himself back up, he threw the ball toward his side.

Gennie snagged it out of the air and she and her Companion scrambled for the North goal.

No one—well, perhaps no one except the South team—had expected anyone to get his hands on the ball that fast. The North was caught unprepared, and pelted after her.

But their Foot were already moving to intercept her.

:Pip!: she called out, and feinted toward the goal while throwing the ball in a fast, shallow arc toward her teammate. It came at him like a comet, but he knew this maneuver of old and he stood up in his stirrups and smacked it with his paddle with both hands, as hard as he possibly could.

The ball flew, high and true, and in through the open door of the North goal.

The crowd of spectators—for there was a crowd—went insane.

:We've made 'em mad,: Mags warned, catching some black looks from the North team.

:Good. Now we tire them out with some football,: Gennie replied.

And so they did.

North got the ball this time, but as Gennie had told

them to do, the team crowded the ball handler and kept the Trainees tied up so that the ball went to a Rider—and then South Riders and Trainees pressed the Riders hard, keeping them away from the North Trainees and from each other. They ran the North Riders all over the field, took them on scrambles over the rises, made them leap the little fences and tear down into the gullies, taking them over every thumb-length of ground. The horses lost their heads over this; they hated being run in this way, and as a consequence they became handfuls, fighting the bits and their Riders, forcing the Riders to use those whips in their hands. Which meant the Riders couldn't use the paddles. And finally, the ball-carrier fumbled, and Pip nipped the ball out of the air in mid-fall, just as the whistle blew for the end of the quarter.

:Now that was what I call some play,: Dallen said with satisfaction. But Mags was looking at the poor horses, who were absolutely exhausted. And the Foot, who were the same; they had run all over the field, trying to stay between the Riders and the goal, ready to fall on the ball, pound it out of the air, or use the long poles they had in stands at the side to pull a Rider or Trainee out of the saddle. In a battle, it would be someone with a pole-arm doing that, and the result could be the death of the formerly mounted fighter. There were two minds about the poles, which had padded hooks on the ends. Some of the senior Heralds didn't want them used in the game. Some, who had seen combat, were adamant about their use. The few rules were still in flux.

They all huddled up again. "We've made them angry too soon," said Gennie, with a glance over her shoulder at the other team's huddle. Mags nodded. "They'll probably try to rush us to keep us off the ball so they can get it first. And we won't manage the same trick to nip in under their noses. They're smart; we'll never be able to play the same trick twice on them."

"I wouldn't doubt they have more than a few tricks up their sleeves," put in Pip. "Three of 'em are my yearmates. Never forget, my team, that the people on all four teams are the best of the best. The only differences among us are the way our coaches are strategizing the game, and the talents they picked for their teams."

"Never forget to play like a team," Gennie reminded them. "There is a difference between a team and a group of the best, and a team will win every time. Stay loose and keep alert. Don't go for the ball this time; go for keeping them away from it. Keep on top of it and just don't let them have it."

They lined up for the second quarter. All eyes were on the ball, and sure enough, one of the Trainees on North rushed the ball, coming in with a clever scoop that might have taken it, if the South hadn't followed Gennie's orders. It was Companions and Trainees this time; the scrum was nothing but white coats and tails. South didn't even try to get at the ball; they just moved in right on top of it and kept it in play among the Companions' legs.

:Where's the ball?: Mags asked Dallen.

:Under Hack's tail, or at least that's where North thinks it is.: North kept pushing and pushing at Halleck's Companion Hack, thinking he had the ball.

:Well, where is it, really?:

:By—whoops!: The North had found it at last, and a smart kick from one of their Companions sent it soaring up the pitch toward the South goal.

But the South Riders had been waiting for that, staying well out of the scrum, and now that the ball was heading their way, they made for it.

:Don't snag it! Keep them off the ball!: Mags "shouted" into their minds, as the North Companions, four abreast, rushed the field, trying to block the South Companions from getting to the North Riders.

But momentum carried them all across the field, and what happened was that all of them converged on the ball at once. One of the North Trainees was swinging down out of his saddle and almost—

"Not today, thanks!" shouted Jeffers, as his horse shouldered into the Companion, forcing him sideways enough so that the Trainee missed his grab. Pip was right after Jeffers, and made the scoop.

But the North was determined not to let them near the goal, and so they were rushed up the field and down again. The North brought their Riders into play—and at the change, their Riders had gone for big, heavy horses. They could shove the South all over the field if they chose.

They looked big enough to eat the whole team and want dessert, in fact.

:Those Riders are too confident of their horses' weights!: Gennie said to Mags, who passed it on. *:Tell Pip to send the ball at the goal anyhow! We'll race them and see what we can do!:*

Pip and his Companion got a good smart kick at the

ball that sent it skittering away across the field toward the North goal at a time when the North Trainees were scrummed up with the South Trainees. Mags knew it when the ball went flying, a breath before the North team knew, and he and Dallen went careening after it. A North Rider on a big black charger went for the ball at the same time. The black was hot and angry—you could see it in his eyes and in the flag of his tail. They were heading for a collision if neither of them wavered. Dallen was cool, calculating, and as Jeffers came streaking up behind them, Dallen applied his weight to the side of the North horse with science. Mags felt the impact all through him, and if it hadn't been for the armor on his leg, it would have been bruised from ankle to thigh.

The blow was tremendous.

Dallen sat down and slid on his tail as Mags hung on for dear life. But when Mags looked around, the black was down and on his side, with all his breath knocked out of him, and his Rider was picking himself up out of the dirt. Neither were hurt more than bruises, but both were out of the game for a little, at least.

:Ha!: said Dallen, and scrambled to his feet, following after Jeffers, who had nipped the ball up right under the nose of the North Foot.

But the North Foot were ready for him and he couldn't get the ball in to save his life, nor could he get the chance to rush them and steal the flag.

Time was called, and that was the end of that quarter.

"They'll bring out fast horses for their Riders next," said Gennie in the huddle. "What have we got?"

"We've got nothing fast," Jeffers told her. "Just sound."

"They'll probably make a goal on us, then," Gennie replied. "It will be up to us to make that goal back, right after, when they least expect it. Or make a try for the flag."

"I dunno," said Mags, who had been up and down the line of the North's Foot several times in the melee. "I don' see 'em givin' us an openin' t' try."

"Then we play what we can get," Gennie said firmly. "Remember that fast horses won't like football, and maybe we can tie them up again. If we can't, well, we'll do what we can."

Off they all went to the line, and the horses that the North Riders were on looked very fast indeed. And the Riders did not want football, they wanted a game, and they had the speed to get it.

They plunged down on the ball like falcons on a pigeon; the Trainees hung back and let them, and they got the ball too, arriving a good stride or two before the South did.

The South tied up the Rider with the ball, but he gave a great heave and sent it flying toward one of the North Trainees.

On the chance that might happen, Gennie had pulled back and put herself between him and them and as she saw the ball hurtling toward her, far too fast to catch safely, she copied the move earlier in the game. She stood in her stirrups, got the paddle in both hands and thwacked at the ball in passing. Not aiming, just deflecting.

So the ball met her paddle and sped off her paddle at an angle, with the speed of her hit and the Northern Rider's tremendous throw, and went screaming off to the sidelines.

:Paddle's broke, I'm out!: Gennie called, and went careening to their side to get a new one.

The entire Northern field went after the ball. Mags caught movement out of the corner of his eye and alerted.

:Hack, Halleck, the flag!: he warned, for those two were the closest, and he and Dallen made a straight run for their own goal. *:Foot!:* he projected, as hard as he could. *:The flag! They're usin' our trick!:*

Sure enough, the North had "stolen" the South's "secret move," which was to send one of the Foot sneaking under cover across the field to steal the flag when no one was watching it. And if they hadn't trained themselves for that, they might not have noticed until it was too late.

The Northern Foot had the flag in his hands as Hack nearly ran him down, Halleck snatching it away as they passed.

Their own Foot chased him back to the safety of his own lines, furious that they had been distracted enough to let him get that close. They shouldn't have. They'd known this could happen and had planned for it to be them that did it.

:Cool down,: Mags advised to them all. *:Ain't no thing. We caught 'er in time. 'Ware goal!:*

Halleck rammed the pole of the flag back in place and rejoined the game just as Gennie pounded back from the sidelines toward the Rider with the ball with a grim look on her face.

Just how grim she was, was clear by the fact that the North was dangerously close to the South goal, taking advantage of the distraction of their Foot's attempt on the flag. She went at the Rider with the ball full-out, shouldered into his Companion, and bringing her fist up between his hands, bunted the ball right out of them. It popped up high in the air and fell back among the hooves, and there it stayed, for the South was not going to let them get it back again.

:Football! Football!: Mags "shouted," and football they got. The fast horses of the Riders got hot and lathered as the South's Companions kept the ball among their feet, not daring to kick it away lest it be intercepted.

Compliments were exchanged among the Riders and Trainees. Horses kicked and bit, and Companions put their heads down and would not be moved. And finally, time was called and it was the end of the third quarter.

"This will be the worst," Gennie said, pulling off her helmet and mopping at her face and neck. "They've got fresh horses for the Riders, and we don't. They want two goals; they need one." She looked hard at Mags, at all of them. "Now's for it, if you see it. Take chances. We won't have another quarter to make up what we lose."

Mags nodded. They all did. They knew what that meant. So did Dallen, who tossed up his head to show he was still in the game.

"Football, my lads. Football. They have fresh horses. They'll drive us in toward our goal. They'll try to get close enough to score. But we can win this one just the same if we keep our heads."

They all nodded. Then it was into the saddle and onto the line, and the first thing the fresh Riders did was get the ball right under Halleck's nose. But he was atop them, and copying Gennie's move in reverse, drove his fist down on the ball, knocking it among the hooves again.

The Northern Trainees had learned by watching, and now it was their Companions who were playing as much football as the South. The time for compliments and kicks was over; both sides scrummed grimly over the ball, hocks were kicked and dust rose above the melee and the Northern Foot came up to join the fray.

This was new! They had left their poles behind!

The Foot circled the outside of the scrum, dancing back and forth, watching, watching. Mags could scarcely believe it, but it looked as if they intended to dash right in there and snatch the ball up from among the flying hooves if they got a chance!

And then it hit him. He glanced at the Northern goal.

There was only a single Foot there to guard it.

Dallen didn't need prompting; he responded the instant Mags' eyes took in that fact. This was what he lived for, a straight, hard run across rotten ground, as fast as he could put hoof to turf. Mags was halfway to the goal before the lone Foot realized he was coming. The man leapt to intercept them, but instead of taking one of the ramps, Dallen gathered himself like a rabbit and made an enormous jump that got his forehooves on the top of the base. He scrambled for a desperate moment with his rear, as Mags threw his weight over Dallen's neck, saved himself, and pivoted. Mags snatched at the flag, just as a roar from the other end of the ground told him that the North had scored.

Run!

They had the flag—but they had to keep it—

And now the entire field had realized what he had done and were heading toward him.

He hunched down over Dallen's neck. Dallen leapt off the top of the goal-structure, aiming not for their own goal, but the side of the field where the very worst of the ground was, the boulders and hillocks and a hundred treacherous things. He scrambled among them like a rabbit, jigging and dancing from side to side, as fifteen Riders and Trainees avalanched toward them at a speed that was insane.

One of the Riders, on a beast built like a greyhound, came up on them first, but Dallen feinted to the fence and the horse shied from it. The horses didn't like the fence—they didn't like the shouting people climbing on it, and they didn't like the fence itself. The North horses could not come at his right hand side, and so the North Companions moved to get in ahead of him and stop him.

The South Riders and Companions weren't going to give them a chance, not if they could help it. And this was bad ground, very bad, and Dallen couldn't move in a straight line across it. The entire scrum piled onto him, threatening to trap him.

:Turn them into the fence!: Mags cried, and they did, crowding the horses, whose nerves stretched and snapped, and crowding their fellow Companions, while

Mags and Dallen ran, slid between them, still heading for their goal.

And that was when Mags saw it. The ball in the Rider's hand, forgotten.

:Pip! The ball!: he yelled, as Dallen gave a leap and a wiggle and nipped under a Northern Companion's bridle.

And then they were clear.

Dallen got a surge of energy from somewhere and put on a burst of speed, as behind him and from the crowd, Mags heard a roar.

He ignored it. They had their job—

A Northern Foot popped up out of nowhere right in their path. The man made a vicious swing at Mags with his hook. Mags and Dallen both ducked, and the hook grazed the back of his helmet and his head—and Dallen hopped up like a rabbit to prevent his feet from being pulled out from under him by the return sweep of the hook.

And then they were past—

And then they were pounding up the top of the ramp and Mags stabbed down with the pole of the flag, planting it next to their own, just as a roar came up from the other end of the field—matched by the roar from the spectators at this end when they saw him safely in and the flag in capture.

And the trumpets blatted, marking the game over!

"One goal up *and* the flag in capture!" crowed Pip, for the hundredth time. "Oh! That was a *game!*"

They were playing it over, move for move, at the

celebratory dinner. Tonight there was no time limit on how long they could all occupy the dining hall, and even the cooks kept turning up with more to drink and tasty snacks to hear about the game. Mags and Pip, who made the final goal, were the great heroes of the hour. Now that the game was over, everyone was friends again, and although they were all too young to be allowed to drink very much, they did toast each other again and again in the small beer, cider, and weak wine they were permitted.

"My eye," said Halleck with satisfaction. "This is something like. I wish my family was here."

"Well now, this was just the first game, so don't go thinking we'll let you get away with this when we meet up again," said the Captain of the North with a laugh. "And East and West were watching, so those clever tricks you used won't work a second time."

"Nothing ever does, my lad," Halleck countered, waggling his eyebrows. "You just be on your mettle, for we'll have new tricks for you the second time around."

Mags kept very quiet, and off to one side, but he was full of silent contentment again.

Tomorrow, something else might crop up to make his life a misery again. But for now . . .

For now, life was good.

"I'M glad you had time for this today," Amily said happily, as she passed Mags another random pile of Heralds' reports. "I didn't think you would, what with Kirball practice and all." The little nook in the library felt as warm and welcoming as his own room now. And today was even better, since he and Amily were alone up here.

"Well, yer Pa's left me alone fer a bit, so thet gives me some time," Mags replied, though his brow furrowed with worry. "I dunno though, I'm a bit afeared I mighta got too . . . watched. What wi' the game an' findin' them foreigners. Mebbe I ain't no use t' him now, an' thet's why he ain't got nothing' fer me t' do." The prospect made him unhappy, for reasons he couldn't quite define. Maybe because he had gotten used to being needed and wanted, doing things that were important, even if only Nikolas knew that he was doing so.

"Only until the East and West game, and only until people forget about the foreigners," Amily replied giving him a pat on the back of his hand. "It will be fine. Father is patient. In fact, he's probably figuring out ways to use this to his advantage—perhaps to get you to play up that you are very physical, rather than intelligent. People who are good at fighting or games are rarely expected to be clever; if you play into that, people will underestimate you. And he knows that eventually you and Pip won't be the only star Kirball players. People will all have their favorites; it's the way that games work out." At his quizzical expression, she elaborated. "People will pick a team to support with their enthusiasm, and they will have favorite players on the team itself. If you stay quiet and uninteresting, they will turn their attention to someone who is outgoing and very vocal. Someone who relishes the attention, but not in a bad way. Didn't you know that?"

He shook his head. "Never seen no games like this afore," he replied, more than a bit surprised at her words.

"Oh." Amily was a little taken aback. "I keep forgetting that you didn't—" She stopped before finishing her sentence.

"Thet I didn' hev a normal kinda growin' up," he finished for her. "Well, thet's good. Cause I kinda won't fit in th' way yer Pa wants me to if people are noticin' thet alla time. If you ferget, it means I'm getting' better at that fittin' in stuff." He smiled shyly at her and was rewarded by another pat on his hand.

She eyed him carefully. "So you have no idea what Gennie really means when she talks about 'giving the other team football' do you?"

He shook his head. "Well, I jest thought it was keepin' th' ball 'mongst the Companions' feet. Kinda explains itself. Tha's not it?"

Amily giggled a little. "No, it's an actual game. Fancy, a girl is going to have to explain football to a boy!" She found this very funny, although he didn't see why. "People play football all over Valdemar. It's very popular. I know enough about it to explain it."

So she did; evidently this was a kicking game with a ball, one that was a little bigger than a Kirball. It was played by two teams—on a flat, rectangular field with a goal at either end. The field was much smaller than the one for Kirball, and was generally grassed over. You were allowed to kick or hit the ball, you just weren't allowed to pick it up and run with it.

"Why?" Mags said, finally, when she got done explaining how villages would compete with each other, and how there were many teams down in Haven composed of players from various Guilds and professions—and many more that were just friends getting together. "Why go t' all that fuss an' work t' do somethin' like that? I mean, 'f I had a day free from hard work, I sure wouldn' wanta spend it kickin' at a ball!" He shook his head. "At the mine, all we wanted t' do when we wasn't workin' was t' hunt fer food an' sleep."

"It's . . . fun," Amily said slowly. "It's fun for the people playing it. It's fun to watch. It's fun to support one team or another. Well, at least it is for people who aren't as desperate as the people in your mine were. When you aren't starving or exhausted, people do all sorts of odd things for fun. Didn't you have fun out there playing Kirball? It looked as if you did."

He thought about it. "Reckon . . . I did," he said, after a moment, feeling surprised. "I mean, I got on 'cause Caellan, y' know, Dean of Collegium wanted me to. An' yer Pa seemed t' want me to. So I did, an' it was kinda like another class fer me. But . . . aye, now ye say, I reckon it was fun." He thought about it some more. "Y'know, I think I'd play it even if it wasn't like a class."

"Well, that's why. And when the East and West meet, you'll see it's fun to watch, too." She nodded decisively, and would have said more, except that they heard the door to the Archives open and footsteps coming toward them across the wooden floor. Two sets of footsteps. They both looked up to see Lena and a handsome man in Bardic Scarlet approaching them from out of the shadows at the door end of the Archives. Mags knew that face all too well.

Bard Marchand, Lena's father.

Now that Mags had leisure to study him, he couldn't say he liked the man any better. The Bard had a classically chiseled face of the sort you would expect to see on a heroic statue. He wore his dark hair a little long, and there was gray at both temples. His eyes were a common enough brown, with disconcertingly long lashes, but despite the long lashes there was nothing effeminate about him. He moved with the confidence of someone who expects everyone else to get out of his way, and he carried himself as if he expected to be the center of attention. He wasn't as heavily muscled as a Herald or a fighter of some sort would be, but he was lean and fit.

Lena had a sort of tremulously hopeful look on her face. But the expression on Bard Marchand's was a bit more difficult to read. It looked a little like avidity, which was a strange expression, considering the circumstances.

"Mags, this is my father, Bard Marchand; he wanted to meet and talk to you," Lena said, and her anxious thoughts were so strong they spilled past Mags' shields. *Please be nice to him, he finally noticed me!* Mags blinked a little to realize that there was something else going on with her as well . . . as the Healer had said, he got an inkling of the emotions that were driving her as well. Certainly not enough to be uncomfortable or intrusive for him, and he was sure he could shield them out if he wished to, but he knew very well how anxious she was even without reading her expression.

"Father," she said, with a touch of desperation. "This is Trainee Mags."

They both ignored Amily, which was uncharacteristically rude on Lena's part.

Mags would cheerfully have snubbed the man—who clearly had no idea that this was the same Trainee he'd sent on a servant's errand to make another servant of the King's Own mere weeks ago. But he couldn't spoil this for Lena.

On the other hand, he didn't exactly have to be "himself" for the Bard, either. This was an excellent opportunity for some misdirection.

:Good idea, Mags.: Dallen was irritated. *:Whatever he wants, make him work for it.:*

"Pleased t' meetcher, Bard Marchand," he said, and immediately put on his thickest accent and an amiable-but-stupid expression. He thrust out his hand; Bard Marchand took it with a bit of hesitation. He pumped the Bard's hand with great enthusiasm and exactly as if he was working a pump handle, before letting go of it.

"Pleased to meet you at last, Trainee Mags," said the Bard, flexing his fingers gingerly, although he didn't make a great show of doing so. That was a little odd. It couldn't have been because Mags had crushed his hand with a hard grip; Mags knew better than to pull that kind of game with a Bard (someone who needed his fingers intact) even if he didn't like the man.

No, he got the flash of an impression that Marchand was keeping himself from pulling out a handkerchief and wiping his hand off only by force of will. As if he expected that Mags would be dirty, or something.

Nice, he thought sourly.

"This here purty filly's Amily," he said, since Marchand was still ignoring the other person in the room as utterly unimportant. Time to display the fact that he, at least, had some manners. "She be Herald Nikolas' daughter."

A flicker of recognition passed across the Bard's face, and a flicker of chagrin as he must have realized that Amily was too important a personage to continue to ignore, especially after that dressing-down he'd gotten from Master Bard Lita. "Ah," the Bard said, turning toward her and beaming the full force of his personality at her as he scooped up her hand and kissed the fingertips. "Enchanted. I had no idea my old friend Nikolas had such a lovely daughter." It was easy to see how the Bard charmed his admirers; although this wasn't—quite—the application of his Gift, the Bard had a full measure of charisma and clearly was used to employing it with great precision.

Amily flushed, but only Mags knew it was not with pleasure. "I prefer to stay quietly out of the public eye, Bard Marchand," she said with an edge to her voice under the sweetness. "I've no taste for court maneuverings, and I suppose you would say I am something of a bookworm. Father indulges my taste for solitude."

"What kin we be a-doin' fer ye, Bard Marchand?" Mags said, letting his voice take on tones of faintly servile admiration. The man lived on flattery, it seemed, so . . . give him what he wanted and see what came of it. " 'M jest a Trainee, cain't think what brung ye up here, 'less ye wanta know stuff's in Archives."

"Oh, I was wondering if you would be so kind as to give me your view of the events of this winter, and the discovery of those vile miscreants in Haven a few days ago, Trainee?" Marchand continued, turning back to Mags with a coaxing manner. "I understand you had a firsthand view of them during their stay at the Palace, and were instrumental in discovering that they were still in Haven." He smiled. "It's all fodder for work, of course. And while I am sure that you have already told others of my calling all about those events, a Bard is doing less than his duty if he fails to get the tale directly from those who lived it. The Dean of your Collegium himself advised that I speak directly to you when I enquired of the matter."

For a moment Mags wondered if that last was a lie. He wouldn't put anything past Marchand, if Marchand wanted something badly enough, including lying about whether Herald Caelan had actually sent him.

But . . . no, probably not. He might be self centered,

but he wasn't stupid, and it would be ridiculously easy for Mags to catch him in a lie, even if Mags was as dull as he was pretending to be. It was very likely he'd be caught out, in fact; Mags would certainly say something about it to Caelan the next time he saw the Dean. After all, Bard Marchand was wildly popular and wildly famous, and it would be natural for Mags to be flattered that he had been singled out, and just as natural to thank the Dean for the opportunity to meet the Bard.

Well, natural in Marchand's eyes, anyway.

:Humph. Indeed. He thinks the world is always watching him.:

:I'd like t' be watching th' back of him as he leaves, right now.:

The fastest way to be rid of him would be to tell him the bare, unvarnished truth in as few words as possible; use that veneer of stupid stolidity to Mags' advantage. Someone as dense as Mags wanted to seem would have little or no imagination, and might be so overwhelmed by the "honor" of Marchand's attention that he could only manage to get out simple sentences.

So that was what Mags did; keeping the tale spare, staring without comprehension when Marchand asked him things like "But what did you think of that?" or "But how did you feel?"

"Don't rightly know, Bard," would usually be his reply, as he would let a puzzled expression creep across his face.

This set him down in Marchand's mind as a singularly unimaginative, stolid country bumpkin, which suited Mags perfectly.

But it was painfully clear as the questioning continued, that Marchand also considered him to be, if not an actual "hero," certainly a proto-hero, and one with a great deal of potential. Precisely what Mags did not want him to think. Marchand kept dropping flattering little comments about how brave he was for one so young, and how he surely had a bright future ahead of him. There was no doubt in Mags' mind that Marchand was not going to be satisfied with this single encounter. He was trying to cultivate Mags.

And Mags kept saying things like "Eh, 'twas all Dallen," and "I didn' git a chance t' think, belike." And it didn't seem to help.

:I'll say this for him, his instincts are very good when it comes to spotting those who are likely to make good song-fodder,: Dallen admitted reluctantly. *:And even better for spotting those who can help him enlarge his own fame.:*

And when the conversation shifted to the new game of Kirball, it was obvious that Marchand's interest was not feigned—though he seemed less interested in the game itself than in the players. Mags was a Kirball champion, at least for now, which also made him a desirable—acquaintance?

:No,: Dallen said sourly. *:Acquisition. Marchand acquires people. People he thinks other people will want to know. I am afraid he has decided that you are a very desirable target, probably more for Kirball than for the business with the foreigners. The latter could have been due to mere happenstance, you being in the right place at exactly the right time, then acting like a Herald should.*

The former is something that is going to be popular, and if Marchand knows nothing else, he is superb at riding waves of popularity. Watch out, or he'll invite you to—:

"I am going to stage a small concert for just a few friends," the Bard said smoothly. "I'm sure you'd like to attend, and I am equally sure my friends would enjoy discussing this new game with you. I'm going to hold it tomorrow night, after the Court dinner."

Mags was about to open his mouth to come up with some excuse why he couldn't attend, when the Bard's next words stopped him dead.

"Lena is going to sing as well, aren't you, my dear?" the Bard said, as Lena nodded. "It's so important for a young Bardic student to get early exposure to audiences other than their friends and teachers. Good training for what is to come. There is nothing so important to a Bard as being able to gauge his audience within a few moments, ascertain what their mood is, and at need, what direction to steer that mood."

Lena looked so thrilled that she was going to be performing in the same venue as her father that Mags could not bear to mar that happiness in any way.

And Marchand surely knew that. He might not know that Mags had helped to steady Lena during her first contest, but he absolutely knew that Mags was one of Lena's best friends and steadfast supporters, and that Mags would never abandon her to face a room full of strangers on her own.

"We'll be glad to come, Amily an' me," Mags said then, deciding that if he was going to be blackmailed into this, he was going to make Marchand pay for it another way. *Snub Amily, ye smug peacock, I dare ye!* "Amily missed Lena's contest; she'll be a mort glad t' hear 'er sing now!"

Marchand was clearly taken aback, but there was no way now that he could just come out and say "but I only invited you" without looking unforgivably rude. "Good, then," he replied, plastering a smile on his face. "I'll be looking forward to seeing both of you. Right after Court dinner; it will be one of the rooms off the Great Hall. Lena can come and fetch you, so you don't get lost in the Palace."

Nice. Treat Lena like a servant, like ye treated me.

:Giving Lena no preparation time for her performance,: commented Dallen.

:'Cept we know her an' we know she'll hev prepped herself all day,: Mags replied. *:He really don't know her at all, does he?:*

:Not in the least.:

"Thank you, dear, for bringing me here and introducing me to your friend," Marchand continued. "Now I must be off, and you must go on to your classes. And I see that I was interrupting some work here, so I am sure I shouldn't continue to do so. Until tomorrow night!"

He turned with a flourish, and made an exit, with Lena pattering along beside and a little behind him, just like an obedient, devoted spaniel.

Amily bent her head over the papers for a moment, and it was clear she was furious. Finally she said something.

"Oh, that man."

It was more restrained than he expected.

"I don' like 'im, not one bit," Mags said, " 'E makes me skin crawl."

"Well, he is clear proof that talent and a Gift don't make you a wonderful person," Amily said sourly. "It makes me wish that there was a better way of selecting Bards than just judging what they can do. Someone like that should . . ." She paused, and then said, unexpectedly, "Do you know why he tries to humiliate my father every chance he gets? Did Father tell you?"

Mags shook his head.

:Oh, this could be interesting.: He felt Dallen settle back, waiting for the revelation.

:Yer a worse gossip than a old woman.:

:It's only gossip if you repeat it. Until then, it's gathering information.:

"Because many years ago, when they were both Trainees, my father was party to something that Marchand would really rather no one else knew." Her lips tightened. "And I shouldn't tell you this, and I wouldn't, except that you are in Father's confidence. What happened was that he was in the same room when Marchand was getting a dressing-down from the Dean of Bardic for some incredibly selfish thing he had done. Father never told me what it was, but given Marchand, he probably used his Gift to get something he wanted to the detriment of someone else."

"Like, usin' it t' hev his way wi' a servant, or somethin'?" Mags hazarded. He could easily imagine that. Anything from getting the servant to do something he wasn't supposed to, or finagling a girl into his bed.

Amily nodded. "Probably wenching," she said, confirming Mags' guess. "They were both about sixteen at the time. My father was the witness to it, so the Dean had him in the office to confirm the accusation. Whatever it was isn't important . . . what's important is that he did something that was in violation of Bardic ethics."

"It couldn' have been huge," Mags pointed out. Then hesitated. "Could it?"

"Well . . . that's the question. I mean, not life-threatening huge, but I would say very serious. The thing is that the Dean really lost his temper with Marchand, and told Marchand with Father there—" She paused, and closed her eyes, as if making sure of the memory. " 'The only reason we allow you to continue here is because, with a Gift as strong as yours, we dare not let you off our leash. You are like a dangerous animal, Trainee, but you are one of us by virtue of that Gift, and the Bardic Circle will not abandon their responsibilities in the matter of how you use that Gift. We will control you, Marchand, if you do not learn to control yourself and abide by the rule of ethics and law.' "

Mags felt his jaw dropping open with shock. Well, that explained a lot. "Anyone else know this?" he gasped.

"The Dean, who's dead now, Father, me, the King, Marchand himself, and now you," Amily said gravely. "Father told me and the King. I very much doubt the Dean told anyone. Marchand knows that as long as he stays just on the edge of the line, so to speak, my father won't ever say or do anything about what he knows. So he doesn't actually use his Gift to get things he wants directly, he just uses it to charm people into wanting to give him what he wants." She paused. "I don't think he's actually evil, just incredibly selfish. I don't think anyone matters to him except as a means to getting what he wants."

"Gah." Mags felt sick. "So thet's why he ain't in the Ruling Circle e'en though he's a Master Bard."

Amily nodded. "Exactly. He will never be on the Council or in the Ruling Circle. The King will always veto him. I don't know if anyone has ever guessed why for certain, but most of the high ranking Bards feel about him the way you do, and the plain fact is they all know he is far too selfish to ever be allowed real political power, because . . . he wouldn't actually abuse it as such, but he would never use it for anything other than what suited his own ends. His 'friends' are mostly what I would call patrons and admirers. In fact, I don't know that he actually has what I would call a real friend."

Mags pursed his lips thoughtfully. This really explained a lot. He knew that Lena's family was very well off, and it wasn't from any income that Marchand might bring in. "Lena's Mama?" he asked tentatively. "She one of those patrons, like? Thet why 'e married 'er?"

"Lena's mother has piles of money," Amily confirmed. "He charmed all of the family, married her, fathered Lena, and now only has to appear home for a few days a year to keep them all dazzled. Or so Father says. I don't see any reason to disagree with that."

Mags shook his head. "Gotta say, what wi' Lena's Pa an' Bear's folks, mebbe I ain't so bad off not hevin' a fambily."

Amily only sighed. "Then there is Master Soren, and

my father," she pointed out. "And Marc's family, Pip's family and Gennie's—more good than bad. Not all families are trouble . . . but I will admit, it does make me appreciate my own."

The East and West teams had played their first Kirball match yesterday, and the dining hall was still full of the babble of people talking the match over and comparing it to the North and South match. You could tell who was discussing the game—which was almost everyone—by the flailing arms and hand gestures. Everyone had an opinion. Bardic Trainees were clearly trying to figure out how to write songs about this. Mags overheard some comparisons between how he and Dallen had taken the North flag to how East Foot Kaven Lockertie had stolen the West flag. So far, the Fetching Gift hadn't even come into play, which didn't much surprise Mags. You'd have to be really, really good to make Fetching work in the middle of the scrum, and as for standing off on the side . . . the moment anyone spotted a Herald Trainee doing that, they would be on him in a heartbeat.

Mags had found that he had, indeed, enjoyed watching—perhaps even more than he had enjoyed playing. But the second full day of non-stop babble about it was beginning to pall, for there were only so many ways that you could replay the match in theory. He wasn't comfortable speculating about what the other teams could and could not do. He certainly wasn't comfortable with talking about his own abilities or lack of them. And he was very glad that Bear was talking about something else.

Bear's herbal medicine kit was coming along. The Healers in general were satisfied with his progress, and he was happy. Mags didn't understand more than half of what he was saying about it all, but it was obvious that things were going well, so he listened and contributed where he could.

Now the idea had expanded to placing one in every village that didn't have a Healer; nearly every village had a midwife or something of the sort, so that would be who would have the responsibility for keeping the kit safe and doling out the medicines.

"I'd worrit 'bout thet kit makin' people think they didn' need a Healer," he offered. "Y'know, jest tryin' one medicine after 'nother till it was too late."

"They do that now, without the kit around," Bear replied, shrugging. "Mostly the medicines and remedies they try are ineffective ones. But you're right to think that, the Healers' Circle debated it for almost a day before deciding it was going to do more good than harm. At least this way, the medicines they'll try are known to be effective, and known to be of standard strength, and not something like dead beetles and bat's blood pounded with the dung of a pregnant goat."

Mags stared at him, fascinated and appalled. "Yer jokin'. No? Thet's s'posed t' be a medicine?"

Bear grimaced. "Not only that, but one with a lot of people that swear by it. Thank the gods it's only supposed to be for going bald, and you are supposed to rub it in your scalp, not eat it. I don't want to think about how you'd stink when you were using it, or what it would do to a scalp wound."

"I'd be more like t' swear at it then swear by it." Mags shuddered. "An' here I thought yer messes was foul!"

Bear shrugged. "Right now I'm trying to work out how to dry that bread mold that works on wounds so that you can get it to sprout again. And how to describe exactly what it looks like so people know whether or not the right stuff sprouted. As it stands, the only way we have to get the stuff out is to take a live batch out by hand and cosset it the whole way."

Mags shook his head. "I dunno. Yarbs an' things, ye kin prolly get people t' believe on'y the stuff i' th' kit works right. But ye start sendin' out mold, an' people'll start thinkin' mebbe you was wrong an' them dried beetles'd work jest fine."

"That's a good point." Bear slowly chewed and swallowed. "I have a favor to ask. Think you could come give me a hand with the Lunatic?"

Mags blinked. This was—unexpected. "Aye but—how? I ain't a Healer nor a Mindhealer."

"Actually, that's the point. The Mindhealers don't want to get near him, I guess their shields aren't as good as yours, or else the way they have to work is completely without shields. When he talks, he doesn't speak Valdemaran, and that's a problem. Sometimes people who've gone mad actually make sense once you figure out what the meaning is behind what they are saying." Bear scratched his neck. "Am I making any sense here?"

Mags nodded. "I'm follerin' ye so far."

"I'm hoping with all your shields, you might be able

to get stuff leaked over that I can use to try and understand what's going on in his head." Bear sighed. "I've got him calmer now, at least. And he's put on a little weight. So we're more or less back to the point where he was during the blizzard."

"I'll give 'er a go," Mags said. "But I ain't promisin' nothin'." He felt a little uneasy saying even that much, but this was Bear, and he would do whatever he could to help out his friend.

He just wished he could have gotten hold of Nikolas to ask him about keeping Bear here. He was pretty certain that if Nikolas made the request, things would be sorted in a hurry.

He followed Bear back to Healers' Collegium, and into yet another part of the building he'd never been before. They entered by a different door than before, one tucked out of sight. Once inside, Bear took him through a pair of double doors at what must have been the other end of the big sickroom. This was a short section with a corridor that looked a lot like the one in the part of Heralds' Collegium that held the student rooms. Except the corridor was much narrower. He couldn't help but notice the very heavy doors to each room, the thick walls (as evidenced by the narrowness of the corridor), and the odd atmosphere of the place. It felt . . . as if everything was slightly wrong, somehow, as if what he was seeing was not what anyone else saw. That made no sense, on the face of it, but if the people kept here were all mad, well, maybe that was the literal truth; what they saw was nothing like what he was seeing.

Sounds were muffled, and the air felt—not stale, exactly, but as if it never moved.

"How many people ye got i' here?" he asked in a whisper. It felt as if he should whisper, as if there were things here he didn't want to wake up.

"Around ten. Most of them aren't as bad as Lunatic. Most of them we can help," said Bear with a sigh. "Not all of them. Got a woman who killed her babies, thinking they were demon-possessed. Now she knows they weren't, so now she keeps trying to kill herself. I don't know what they're going do about her. Husband wants her sent home so that she can kill herself. Says it's only fair, that she'd hang for murder now that she knows what she did, so we might as well let her hang herself. The Healers don't want that to happen, so they keep her here. She just keeps getting worse. Mindhealers can't do anything with her now."

Mags winced. "Nothin' good gonna come of that, no matter what. Keep 'er, turn 'er loose, whatever. Even if she stops tryin' t' kill herself, law might hang 'er."

"I know. Makes me glad I'm not a Mindhealer. Here we are." They stopped in front of one of the doors, and Bear took out a key to unlock it. "Not sure what you want to do, but based on how the Mindhealers reacted, I'd be careful about dropping shields."

:I can get them back up for you faster than you can for yourself,: said Dallen.

"Dallen reckons he kin help," Mags reported.

"Good, that's something the Mindhealers didn't have." Bear swung the door open and they went inside.

The room was absolutely stark and bare, although

Mags got the feeling that this was because of the occupant rather than some omission on the Healers' part. The only furnishings were a bed, a table, and two chairs. All were made of metal and bolted to the floor; the table and chairs were under the window, the bed pushed up against the wall. The walls were utterly smooth and featureless—if nails had been used to put them up, there was no sign of them, no way to pry one out of the wall and use it as a weapon or to harm yourself. Nevertheless, walls, floor, and ceiling were all a soft, soothing rose-ocher color, and someone had carefully painted wonderful designs on them in darker rose and cream. The single window in the wall had a metal grate with small holes in it bolted over it, protecting the thick glass panes from the occupant. It looked out over a bit of garden.

The foreigner was on the bed, at the head of it, curled up in the corner against the wall. His back was wedged into the corner, his arms were wrapped around his legs, and his chin was propped on his knees. He regarded them with unfocused and uninterested eyes.

"How are you doing today?" Bear asked. The man blinked once or twice, and mumbled something Mags couldn't make out. It didn't sound Valdemaran.

"You really need to try and speak a language I can understand," Bear said, gently. "I can't help you if I can't understand you."

The man muttered something else.

Mags wasn't getting anything at all from him through full shields, so, cautiously, he dropped the first one.

Very faintly, he began to sense something. Now, the

good thing about Mindspeech was that it was always in a language you understood—which only made sense, really, since it was thought to thought, and shouldn't need a translator. And right away, Mags understood why the Mindhealers hadn't wanted anything to do with this man, if it was true that they had to drop all their shields in order to treat him.

First, there was the dim sense of incredible fear. Then came the man's thoughts, which were, strangely enough, completely organized and circular. It was almost prayer-like, as if the repeating loop kept whatever the man was afraid of away.

The problem was, this was babble. Babble with an undertone of stark terror. Mags was getting that panicked fear even through very good shields, and Mindhealers tended to be Empaths, people who picked up emotions rather than thoughts. It would have been torture for them to encounter that much sustained terror, and then to have that babble running around in your head—assuming they were also Mindspeakers—well, he would have thrown up his hands and walked off too.

"... and all the things that are not there, they flock and fly and stare and stare, and all their eyes are big and bright and burn away the dark of night, and there is nowhere left to hide, they're everywhere, they get inside, and even though they are not there, they're watching watching everywhere, and more and more come every day, oh gods I wish they'd go away, and all the things that are not there, they flock and fly and stare and stare ..."

Mags got the thoughts just like that, as a kind of poem. Which ... maybe made sense, since almost all the books the foreigners had left behind them had been of poetry.

"He's babblin' about things that ain't there, how they stare at 'im and won't go 'way, how they've even got inside 'im," Mags reported with confidence. "Tha's basically it. Same thing, over an' over. I think he thinks th' words keep th' eyes outa his head. 'E's still seein' things w' eyes starin' at 'im, an' more of 'em all the time. 'E's jest scared 'bout to death."

"That's more than anyone else got from him," Bear said thoughtfully. "And—yes, unless I drug him to sleep, he's always frightened, his heart is always racing. So he's still on about the eyes. I don't think there's any doubt Lena was right. I am going to have to dig deeper in the Archives."

"Fer what?"

"Something that will shut off—well, whatever it is that he has that is attracting these things," Bear said.

Mags blinked at him. "Ye mean, ye think he ain't seein' things that ain't there, 'e's seein' things that are?"

"Best explanation I can come up with," Bear replied. "I've tried just about everything else that would shut down a hallucination. So what's left? They aren't hallucinations."

"Huh," said Mags.

They went out, leaving the poor man to his horde of invisible tormentors.

THE moment Mags woke up, he knew by the sinking feeling in his chest that there was trouble, and it was aimed at him. Again. And once he knew that, he could feel it all over again, that pressure of unfriendly, accusatory regard out there.

:Wha' happened whiles I was asleep?: he asked Dallen immediately. He squeezed his eyes closed, forcing down the nausea that this called up in him. Dear gods, he hated, hated this. In a way it was worse than anything he'd endured at the mine. There, at least, no one had actually hated him.

:The damned Foreseers had more of their visions,: Dallen replied with disgust. *:Still just as vague, except that one of them said he saw you, specifically, with your hands covered in blood, and nothing but you. And it was someone who'd come to see the Kirball game and knows what you look like, so we can't wonder if it is a case of mistaken identity. So it's all to do all over again.:*

Mags tightened his jaw. *:Dammit.:* He felt his spirits

sinking lower, felt that certainty that it just wasn't even worth getting out of bed anymore. *:Knew it couldn' last.:*

Maybe what he ought to do is just give in to the depression and curl up in bed and never get out again.

:That's all right, we'll weather this. Just do as you did before. Keep quiet and stick with the team. They all know you, better than anyone but me. You can do this, Mags, don't let these fools make you give up. As long as your team is around you, no one will do or probably even say anything.: If Dallen was picking up on his despair, the Companion wasn't actually addressing it directly.

:But they'll think it,: Mags replied, the nausea, the ache, all coming back. *:An' they'll talk about it behind m' back.:*

He got the sense that Dallen would like to help, but had no idea how to. It was the same old thing all over again, with the difference that this time he'd been "seen" with blood on his hands. Blood on his hands? Was it a metaphor? If it was, then in a sense every Herald had or would have blood on his hands. They were often responsible for life and death decisions. Their judgments condemned people. What they uncovered condemned people. Messages they carried condemned people.

And of course, they fought in battles alongside the Guard. That, after all, was what Kirball was about, preparation for war. So all Heralds would have blood on their hands, eventually.

For that matter, he'd already been responsible for people dying. There were the murdered mine kids he hadn't been able to prove were even dead. And most of all there was that crazy killer that had kidnapped Bear.

That man was dead literally at his hands. Who was to say that this so-called vision wasn't about the past rather than about the future?

It was so unfair.

For a long, long time he contemplated the idea of just not bothering anymore, of turning his face to the wall and telling the whole world to hang.

But . . . Dallen wouldn't let him. And anyway, if he just sank into depression and gave up, what would that do to Dallen? That would pile being unfair to the one creature that had always been good to him on top of the general unfairness of the universe.

He dragged himself out of bed reluctantly, and prepared to face the ordeal of breakfast.

It was not quite the ordeal it had been the first time all those wretched Foreseers had spread their stories, since the Trainees of his team had already gotten wind of what was up, and had filled in the others as they waited for Mags. But once again, he was getting the suspicious looks, and once again, certain folk who were dubious of anything that was not Valdemaran were allowing their prejudices free range.

How stupid was that? Why should where your parents came from have anything to do with whether you were a good or a bad person? Especially when you couldn't even remember them?

Unfairness piled on top of unfairness.

He managed to get through the day, unconsciously taking that hunched-over, defensive, hunted posture the whole time. He didn't even realize what he was doing until he straightened up for Kirball practice and felt his muscles unkink. But that didn't stop his mind from sending his body right into that same posture again once practice was over.

Over the next two days, things remained the same, with the same waking-to-sleeping tension. The only good thing was that the weather was warming up enough that when he wasn't in class or at practice, he could study out of doors. So that was where he took his books and stayed until there wasn't enough light to read by, hidden in some little cluster of bushes in Companion's Field. That kept him out of his room in the stable, where he would sense the thoughts of everyone who came near the stable.

It was very peaceful out there. Any sounds from the Palace and Collegia were muffled, any spilled-over thoughts too distant to bother him.

Actually, it was more than peaceful—even though it was a bit lonely. Still, he'd always been lonely, and only during the past half-year had he been anything but lonely. You just didn't make friends at the mine. Even the kiddies he'd sporadically helped hadn't been friends.

As he packed up his books to go back to his room and try to sleep, he thought about that. This time last year, he was at the mine. He remembered very well how he had welcomed the warmth after the killing cold, and welcomed other things too—because spring meant all sorts of things were edible that were not, later. And if you could get away into some of the forest around the mine and you knew what to look for, you could find them.

Strange how last spring he had been as close as he ever got at the mine to being happy. But he'd had a belly full of greens almost every night, and back at the mine, a full belly meant you were happy. Lion's-tooth was sweet when it first came up, not bitter, and it was one of the heartiest weeds there was, so there was a lot of it. Cattail root was delicious, but impossible to harvest in the winter unless you wanted your feet frozen solid, and you had to be sure you were getting it, and not water iris, which was poisonous. There were tiny wild onions too, mushrooms (though you had to be careful of those as well), sorrel, the tips of birch twigs, brooklime, clover, cow-pea, mustard, violets, pigweed, sow-thistle, jewelweed, shepherd's purse, pokeberry, plaintain, knotweed, and very young nettles. There were other things you could eat if they were cooked, but how could any of the mine-slaves get a fire, much less a pot? So they had to confine themselves to what could be eaten raw.

With so many years of mine workers foraging nearby, there were no berries within a reasonable distance of the mine, and the most obviously edible things were also long ago grubbed up and eaten. But if you knew what you were looking for and you were prepared to graze like a goose, spring was the one season when you could actually go to sleep with a full belly if you could slip away for a while.

Now, this spring, he could sleep with a full belly every night—if only his belly wasn't so knotted up with tension that it was hard to eat anything at all. Such irony.

As one day turned into another, he found the Field to be his new sanctuary, safer even than his room or the Heraldic Archives.

As he would sit studying, sometimes his attention would be taken by one of the things he would immediately have pounced on and devoured this time last year, and he was reminded that no matter how uncomfortable things were, they were so much better than they could have been. He might not have survived this past winter. Even if he had, right now he would have been half starved, always tired, always afraid.

But it was hard, very hard, to try to keep his spirits up. The constant weight of unfriendly regard on him wore his spirit down.

It was harder still to have to come to meals and the occasional study session with Bear, and see poor Lena. Lena had gone from bright and happy—even if her happiness had a false cause, it was real happiness—to crushed and bewildered.

That first little "informal concert" had been the last that Mags had been invited to. And, he supposed, the last that Lena had been invited to participate in. With the dark stories in the wind again, Bard Marchand had pulled back from Mags abruptly, not even acknowledging that he knew the Trainee if they happened to cross paths. And that meant Lena was no longer of any use to him. She didn't say anything, but Mags could tell, by the way she drooped and looked forlorn, that her father had once again abandoned her as well as Mags.

He actually felt worse for her than he did for himself.

He wouldn't have said anything to Lena about it, though, but Bear brought it up. Actually, Bear brought it up several times and finally, one night, wouldn't let go, asking her "What's wrong?" until she finally answered.

"I never see Father anymore," she said unhappily. "I don't know why, or what I did to offend him but I never see him at all now, and he doesn't reply to my notes."

And again, Mags wouldn't have said anything, but Bear had evidently had enough of this. He got that stubborn look on his face, pushed his lenses up on his nose with one finger, and leaned over the table.

"He won't see you because Mags is in people's bad books again, and therefore, Mags isn't on the list of people he looks good knowing," Bear said, bluntly. "All he ever wanted was to meet up with Mags and make it look as if Mags was a friend of his. You were nothing more than his way to get to Mags easily. He just doesn't care about you, Lena; all he ever cared about was that everyone would know that he knew the Kirball star and the hero of the hour, because he collects people like that just to get an advantage."

Lena turned shocked eyes on him. "How—why would you say such a thing?" she cried, looking as if she was about to cry. "Father never—Father wouldn't—he's a famous Bard, why would he do something like that?"

Mags sighed. He couldn't leave Bear to take this one alone. "He's sayin' it 'cause it's true," he said. "Nobody wanted t' tell ye, but thet's what he's like."

Lena looked from him, to Bear, and back again, stricken dumb.

"Lena, what has he ever done for you, for your family, besides remind them once a year how lucky they are that he married into your house?" Bear urged. "Where does his money come from? Your family, and whatever gifts he gets from his patrons. Does he ever send any of that back? No. Who got you your first music lessons? Him? No. Your ma. Who saw to it that a Bard heard you play and sing so you could get sent here, him? You'd think that would be natural, wouldn't you, once he found out you were a musician? But no. It wasn't him, it was your grandpa, you told us that yourself. Had he ever heard you sing and play before you got here? No."

"Did 'e even recognize ye when 'e sent me off on that errant?" Mags added softly. "Not thet I noticed. In fact, you was pretty upset 'bout it at th' time, an fer a goodly while after. I' fact, you was upset 'bout it right up till he started payin' 'tention to ye. Aye?"

Bear took Lena gently by the shoulders and shook her a little. "Lena, think. Think about it. Haven't you felt him using the Gift on you a little, and using his personality on you a lot, to get you to forget all that? Haven't you felt him pressing you to worship him the way Amily worships her pa?" He didn't let her answer; he looked at Mags instead.

:Tell her I have,: Dallen said sadly. *:Of course, that is unethical, but he used his Gift so little that he could always claim he didn't realize he was doing it because he wanted his daughter's regard back. And he would probably be believed.:*

"Dallen says he has," Mags told her. " 'Cept, of course, Amily's pa deserves thet sorta worship, aye? Ye jest have'ta see 'im with her, how much he takes care'a her, how he makes sure she's all right afore he goes an' does things. Mebbe he gotta think'a Valdemar an' th' King first, but he makes sure someone is lookin' out fer Amily. Like Master Soren an' Lydia. Yer pa? He ever make sure ye got so much as a spare harpstring? He ain't done nothin' t' deserve nothin' from ye, if ye was t' ask me. He never done nothin' t' get ye here, an' aside of that one concert, never done nothing for ye when ye got here. Never made sure you was all right. Never made sure there was someone t' watch out fer ye."

"You have the Gift too, Lena," Bear urged. "Use it! Shake off what he did to you and see him!"

A hundred emotions, all negative ones, chased themselves across Lena's face—and then her face crumpled, she buried it in her hands, and sobbed.

"I thought he loved me!" she wept into her hands. "I thought he finally loved me."

Both Bear and Mags made a move to hold her; Mags pulled back and gestured to Bear to comfort her. Pushing his lenses up on his nose, he pulled her into his shoulder and let her sob.

"One day someone is going to not get charmed and beat the stuffing out of him," Bear said, in a growl. "And the sooner that day comes, the better. But let me tell you something, Lena. One day, when people say 'Bard Marchand,' it will be you they are thinking about and not him. And one day, when someone says 'Tobias Marchand,' others will wrinkle their foreheads and say, 'Don't you mean Lena?' and they'll have to be reminded that Tobias happened to be the father of the really, truly famous Bard Marchand."

Mags nodded in silent agreement.

"Families," Bear added, in tones that indicated that something more had shortened his temper than just having to work with difficult patients.

"Wha's got ye riled?" Mags asked.

Bear sighed. Lena sobbed on, oblivious to what they were saying. Well, Mags couldn't blame her. This was a horrible blow to her. Here she thought her father had finally noticed her, was impressed by her, and had come to love her. The fact that all these emotions had been created in her by her father in order to manipulate her was probably unbearable right now.

"Got a letter from my family," he growled. "My brother's turning up. Head of the Sweetwater House of Healing, if you please, and he's going to demand that I do my duty to the family, come home, and get married on Midsummer and start spawning babies. They still haven't given up on that."

Lena's sobs were easing off. She sniffed wetly and Bear offered her a scrap of clean cloth. She took it, pulled away from him, and he reluctantly let her go.

"M-maybe you just ought to go along with that for a l-little," she said, with a faint stammer. "At least your family cares about you, and if you just give them what they want for a moon or two, you can come back here—"

"I don't want that girl," Bear snarled, sounding startlingly like his namesake. "I don't love her! I am not going to get shackled up to some girl I hardly know just so my parents can be grandparents, and it's not as if they aren't already, because they are. If I marry anyone, it's going to be someone I love and would do anything for, not someone my parents picked out because they're neighbors! Someone like—" he paused. "Never mind. It just won't be her."

Lena stared at him, startled by his vehemence. He looked down at his hands. "Sorry. That kind of just jumped out."

"Nothin' t' be sorry fer," Mags offered. He shook his

head. "Sometimes it seems like we all oughta just run away from here, an'—an' that's when I run out, cause I dunno what we'd do t' keep ourselves fed an' housed up."

"I could always be an animal Healer," Bear said sourly. "At least animals are always grateful to you. Nobody thinks you're second-rate because you treat them with medicine instead of a Gift. Animal Healers are always in demand."

"I could be a traveling minstrel," Lena answered, wiping her eyes and blowing her nose. "I'm good enough for that right now. Maybe we should do that. Run away and do that. Show them all."

Mags shrugged. "I got nothin'. All I know's mine work. Jest end up i' the same situation, jest wi' a better master. Mebbe. I misdoubt Master Cole was th' on'y mine owner t' treat 'is miners thet way."

And Lena sighed. "Traveling minstrels starve a lot," she said forlornly. "And my father still wouldn't notice or care."

"Well then," Bear said stolidly. "No running away."

They all sighed, and looked at one another.

As Mags made his way back to his room in the stable that night, he resolved one thing. He was going to at least ask King's Own Nikolas if he could help Bear.

If, of course, he could ever see the man.

He decided to take the bull by the horns—or at least, the heifer. He was going to help Amily that evening, since Nikolas hadn't shown up at his room or even given any indication that he was *ever* going to continue the lessons again, so he would ask the one person who surely *knew* where her father was.

"Lissen," he said, before they got down to work. "Gotta ast ye somethin'."

She raised her eyes to look at him. "Of course," she replied.

"I need t' see yer Pa. Nikolas," he said, looking her in the eyes.

She looked away, but laughed, though it wasn't exactly the laughter of someone who was hearing a joke. "We all need to see him," she told him, still not looking at him. "He has become a phantom. I know he's still here in Haven, because dirty plates and filthy uniforms appear in our rooms and have to be taken away, but I haven't actually seen him personally in the last few days."

Ever since th' new set' a visions, Mags thought bleakly. *Aye, that figgers. Bet he reckons it's me after all an' he's tryin' t' find a way t' stop me.*

"Well, when ye do, tell 'im I need t' see 'im?" he pleaded. "It's pretty important."

"If I see him I will," Amily replied, looking uneasy, and maybe a little guilty. "But sometimes he does this and I don't see him for—well, once it was for three moons."

Well that would be a bit too late . . .

But it would be ungracious to act like a boor about it. Amily couldn't help what her father thought or did. "All right," he replied. "Thenkee. Now, hand me my share, aye?"

She did so, and he couldn't help but note that her hand was shaking a little as she did it.

Bear's place at lunch was empty.

For a moment, Mags had the crazy thought that Bear's brother had arrived and essentially kidnapped his sibling—but no, that wouldn't be possible, would it? Surely no one here would allow that.

:Dallen?: he asked first, before voicing the question aloud.

:No clue,: the Companion replied. *:Let me ask some of the others—though, mind you, we usually don't know what's going on up at Healers' Collegium. They have good shields and don't leak much.:*

"Anybody know where Bear is?" he asked aloud. His only response was headshakes.

Well, there was no point in worrying about it. Bear was often called away; this was probably just another one of those times.

They were almost done with the meal when Bear turned up, finally, looking bad. Ragged. He dropped down into his seat and stared dully at his empty plate, a plate which Gennie and Mags took, filled with the left-overs and shoved in front of him.

"Eat!" said Gennie.

"He's dead," Bear said, mechanically picking up a

fork and getting a mouthful. "I don't understand it. He just . . . died. He shouldn't have died. I was crazy-careful about dosages and combinations. I tested everything on myself first—"

He stopped, as if he had said too much. No one else seemed to notice the gaff, they were all staring at him in puzzlement.

"Who died?" Halleck asked.

"Lunatic," Bear said dully. "The crazy foreigner. I just don't understand it. I thought I had his fear and his heart rate under control. He was fine last night. I made sure he took everything. The new stuff I gave him was working, at least I think it was, there were moments when he was even coming out of that fear-fit he was in . . ."

"Oh, him." Halleck shrugged. "Bear, I know he was your patient, and you have to feel bad about that, and I know that the senior Healers trusted him to you to treat, but face it, they only did that because they couldn't do anything with him. They'd already given up on getting him sane, and everyone else had given up on getting any information out of him. So it's not as if it's a tragic loss . . ."

Halleck trailed off, seeing that he wasn't getting through to Bear.

Mags knew why. Entirely apart from the fact that Bear took the care of every patient he had very seriously, there was the implication that his skills were nowhere near as sharp as he and everyone else had thought. Failure put him one step closer to being hauled home, and his brother was due here any day.

And Mags hadn't exactly done anything about getting Nikolas to intercede for him.

Of course, that was because Nikolas wasn't anywhere to be found, but that was beside the point. He hunched over a little with guilt, and finished his lunch in a hurry.

"'M sorry, Bear," he mumbled as he got up to leave. "I don' think 'twas yer fault, if thet means anythin'."

Bear didn't even look up.

Mags heard the shouting long before he got to Healers' Collegium. One voice was Bear's; the other was very like Bear's, just deeper. The accent was even the same, which pretty much identified who it was.

Bear's brother was here.

". . . and now you see what happens when you think you can muck around with midwife potions and try to do what only a skilled and Gifted Healer can!" shouted the deeper voice. "You are in way over your head, Bear! We should never have allowed you to come here; you let a few early successes go to your head and they made you think you could actually do what only a real Healer can, and now you see the result! You managed to kill a valuable asset to the Crown!"

Mags hesitated. Should he leave? He had no right to listen to this.

But he couldn't seem to make his feet move.

"I didn't—"

"Bah, don't tell me that, I know you, I can read you like a Mindspeaker. Even you think you killed him!" There was steel in that voice, the steel of someone who was absolutely certain he was in the right, and no one was going to tell him any differently. "It's time you stopped mucking about with potions and accepted your responsibility to the family. You are coming home and getting married. If you want to spend your time dosing animals when you get there, fine. But no more of this 'herbs can replace a Healer' idiocy. Good gods, that medicine chest notion—that is appalling! How many more people do you want to kill with that?"

"They'd die anyway," Bear shouted back. "At least this way they have a chance!"

"You don't know that! In fact, it's far more likely that they wouldn't die without all those leaves and roots, because they would be wise and send for a Healer right away, instead of mucking about with beans and flowers until it's too late for a real Healer to save them!"

"The Circle—"

"The Circle will see it my way after this," the brother said, scornfully. "Killing a patient tends to make them wake up and take the blinkers off. So you just resign yourself to doing what you are told for a change. And start packing. There's going to be a wedding at Midsummer if I have to drag you to the altar tied up."

Silence, the slamming of a door, then the sound of something breaking.

Slowly, carefully, Mags approached the door to Bear's conservatory. He tapped gingerly on the window.

Bear opened the door, and glared at him. "I suppose you overheard all that," he snapped. The young Healer Trainee was disheveled and red-faced with anger. His hair looked like a bird had made a nest in it.

"I gotta think yer whole Collegium overheard thet," Mags said tentatively.

Bear snorted.

"I—" Mags hesitated. "I dunno what I kin do t' help—"

Bear exploded. "Well you should have thought of that when I first told you about it. You should have gone to Herald Nikolas and gotten him to help me! But no, you selfish pig, all you could think about was being a Kirball hero and how persecuted you are, and making everyone feel sorry for you."

That was so unjust it took Mags' breath away.

Bear had clearly worked himself up into a towering temper. "It's all about you, isn't it? It's always all about you, the incredible savage mine-orphan who now gets invited to private Bardic concerts and hobnobs with the King's Own! The big champion of some stupid game that somehow makes him a hero!" Bear's eyes were dark and furious. "And now here you are, all so hurt and persecuted because a couple of idiots have a bad dream, and a couple more idiots believe it, and now everyone feels sorry for you and tries to make you feel better and they don't give a hang about what's happened to the rest of us while you mope around feeling so sorry for yourself!"

Mags could only stand there, stunned, his chest getting tight, and his throat getting choked.

"Meanwhile, people who are actually running themselves ragged doing things to try and help people are told they're useless and fools, and they're going to kill people, and they just have to come home and stop mucking about with mudpies and take care of sheep and goats, because no one cares if a sheep or a goat dies!"

Mags opened his mouth, but nothing came out. His words felt cut off in his throat. Bear glared at him, and the look in Bear's eyes was very like hatred.

"The hell with you!" Bear shouted. "You can't even be bothered to help a friend! I hope—I hope—oh bah!"

He slammed the door in Mags' face.

Mags blinked, feeling a welter of emotion rising in him. Anger, because nothing about that was true or justified. Indignation.

But mostly grief. Now even Bear had abandoned him. How alone did that make him?

He wanted to wrench the door open and give Bear back as good as he'd gotten—but he couldn't think of anything to counter what Bear said. *You don't know what I've been trying to do for you*—well, yes, but there was only his word for that, and it was pretty clear that Bear would just think he was lying. *I never wanted any attention*—well, Bear clearly didn't believe that now, and saying so wouldn't change anything.

How long had this been festering inside his friend? Or . . . not friend anymore.

He wanted to turn to Dallen for comfort, but what if Bear was right? It didn't feel to him like Bear was right, but how would he know? And would Dallen actually tell him, or just make soothing noises?

Amily wouldn't talk to him now, except about commonplaces. His teachers were avoiding anything but their subjects with him. The team never talked about anything but Kirball around him. Now Bear—

And Nikolas. Had Nikolas really vanished? Or was he only "invisible" to Mags?

He had to think the latter.

That meant the only real friend he had left, apart from Dallen, was Lena, and now that Lena knew her father had only used her to get to Mags, how could she ever want to stay friends with him? Worse still, once Bear told her that Mags hadn't lifted a finger to help him stay, why would she want to stay friends with him?

She wouldn't, of course.

Who would?

:I would.: The depression in Dallen's mind-voice took him aback. *:Mags, you are not a bad person. I believe that there is a good explanation for what the Foreseers saw. I do not believe that you would ever harm the King, or anyone that didn't try to hurt you or your friends first. I believe that you have done all that was in your power to help Lena and Bear, and all your friends. I believe that.:*

:You're 'bout the only one, then,: Mags couldn't help but respond.

There was a long pause. *:Unfortunately . . . you may be right.:*

THERE was no practice today, and the members of the team had scattered to the four winds to enjoy their free day in picnics and trips to the market in Haven and other enjoyable pursuits.

Bear was not speaking to him. At all. Last Mags had heard, the Healers' Circle had not bent to the will of Bear's brother nearly as readily as that worthy had assumed they would, but there were certainly some questions about Bear's dosages and skill with herbs and willingness to call in help. And a thorough investigation was underway concerning the Lunatic's death. Of course, none of this satisfied Bear in the least, or did anything to keep his brother from insisting that he was going back home.

Amily was nowhere to be found. She had not shown up in the Archives for three days running, and when Mags had dared to try the quarters that she and her father shared, the servants said she had been gone for that long. She often went to stay with Lydia when her father was absent, so they told him. But at this point he was not at all certain of any sort of welcome at Master Soren's house either, so he didn't even try to find her there.

Lena, so the disapproving proctor said, had closed herself in her room again and wasn't speaking to anyone. Mags couldn't tell if the proctor disapproved of him, of Lena closing herself off from everyone and half-starving herself because she was unhappy, or felt he was to blame for her behavior. Maybe all three.

Right now, less than a candlemark to sunset, Mags was standing on the stone bridge over the Terilee River, watching the water rush by beneath him, and wondering despondently if drowning hurt very much. Drowned people looked peaceful. Well, except for the staring eyes.

:Yes,: Dallen said, interrupting his morose thoughts. *:Yes it does. Very much.:*

He sighed. *:Cain't find nothin' quick or thet doesn't hurt. Them flyspeck 'shrooms hurt a lot too. And so does water iris. There ain't no cliffs 'round here t' toss myself off, they closed up Bell Tower so ye cain't throw yerself outa there, on'y th' Palace towers're tall 'nuff, an' no chance me getting' inta one'a them towers . . . :*

:Stop that,: Dallen ordered, desperately. *:Don't talk like that. You aren't going to drown yourself or throw yourself off a tower or eat poison. You are my Chosen and we have each other. We will get through this.:*

Right now he was so far from imagining how they would that not even Dallen could persuade him. *:Ye heard? They're talkin' 'bout Black Companions again. An' 'bout Black Heralds. Ev' crazy idea they had afore, they got goin' now, an' people're startin' t' think 'bout* *takin' 'em all serious. Someone's even floatin' the ideer that there's some kinda second soul'r somethin' in me, an' it's hidin' behind me an' controllin' me an you. People are listenin'. An'—:*

He couldn't go on. And it wasn't as if Dallen wasn't already aware of this. What Mags knew, he knew, and he probably knew a lot more than Mags did. In fact, he was starting to spend an awful lot of time by himself in Companion's Field, as if even the other Companions were starting to doubt him and his Chosen.

:Ye'd be better off w'out me,: he said dully. *:Go Choose someone else. Ain't nobody'd miss me, and plenty'd be happy t' get rid'a a big problem. An' I know damn well ye kin Choose agin, specially if I'm so bad rotten. It's all right there i' those Archives an' Reports I been sortin' through.:* He felt his throat closing up. *:Hellfires, I'm startin' t' believe all them stories.:*

:Don't be ridiculous! You are not bad! Look at everything you've done; it was all to help people!:

:Reckon Bear 'n Lena'd argue wi' ye.:

:Exercise,: Dallen said desperately. *:We need something to take our minds off this. The Kirball field will be empty. Let's take the fastest run we can over that. A hard workout, the sort of thing we can't do with the team.:*

Mags was about to object, then sighed. He just didn't have the will to fight Dallen on this. It wouldn't help anything, but it wouldn't hurt anything either, and it might exhaust both of them enough so that their minds stopped spinning in the endless circle of "we have to prove we're innocent, but it hasn't happened yet, so how can we prove we're innocent, but we have to prove we're innocent . . ." Mags was irresistibly reminded of the poor Lunatic's mind, and how it kept going round and round the same cycle of words.

Aye an' mebbe tha's what makes me snap an' kill the King. That would be an irony of monumental proportions—that the very suspicion and hostility that was being heaped on him was what would cause him to lose his mind and turn into some sort of insane killer. So the people that were the ones convinced he would do this thing in defiance of all logic and past behavior would be the very ones to make him into the monster that would do it in the first place. He thought about trying to put that to someone in authority—

But who? Nikolas had vanished, the King certainly wouldn't see him, Herald Caelan was only the head of the Collegium, not someone who had any sort of say in what went on outside it. And anyone else would likely laugh at him, or think that this was yet more evidence of his unstable—or evil—nature.

Well, being exhausted would not be bad. And although there was no way he was going to go into the Collegium and take a hot bath afterward, it was just warm enough to do the same thing in one of the Field ponds without freezing to death. Plus, if he put a hot brick in his bed to warm it up, the combination of being chilled from the bath and the exhaustion and getting into a warm bed would put him right to sleep.

Mind, that would do nothing about the nightmares. He hadn't had a night that was free of them since all this started. And the last of Bear's nightmare potion was long gone. Even if anyone else at Healers' Collegium had known how to make it, the question was whether he was going to trust them enough to drink something they'd concocted. Bear was very popular among the Healers, and while they might have some qualms about his skills, they had none about his personality, and very little about his right to be here. They probably all blamed him for not using his influence on Nikolas too.

So would he trust something that had been made by someone who wanted to punish him?

Prolly not. They'd be as like t' give me somethin' that made the nightmares worse. Or jest somethin' t' give me a bellyache.

But he'd heard worse ideas than Dallen's. *:All right. But it's gettin' on t' twilight. It'll be hard for ye t' see. I don' want ye to hurt yersel', strain a tendon or summat. That'd jest be the end. Team'd never forgive me.:*

Dallen's mind-voice was full of relief. *:All the better to simulate, oh, a battle that's going long, a sneak attack by the enemy on our camp, or—oh, something else going wrong around twilight. I'll be able to see well enough. Besides, we know that field like I know my stall; we could probably run it in a night of moon-dark.:*

:All right,: Mags agreed reluctantly. *:I'll come saddle ye. If'n thet's what ye really want.:*

He left the bridge and trudged down to the stable, and selected a saddle and bridle from among Dallen's neatly-stored tack. It should be neatly stored. He'd spent enough time cleaning, mending and putting it away today. He didn't actually saddle Dallen so much as strap on a very light riding pad, meant to keep Companion and Chosen from chafing each other, and as close to riding bareback as you could come. And, as usual, the special bitless bridle, light and well worn and comfortable as bridle made of ribbon for him.

Dallen was impatient, and instead of walking, they galloped down to the Kirball field, where already the setting sun was turning things a bright red-gold. There was no one there, not even one of the groundskeepers. This, of course, was exactly what Mags wanted. No one around. He relaxed a very little. Not much, but a little.

:Is there a particular route and obstacle set you want to take?: Dallen asked, dancing in place to loosen up his hocks and warm up his muscles.

:Yer choice,: Mags replied, settling himself in Dallen's saddle, in the one place in which he still felt at home. *:You were the one that wanted t' do this, so, you figger out what ye wanta do. I'm jest the baggage.:* He hunched himself down low over Dallen's neck, and rested part of his weight in the lightweight stirrups so that he could shift it at a moment's notice.

The instant that Dallen sensed he was ready, he gathered himself and launched himself at one of the goals as if he had seen a starting flag go down. Mags shifted his weight smoothly as Dallen dodged imaginary foes and headed for the goal at his top speed.

He didn't gallop up and down the ramp, either; he repeated the move that had won them the North flag, making a huge, straining leap for the top of the goal, managing to scramble up it anyhow as Mags shifted his weight practically over the Companion's neck, whipping around on his hindquarters and leaping back down again.

From there, it was a high-speed scramble over the hillocks of "the bad side." Mags kept in tune with him, shifting his weight to assist as they plunged toward the other goal. Dallen glanced to the side; Mags felt the turn coming. Dallen pivoted to the right, jumped down into a gully and scrambled up the other side like a goat. At the top he leapt into the air and did the sort of kick-out that he would do if there were soldiers right behind them. Warhorses did this sort of thing too, but they had to have the signal from their riders. Companions didn't need signals because they could think, but they did need to be perfectly in tune with their Chosen so that the human wouldn't fall off or otherwise botch the maneuver.

Mags rode it out as easily as if he was sitting on a chair.

When Dallen came down again, he flung himself at top speed at the ramp, galloping up to the top and back down again, then wheeled and did it again, wheeled and did it a third time, coming to an abrupt halt on the top of the goal where the flag would be. There he reared and hopped forward three steps, flailing with his forehooves the entire time—nasty strokes that would bash in the face and helm of anyone foolish enough to be in front of him. Mags clung to his back like a burr, and with a mad leap they were off again.

This time it was a bit of steeplechase, with Dallen running neck-or-nothing at every obstacle in the field, and vaulting it cleanly, no matter how wrongly he came at it. They zig-zagged over the field that way, ending up back at their start, where he leapt and releapt the highest hedge in the field, a bit of brush that had been there long, long before this section of the grounds had been made into the Kirball field. He was over and over it four times like a goat or a rabbit, then wheeled as neat as you please and made for the boundaries.

This time it was a straight run along the fences, so close that Mags' leg brushed the wood. Not that there were no obstacles here—no, there were ditches and gullies to leap or scramble through, those wretched hillocks to negotiate, bits of fence and hedge to get around or over. But this was good practice for war as well as Kirball. Horses didn't like fences, and running along one had the strong potential of making them spook, or at least nervy.

The only things that there weren't here on the Kirball field, things that you might find on a bad piece of ground, were big boulders. Even the goals were made of stuff that looked like stone, but wasn't. This was because accidents happened, and a horse or a Companion running full tilt into rock would be dead, and maybe Rider or Trainee with him. There was turf, there was dusty dirt and mud and soft sand, but there was no rock anywhere in the field, except for pebbles in the bottoms of the gullies. And even those were softened by sand.

The full circuit of the boundary they went, and Dallen was just fully warm now, with maybe half a candlemark or more of this in him. Mags was sweating, but somewhere in the back of his mind he knew that Dallen had been right, that this was exactly what they needed to do to get their minds clear, at least for a little bit.

The last light of the sun was gone, and the blue dim of

twilight on them. Mags felt Dallen decide for a gully scramble, taking the field as he had before, but the "low road" rather than the high, running through the ditches and gullies instead of leaping them. Dallen wheeled and made for the nearest, which was barely big enough to fit them. Mags felt the walls of the ditch brush his legs, and made himself even smaller on Dallen's back.

Up and out of the ditch, and then down into the next, along it for three lengths until it ended and then up and down into a twisting bit of natural run-off gully with better sides but worse footing.

Dallen gathered himself, leapt and came down again in a third ditch, scrambled along it and scrambled out again at the end.

He wheeled, intending to execute an uphill leap and scramble, taking an obstacle the opposite way from what was intended, starting low and ending high. It was a mad maneuver for a horse, only slightly less mad for most Companions, but Mags knew this of old, and was ready for it.

And a blow to his mind knocked all sense and all preparation out of him

It was a scream of incredible rage, hate, loathing—a howl that was only mental, but nevertheless it was like a dagger through the eyes.

Mags' mind had brushed up against something murderous, so vicious it was like a swipe of razor-sharp claws across his mind. He cried out without meaning to, and the thing was gone, but the damage was done. Dallen had been caught and thrown off in mid-stride; he came down wrong on his leap, blundered and slipped, felt himself toppling, felt Mags about to go head-first into the ditch where he would surely break his neck.

Mags felt the jump go wrong, felt Dallen falling out from under him, knew he was not balanced at all, could not get his balance and saw his own death coming at him too fast to stop.

Then Dallen somehow flung himself over sideways. Mags found a balance-point, instinctively kicked himself free of the stirrups and tumbled off to the side.

Just as he heard the terrible double crack of both of Dallen's forelegs breaking, and felt as well as heard Dallen's scream of agony. He convulsed. Dallen, thank the gods, was paralyzed by the pain.

He screamed too, mentally as well as physically, dropping all his shields and shrieking a mindless call for help.

He scrambled on hands and knees to Dallen and weeping, sat on Dallen's shoulder so he wouldn't thrash, clasping his hands around the breaks to make sure they didn't get worse. He could feel the bones grating under his hands, but they hadn't broken the skin.

And meanwhile, he screamed for help, again and again, until his mind felt as raw as his throat. Dallen was voiceless now, mentally as well as physically, paralyzed by the pain, his sides heaving and his breath wheezing through clenched teeth.

This was a killing injury for a horse; any horse that had broken both legs like this, unless he was extraordinary indeed, would be put down. They'd done that to one of the mine ponies once, even though Master Cole was a man who would have—and did—work his ponies until their hooves were worn down to the frog and their hocks and knees were as swollen as ripe squash.

Finally, after what must only have been a few heartbeats, but felt like an eternity, rescuers swarmed the field. A flood of lanterns poured down the hill from the Collegia, people shouting at one another to "get this" and "bring that." They leaped the fence and completely overran the two on the ground, shoving Mags carelessly off Dallen. He stood up and was further shoved off to the side, and kicked when he didn't move fast enough.

Healers were there first, and in moments had shunted much of Dallen's pain away, blocking the part of his mind that felt it. When the pain had been eased, they grabbed his forelegs in the light of the lanterns, and the bones were quickly aligned properly and roughly splinted to keep everything in place.

Mags shut down his shields, hugged himself, and shivered, weeping without any shame. All he could think about was Dallen, and how this surely was all his fault. He should have been smart enough to see this was a bad idea . . .

His eyes poured hot tears; he could scarcely breathe, his chest hurt so much. He would have given anything to take the last candlemark back.

More men came running, bringing a huge pieces of wood and metal, and more lights. Once they could see, they assembled an enormous frame of beams and bars and pulleys, while the Healers continued to keep Dallen eased. Some of the rescuers dug under Dallen's body to slip a sling under him, then bit by painful bit he was hoisted up until there was no weight resting on his legs at all and he dangled from the frame like a trussed chicken in a market.

Now two of the huge, patient horses that hauled enormous carts were brought up; they normally towered over Dallen by a good four to six hands. His sling was fastened to their harness, so that they carried his weight; he was let down off the frame so that they carried him between them, like two men carrying an injured fellow between them on a stretcher. They moved off; Mags followed, speechless with grief and guilt.

Behind them, the men disassembled the frame as quickly as they had put it together. The sound of hammers followed them up the hill.

They made their way, step by painful step, toward Healer's Collegium. It took another eternity, and every step was as painful to Mags as if he walked on knives, as if it was his legs that were broken, and not Dallen's.

He wished that they had been. He wished with all his might that Dallen had not saved him.

:No . . . : came the gasping mind-voice feebly. *: . . . was worth it . . . :*

But this was all his fault! He knew that going that hard and fast over the course was bad enough by day, and yet he had agreed to it! And it had been his mind that the Other had brushed against! He was too open, it was his fault, he must have let some shields down without realizing it. It was all, all his fault, and he could never say he was sorry enough to make up for this.

Limping, bruised, and bleeding heavily from a cut on his forehead, Mags followed, ignored by everyone intent on getting Dallen safely into his stall in a special small area at Healer's Collegium, a little stable especially for injured Companions who were too badly hurt to be in their own stalls.

When, after an agonizingly long time, they finally reached the stable, it was to find the waiting stall already prepared. There was another sling arranged on the rafters above the stall, one with a pulley so that Dallen could be let down from time to time to sleep on his side. But now he was transferred to this sling, the big, patient horses were led away, heads nodding with each step they took. Healers swarmed over the Companion, properly setting his legs, then encasing them in strips of cloth dipped in plaster wound around and around them so there was no way for the broken bones to move. Then a bottle was thrust between Dallen's teeth and he raised his head, head and neck trembling, so the contents poured down his throat. Then he set his chin down into a second sling so that his head didn't have to dangle and let the drugs take over.

And slowly, for the first time since Dallen had Chosen him, Dallen's Mind-presence faded from Mags' mind, leaving only a vague and undefined something in the back of his head.

Mags curled up in a miserable heap on the straw in Dallen's stall, crying silently. Dallen hung from the sling like a lifeless chunk of meat, and only the slow heaving of his sides and the vague presence still like an echo in the back of his mind gave him any indication that Dallen was even alive.

All he wanted to do was die. How could even a Companion survive something like this without being crippled for life? If he hadn't been so . . . so stupid, so despondent, Dallen would never have suggested the reckless run. If he hadn't been so careless as to let down his shields, even though he didn't remember doing so, this wouldn't have happened. If only he had insisted on not doing this at all, or insisted on stopping as soon as the last sun vanished, it wouldn't have happened. It was all his fault.

A heavy, horrible silence hung over everything here, a silence that was not even broken by his sobbing. He had learned the hard way how to cry silently a long time ago. So when Lena came running into the stall, his presence took them both by surprise.

He sat up at the sound of frantically running footsteps, and turned toward the stall door, and Lena's shocked face stopped the breath in his body and the sobs in his throat.

"Da—" she began, then registered his presence. Her face changed from anguished distress to—well, he couldn't read it.

"Mags, what is wrong with you? How could you have been so horrible? You aren't stupid, you knew better than to run that course in the dark! Why did you do this to Dallen?" burst out of her, her voice shrill with accusation. "Why did you hurt him?"

Well it looked as if he was not the only person to blame himself.

"I didn' do it!" he snapped, without thinking, lashing back defensively. He went in an instant from anguished to angry. It sounded as if she thought he had taken a crowbar to Dallen's legs! "It were a horrible accident! We was runnin' obstacles! An—something—"

"Why were you running obstacles in the dark?" she retorted, interrupting him before he could tell her about the murderous mind he had brushed up against, her cheeks red with fury. "How stupid is that? What were you thinking, why did you make Dallen do that?"

"I didn' make him do anything!" Mags shouted back, then glanced guiltily at the poor hanging Companion. If he hadn't been so low, would Dallen ever have suggested such a thing? " 'E was the one that said we should do it!"

"Did he want to, or were you so drowning in feeling sorry for yourself that he would do anything, no matter how stupid it was, to get you out of it?" she shouted back. "Bear was right! You don't care about anything but yourself! You won't even take responsibility for this! You're horrible! You're a horrible, horrible person and you probably are going to try and kill the King, because anyone that would do this to Dallen would do anything!"

He almost jumped up out of the straw and hit her. He did jump to his feet, and he had to fight with himself not to hit her, or grab her by the shoulders and shake her until her teeth rattled, or shove her to the ground. His hands clenched and unclenched, his chest heaved and hurt, and his head spun in circles.

And the awful thought went through his mind then

that if Dallen died . . . if Dallen died, he wouldn't care about anything. He would go crazy. If he could have to fight not to hurt Lena right now, there would be nothing holding him back if that happened. He'd just want everything else to hurt as much as he did. And no matter who it was that was in front of him at that moment—if they came at him the way Lena was now, there was no telling what he would do to them.

Maybe that was it. Maybe that was what the Foreseers had seen. The moment when he snapped and did the unthinkable.

Meanwhile words, awful, hurtful words poured out of his mouth, and he could do nothing to stop them. "Get out, ye worthless bint!" he screamed back at her. "Ye get in 'ere on the strength of yer pa's reputation, an' ye cain't even sing a simple song in front of people wi'out sommun holdin' yer hand an' tellin' ye wot ter do, an' ye dare tell me all thet stuff? Ye close yersel' in yer room an' sulk fer days ev'time summat goes wrong, ye make half yer Collegium try and cosset ye back t' actin' like somethin' other than a wee babby, an' ye tell me I am th' one thet on'y keers fer hisself? Ye tell me I am th' selfish one? Aye, the world circles 'round poor wee Lena, an' ain't nothin' else matters, not even though m'best friend broke both 'is legs savin' me! 'Tis all 'bout you! Get out! Leave me alone!"

Her mouth hanging open, she stared at him, as if she couldn't believe what she had just heard. Then, with a sob that wrenched its way out of her chest, she whirled and ran for the door.

With an identical sob that felt as painful as it sounded,

he dropped back down to the straw, sure that his cup of misery had overflowed.

He'd said unforgivable things to her. She would—no one would—ever forgive him, ever trust him again. The moment Amily found out what he had said, she would hate him forever. Everyone would hate him.

And rightly. He was destroying everything around him, as surely as if he was running about the Collegium with a knife, slashing everything he cared about to ribbons.

Maybe that awful thing that had brushed up against his mind wasn't from outside; maybe it had been from inside him!

Maybe that wild rumor was true—and there was something hateful, malicious inside him! Maybe it—this thing that was the real Mags—had broken out for just a second, and he had seen and felt what he really was inside!

Blindly he ran for the door, and just as blindly tore down the path to his room. He stumbled and fell several times, picked himself up without a thought and kept running. He raced past the accusing eyes of the other Companions and into his room and slammed the door behind himself, locking it.

Then he dropped to the floor, arms wrapped around his chest, sobbing silently again. His eyes swelled and burned, his chest ached, his throat was so choked he could scarcely breathe. All he could think about was what he had said to Lena—what she had said to him. What he had done to Dallen.

No matter that he had destroyed his own life. He'd also destroyed Lena's and Dallen's.

He jumped as an angry pounding on his door startled him.

"Mags! Mags! Answer me! Answer me, you right bastard!"

It was Bear.

"Come out of there, you coward! Get out here so I can pound you! I'm going to whip you like the mad dog you are!"

Of course it was Bear.

"Who else, what else are you going to ruin, eh?" he shouted furiously, pounding with what sounded like both fists on the door. "Who's next? Who else are you going to betray? You've already destroyed Dallen! Dallen's probably never going to walk again without pain, much less ride a circuit! What kind of Companion can't ride a circuit? And you sent Lena into a state where all she can do is cry! You couldn't even bother to lift a finger to save me from what my family is going to do to me, you selfish bastard! Who else are you going to destroy? Gennie? Amily? The King?"

There it was. Bear believed it too. And if Bear believed it—it had to be true.

"You don't belong here!" Bear screamed. "You don't deserve a Companion! You don't deserve to be a Trainee! Why don't you go crawl back into your hole in the ground where you came from?"

Why indeed?

Bear was right. He didn't belong here. He was a blight. An infection. An animal, a mad, dangerous animal. He shouldn't be around decent folks.

The Foreseers were right.

Bear pounded and pounded on the door, yelling, but Mags wasn't listening anymore. He was kneeling on the floor, his arms wrapped around his chest, sobbing and rocking, sobbing and rocking, until Bear finally gave up and went away.

Mags' mind ran around and around in circles, like a mouse trapped in the bottom of a water jar. The candle in his lantern burned down, then out, and he remained where he was on the floor, still curled up around his pain.

There was nothing he could do. There was no way to make any of this right again. All he would continue to do would be to make things worse.

No wonder Nikolas had "disappeared." He must have been the first to realize just what a bad lot Mags was. Maybe his parents hadn't been bandits after all, but everything else that Master Cole had said about him was right. He was bad blood, not worth anything.

The best thing he could do right now would be to die—

But no, Dallen was still bonded to him. If he died, in the condition that Dallen was in now, Dallen would probably die along with him.

But Dallen could re-Choose. He knew that was possible. It didn't happen often, and usually only when a Herald died, but it could happen. Tylendel's Companion had repudiated him, and presumably had been intending to re-Choose.

Dallen could surely do the same.

And he, Mags, could force the issue.

Yes, that would be the very best thing that he could

do. In fact, it was the only honorable thing left for him to do.

And that was where his mind finally stopped, frozen. With the conviction that this was the only possible answer to what he had done. And so he remained, sleepless, curled on the cold floor, in the dark, until at last the first light of dawn filtered in through the window.

MAGS knew that if he hesitated, if he said or did anything, if he even gave a hint of what he was about to do, someone would try and stop him. Stupid, but there was always someone who thought that the unsalvageable could be saved. Right now he didn't want the temptation to change his mind or the effort it would take to fight the well-meaning. So he shielded himself completely. Dallen was in no condition to pick his thoughts up, but others might.

Not that the Companions were likely to do anything about him. They would probably be only too happy to see the last of him.

He wasn't going to leave more of a mess than he had already created, however. He would make it easy for the rest to erase him, his presence, his life from this place. So he set to work, putting all of his books and class supplies on the table, packing his personal possessions in a basket, then carefully folding all of the clothing he had been given and laying it on the bed until the only things left were the clothes he had arrived in. He didn't feel bad about taking those; after all, they had been cast-offs in the first place.

He dressed in the ill-fitting, un-matching shirt and trews, pulled on the much-patched boots, and peeked around the door to ensure that the Companions were still drowsing. His preparations hadn't taken long at all, the stable was dark, lit only by the two night-lanterns at either end. Making no noise, he slipped out of the stable before anyone, even the grooms that served this stable, was awake. He crept across the grounds as he had learned to creep and hide back at the mine when he was sneaking about looking for food. The sun wasn't even up yet. He scuttled from bit of cover to bit of cover, and not even the dawn-rising gardeners saw him leave.

The Guards had a bad habit; they watched and challenged people trying to get into the Palace or the Collegia, but not the ones leaving. So once he reached the gates where the lowest of the servants came and went, he stopped skulking; he went through the gates and just walked off the property in the wake of a delivery cart, and they didn't give him a second glance.

But now, dressed as shabbily as he was, he quickly had to move to the "back" of all those fancy manors and near-palaces that were up here. He needed to get off the main road where he would be conspicuous, and into the alleys and lanes behind them, where people like he was "belonged."

The first thing was, he needed a job. If he was going to stay alive, at least until Dallen decided to repudiate him and find someone else, he needed to keep himself fed and sheltered. And . . . that wasn't as hard as he had made it out to be when he and Bear and Lena talked about running off. If you didn't care how well you lived, only that you stayed alive, there were plenty of things he could do. None of it was interesting or rewarding, but why would that matter now? All he cared about, really, was that it be hard enough work to keep him from thinking and let him fall into the same exhausted stupor he had when work at the mine was finished.

And certainly, there was plenty of potential for being abused and mistreated, but that didn't matter in the least to him. Right now, he didn't really care how well or badly treated he was. It came to him after a moment that he'd actually welcome being punished, since he certainly deserved it.

The way to find a job like that was to ask for it. While there were places down in Haven where those looking for work could be hired, more often than not, the sort of thing he was looking for came to a person that presented himself at the right time, and in the right manner. He was clean and neat, which argued for being reliable, and he was dressed perfectly for the sort of person that would be in the lowest ranks of the unskilled servants; exactly the right sort of "shabby." No one would trust him with horses, for instance, not even in mucking out the stalls, but they'd be happy to offload all the dirtiest, nastiest kitchen jobs on someone like him. Scullery jobs, that was the thing, jobs that went, even at the Pieters' mine, to people who were paid in little more than food and a place to sleep on the floor.

One by one he went down the line of manor houses.

At each, he presented himself at the kitchen door, looking for work. In late afternoon, he found a place, as one of the pot-scrubbers. There was no one lower. Potscrubbers—who also scrubbed the kitchen floor when the day's work was done, and hauled out the garbage—frequently deserted their posts, so someone was always looking for replacements. He didn't have to look as if he was eager; stupidity was an asset in such a job. No one cared if his eyes were swollen and red with weeping; all they cared about was a sturdy body and just barely enough intelligence to do the work.

He tapped on the door—he didn't even know whose house this was, only that it was moderately sized, and wasn't Master Soren's. A frazzled kitchen-maid answered it. Her apron was splashed and stained with whatever she had just been working on, and there was flour in her hair.

"Got work?" he asked, dully.

"Mebbe. Stay here," she replied, and scuttled off. She came back with a broad man in a white shirt and enveloping apron.

The red-faced, balding cook eyed him, frowning. "One of our boys ran off. You gonna run off?"

"Nossir," he mumbled, not looking at the cook, since that would be insolence.

"I 'spect hard work outa you. You don't work, you get beat. You understand?"

"Yessir." He looked at his feet.

"You get eats, and a bed at the fire. Twice a year, get a suit of clothes and three pennies. Understood?"

"Yessir." He bobbed his head. "Thenkee sir."

The cook shoved him inside the door, then to a place at a sink already full of hot water, soap, and pots. "Get to work."

Evidently, the staff here was considered large enough to keep two potboys busy; the other one was younger than Mags, but they were about the same size. And the size of the stack they were to clean was daunting. So, the household—or the cook—was frugal when it came to staffing. There was too much work for just two small boys, unless one of them was Mags, who threw himself into the job in a way that made the cook grunt with surprise and satisfaction.

This, at least, was one thing he could do right. With pumice stone and harsh soap, he attacked each pot as if it was his life. Unlike his life, he could clean this mess up. The cook was not stingy about hot water and soap, ordering them to change it whenever it got merely warm and not when it was as foul and cold as a sewer.

He did two pots for every one of the other boy's, which made the other boy glower at him when the cook shouted abuse at him for not keeping up. Mags didn't care. It wasn't as if he was going to try and make friends ever again. So he kept his head down and his shoulders hunched over, and eventually the boy stopped bothering even to glare at him.

The other boy reminded him of the mine-kiddies, with his sullen looks and grunts instead of speaking—shoulders hunched much like Mags, and hair falling down over his face and into his eyes. But he didn't look ill-fed, and there weren't a lot of bruises on him. Maybe the cook beat him for assumed shirking, but it didn't look as if people in this kitchen were beaten for no reason other than that the cook wanted to beat someone.

All afternoon they scrubbed the luncheon pots, which were snatched out of their hands as soon as they finished and pressed into service for dinner. Mags concentrated every bit of his mind on getting the pots so clean they were slick under his fingers. When the last of the pile was clean, he turned to look for more.

There weren't any, and the other boy scuttled across the kitchen, a rapid sort of slinking walk that, again, was much as the mine-kiddies used to do. He sidled over to a table in an alcove, where the remains of the kitchen staff luncheon was. After a moment, Mags trudged over there too.

It appeared that the kitchen staff was fed on what the masters of the house left over, and right now, after everyone else had picked the remains over, what was left for him and the other boy looked like the aftermath of a plague of insects. Mostly what remained were odds and ends of bread, the crusts from pies, and some bits of vegetable. Some pickles. A little fruit. In terms of bulk, they wouldn't go hungry. The other boy pounced on anything that looked like it had gravy or sauce on it, hunted for scraps of cheese or shreds of meat. He gathered his finds greedily to him, glaring at Mags.

Mags didn't even bother picking things over, he just shoved whatever was nearest into his mouth, not even tasting it, just mechanically chewing and swallowing until his stomach told him he was full. Dully, he noted the other kitchen staff looked all right—not starved, and they didn't cringe much. It looked as if he'd fallen into a situation where he was going to survive all right.

They weren't given a moment of rest though, and no time for the sort of banter and gossip he'd seen in the Collegium kitchen—and others. They were working every moment, the head cook looming over them and lashing them with words, if not his fists. As Mags watched, he figured out what the pecking order was, and who was best to steer clear of. Then the cook, who had kept a fraction of his attention on them the whole time shouted at both of them. "Get your lazy bums over here, you two! Pots are piling up!" So it was back to the sink.

The kitchen was hot and noisy, the cook shouting at his helpers, the cook's helpers shouting at the kitchen maids, and the maids shouting at each other. Pots and pans clanged and clattered, people bustled about, ran into each other, and cursed, people did things wrong and got yelled at or hit with a ladle or a ham-like hand—not a beating, but definitely a heavy cuff. And he and the boy just scrubbed and scrubbed and scrubbed, while the sweat poured down his face and back, and the air filled with the smell of baking pie and cake and roasting meat and savories and complicated dishes involving cheese and spices.

The boy yearned piteously in the direction of the spits, where big roasts were turning. Mags felt apart from it all—he could remember being someone like the boy, for whom a taste of meat was the highest possible dream. And he could remember another Mags, who had rejoiced over his good fortune in landing somewhere like the Collegium with all its wondrous food. But he was neither of those boys. He was hollow and indifferent to his surroundings, and all he wanted was for exhaustion to numb his mind and make it impossible to think. He couldn't help observing and filing it all away, but it dropped into an empty place in his head, a place where things that had no use would go.

Then the serving maids arrived, and were laden with trays that in turn were loaded down with food. The first course went out—coarse stuff for the servants that ate in hall, the best things for the master and his table.

Food went out to be served, remains returned from the hall and were piled on the table in the corner, atop the remains of the luncheon. Except for what came back untasted, which went into the pantry—probably to reappear at breakfast—and a few things that were set aside for the cook's private table.

The pots continued to pile up, he continued to finish two for every single one of the boy's, and finally, as clean pots were taken away and stored for tomorrow, or set up to cook porridge and the like overnight, the pile of stuff waiting to be scrubbed began to decrease. People gathered at the leftover table, squabbling over the best bits, heaping what they wanted on crude wooden plates or the leftover bread-trenchers from the lower tables up in the dining hall. The helpers ate first, then the kitchen maids. The helpers left after eating; the maids stayed to clean. This was no slattern's kitchen; it was clear the cook here might be penny-pinching, but he knew his business. Every surface was scrubbed clean, every dish put away clean, only the floor was left to do.

The maids finished their cleaning, and left, probably for real beds somewhere. The cook was still making his leisurely way through his own dinner, one eye on his winecup and the other on the staff.

Finally, there were only two pots left, and the boy scuttled to the table like a rat to scramble up onto a bench and stuff his face, leaving them to Mags.

Mags scrubbed them clean without a word, which evoked another grunt from the cook.

When he was done, he trudged to the other side of the table and picked up and ate whatever was nearest. He couldn't have said if anything was bad or good, he was only interested in getting eating over with so he could go back to work. He couldn't taste anything anyway.

The boy crammed food into his mouth with both hands and one eye on the cook, the other on Mags. Probably he was getting ready to grab anything Mags uncovered that looked better than what he had, but nothing turned up on Mags' side of the table. The cook finished his dinner, heaved himself up, and evidently that was the signal for eating to stop.

"Clean up," the cook said. The boy scuttled off and came back with a big hessian bag, grease-stained and grubby on the outside. He gestured to Mags to help him, and together they scraped everything off the table and into the bag, which was put outside the door.

Mags followed the boy's lead without a word while the cook watched them both, arms folded over his chest. The boy kept glancing furtively at the cook, as if he was expecting a cuff to the head. The cook, however, kept most of his attention on Mags.

Next, they scraped all the crumbs off the table they'd eaten from, throwing them at the cook's direction into the fire, and scrubbed down the table with soap and water and pumice-stone.

So that would be why no one got sick from the left-overs on the table.

The boy got brooms for them both, and they swept the floor, throwing the sweepings out the back door. Then they got down on hands and knees, with buckets of water and soap and big bristle-brushes and scrubbed it as the cook watched. Oddly, the cook washed his own plates and cutlery, but that might have been because he didn't trust them with it. When they were done, he grunted approval, reached into a cupboard, and pulled out two bundles of bedding.

These proved to be a couple of thick sacks made of multiple layers stitched together, a patchwork of old, worn blankets. The cook tossed one to each of them. Mags caught the one thrown to him and watched the boy to see what he did with his. The boy moved his sack to the best place by the fire, pulled off his shoes, stuck his legs into the opening, and wriggled until he was all the way inside it with just his head sticking out.

Mags copied him, and the cook grunted with satisfaction again. "Don't think to steal anything from the pantry, boy," he warned as he put the rushlights out, so that the only light was from the dying fire. "I'll beat both of you senseless if anything is missing or nibbled. Both of you. So no use thinking you can nick something and get away with it by blaming the other."

Then he left, and the kitchen was quiet except for the sound of the fire and the other boy breathing.

Mags became aware that his arms ached from scrubbing, his back ached from bending over the sink, and his legs and feet ached from standing on stone all that time. He welcomed the pain, even as his muscles began to stiffen and hurt more. Pain on the outside was easier to deal with than pain on the inside.

Nevertheless, black sorrow descended on him, and with his arms pillowing his head, he cried, silently sobbing himself to sleep.

A kick in the side roused him. He sat up in his cocoon of bedding with a groan, and was rewarded with another kick. He managed to squirm out of the bedding, and it was snatched away from him by a maid and bundled into the top of the cupboard.

The room was full of sleepy people, complaining, ordering each other about. He and the boy were put to fetching firewood from the pile outside, and the roasting fires and the big ovens were set to burning hotly. The bag of meal-remains they had left outside last night was gone. He remembered, now that he thought about it, that he had noticed chickens in a pen in one corner of the kitchen-garden. It probably went to feed them. Another evidence of frugality, that they kept hens to have their own eggs and roasting birds.

Last night's bread was shoveled out of the oven and laid out in order of quality, to be served at breakfast. Huge pots of pease-porridge and oat-porridge emerged from the ovens as well, the staple breakfast food for the servants. Serving maids appeared, caps a little askew and yawning sleepily; they were swiftly burdened with great trays of bowls full of both, or baskets of bread. The servants would eat earliest of course, and not with the masters, who would lie abed and probably be served there.

As the porridge kettles emptied, they came to Mags and the boy, who began their work. The bowls and utensils from cooking the better foods came to them too, and they labored to keep up.

"New potboy?" asked one serving-maid of one of the cook's helpers.

"Aye. Thick as two short planks, but does the work," came the reply. "Hasn't said a word since he was taken on yesterday."

"That'll suit Cookie, then," came the laconic reply.

"It'll suit Cookie better if he's too thick to count to three," said the helper. "Cookie'll give him two pennies and keep the third."

The maid snickered.

Mags kept scrubbing, concentrating with all his might, the way he used to concentrate on chipping out a stone without fracturing it, on getting every last fragment of food from every pot he was handed. When he and the boy ran out of pots, they were sent for more wood, or to haul in bags or baskets of coarser foodstuffs from a root cellar, or to carry the garbage from the cooking out to the chicken pen. They emptied out the peelings and ends and bad spots, the leaves and the burnt bits of bread into the pen and the hens fell on the bounty, clucking and fighting over the best bits, like the servants in the kitchen. Then back they went to scrubbing. Mags bent over the work, always with an ache in his soul that felt as if someone was squeezing his heart in a vice.

At least he could do this. And he could do it well. He could do it without hurting anyone.

And when he started to weep, he could put his head down over the basin, let his hair fall to cover his face, and no one would be the wiser.

So there it was. This, for now, would be what remained of the wreckage of his life.

The days blurred one into another. The days lengthened, and the kitchen grew hotter by day because the weather outside was warmer. He and the boy worked stripped to their trews; the women in shifts and chemises. He threw himself into the scrubbing and anything else that was given to him to do—and seeing that, the cook gave him every task that two hands and no mind to speak of could perform. He was set to scrubbing the soot from all the walls, and bleaching the stone floor with lye. He did it all without complaint, without a word.

He couldn't hear Dallen at all. He began to think that if Dallen had not actually repudiated him yet, it was only because Dallen was not in any physical shape to. As soon as Dallen was as healed as he could get, the Companion probably would do exactly that. And in the meanwhile the silence meant that Dallen had decided that Choosing Mags had been a terrible mistake, and this was the way to keep him isolated until the Companion could be rid of him.

It hurt, it hurt terribly, but he had to acknowledge that everyone was better off without him.

And all he was waiting for now was for that ghostly, silent presence in the back of his mind to one day become an echoingly empty place.

When that happened . . . well, then he would decide what to do.

And it occurred to him that once Dallen left him, there was one option he hadn't considered—a painless, easy way to put an end to everything. One that now, in retrospect, he wished had happened last winter, in that blizzard.

All he had to do was be patient and wait for winter. Whether or not a blizzard came, there would be snow. Then all he needed to do would be to walk out into it, until he started to feel sleepy; he could ignore the cold, he had done so before. Then, when it was too hard to move, too much effort to keep going, he could sit down, close his eyes, and let the snow take him and his misery away forever.

:MAGS. . . .:

The voice in his mind echoed through the nightmare. He always had nightmares, worse than ever before, far worse than he'd had at the Collegium. The cocoon-like bedding at least kept him from thrashing—not that anything would wake up the boy—but he had them every night. The odd thing was, even though they were horrible, and even though he woke up from them with the top of his bedding soaked with tears and the rest damp with sweat, he welcomed them. He always woke exhausted, which left his mind in a numb fog. And a numb fog was preferable to thinking.

:Mags. . . .:

After days of working here—he still didn't know who he was working for—his body knew when to wake up. Had to be before Cookie came in, since he would kick them awake. Which, oddly enough, seemed kind of fair, to Mags—Cookie didn't kick Mags hard enough to break anything, and he and the boy did have to clear away from in front of the hearth so that the fires could be built up again, and the big water kettles swung into place on their cranes to heat. Cookie was a strange combination of brutal and fair. He never meted out punishment to anyone who hadn't earned it, but those who earned it got the receiving end of a beating just short of breaking bones. Cookie was exact in doling out precisely enough punishment that the recipient was still capable of working. The boy had gotten two beatings since Mags had been here, both for shirking. So far, aside from morning kicks, Mags was unscathed.

He woke straight up out of the nightmare; he was just in time to hear Cookie's heavy footsteps in the passage outside the kitchen. The voice still echoed in his head as he struggled out of his cocoon and rolled it up into the bundle that Cookie preferred, shaking his head a little to clear it and knuckling his eyes to get the fog out of them.

It wasn't Dallen, of course. Dallen was surely only days away from withdrawing from Mags completely. Maybe that was why he was hearing the memory of Dallen's mind-voice in his dreams, the few dreams he had that weren't nightmares, the ones on going to sleep and again on waking.

"Bath," said Cookie, when he saw Mags waiting beside his bundle. He gestured to the door, and Mags went out into the yard while Cookie kicked the boy awake. Cookie set a great deal of store by cleanliness, and every other day was a bath day for the potboys. "Bath day," in the sense that they went out into the yard, stripped down to singlets, doused themselves under the pump that stood out there, washed with the same soap they used for the pots, washed their clothing the same way, put it on wet and came back to work. Small wonder they'd actually need a new suit of clothing every six moons. Mere cloth couldn't stand up to that sort of treatment every other day.

He was already clean by the time the boy came out to the yard with a bruise along one side of his face. Mags wondered what he had done to anger Cookie this time. It didn't seem that difficult to avoid a beating. All you had to do was work hard, not steal, not be insolent or waste time. Just how stupid was the boy?

When he took his place obediently at his sink, he noticed that Cookie's eyes were bloodshot, and he held his head as if it hurt him. Last night had been some sort of feast, and a lot of bottles had gone up to the dining hall from the locked cellar. It appeared that Cookie had helped himself to at least one. Well perhaps the boy hadn't been at fault this time.

Better stay extra quiet today, at least 'till Cookie gets his head back.

It was one of those rare moments these days when he actually thought something, a real thought, instead of just letting fatigue keep his mind numb and as empty as possible.

:Mags!:

His hands closed convulsively on the pot and pumice-stone, and powerful emotions he couldn't name washed over him and drowned him for a while. Meanwhile, as he had schooled it to do, his body kept mechanically on with his task.

No, it wasn't possible. Dallen wasn't trying to speak to him.

No—wait. Dallen was going to repudiate him. That was it—he'd finally come to his senses, and in order to repudiate Mags, it had to be that Dallen had to actually say as much to him. And although the deepest part of Mags was screaming "No!" most of him was bracing itself and acknowledging that it had to be done. He cautiously opened himself to Dallen a little. Just enough so that Dallen could say what he had to and get it all over with.

Dallen probably had a lot to say, too, now that he had spent so long in so much pain. That was it—Dallen was only calling him so that the Companion could tell him how worthless he was before casting him aside.

:Mags . . . : the mind-voice started to fade away, with a sense that Dallen was dropping off into a stupor again. But the last words were clear. *:Mags . . . come home!:*

If he had not long ago trained his body to keep doing whatever task it was he had been set while his mind either dropped into a stupor of its own, or ran in frantic circles, he would have earned a bruised face himself at that moment. His thoughts reeled. This wasn't possible; Dallen could not possibly want him back. And even if somehow, his Companion was too insane, too stupid, or too softhearted to repudiate him, the rest of the Companions would properly never permit him to return to the Collegium. Not ever. He was a danger to every Companion and Chosen in Valdemar. And Bear was right, he just plain didn't deserve to be up there.

Well, there was only one thing for it. If Dallen would

not do what he should, Mags would continue to force the issue on him. Someone had to do what was smart, what was right. He was on fire with the need to protect Dallen from himself, protect the Collegia, the Heralds, everyone up there on the hill from him.

As he scrubbed and rinsed, he carefully, painstakingly, built up a wall in his mind, layering it over what he already had in place, closing Dallen out completely. Normally he would not have had the energy for this, but with all that welter of emotion behind him, for the moment, he could do just about anything.

Let Dallen wear himself out against that wall, and give the other Companions time to convince him what he must do to save himself. Whatever selfish, poisonous thing was inside Mags, whether it was some parasitic, strange other personality, that had attached himself to him, whether it was his real self and the "Mags" he thought was himself was just a kind of mask, or whether it was just because underneath it all he couldn't control the evil inside himself, it must never be permitted inside the walls of the Collegia again. One disaster had been enough. There was nothing about him that belonged up there.

That done, he let the fires that all those emotions had ignited burn out, let himself sink into apathetic despair, let weariness of body and spirit take over, and numb his mind into the state of not-thinking again.

This was the right thing to do. This felt right; it was right. This was the only thing that was right, in all of his dreadfully wrong world. He had to stick to it. He couldn't be saved, but at least he could save Dallen.

The numb state lasted until the luncheon pots were done and he and the boy were feeding at the communal table. As ever, the boy's hands scrabbled among the crusts and bread for anything good, and he stuffed what he found into his face so fast that Mags wondered why he never choked. The boy seemed to live for food, in a strange way that even the mine-kiddies had never matched. He and the boy never left this table hungry—they might not be well fed, but they were certainly full. So why was it the boy tried to stuff himself as if he thought he would never eat again? The boy's behavior made no sense to Mags. The boy seemed to live for and obsess over food. It was a mystery.

As ever, Mags methodically ate whatever was nearest, without regard to its condition; it was all so tasteless to him it might as well have been dead grass. He ate to keep his stomach from complaining, to get him through another day. But there was no reason to be as fixated on food as the boy was.

:Mags!:

He started, and checked his mental wall as the boy looked at him curiously for a moment, then fell back to eating. The wall was still there. There was no way that Dallen could have breached it.

:Mags, come home!:

How was Dallen talking to him? Never mind, this needed to be put to a stop.

No! he thought and *:No!:* he shouted back. *:I'm—ye need t' stop this, Dallen! Ye need t' cut me off!:*

There was no reply, only the sense of stuporous slumber again. Mags shook his head. He must have imagined it. Or else, he'd half fallen asleep, sitting here, and dreamed it.

Or else he was going crazy. This was not at all unlikely, actually. Being insane would actually be something of a relief. If he could blame the way he had hurt Dallen and treated Lena on insanity, well . . . it might ease his guilt a little.

Mad, bad, and dangerous to know, he thought, up to his elbows in soapy hot water. In a way the idea that he might be insane was oddly comforting. Insanity would explain why he had lashed out like that. Well he could be all three here, and it wouldn't matter. No one would care if he was mad, or evil inside, as long as he cleaned the pots. He had no friends, he had no access to weapons of any kind, he was not in charge of anything dangerous. He couldn't hurt anybody here, he was never going to make a friend to be hurt again, so the danger of knowing him was not an issue.

The afternoon was always the hardest part of the day. The scents of the cooking and baking were enough to convince even a full belly that it wanted more. The boy always slowed down, knowing that this was the busiest part of Cookie's day, and that Cookie wouldn't see him shirking. And today the kitchen got so warm it was hard not to fall asleep where he stood. If he closed his eyes even for a moment he would find himself slowly tipping over toward the water and come to himself with a jerk, and today was no exception.

He couldn't imagine how the others stayed awake. Maybe it was just that they all had more sleep than he ever did. Certainly the boy was as alert as a hungry rat, watching the roasting meat, hoping for a moment of distraction or inattention when he might be able to dash in with a bit of the bread he'd stuffed into his pockets and sop up some of the juices collecting in the trays under the spits. Those were supposed to be reserved for sauces and gravy, and Cookie guarded them jealously, but the boy never gave up hope of getting some. He'd actually succeeded, probably more than once, or he never would have kept trying, but Mags had seen him manage the trick once. Once, when the rest of the kitchen had been busy and Cookie had gone after something from one of the locked cellars or pantries where the expensive things like wine and meats were kept.

Today the boy got the moment of distraction he'd hoped for, and more. The door was open to let in what breeze there was, and suddenly, without warning, one of the biggest wasps Mags had ever seen soared lazily inside; it was a huge black thing, easily the size of a man's thumb. Perhaps it had been attracted by the scent of the fruit being made into pies, or the jellies in their bowls. One of the kitchen maids spotted it, pointed, and screamed.

Then she made the mistake of flailing a towel at it without actually hitting it. That made the insect angry, and it dove aggressively down out of the air and attacked her, darting in, landing on her long enough to sting her on the neck. She shrieked with pain, while the other maids screamed and flapped their towels and aprons ineffectually at her, missing the insect altogether and further enraging it; it zig-zagged around the room, looking for more enemies to sting.

The whole kitchen erupted into a bedlam of screaming, flapping towels, people ducking out of the way, while the enraged wasp tried to find itself another target.

Mags abandoned the sink and ducked as low to the floor as he could get, making himself less of a target, as the boy saw his chance and made for the roasts. Cookie waded in at that point, as the wasp landed on the back of one of the cook's helpers to sting him. Cookie smacked the victim and insect with his huge hand, smashing the wasp, and sending the hapless helper tumbling over into a cupboard. The maids, sure that the insect was still in the air, flailed and screamed with their eyes closed—or like Mags, ducked under the table, unaware the danger of being stung was over.

Mags glanced toward the fire. The boy was stuffing his face, not only with juice-dipped bread, but with strips of crisp skin and meat he tore off the roast with his bare hands. If Cookie turned right now—

"Shut up, you lot! Shut your faces, it's dead!" Cookie roared for silence, whirled, to glare at the hysterical mob of maids, and caught the boy with both hands and his mouth full.

Cookie's face, already red, went purple with rage. He strode across the kitchen and seized the boy by the collar, hauling him to his feet and shaking him like a terrier with a rat. "Thief!" he raged. "You little bastard of a thief! Oh, you're for it now!"

Even the maid who'd been stung stopped crying and watched with open-mouthed fascination as Cookie shook the boy until his eyes rolled up in his head. The boy probably pissed himself with fear too, but he and

Mags were so soaked with sweat and dishwater you couldn't have told.

Mags had to look away, then, as Cookie delivered one of his carefully calculated beatings. The meaty sound of an open hand on flesh filled the kitchen, as the rest of thes staff watched or turned away according to their natures. It didn't go on for very long; Cookie knew that they were behind on preparations now, and he wasn't going to waste any more time on the boy right now than he had to in order to maintain discipline. The sounds of the flat of a hand on flesh didn't last as long as Mags thought it would. Maybe because Cookie was desperate to get things back on schedule. As Mags looked up again, Cookie dragged the boy back to the sink, dropped him there, blubbering.

"Now get back to work!" Cookie roared, whirling round. "I'll give you another dose of what's coming to you when the work is done! You've wasted enough of my time for now! That goes for all of you!"

Mags got up off the floor and went straight back to work. Sniveling and sniffing, so did the boy. There was some harsher punishment coming for him, probably more beating, possibly something else. Mags was as sure of that as he was that the sun would rise, but right now Cookie wanted his pots clean before he wanted the boy punished.

And into the silence in his own head, came that mind-voice. *:Mags.:*

Hellfires!

How was he getting into Mags' head?

:No!: he shouted back. *:Dallen, no, ye don' want me!*

They're right, I got this horrible thing i' me, ye felt it yer-self! It's—I dunno how t' get rid of it, an' it wants—:

:It's not something . . . in you,: Dallen replied with difficulty through his haze of drugs. *:We know. Others . . . in Haven have felt it.:*

Mags almost stopped washing pots. He actually froze for a moment, and only a blubbering sob from the boy woke him enough to continue the work. He scrubbed feverishly, no longer sleepy.

:Whadya mean?: he demanded.

:Others . . . felt it. Down in Haven, not up here on the hill. A Healer, a Temple Foreseer, and a priest with the Gift. Not so strong as you did. But felt it. It's—he's the foreigner. He's the one. It's not you. They know that now. Mags, come home!: Dallen pleaded.

He shook his head; as tempting as it was to believe that he had been exonerated, he now had some real crimes on his own doorstep, and those couldn't be rationalized away. *:That doesn' touch whut I done,:* he replied, trying not to cry, himself, as the boy blubbered and whinged next to him. *:I hurt you. I said 'orrible things ta Lena an' Bear.:*

:Things with some . . . truth in them,: Dallen replied, fighting against his drugs. *:And they said horrible things to you. But you are the one that took them to heart and ran away.:*

:'Cause they're true.: Mags cringed, contemplating that dark place inside himself. *:I don' deserve you, an' I don' belong there.:*

:That will be quite enough, Trainee Magpie.:

The sonorous mind-voice wiped out every thought,

everything he was going to say, and made his head ring. He'd heard it once before. In the stable, when Rolan chose to broadcast his thoughts. He'd never been the sole focus of that mind-voice before, and it felt a little like having lightning strike at his feet.

:Everyone has darkness inside them. Heralds are no exception. The difference between Heralds and villains is that Heralds overcome their darkness. The difference between Heralds and cowards is that Heralds face their darkness and cowards run from it. The difference between Heralds and the cruel is that when Heralds slip and allow their darkness to speak, they are truly remorseful and make amends, thus allowing the wounds they caused to heal instead of fester. So, Trainee. Which are you?:

Mags waited to see if Rolan was going to say anything else. The inside of his skull reverberated like a bell. But Rolan said nothing else. Perhaps he was waiting for Mags' reply—or perhaps he was on to more important things, leaving Mags to make up his own mind.

:Come home, Mags.: Dallen's weary mind-voice fell into the silence like a feather. *:Amily and Lena are frantic with worry. Bear has told his brother that he will not leave until you are found.:*

Mags bowed his head, and tears fell into the dishwater as the grief at what he had done overcame him yet again. *:But I hurt ye!:*

:But I was an idiot, galloping in the dark,: Dallen countered. *:Rolan has spoken, and you heard him; he stands by you as I do. The others have spoken to their Chosen. That evil creature, whoever he is, has been sensed*

by others. Everyone knows it is not you. We need you. I need you. Come home. Please.:

He was afraid to believe. And yet, Rolan had spoken. If he couldn't believe in Rolan, what could he believe in?

With a sigh, he gave in. *:All right,:* he said *:But not right now.:*

As he let down the walls he had built to keep Dallen out, he sensed Dallen's surprise and shock. *:But—why not?:*

:Because there's a kitchen fulla people waitin' on clean pots, an' the on'y other person t' wash 'em is a beat-up layabout,: he replied stubbornly. *:If I'm gonna act like a Trainee, then I ain't runnin' out with a job half done. I'll leave after it's all cleaned up. Not afore.:*

Cookie had gone to bed early, and the boy's continued punishment for his theft of meat was to be beaten again, then locked in the root cellar to sleep, among the mice and rats and black beetles that crawled in the place. This left Mags alone in the kitchen, absolutely unguarded, since in the couple of weeks he had been here, he had shown nothing like intelligence enough to get into any mischief.

He felt he had done his duty at this point. He'd done everything he had been asked to do and had been fed on scraps. They had gotten more than they had paid for out of him, and he owed them nothing. The boy and one of the scullery maids would have to wash the pots tomorrow, until someone else turned up at the door looking for work. Someone would. Someone always did.

Once the entire place was asleep, he checked the kitchen door. As he assumed, it was only locked from the inside, and it was easy to slip out.

Of course now, if there had been anyone watching the place, looking for an opportunity to steal, they would have thought that it was their lucky night, for he slipped out without locking the door behind him. That wasn't very likely, though, and as he dropped his shields a little just to be sure, he sensed no one within easy reach was awake, much less preparing to steal something.

Somehow, even though he had thought that his mind was in a completely numb state, he realized he had been observing everything about this house the entire time he had been working here. Nikolas' training had proven too strong to overcome. He knew exactly how to get out of the yard; use the barrel where the chicken manure was deposited every day—it was quite valuable for the garden plants—to get onto the roof of the coop where the chickens slept locked up at night. And from there, make a leap to the top of the wall, and tumble over. That would put him down in the alley.

He had to be careful, of course. The barrel was none too stable, and the roof was not meant to hold the weight of a man, just to keep the weather off the chickens. But being careful was what he had been taught on the personal obstacle courses; moving slowly and testing your balance and the ability of the surface ahead of you to take your weight. Think every move through before you do it.

He eased himself up onto the barrel, using his arms only, as if he was about to try and do a headstand. He noted as he did so that his arms were a lot stronger than they had been—but also that his endurance wasn't quite as good as it had been. Well, he could certainly recommend pot scrubbing as a way to build up arm strength, but a diet of scraps—and those mostly bread and crust—clearly didn't do much for the muscles as a whole. Moving at a glacial pace, he got his feet on either side of the barrel rim so that he didn't go through the top. He stood up, then reached up to the roofline. He felt along the roof edge, found the support beams for the coop roof, and slowly put his weight on them. They held.

He eased himself up onto the roof, spread his weight out over it by lying flat on it, waited for a moment while his arms recovered. After all, it was not as if he had to do this in a hurry. Once his arms stopped aching, he crawled to the side nearest the wall. There was just enough moonlight to see by; he found the beams on the other side of the roof by feeling under the roof edge, and slowly stood up with his weight on the beams and not on the roof between. He took three deep breaths, and jumped, hands outstretched.

His hands caught the top of the wall, and he pulled himself up onto it. Not easily, his arms protested a lot, but he managed to get a leg over, and after that it was a simple fall and tumble down the other side. He got a little bruised doing so, but on the whole, it wasn't a bad fall. He stood up, brushing himself off—then stopped. Why bother? He wasn't exactly clean to start with.

:Mags? Are you coming home now?: the drug-sleepy

voice in his mind was as comforting as salve on a raw wound. He almost started crying again.

:Aye. Jest need ye t' rouse sommun t' get th' Guard t' let me past th' gate. Or I kin wait outside 'till mornin' an' ye kin ask sommun then. Reckon I kin find a place t' hole up till—:

It wasn't a brush, this time, as that terrible mind impinged on his. It was more like a spear piercing his brain. That mind, that angry, murderous mind, actually hurt, burned, as it touched his. So angry, so hateful, that his knees gave and he sat abruptly down in the alley.

It wasn't cushioned by anything, and this time he knew. This was not inside of him, some hideous passenger in his head. No, this was a fully formed personality, older than he was by a couple of decades, and its anger and hate carried with them brief glimpses of memories of places and people and things that he had never seen, much less dreamt of.

It was utterly unaware of him, this mind. Either this was not someone with a Gift for Mindspeech, or more likely, it was not someone who was aware that such a thing existed, or was trained in how to use it. And Mags had no idea why he could listen in on it. There had to be some connection between him and the one who harbored such horrible thoughts—but what?

He considered trying a probe, but something held him back. It wasn't ethics; the man thinking these things was a clear danger to Valdemar, and a mental probe was exactly in order here. It was something else, some subtle sense of warning. The man himself might not be aware of Mindspeech . . .

But slowly, Mags became aware that there was a shadow there, hovering behind the mind in question. He thought perhaps it was something that had been put to guard him from outside. That was what was making his actual thoughts so obscure and hard to read. And that shadow . . . there was definitely something about it that made the hair on the back of Mags' neck stand up, the way it did when a large and dangerous dog growled. Danger. Definite danger there.

So he clung to the contact this time rather than trying to shut it out, and tried to glean what he could from the fragments he picked up. Oh, he wanted to shut it out, the pain of being touched by it was as bad as anything he had ever known—but this was important. Every fragment of information he could glean was more that could tell the Heralds who it was, and where he might be.

There were fleeting memories of the Palace—and that suite that the fake envoys had been in. So . . . yes, this was one of the foreigners. He sensed Dallen struggling to stay awake and take all this in, but he couldn't spare anything to help at the moment, as it was taking every bit of his concentration to absorb the bits and pieces he was getting and put them together into a coherent pattern.

Oh, the man was angry, so angry. Mags could scarcely believe that anyone could be that angry and still be as under control as this man was. It was as if his rage was the food he lived on, the fuel for the furnace that forged him.

This was nothing like the mad mind of the assassin;

this rage was as cold as the mad one's had been hot. Calculating, that was what it was. He might be insane—in fact, Mags could not imagine how anyone who was carrying around this much anger could not be insane—but he was as meticulously organized as a fine clockmaker. This man did nothing without examining every possibility and figuring out where it could take him. That was part of why it was so hard to read his thoughts—he actually thought these things through, several of them at a time, much faster than Mags could follow just one! Brilliant, he was blindingly brilliant.

And yet, there was something about that mind that was very akin to the mad one. It was not in the level of organization, and not in the level of intelligence. It wasn't the anger, although the mad assassin had been very angry. It felt almost as if—as if the two, this man and the assassin, had been related, physically related in some way. Could there be, in fact, a kinship connection? There might be!

He repressed the thought that perhaps the reason why he was so sensitive to these minds and no one else was, was because there might be a kinship connection with himself. That wasn't important right now. And as Dallen had stressed to him, just because your parents had been bad, it didn't follow that you would be.

What was important was figuring out where this man was, and what it was he was going to do.

It was very like trying to ride the back of a wild and dangerous, ravening beast—a beast that had no idea Mags was there. All he could do was hold on for the ride and hope the beast didn't notice.

After several moments, he still couldn't tell which of the foreigners this man was . . . he only knew which one he wasn't, because this mind was nothing like the mind of the man he had seen down in Haven and followed to the travelers' inn. And there had been no kinship connection there, either.

He closed his eyes tightly and concentrated with all his might, but could not even get a sense of direction from that mind. All he could say for sure was that it was down in Haven somewhere. He got flashes of what looked like a great many people eating and drinking together; another inn, but it could have been one of dozens. Even if Mags had been able to recognize it, there was no guarantee that the man would stay there for any length of time. In fact, given that they had been discovered now, it was very unlikely that they would take any two meals in the same place.

There were layers to the man's anger. There was a fundamental rage that drove him all the time, waking and sleeping. And there was a hatred for Valdemar atop that—but not the sort that he would expect to find in, say, a Karsite, who hated and feared everything that Valdemar represented.

No, this was a more generalized hatred. He didn't want to be here, he hated this place, it wasn't home, the people were soft and simple fools, their Heralds were unnatural and perverted creatures with a sick and twisted bond to their horses, and he wanted to be gone as soon as possible.

But he couldn't leave. He had a task to perform here.

Frustratingly, Mags could not get a sense of what that

task was. Only that there was a very important task to be accomplished and he had not been able to do it.

And atop that, another level of anger and acute frustration that there was something he needed, desperately needed, in order to finish that task. And it wasn't something that he could just buy or make or have made. It was something personal and very specific. He had thought he had it, but he didn't. He must have left it, because it was missing, and now he could get nothing done. Try as he might, Mags could not get a sense of where the man thought he had left this thing, much less what it was.

Right now, getting that thing back, whatever it was—that was his primary goal. He thought now he knew where it was. He was working on several plans simultaneously to get it. It was all those plans, being thought through together, that made it impossible to see what the object was and where it was.

:...oh...now I understand.: Dallen's mind-voice was a whisper, as if he, too, was afraid to disturb that mind.

:Understand what?: Mags demanded.

:Later—:

The mind buzzed with these plans, to the point where Mags couldn't follow any of the threads of thought at all. Plans branched off plans, and the mind worked at all of them, simultaneously, until Mags felt dizzy—

Then, suddenly—the mind was gone.

:What happened?: he said, alarmed. *:Did I—did he—:*

:I don't—think so,: Dallen replied with difficulty. *:I don't think he knew you were there. I think...I think*

there is just something that links you randomly. It holds you together for a bit, then he spins away and the connection breaks.: Mags sensed a lot of pain, physical pain in Dallen.

:What're ye doin', ye gurt fool?: he demanded, alarmed, *:Ye ain't tryin' ter walk are ye?:*

:No . . . no. I just let my pain drugs wear off, so I can think and talk to you. It's worth it. A little pain is not an issue with something this important in the offing.: There was a sense of a weak laugh. *:I will muddle through.:*

Mags wanted to throw his arms around Dallen's neck and beat him with a stick at one and the same time. He was so glad that Dallen had been able to follow all this, so glad that Dallen would be able to tell all the other Companions immediately. And he wanted to beat the big moron for hurting himself to do so and shrugging it all off.

:I promise I will drink them very soon now. I think there is something up here at the Collegium that has been preventing you from making that connection quite so often,: Dallen continued. *:There are a lot of shields here, and every Gifted tends to naturally create a differently sized shield as well. Some don't even have a specific person that they are tied to, and are probably the result of many Heralds and Healers being in the same place for a long time. Most of those shields don't extend much past the surface of one's own mind, but some can extend to cover the Collegia and Palace as well. Those big ones aren't strong, and they are entirely subconscious, but having several of them in place could have interfered with you making conscious contact with that mind before.:*

:Could thet be where m'nightmares're from?:

:Oh yes. In sleep you are more likely to get seepages. And it was just our bad luck that we were on the Kirball field, outside those shields, when whatever it is happened that allows you to link briefly with that madman.: He got a sense of Dallen wincing as his poor legs complained to him.

:Gods.: He breathed heavily, as if he had been running. *:An' if I go back—no chance up there thet I'll hook him again. Then no way, I cain't go back up there. Not if I'm gonna have any hope of findin' him.:*

:Not when we have no idea how you link to him, not when it seems to be triggered by something on his part, and not when we don't know when that is going to happen,: Dallen agreed unhappily. *:Oh Mags—I am sorry.:*

:Eh, 'sallright.: He actually felt a little light-headed, giddy, with the revelations of the past candlemark or so. Lena had clearly forgiven him, Amily had not abandoned him nor given up on him. The Heralds now knew—or would soon, when Dallen reported to them—that he was not "the foreigner" although he was somehow involved. That image of him with blood on his hands was troubling, but there were so many interpretations of that even as a real vision and not something symbolic that it wasn't even remotely likely that one of them was "Mags kills the King."

Though what evoked fear right now was the thought that it was a vision of "Mags interrupts the person that kills the King . . ."

Aye, but Foresight ain't absolute. Ye kin change things. People do't all th' time.

And as Dallen had confirmed, those nightmares he had been plagued with had an explanation too. The sleeping mind was a lot more susceptible to mental links, and he could be linking to that madman every time he slept. Which was a scary thought, but not nearly as scary as the idea that he had been creating those horrible dreams himself.

:I cain't come back,: he said slowly. *:Not if them shields ain't somethin' that kin be taken down.:*

:I don't think most of them can be,: Dallen said reluctantly. *:There are some that are as old as the Palace itself.:*

:Then I gotta stay here, in th' city. I gotta wait fer th' next time I get linked up. I gotta either find this feller, or figger out which one he is, or figger out what he's gonna do.: The logic was inescapable.

:Or all three. I agree,: Dallen said mournfully.

:Hellfires.: He sighed. *:All right. Let's make us a plan an' fast, so's ye kin tell Rolan an' the rest an' they kin do what they're gonna do, an' ye kin get drugged up.:* He smiled to himself. *:Ye gurt fool.:*

THE first order of business was to find a place to wait until dawn, or thereabouts, when someone in authority could wake up and decide what to do about Mags. And up here would not do. There were too many private guards and not nearly enough places to hide.

So Mags made his way as swiftly as he could in the opposite direction to where he really wanted to go, because right now the idea of being safe in his room again was so desirable it that it was all he could do to hold to his plan. He went further down into Haven, to find a place where he could get a little sleep while he waited for dawn.

While he trotted down the alleys—because anyone who was skulking and moving from shadow to shadow would attract suspicion, and anyone who was moving without any attempt at stealth would be assumed to be here on some business—he went at the problem logically. He needed somewhere he wouldn't be disturbed, and somewhere flat so he could sleep. He needed sleep, or he'd be even more vulnerable than he already was. It had to be somewhere he wouldn't be seen, and out of the way of traffic. At the Collegium, at the mine, that had been easy—wriggle into cover under some bushes. But this was a city, and there was nothing like that to speak of—what little there was grew in parks and private gardens. The weather was good though; he just needed some place out of the way, and flat enough that he could get some sleep.

Then a glance at one of the great houses he passed to see how high the moon was gave him the answer. Out of the way, and flat? What could be better than a roof?

Most roofs were not actually flat, of course, but he knew there were places where cornices joined and roofs butted together that would give him something he could wedge himself into and not worry about falling off.

So as he got down into the part of the city where the everyday folk lived, he started looking for an inn—because an inn had people coming and going at all hours, and a little activity around it would go unnoticed if he was careful.

It was not more than a candlemark later that he was wedging himself into exactly the sort of nook he had envisaged, and even better, it actually was flat, a flat space behind a set of four chimney pots. And as an added incentive, the chimney pots were keeping it warm, for the air was still cold at night, especially up here where there was wind whipping around the rooftops.

Now that he was up here, secure—it all hit him at once.

Mostly what hit him was a relief so profound it felt as if all his muscles went limp at once.

He had already cried far, far too much, so he didn't begin sobbing now. Instead, he found himself smiling for the first time in—well—since the second lot of visions began. Weeks, anyway.

It didn't matter that he had a daunting task before him. For right now, this moment, all that mattered was that he was a Trainee again. He would apologize to Bear and Lena and somehow make it up to them. Dallen was going to heal, and if Bear was right and he couldn't ride circuits, well Mags could serve in Haven. What mattered was it really had been an accident, though they had both taken the foolish chances that contributed to the accident. What mattered was that though there was a nasty part of him, it wasn't a monster. Rolan was right.

He yawned hugely and curled into the warm chimney pot a little more, his muscles feeling as if they were made of butter.

And the next thing he knew, it was morning.

He watched the sun coming up over the rooftops, and waited for Dallen to rouse.

:Mmrph.:

:Mornin'.:

:I am glad you did not say 'good.': He got a sense of the ache in Dallen's legs, and winced.

:Talk to anybody yet?: he asked, not expecting an answer.

:Actually, yes. Rolan, and Nikolas via Rolan. It will take some time to convince people outside of the Heralds up here that you are not a great villain. Nikolas wants to know if you think you can survive without direct contact

from up here for a while. I think he has some concerns that our foreigners might not be working alone.:

:Ye mean if it gets out thet I kin see this feller's mind, I could be in trouble?:

:Exactly. Nikolas wants to keep this information confined to the Companions, himself, and the King for now. He can't get away to help you, and we certainly can't send the King down with a packet of money and clothing.:

Mags chuckled at that image.

:And a Companion trotting up with saddlebags for you would be just as conspicuous. So can you manage on your own?:

Mags considered that. *:Dunno why not. Don' think I should try getting' 'nother job, though.:*

:I agree. Your 'job' is hunting down our quarry. You need to be mobile.:

:So I need somethin' that'll let me lounge 'round streets an' do nothing an' not look suspicious.: He considered that for a moment. *:Blind beggar. People'll gimme money. I kin sleep rough, an' I kin scrounge fer more food. I ain't picky 'bout what I eat.:*

Dallen was silent. *:I had thought about beggar. Blind didn't occur to me.:*

:I kin drop a liddle shield an' use other peoples' eyes t' watch crowd—an' the bandage'll cover m'face, so if the furriners see me, might not recognize me.: He thought some more. *:I kin snitch some wax an' seal m'eyes shut w' it, case summun snatches m'bandage off.:*

The thought was the parent to the deed. He was already making his way quietly off the roof and into the stable attached to the inn as he spoke.

And on his way out of the inn-yard, he got his first stroke of good fortune. A fellow in a hurry to leave discarded half a meat pie in the dust as he mounted his horse. Mags snatched it up, dusted off the worst of the dirt, and devoured it. There was breakfast, and he had certainly eaten worse.

He needed wax, a rag, and a staff. The last would be easiest to get. He managed to steal a rag from a rag-and-bone-man's cart as the man made a collection. That left the wax.

Wax was valuable. He considered using mud instead, but he was afraid of getting something into his eyes that would infect them. What to do . . .

:Turn right,: Dallen said suddenly into his mind.

Mags didn't argue. He went down the first right-hand street he came to, and discovered himself in the chandler's street—but in the alley, not the street itself. And although wax was valuable, and candle ends would always be collected to be melted down and made into new candles, he soon realized that tiny bits of it were not so valuable that here anyone bothered to pick them up out of the alley. He prowled the expanse with his nose practically pressed to the hard-packed dirt, picking up a drop there, a drip here, and pressing them together in his hands. With patient gleaning, by the time he got to the end of the alley he had a nice ball of wax about the size of his fist, and it was a pleasingly unpleasant color as well, close enough to flesh-color to blend, and mottled with threads of red, blue and ocher. If he made a flat sheet of it and pressed pieces over his eyes, it would look at first glance as if he had had a horrible accident and his eyes were covered with scar-tissue. It wouldn't pass a close muster, but most people wouldn't look a second time.

And the staff was easy; he just went through the alleys of the better homes again, and found a place where the gardeners were doing tree trimming, dashed in and nicked a piece when the gardeners were too busy to see him. As an added bonus, in the garden-midden he found what had been an ornamental bowl for flowers, which now had a chipped rim and a big crack in it. That would do for his begging-bowl.

By midmorning, he was established. He settled himself just out of the way of foot traffic, his eyes sealed with wax and bandaged, his staff across his lap, and the bowl, which looked nicely forlorn and battered, in front of him.

He dropped some of his shields, ever so cautiously, and let the thoughts, and particularly the images, of the people passing by seep into his mind. Uppermost for the most part were concerns about where they were going, so he got lots of glimpses of the street and the people in it.

Until the madman somehow connected with him again, this was Mags' best hope of finding him; looking for the foreigners through the eyes of other people.

Now and again he heard the metallic sound of a small coin falling into his bowl. When he did, he murmured a quiet thank you, groped convincingly for the token, and stuffed it in his pocket.

Dallen was a comforting presence in the back of his mind again, even if the Companion was mostly drugged and comatose. There were a hundred questions he wanted to ask, and unfortunately, right now, he couldn't.

Foremost was the suspicion that at least part of the reason why Nikolas wasn't giving him help was that the King's Own was testing him again.

If that was so, well, he was actually all right with that. He still felt as if he needed to be punished—or at least to atone in some way—

Maybe someone else would have resented this, but he was trying to be honest with himself, and if he had been in Nikolas' shoes, he'd have done the same. After all, Mags had run away from the Collegium; Nikolas had to be sure that he could count on Mags to do what he was asked to do.

So Mags had to prove himself, show he was still able to perform as he had been taught, and do so without any outside support.

While he watched the passing crowd through the eyes of the crowd itself, he pondered where it might be likeliest to find the foreigners now. Would they have tried to hide themselves in the slums?

Don't think so. One of the things that Nikolas had taught him was that each block in the poorer sections of Haven was like a village. Everyone knew everyone, and they all knew each others' business. For a lot of foreigners to suddenly intrude—well, they would stand out. It would be obvious that they weren't poor, no matter how they tried to disguise themselves. And—hmm.

Another question to ask Dallen: just how widespread were the stories about foreigners' plotting the King's death? If such tales were current all over Haven, there were plenty of people who would report their presence to the Guard, no matter how they themselves felt about the Guard, or whether or not they were lawbreakers. Because there was bound to be a reward tied to their capture, and there is nothing like a reward to make the former lawbreaker turn law-abiding citizen.

So he could probably dismiss the slums.

On the other hand, they had stolen horses now. They didn't have to be in Haven at all. They could be anywhere within half a day of the city, though it was likeliest that they were closer than that.

So if I was one'a them, what would I want right now?

The one he was linked to had clearly wanted something, and it was an actual object. Mags had the impression that very recently he had decided he had left it behind somewhere. There was no doubt it was important, very important.

Maybe that was why he was back in the city! They must have stayed at a lot of inns in order to keep from arousing suspicion by staying too long in one. The lost object would probably be in one of those inns.

Now, the inn Mags had found them living at was not exactly a cheap one—not luxurious, but not cheap. He doubted that they would ever stay in a cheap place. In a decent inn, when you left something behind, the innkeeper held it until you turned up again and asked for it; it paid them to do such a simple service, for it guaranteed repeat customers.

Perhaps one way to go about this would be to consider just where in the city a foreigner could stay without causing comment in the middle of winter, besides that row of inns on the Trade Road.

Well . . . time to consider what he had learned from Master Soren, and at Master Soren's gatherings. There were only a limited number of kinds of merchants that would need housing in the middle of winter. If the foreigners were trying to avoid detection, they would have to be careful about what they were trying to pass as.

One thing sprang instantly to mind. At the Midwinter Festival, he had overheard a conversation with a Master Goldsmith. If he recalled this correctly, the man had been recounting—with great pleasure—the long negotiation he was having with a particular gem trader who had decided to overwinter in Haven purely to keep the bargaining going. So gold and gem merchants would remain . . . particularly if staying would get them a really good bargain.

They was sportin' a mort'o sparklies, he recalled. *Huh. I wunner if they was like t' sell any on 'em?* If so, the gems they were selling would lend verisimilitude to pretending to be gem traders. And no one thought twice about gem traders being foreign. In fact, if he had been in their shoes, and had not established an alternate safe house down in Haven, that would be exactly what he would do. Well, unless he thought of something even safer.

Well, that gave him an outline for another course of action. Investigate the inns—and there couldn't be many—where the goldsmiths were. That could be a bit difficult in his current disguise, but not impossible.

Do wool sellers overwinter? It would be easy enough to find that out with a day or so of lingering in that part of the city.

Horse and cattle traders—no. There were horse fairs from Midsummer on, but they stopped at the first snow. There was a cattle fair for weaned calves at Midsummer, then nothing until the fall, but by the time the first snow fell, cattle traders were safely back home. No use looking there. Same for sheep and other livestock. Besides, aside from exotic breeds of horses, like Shin'a'in, the sellers were all Valdemaran.

Spices, dyes and medicines . . . maybe. He'd have to lurk again.

Grain . . . no, and anyway all sellers would again be Valdemaran, not foreign.

He wracked his brain. A merchant that was foreign would have to be selling something exotic and very expensive, and in order to overwinter, he would either have planned to be here, or got caught by surprise.

All right. That narrowed things down quite a bit.

Weapons . . . no. That would make them stand out, which was something that they wouldn't want to do.

What about a reason for being in Haven that had nothing to do with selling anything?

Aha. Scholars. Virtually every Temple had a library and archives. Now that might be the answer. If they were pretending to be scholars, they could move from inn to inn without causing comment, and only needed to go out "to study" during the day to keep up the ruse. No one thought twice about scholars being foreign, peculiar, or reclusive.

And that led to another, sobering thought. What if all those trips down into Haven on the part of the bodyguards had NOT been to get drunk, but to scout out potential places where they could all go should they need to abandon the Court?

He hoped that Nikolas had thought of that.

Never mind. Concentrate on what he could do; that was the important thing right now.

He picked up his begging bowl and held his staff out in front of him, sweeping it back and forth in little arcs to "feel" his way. Which he wasn't actually doing, of course, he was using other peoples' glimpses of him to figure out where he was going. It could have been disorienting had he not gotten used to it while he sat in his corner this afternoon; it was a bit difficult to do, but not disorienting—like trying to thread a needle by looking at it in the mirror.

That only made him go slowly, and with the appearance of fumbling a bit, which was all to the good; it added to the realism of his performance. It amused him a little to think that all he needed now would be for some kind-hearted soul to take his elbow and offer to lead him where he wanted to go.

He had made sure to get up and move only when the crowds had thinned out so as not to inconvenience folk too much. No one appeared terribly irritated by him, and most simply cleared out of his way with no fuss.

Since the last place that his quarry had been was that section of inns on the Trade Road, that was where he headed; his first position hadn't been too far from there, so that was all to the good. It took him about a candlemark to slowly walk there, find a reasonable place to set up—visible, but out of traffic—and settle in. He thinned his mental shields a little more, this time hoping to pick something up specifically about his quarry. A few moments later, he heard someone speaking—to him.

"What happened to you?"

The tone sounded more suspicious than concerned. He refocused on the nearer stray thoughts, and got an image from people around him as well as the man himself. Ah, the person in question was a City Constable, checking to be sure that he was an "honest" beggar. He hadn't known that they checked on beggars; good thing that he had made his preparations!

"Burnt, sir," he said softly, and slipped his bandage a little. It was dusk, and what looked passable by daylight was hideously convincing by twilight. "Accident."

He felt the man's involuntary recoil and had to suppress a smile of satisfaction. He pulled the bandage back up.

"I'm sorry for you, lad. You can set up here," the man said, and Mags heard his footsteps going off.

Once again, Mags set to listening in on unguarded, errant thoughts. It was a lot like working in the mine, actually. A lot of tedious chipping and sifting through things you couldn't use and didn't want, hoping for a sparklie.

The Constable returned—this must have been a regular patrol for him—and paused. Through the eyes of a curious passer-by, Mags watched him lean down and felt something warm placed in his hand; a chance thought from the Constable himself told him what it was—a meat pie!

"Oh, thankee, sir!" he said, his voice warm with very real gratitude. It had been a very long time since that half pie this morning, and this was what some of the inns called a "Drover's Pie," twice the size of the normal ones, with meat in one half and apple in the other. "Been a good bit since brekky."

"Eh, inns on the Row feed Guards and Constables free," the man said with a trace of embarrassment. "They give us too much, and I thought you could use it."

"A kindness still be a kindness, sir," Mags replied. "Ye took thought, aye? Many wouldn't. Thankee."

The man was pleased, if still embarrassed, and moved off on his rounds.

Mags savored the aroma of the pie; it was a good one. He bit into it, by purest chance getting the meat end, and slowly chewed and swallowed. It was a very good pie, made all the better by the fact of the Constable's kindness.

:Damn,: Dallen muttered sleepily.

:What?:

:I'm not there to get the apple end.:

Mags almost laughed.

He stayed there until long after dark, "listening," waiting, patient. A few more coins dropped into his bowl, he got some tantalizing hints about his quarry when someone asked about the increased patrols and the inn servants talked about horde of Guard and Heralds that had descended on an inn further down the road.

:Dallen, did th' foreigners leave anythin' behind when they scarpered off?:

:Nothing but the Lunatic,: Dallen replied. *:Otherwise the place was scoured clean.:*

So, whatever it was that—damn it, he had to give his quarry a name.

Temper, he decided. For the man certainly was in a towering temper.

. . . whatever it was that Temper had left behind, it hadn't been at the last inn. And he learned that the Constables and the Guard had been to every inn on the row with descriptions of the foreigners, asking if they had stayed there. They had, of course. But again, they had left nothing behind. In fact, they were careful not to leave so much as a stray hair or a nail paring behind, which had struck the innkeeper whose thoughts Mags was watching as being odd.

He got nothing more after that—well, nothing pertinent, although he did learn that at astonishing number of married men brought clandestine lovers to these places . . . As the night weathered on, and the inn common rooms began to empty out, he caught the thoughts of the Constable again. The man was approaching, a bit reluctantly . . . hmm. Mags wondered what he was about to say.

"If you were to curl up farther back in that nook to sleep," the Constable said, standing over him, "You'd be out of the way and I wouldn't need to ask you to leave for the night."

Mags chuckled. "Thankee sir, but I got a safer place. Time fer me t' be gettin' on then?"

"I'm afraid so," the man said apologetically, as Mags got to his feet with the help of his staff, and picked up his bowl. "We're not supposed to allow people to sleep on the street. Rules are rules."

"Rules're there fer a reason, sir. Reckon it keeps them like me safe, too. Be fair easy fer someone to decide he didn't care for the look'a me an' give me a kick or three. Goo'night t' ye."

"And to you," the Constable replied, relieved that Mags had made no fuss. "And good luck."

Mags made his way down the street, a little hampered by the fact that there weren't a lot of people about whose eyes he could use. But as soon as he was well out of sight of the Constable, he ducked into a darkened doorway, and with relief, peeled the wax off his eyes.

With wax and bandage tucked away safe, and his bowl and staff under his arm, he made for the part of town where he had found his cozy sleeping spot at a quite brisk pace, energized by the unexpected bonus of that pie. On the way he had the good fortune of running into a street vendor who was just packing up, who was happy to sell him the remainder of his stock for the handful of small coins Mags had been given today. Though the skinny sausages and tiny, bite-sized pies the man handed over were beginning to dry out, and had been made of the cheapest possible scraps and innards in the first place, nevertheless Mags had not scrupled to eat a half pie dropped in the dirt this morning, and he wasn't going to cavil at eating these now.

He got a drink at a public fountain and horse trough in a square on the way to his goal, after devouring the sausages (since the pies would keep better). There was a line of workmen having a bit of a wash-up at another public horse trough, and he took advantage of the opportunity to do the same.

By now, inns were closing their doors, and he was in a good position to scramble up to his chimney pots without being noticed as drunks who were disinclined to pay for a spot on the floor to sleep off their liquor were turned out into the street. With the staff tied to his back and the bowl inside his shirt, he made it up before the local Constable came by on his round.

He tucked his pies right up against the chimney-pots to keep them warm and settled in.

:Anythin' from anybody?: he asked Dallen.

:Nikolas is testing you in part,: Dallen replied dryly. *:As you suspected. But there is reason to think there is someone up here who is in contact with our quarry. Whether it is someone at Court, a servant, or even a Guard . . . we can't tell. And whether the person is in collusion or being duped . . . we can't tell that, either.:*

:'Till I actually find something, don't matter,: he replied.

:They're moving me back to Companion's stable tomorrow,: Dallen continued. *:Healers' only has one stall for Companions, so, there it is. I've been politely asked to vacate and agreed. I'm allowed to stand on my own a very little bit, and the rest of the time I can lie down, so . . . time to give the stall back in case someone worse than me is brought in. It will be nice to be in my own stall again. And they will still keep working on me.:*

:Wisht I was there,: Mags replied wistfully. *:Well, cain't be helped.:*

:And I wish bones healed faster.:

Mags hesitated, then asked the question that had been haunting him. *:Bear said—:*

:I am quite aware of what Bear said,: Dallen replied dryly. *:Allow me to point out that Bear has never healed anything but a horse, and cannot possibly know what to expect from a Companion. I am healing fine, and my legs will be just as strong as before. You and I will be playing Kirball as soon as you get back up here. Or . . . all right, maybe not quite that soon, but certainly before Midsummer.:*

Mags heaved a sigh of intense relief.

:Companions are not often crippled, except by age,: Dallen continued. *:Bear couldn't know that, of course. It's—well, for the same reason we stay white. So rest easy, Chosen,:* he added fondly. *:We'll soon be Kirball champions again.:*

:Ha!: Mags replied, happily curling up to sleep. *:Ye mean you will! I'm jest the baggage in yer saddle!:*

:Hmm.: Mags got the sense that Dallen had taken his medicines again, and was about to drowse off. *:I won't deny that the mares have been very attentive. Very . . . atten . . . tive.:*

Mags chuckled quietly, and drifted off to sleep.

EVERY day, Mags set up in one of five places where he thought that the foreigners might be hiding. It wasn't at all difficult to get himself established; he had learned something about the beggars just by things Dallen warned him to be careful about. Now that he was out here, he learned a lot more by catching their surface thoughts. Mostly what he figured he needed to do was set himself up in such a way that he didn't annoy them. They could be surprisingly competitive, so he needed to make sure they saw him as nothing like a threat. He hadn't realized that part until he came to set up among them during the day; he had been lucky his first night, setting up quite by accident in a quiet spot that none of them wanted. Now he had to be more careful.

And after dark, he prowled some of the darker corners of Haven, keeping to the shadows, just in case, against his own judgment, the foreigners might have taken shelter among the poor and the criminal. But by day, and even into the night until the inns closed their doors to anyone not paying to stay the night, he haunted his five districts, moving once around noon and rotating them so that he never visited the same one twice in a row.

The Constables of the five areas he frequented got to know him—he called himself "Trey"—and looked out for him, which was good, because he wasn't an aggressive beggar. Most beggars called out their sad stories to passers-by, and made a great display of their infirmities. Mags, obviously, did not, because the one thing he did not want to do was to draw attention to himself. As a consequence, his takings were fairly meager. On the other hand, he never once got into a fight with one of the other beggars. Usually those fights were verbal, but not always. Besides, he couldn't afford either the attraction or the distraction that a fight would cause.

The Constables always saw to it that he had a decent midday meal at least, but things would have been very lean indeed if he had not resorted to a combination of theft and scavenging.

Now, it would have been dissembling to say that he only stole from those who deserved getting stolen from—but he really was in a good position to determine those who did deserve a bad turn, and most of the time he managed to be no more than an inconvenience or an embarrassment. And one thing was absolutely true: he never stole from anyone who couldn't afford it.

And at any rate, it was never anything worse than snatching a bit of food—usually by nipping in through a hall window at an inn and helping himself to meals left at the doors of people who had hired the room for reasons other than a place to sleep. In short, he stole from men entertaining women who were not their wives in private and very expensive rooms. He never took money, although the opportunity presented itself, nor other property, though that came within reach of his fingers even more often than money. He had discovered he had a positive talent for scampering about on rooftops, which, considering how much of his life had been spent underground, was supremely ironic.

It wasn't at all difficult. There were never more than a handful of these "special" rooms in an inn, and all were on the top floor, just below the servants' attic rooms. All he had to do was wait until a post-assignation meal had been left discretley at the door, swing in through a hall window, stuff his shirt full, and scramble out again. It never took him more than a few moments. And to be honest, these little feasts were so extravagant he doubted that much was missed.

He did not use that talent for roof exploration in the poorer quarters, however. There were plenty of souls who lived there that were far better at it than he was, and most of those people had sharp tempers and sharper knives. No, he kept to the ground, to the shadows there, finding places he could hide and listen.

It wasn't pleasant. The alleys here were only cleaned by rain, and it was a good thing he had a strong stomach.

Although he caught a few, brief whispers of Temper, somewhere off in the distance and never for long enough to get an idea as to direction, never again did he feel the full force of Temper's thoughts, except in sleep. He slowly came to understand that as he had suspected, these actually were Temper's nightmares, not his.

And that was where things took a very odd turn indeed. Waking, the man was tough, ruthless, and utterly immoral. In his dreams, he was the victim. The man spent every night fleeing from or fighting with something he knew would destroy—had destroyed—everything he cared about. It had been Mags' own memories that had colored what he had gotten from Temper, and turned the dreams more personal. In his dreams, he didn't know what the thing was he fled from or fought. Temper, however, knew very well what, or who, it was. But since it was a dream, Mags had no way of controlling it, to see the situation through Temper's eyes, so the shadowy hunter remained a mystery.

It got even stranger once he realized that. He began to suspect that Temper was no mere hapless victim, but that he had given himself into the situation willingly. That he had sacrificed the very things he loved for the sake of power. And strangest of all, Mags got the impression that the very thing he fought was the thing he served.

In fact, the thing he fought was the thing he himself most wanted to become. Or, perhaps, replace.

No wonder he was insane.

Mags wanted to feel sorry for him, and couldn't. The man was, in every sense, a monster. The longer Temper remained at large, the more danger he posed, because Mags knew that he was tenacious; either out of fear of his master, fear of failure, open-eyed ambition, or a combination of all three, Temper would not leave a job until he was called off, or the job was completed.

Aside from all that, this was, oddly, one of the most satisfying times of Mags' life.

He was doing something important. And yet, he was more free than he had ever been. He answered to no one except himself. And he had Dallen. Certainly he was living and sleeping rough. Certainly there were nights of an empty belly, days in the misery of a pouring, cold rain that would be followed by a night in the open hoping that someone would put a fire in one of the fireplaces served by his chimney pots. But if he succeeded, it would all be worth it.

He was learning more about Haven than he had ever gotten from books, or even from Dallen. And since most of what he did was absorptive observation, he was learning far, far more about people than he ever dreamed possible. Those little glimpses he got of their unguarded thoughts were telling him more about what it was like to be someone who had a normal life than he would have under any other circumstances. It tended to "leak" over, too; more than once he found himself looking at things from two sides—the way "Mags" did, and the way a "normal" person did.

And he learned that he was not as much of a freak as he had thought he was. He learned that most intelligent people seemed to spend their lives feeling as if they didn't fit in, that almost all of them felt like strangers inside their own skins, even when among their own friends. All of them seemed to be lonely, more or less. Many, to his surprise, were certain that there was a terrible darkness inside them that would utterly revolt anyone that knew about it.

Now, it was true enough that his situation was unique; he really was something of an anomoly. But he wasn't alone in feeling like such a complete outsider that he might as well have been raised by wolves. It struck him as so very strange, and yet, maybe not so strange. All of these people were alone in their own heads, isolated inside their own skins. They didn't have, never would have, what he had with Dallen.

That made him both less alone and more alien than any of them. But then again, that was the case with all Heralds.

:It's a wonder we don't all go mad,: Dallen said, sleepily. *:Except we keep each other sane, I suppose.:*

:If yer sure ye're not crazy, don't that pretty much mean ye are?: he replied, and got a woozy chuckle.

Days went by without so much as a hint outside of his sleep-time of Temper. He began to wonder if Temper had somehow detected him, and was now effectively shielding his thoughts.

Or maybe that shadow he had sensed had, and was.

That being the case, he was going to have to go back to scanning the crowds, using nothing more than his eyes.

Or rather, other people's eyes.

He tried, briefly, to use animals, but there either wasn't enough mind-power there for him to skim off what they saw, or else he just wasn't in tune with them. But the more he practiced, the better he got at it, until he was able to see what was going on several blocks away.

And that was how it happened that, three days after

Dallen was moved back to his old stall, late at night as the inns emptied out, Mags thought he spotted someone familiar.

It was not the hair, which had been cut roughly, nor the clothing, which was nondescript. It was a way of turning the head, of walking, betraying an arrogance that was only partly hidden. It was a barely contained force that made people give the man a wide berth.

He sifted through all the surface thoughts as fast as he could until he came to the right ones. And he knew they were the right ones, because he sensed that shadow again, hiding them.

But it was only partly successful. The shadow was keeping Mags from the direct connection that he had had before—but it couldn't stop the man's thoughts from leaking out over his rather fragmented natural shields.

There was something about those shields . . . why should they be shattered like that? Most people that weren't Gifted either had no shields, or were so strongly blockaded they might just as well have been lumps of stone. Mags got another impression, a feeling more than any actual information, that once upon a time, this man actually had possessed good natural shields, but something had fractured them, and now his surface thoughts were anyone's to read. Mags could not imagine what circumstance could have done that. In his experience, shields could be brought down, or forced down, or destroyed entirely as the mind that created them was destroyed, but they couldn't be shattered like that and then left in pieces.

He reminded himself not to be distracted, and put his attention back on gleaning every tiny bit of information that he could from those thoughts.

As the last time . . . Temper's main emotions were immediate irritation with the people around him, layered over loathing. He really, really hated Haven and Valdemar, and the people who called Valdemar home. He desperately wanted to leave. Mags got glimpses this time of the place that the man considered home, proper, secure.

It was . . . nothing like he had expected. It was like a huge Guard barracks, if the barracks themselves had been run by a fanatic for order and rules and had been the size of a city; very regimented in every way, very disciplined. Rigid. There were few recreations, and those few were strictly controlled. Every aspect of life, from infancy to old age, seemed to be dictated by the handful in power, and the one aspiration that everyone had was to rise to become one of those that made the rules. You were told what to do, what to believe, what to learn and what to think, and no deviations were permitted.

That was the impression that Mags got, anyway. Small wonder the cheerful chaos that was life in Valdemar revolted this fellow to the core. To his mind, to live without a rule for everything was to live like an animal.

He was moving off, and soon he would be out of Mags' mental reach. No hope for it. Mags would have to follow.

It was dark enough that Mags felt safe in discarding his disguise altogether, pulling off his eye-wrap and the wax, leaving his bowl and staff behind so that he could hurry to catch up to the man before he got out of the distance at which Mags could keep picking up those surface thoughts.

At first, Mags thought that he was going to return to wherever it was he and the others were hiding. That thought was uppermost in his mind, although Mags got no sense of where that might be, and he was walking away from any of the areas that Mags had thought likely.

But then, something else, another goal began leaking out.

The object. The thing he had lost. Now Temper knew exactly where it was. Tonight he was going to get it and he was only killing time until he reckoned it was safe enough to go after it.

Just as he thought that, Temper turned his head to look over his shoulder and his eyes fell directly on Mags—who fortunately, was limping along, looking not at the man, but at the ground, the better to concentrate on following Temper's thoughts. He fought the urge to freeze or hide and kept on walking, as if he, too, had a place to go and wanted to get into it.

He saw himself through the man's eyes. Sensed instant analysis.

And, while he tried not to cringe in fear, he sensed instant dismissal. To this man, the wretched creature that was limping along the street behind him posed no sort of threat. This was one of the poorest of the poor, in rags, filthy. Undersized, and carrying no weapons. Of no consequence.

Mags heaved a sigh of relief as the man went on to examine, analyze, and dismiss everyone else around him. He hadn't recognized Mags from the Collegium, and he didn't realize he was being followed.

That was when Mags sensed the cutpurse who was hiding in the alley ahead; then sensed that the thief had spotted Temper. The surface thoughts of the thief, desperation crossed with greed, alarmed Mags, and he stopped, bending over to fumble with a shoe while he tried to figure out what was going to happen, and if he could do anything about it.

The would-be thief was a boy, not a man, a boy no older than he was. A boy with a master to answer to, and who, so far today, had nothing to bring back to him. Coming back meant a beating or worse, and no supper. The boy looked at Temper with the eyes of a hunter and saw good clothing, a man well-fed, with no obvious weapons. That was enough; the thief made his decision. Before Mags could even think of something to try and stop him, the boy was moving.

His was the cut-and-run style, rushing at the victim from under cover, cutting the bands of the belt-pouch, and dashing off with it. Effective only when conditions favored a swift escape, it was well-suited to a night-thief, and to thefts where crowds thickened and thinned again, hampering pursuit.

The boy thought he had such conditions—night, the alley, and a half a dozen escape routes on the other side of the street.

He was wrong.

The man heard the running footsteps; his instincts all came alive, and an unholy glee came over him.

The rest was a blur to Mags, caught as he was between

the thoughts of the cutpurse and the thoughts of Temper. Temper threw off such violence that it rocked Mags back on his heels, but it was precise and calculated violence, and an acute pleasure in what he was about to do that was very nearly pain in and of itself.

The man moved at the last minute; the boy's outstretched hands missed the tempting purse. There was a moment of anger and bewilderment on the part of the thief as his hands closed on air.

Then a flash of terrible pain and incredulity.

Then nothing.

And in the street ahead, all that anyone would have seen was the thief make a rush, the man step aside, and the thief falling to the ground as if he had stumbled. Except the thief didn't get up again.

Temper passed on, leaving the cooling body of the boy in the street. It happened that quickly. One moment the thief was alive, the next, dead.

Mags could scarcely believe it; shaken to his core, he sought for Dallen, but found only that haze that meant Dallen was heavily drugged, and nothing would rouse him.

He recoiled from Temper's thoughts, as the man savagely reviewed the three steps he had taken to break the boy's neck with the pommel of his hidden dagger, so as to leave no obvious signs of violence on him for the Watch to find. Temper lingered lovingly over each move, each sensation, culminating with the climax of the weighted pommel striking exactly the precise point where the skull joined the spine, the single point that would kill the cutpurse instantly—lingering over the feel of the butt-heavy dagger in his hand, the solid impact with the skull, the sight of the boy sprawling just a little ahead of him, momentum taking what was already a corpse into a slide on the street. It was a perfect kill. Nothing could have been better—except, perhaps, if he'd had the leisure to strangle the thief with his bare hands.

Temper loved this. This was how it should be. This was what he should be doing, not skulking around, trying to find the—to find the—to find the—

Book! Mags realized as he finally "saw" what the man had been looking for all this time. He recognized it. He'd handled it himself, all unknowing.

It was the book of poetry with the pictures of flowers in it that had been left behind when they vacated, kicked under a couch and forgotten in the haste to depart.

The book of poetry. But—why?

Temper had been working for moons to discover who had it, what had become of it. Without the book he couldn't—he couldn't—

Before that thought could emerge, Temper's goal swam to the forefront of his thoughts. The Palace. No . . . the Guard Archives. That was where their possessions had gone when everything possible had been gleaned from them. Temper had finally determined this, after weeks of finding where the Palace Guardsmen went on their nights off, and pouring wine down willing throats to lubricate them. Now he was heading for the Palace to get it back.

And there was no way for Mags to alert anyone, not this far away. Dallen was sleeping like the dead.

Now Temper's thoughts were overlaid with agitation and anxiety, born out of the fact that the man knew he had orders, yet did not know what those orders were. In his world, following orders was of absolute importance, yet he could not follow the ones he had been given, because he didn't know what they were. How could he not know what they were? That didn't make any sense.

The book—the book—

What did the book have to do with all of this?

Mags tried to think what on earth there was about the book that had escaped everyone. Every single soul that knew how to look for such things had examined it. There were no false covers, there was no invisible ink. There was no way for packets of orders to be hidden in it.

So why—

Mags didn't dare pause, for Temper, acting with that terrible urgency impelling him, was making his way from shadow to shadow with a speed that Mags could scarcely believe. The only possible way Mags had of trying to contact anyone up at the Collegium was to stop and concentrate, but he didn't dare stop. If he did, he'd lose the man; if he lost the man and couldn't say where or how the man was going to get in, the only choice would be to rouse the Collegium. If he did that, Temper would see and know that he had somehow been exposed, and he would vanish again. All that Mags could do for the moment was to stick with him, and hope that once they were on the grounds he could get hold of someone to raise a quiet alarm and ambush Temper as he searched for the book—the book—why the book? Why that book?

Then, like a gift, another set of images flashed across his mind and into Mags' grasp. And suddenly Mags knew why he wanted it. The thoughts were carried on waves of frustration and despair.

The book was the key to a cipher he, and the rest, were using to communicate with their superiors.

It was nearly unbreakable too, unless you had the key.

The key was simple enough. Every fortnight it would change to the next set of lines in the given poem. Letters of the alphabet were assigned to the letters in those lines. There were further complications involving maths that Mags barely glimpsed and which made his head spin, but the basis was the changing lines of poetry in that book.

The irony was, since no one in Haven had had any idea that they were getting secret orders—from whom? Mags couldn't tell, that wasn't in Temper's surface-thoughts—the orders probably could have been written plainly.

The problem was, Temper and his cohorts had come to the end of the poem they were using. The last message gave the number of the page the next one would be on. But they hadn't memorized that, so even if they had memorized all the poems in the book, the odds of then remembering which one was on which page was rather slim.

And they couldn't tell that to their masters. The message delivery all went one way. Nor was there any possibility of getting another copy of the book.

Not without going home. And anyone going home to

report such failure would be killed. There was very little tolerance for mistakes; none at all for a mistake like this one.

The man Mags called "Temper" slowed his pace.

They were now among the homes of the well-to-do. There was great danger of being spotted here, there were many patrols of both the Watch and the Guard, and they were more alert to subtle signs of an interloper than were the ones down deeper into Haven, who watched mostly for overt violations of the law and crimes being committed openly on the streets. This was how Mags had gotten away with purloining so many dinners. Innkeepers and householders were expected to see to their own security. After all, there were only so many Watchmen and Guards, and far too many windows, doors, and roof-hatches.

Ah, but here Mags had the advantage. He knew this part of Haven much better than Temper did. Now he could run ahead, while Temper only skulked—

Or so he thought.

To his chagrin and incredulity, he sensed Temper straighten, take a folded, sealed packet out of a pocket, and with that in his hand, stride confidently up the middle of the road. He was a man with a message to deliver, and no one was going to look at him twice. No, Mags would have to skulk; not even in the darkness was he going to pass as someone who belonged up here, as ragged and filthy as he was.

At least he knew the area; he knew who had dogs, who had private guards, whether or not those guards were vigilant. So he followed Temper just out of sight, keeping walls and other obstructions between himself and the foreign agent, so that if Temper heard the sound of Mags' bare feet on the pavement, he'd see nothing if he turned to look.

He didn't seem to hear anything, however, and Mags kept up a running, mostly inarticulate prayer that he wouldn't.

Mags was very aware of the nearness of the Palace, the looming walls that surrounded it, and that they were drawing nearer to it with every moment. There was an open space, officially designated as a park, between the last of the Great Manors and the walls around the Palace and Collegia.

Here, the man paused; his mind closed to Mags' as he searched intently for something. This was the back of the Palace, not far from Companions' Field. There was nothing like a gate here; surely he wasn't going to try and get over the wall!

Even as Mags watched, that was exactly what he did.

He raced across the open lawn, and if Mags hadn't been watching him, he would never have seen him go. He took advantage of a cloud passing over the moon to run to the wall in that moving shadow.

Then, impossibly, he jumped for the wall and scuttled up it like a spider, disappearing over the top.

With a spasm of despair, Mags followed in his wake.

MAGS discovered why Temper had chosen that particular spot to go over the wall. A massive vine of some sort had grown up along it—it had rightfully been killed, but *someone* had carelessly left the main stem embedded in the wall. It was just as good as a ladder.

That must have been how he and his cohorts had fled the Palace in the first place, after the blizzard. Whoever had left this thing here was going to get the sack at least—

But that would be later. Right now—

Mags tumbled over the top of the wall and rolled to land. Temper had a good lead on him now. They were right at the edge of Companion's Field. From Temper's fleeting thoughts, he had a good many paces lead over Mags at this point. Mags hurried to narrow that lead, and spotted the man—the shadow, rather, if he hadn't been watching Temper's thoughts, he wouldn't have known it was a man—hiding in the shadow of the end of the stable that contained Mags' own room. Mags took cover himself, and waited for Temper to make the next move.

But if 'e goes straight fer the Guard Archives, I kin get t' th' stable, an' get one'a the other Companions t' wake up 'is Herald and—

And that was when it all went horribly wrong.

Temper was in sight of the Companion's stable. His mind flashed over with that unholy glee and excitement, and the image of what he was going to do to distract everyone from his raid on the Archives branded itself into Mags' mind.

He was going to barricade the doors, and set fire to the Companions' Stable.

Horror washed over Mags. Oh, the others would be able to get out—they could batter the wooden doors down, and no Companion was going to be as terrified by fire as a horse. But Dallen couldn't. Dallen was drugged and the next thing to immobile. He would be trapped in there while the stable burned around him. The moment the others broke the doors down, flaming debris would fly inside, setting fire to all that straw and hay—

He'd be trapped, helpless.

Terror ripped through Mags like a lightning strike; there was no time to spare, no time to use Mindspeech to wake the people he knew, no time to do anything except rouse everyone his thoughts could reach, and fast. Except he didn't know how to do that the way that, say, Rolan did it. He could "shout," but only to the limited number of people he knew. So he did what he had been told, over and over again, never to do.

He dropped his shields. All of them, even the ones

that had been up and protecting him before he even knew there was such a thing as a Gift, before he really knew there was much of a world outside the mine. Everything went down, so that he, in turn, could reach everyone.

And as the dozens, hundreds of minds up here rushed in on him, battering him from all sides, he screamed his warning into them. Even into the mind of Temper, who was frozen in place for a moment as the image of what he had intended to do came flooding back at him, laden with a burden of warning, panic, and terror.

The response came back to Mags, redoubled. All those minds, some shocked awake, all taken by surprise, all jolted by his panic and responding with panic of their own. *What! What! WHAT!!*

Feeling as if he was in the center of a cave-in, Mags struggled to get his shields back up. Struggled, and failed. It felt as if his head was going to break into a million pieces; a hundred images flashed in front of him, and he couldn't tell which belonged to him. Voices in his mind babbled, shouted, at him, and he couldn't understand any of them. His brain burned and it was all he could do to stand erect and he felt his very hold on sanity slipping.

But Dallen was in danger.

Dallen was in danger.

Scarcely able to see for the conflicting images in his head, stumbling and disoriented, nevertheless, he rushed for Temper. Dallen was in danger. That was all that mattered; he had to get to Temper before Temper could move.

He reached the man just as Temper recovered from

the mental blow, and somewhere under the battering of a thousand confused thoughts, he knew that he had never done anything this stupid before . . .

He lurched at Temper with his hands out, staggering like a drunk, barely able to control his own body enough to run at the man. He—*and a hundred others through his eyes*—saw Temper pull his dagger and slash at him with it. Temper was moving slowly though, very slowly, not like—*a hundred others saw/felt the memory of Temper's kill*—when he murdered that poor thief.

Temper recoiled, his mind reflexively lashing out. Mags stumbled and fell, which is what saved him from Temper's first slash.

Enraged, afire with uncontrolled anger, Temper came at him again, just as—*a myriad of confused minds tried to shove him away*—Mags managed to get to his feet. Temper slashed at him again—not the controlled and calculated movement of a skilled knife-fighter, but the flailing of someone who barely knew which end of the knife to hold.

It didn't matter. The knife scored a painful slash across Mags' ribs.

The pain was what saved him, momentarily at least.

As the blade burned across his chest, that same pain made his shields snap back up.

He gasped with mingled agony and relief as his mind cleared. Unfortunately, so did Temper's. The man's stance changed immediately, and he snapped into a knife-fighter's crouch. Mag knew in an instant that he was in trouble. The best he could hope for would be to stay out of reach.

Which, as Temper's arm lashed out, was not looking likely; he moved faster than anyone that Mags had ever seen. Mags managed to evade him, but barely, and Temper was right on top of him before he had any right to be.

Mags' shields dropped again; he staggered as too many minds to count shrieked into his. Nearest was the white rage of Temper, incandescent with fury—and somehow, Mags reflected some of that incoherent anger right back at him, causing him to stagger and miss.

Vaguely he was aware of every window in Heralds' Collegium lighting up, of people boiling out of the building, of the Companions in their stable beside him screaming with rage and battering at the barricaded doors. Temper slashed at him again, then rushed him.

Temper's shoulder hit him right where he'd been cut; he gasped with pain, and his shields snapped back up again. He managed to shove Temper off, and stagger a few paces away.

Temper rushed him again; he ducked to the side, getting another cut across the bicep in the process.

The pain kept him steady, kept his shields up, but he was fighting for his life, and he knew it. And he was in worse shape than he had been when he'd been fending off Bear's kidnapper. He was wheezing already, and his side burned.

Temper's eyes narrowed, and he glanced to the side. People seemed to have figured out that the stable was where they should be, and a mob was heading in their direction.

Mags half expected Temper to say something when

his eyes returned to Mags. He didn't. In fact, he gave Mags no warning at all.

One moment he was crouched a few arm-lengths away. Mags didn't even see him start to move.

Then Mags' back hit the stable wall, knocking the breath out of him. Temper's forearm was across his throat.

And white-hot pain lanced out from the center of his gut.

He screamed and his shields went down—he blasted his agony out and Temper staggered back, both hands to his temples. Mags lunged at him, his gut still on fire, both hands going for Temper's knife. He had to get it away from the man—had to, or he was dead.

He grappled with Temper, feeling his strength ebbing. Somehow he got both his hands on the knife-hand. His knees gave, and he pulled Temper down as he dropped to the ground. Somehow Temper ended up underneath him. He smashed Temper's knife-hand on the ground but the man would not let go of the blade.

Mags snarled, stooped, and bit the hand holding the knife, his teeth sinking into the flesh below the thumb until he drew blood, tasted the flat, sweetness of the blood, felt bones snap under his teeth.

The dagger fell away, into the dirt.

Mags snatched it up.

Now it was only one mind, filling his, and overpowering it with anger and death. His eyes widened and he ground his teeth with rage. He didn't even think—he just picked up the knife in both hands and drove it down into the thing underneath him, over and over and over again—

Temper uttered a surprised sounding gurgle—and died.

The rage died with him.

Abruptly emptied, Mags sat there for a moment, the bloody knife still poised in midair.

Then someone else hit him from the side, and his gut erupted with fire again. He curled in around the agony, blood oozing into his hands as he clutched his middle. His shields came down, snapped up, came down, snapped up, as the world spun around him and—dozens of babbling, angry voices—his gut screamed and—*Who, what, why, who*—his vision blurred, he looked up to see the King with the knife in his hands, and the front of his Whites dyed with blood, and—*blood, death, rage, rage, rage*—he looked down to see his own hands dripping with blood and—*who, death, what, blood, rage*—

Somehow he staggered to his feet. Somehow, with one hand clutching his stomach, he started to reach out. Somehow—

Then all the voices in his head shrieked at once, and he reflected, blasted it all back at them and—

He felt impact at the back of his head.

Then . . .

An explosion of light.

He went down. But he held to a thin, thin strand of consciousness, falling in and out of blankness.

". . . how did he get in . . ."

". . . how did both . . ."

". . . saw him stabbing . . ."

Shouting. Hooves battering wood. Splintering wood.

Blankness. Then, something white, enormous, big as a

house, and white, standing over him. Warm, sweet, hay-scented breath washing over him, taking some of the pain. Closing off some of the minds screaming in his head.

"Rolan! What in the name of—"

A snort. A hoof pawing the ground impatiently beside Mags' head.

"That's who? Mags? Then who is—"

"Never mind that, for the gods' sake, get a Healer here!"

And that was when, mercifully, it all began to fade, voices, pain and all, leaving behind nothing but quiet, darkness, and peace.

He woke up with the warm sunlight pouring down on him, and the familiar sharp scents of herbs and soap around him. *Huh. Reckon I know where I am.*

:I rather thought you would. Welcome back, Mags.:

:So how beat up'm I this time?: He was disinclined to move, because he really didn't want to spoil things with pain right now. He could feel a lot of bandages around his midsection, though.

:A slash across the ribs, one across the bicep that is rather deep, and three gut-wounds that by some miracle did not touch anything vital. Altogether, considering who you faced—:

He restrained a shiver, because it would hurt. *:Damn lucky. I saw 'im take out that thief. I seen lightnin' strike slower. Did I kill 'im?:*

Dallen sighed. *:Unfortunately, yes. Then again,*

questioning might not have gotten anything out of him anyway.:

Mags didn't consider it unfortunate at all, but he didn't say anything. Considering how slippery Temper had been, there was no telling if they would have been able to hold him, much less question him.

:Which one was he?:

:Surprisingly, not the chief of the alleged delegation. In fact, I am not sure you ever actually saw him when they were all up here at the Palace. He was one of the underlings, not one of the bodyguards. Or at least, he was feigning to be.:

:Huh.: Mags considered that. *:That makes sense, actually. Best place t' hide.:*

:So I am told. Well, it looks like both of us will be ready to start Kirball practice at about the same time.: Dallen seemed inclined to change the subject, but Mags wasn't going to let him.

:So who hit me?:

:Which time?:

Mags thought about that for a moment. *:Who hit me i' th' head?:*

:That would have been Herald Yvanda. I am told she smacked you with a large branch.:

That would account for the big bump back there. *:Who knocked me offa Temper?:*

:That would be the King. He was the first one there, because he was actually in the stable. He had to climb up into the loft and get down out of the hay door.:

:Bloody 'ell.: Mags wasn't sure whether to be appalled or full of admiration. Both, probably.

:There are going to be some changes made to the stable,: Dallen added, a bit grimly. *:More than one door, and breakaway hinges. I'm afraid that the place is built a little too well.:*

:Aye.: He thought about how close Dallen had come to being roasted, and this time couldn't hold back the shudder.

:But now the vision is explained. It was your blood the King was covered in. They were rather appalled when they saw how thoroughly you had dispatched the man you called Temper, but then most of them had been experiencing what you did as your shields went up and down, and on reflection, the general consensus is that they are surprised you hadn't diced him into a thousand pieces.:

He thought about that. *:Reckon it was because I was runnin' outa strength an' blood.:*

:Very probably.:

"I know you're awake," said Bear, startling him into opening his eyes. "You aren't going to get out of taking my potion by pretending you aren't."

"Oh, ye reckon?" he said. Then, feeling extremely awkward, "Look, I'm sorry—fer what I said—"

"I'm not. There was enough of it that was true that Lena and I needed to hear it, and better from you than someone else." Bear handed him a glass. Whatever was in it looked vile. "However, to get back at you, I have made sure these potions are all made from the worst possible tasting alternatives in my list."

"Figgers." He held his breath and drank it down.

It was bad enough to make his eyes water. "Ye weren't lyin'!" he gasped.

Bear just smiled, and pushed his lenses up on his nose. "My brother went home," he said, looking very smug. "I don't know what was said to him, but he left without anything more than a really irritated good-bye. He really hates being told that he's not the last authority on everything. He gets treated that way by everyone in his House, and he thinks he should always be treated that way."

Mags thought he detected more amusement than anger in Bear's tone. He smiled, and felt his eyes starting to close.

"You get some rest," Bear said, as his lids fluttered shut.

Another Healer woke him so that he could get some lunch, gazing sternly at his rather bony torso. "All that work to get some meat on you, and you go and make it all to do again," he scolded. Then he ordered the food, and Mags had a bit of a hard time getting through it all. "I hope the next time you get into trouble," the man added, a little crossly, "You don't decide to blast all of us out of our beds."

"I didn' reckon I had time t' call people one at a time—" Mags began.

"Well next time 'reckon' on something else. Get the proper Mindspeech training. And finish that food." The Healer seemed to think he had won something, and exited. Mags just shook his head. He still didn't understand people.

The next time Bear came, he brought Lena, and Mags steeled himself for his apology to her. But she didn't even let him begin it.

First she fussed over him a great deal. Evidently having actual wounds from a weapon rather than just bruises impressed her a lot. Which was odd, because the bruises had hurt a lot more.

Then when he had reassured her for the third time that he was going to be all right, she looked sheepish, then guilty, then asked all in a rush, "Then if you are going to be all right you won't mind my father coming to ask you questions?"

Aha. Mystery solved. *'Er Pa is suckin' up to 'er again.*

"Well, fer you," he replied. She beamed at him, and evidently all was forgiven.

Amily turned up while he was still talking to Lena and Bear, and the little smile she gave him warmed him more than the sunshine had. None of them wanted to speak of anything but commonplaces, catching him up on what had happened while he had been on his self-imposed exile, and since his head wasn't working all that well under the influence of the medicines, he just lay back and let them chatter.

It was when Nikolas turned up that he woke up all the way.

It was just twilight; someone had come around to light the lamps, but there weren't many of them here as the patients were generally encouraged to sleep as much as possible. Mags was drowsing a little when he sensed the familiar presence, and opened his eyes to see Nikolas just standing in the doorway.

The King's Own smiled crookedly when he saw Mags had spotted him. "For someone who never saw a Herald before last year, you're upholding our traditions very well," he said.

"What?" Mags asked. "Ye mean, Heralds being targets?"

"Exactly." Nikolas entered and took the chair beside the bed. "We've just finished a literal house-to-house search of Haven. The rest of the foreigners are gone."

"He was the 'mportant one," Mags said, not at all surprised. "I reckon 'e was th' one that kept 'em all here."

"Likely." Nikolas nodded. "You are going to be in for a rough couple of days, I fear. Rolan and I are going to go rummage through everything you picked up from him while it is all still fresh in your mind. We might glean some clues from it, if not answers."

"Oh." He grimaced. That was going to be very unpleasant, but he wasn't exactly in a position to say "no."

"I apologize for not being available when you needed me, Mags," Nikolas was saying, while Mags was still thinking over the need to go through all those nasty thoughts and images yet again. "I was involved in something very tricky. I still am, actually, but it's at a stage where it has to lie fallow for a while. I can't tell you what it is, obviously."

Mags nodded.

"What I will tell you is that for the next four to six moons, I think you can consider yourself free to be a normal Trainee." Nikolas grinned. "Or at least, as normal as Trainees ever are. Play Kirball, humor Marchand, go have Midsummer Festival with Lydia and her friends, flirt with my daughter—"

He laughed when Mags blushed hotly.

"What, did you think I hadn't noticed?" he asked

mockingly. "Just how preoccupied with my duties do you think I am?"

Mags blushed again.

"You will be doing something actually quite important when you do all these things, Mags," Nikolas continued, sobering. "You'll be integrating yourself with the rest of the Trainees. You'll be establishing yourself, not just to them, but in your own mind, as one of the Circle. Do you understand what I am saying, Mags?"

Mags blinked thoughtfully. "I . . . think so, sir."

"Believe it, Mags. Because there is not a bit of doubt in anyone else's mind after last night." Nikolas stood up to go. "There is no one, in all of Valdemar, more fit to be a Herald than you."

The words echoed in his mind and followed him down into sleep, bringing healing in their wake. There were unanswered questions, still, and a great many of them. But for now, they could wait.

Mercedes Lackey & Larry Dixon

The Novels of Valdemar

"Lackey and Dixon always offer a well-told tale"
—*Booklist*

DARIAN'S TALE

OWLFLIGHT
978-0-88677-804-2

OWLSIGHT
978-0-88677-803-4

OWLKNIGHT
978-0-88677-916-2

THE MAGE WARS

THE BLACK GRYPHON
978-0-88677-804-2

THE WHITE GRYPHON
978-0-88677-682-1

THE SILVER GRYPHON
978-0-88677-685-6

To Order Call: 1-800-788-6262
www.dawbooks.com

DAW 26